WISHFUL THINKING

Jemma Harvey

C

CENTURY · LONDON

Published in the United Kingdom in 2004 by Century

1 3 5 7 9 10 8 6 4 2

Special thanks to Harry Graham's niece for permission to quote
'Calculating Clara' © 1899

'One Perfect Rose' by Dorothy Parker © 1926 Excerpt quoted from
The Penguin Dorothy Parker, Penguin 1977. Reproduced by permission of
Pollinger Limited and the proprietor.

'Nobody's Chasing Me' Words and Music by Cole Porter © 1949 (renewed)
Buxton-Hill-Music Corp, USA. Warner Chappell North America Limited, London
W6 8BS. Lyrics reproduced by permission of IMP Limited. All Rights Reserved.

Century
The Random House Group Limited
20 Vauxhall Bridge Road, London, SW1V 2SA

Random House Australia (Pty) Limited
20 Alfred Street, Milsons Point, Sydney, New South Wales 2061, Australia

Random House New Zealand Limited
18 Poland Road, Glenfield
Auckland 10, New Zealand

Random House (Pty) Limited
Endulini, 5a Jubilee Road, Parktown, 2193, South Africa

The Random House Group Limited Reg. No. 954009
www.randomhouse.co.uk

A CIP catalogue record for this book is available from the British Library

Papers used by Random House
are natural, recyclable products made from wood grown in
sustainable forests. The manufacturing processes conform to
the environmental regulations of the country of origin

Typeset in Sabon by Palimpsest Book Production Limited, Polmont, Stirlingshire
Printed and bound in the United Kingdom by
Mackays of Chatham plc, Chatham, Kent

1 8441 3386 9

WISHFUL THINKING

Jemma Harvey lives in Brighton.
Wishful Thinking is her debut novel.

There are two tragedies in life. One is to lose your heart's
desire. The other is to gain it.

G. B. SHAW: *Man and Superman*

There is wishful thinking in Hell as well as on earth.

C. S. LEWIS: *The Screwtape Letters*

Chapter 1

How now, you secret, black, and midnight hags!
SHAKESPEARE: *Macbeth*

It all began the day we went to the Wyshing Well.

(Of course, it didn't really, because things never actually *begin*, they just continue on from stuff that's happened before, but that's where I'm going to start.)

The well was in the gardens of the Bel Manoir, a Palladian mansion recently converted into a hotel and restaurant, complete with understated Oriental décor – the Prince Regent effect without the vulgarity – and a celebrity chef presiding over the cuisine. (He presided but I doubt if he actually *cooked* – unless there was a TV camera around.) We'd been lunching there with one of our authors, Jerry Beauman, to celebrate his release from prison. Georgie didn't like the choice of location at all – the prices on the wine list went well into four figures – but Beauman is one of our Big Names so she had to agree. There wasn't much to celebrate, in our view. Beauman had been doing time for some sort of financial fraud so elaborate even he claimed he hadn't understood what he was doing, although the judge hadn't believed him. All Jerry could do was make the most of the rather dubious publicity and spend his gaol-time

1

working on a new book about a wronged hero, duped by a villain who envied him his glamour and success, incarcerated despite his innocence until following his release he is finally able to turn the tables on his accusers and vindicate his good name. I wasn't listening to his account of the plot over the meal (I'm not his editor) but I knew what it would be. I was only there because the Publishing Director couldn't make it. Georgie (Georgina Cavari, Publicity) grabbed the wine list in her capacity as official hostess and did her best to keep the bill down. Unfortunately, Beauman is a major seller, if not quite as major as he boasts, and since there really is no such thing as bad publicity for a writer we toasted him with sinking hearts, knowing the book would be a huge success. At least, it would be after Laurence Buckle – who *is* his editor – had done the necessary revisions.

Once Jerry had swanned off with poor Laurence in attendance to discuss the manuscript Georgie, Lin and I tottered into the garden to recover.

We're the heroines, so I'd better tell you something about us. Just quickly, for now. I'll do the flashbacks later.

If I take us in order of age, I start with Georgie. She's forty-two, but you wouldn't know it. I've heard some of the girls saying: 'If I look half that good when I'm her age . . .', the way people do, only I don't join in because I don't look half that good *now*, and I'm twenty-nine. She's nearly as tall as a model and has a double-D bust on a size eight figure and the kind of skin that looks as if she should be advertising face cream for the older woman: 'Because I'm worth it.' Her hair is a short, professionally-tousled mop streaked several different shades of blonde, and she has big brown puppy-dog eyes which effectively conceal the fact that she's a cynic, pragmatist and optimist by turns, and sometimes all at once. She used to be married to an

Italian count but, as she says, 'the *conte* didn't count'. Titles are two a penny in Italy, apparently, where everyone is a member of the aristocracy or the Mafia, or both. She lives alone in a house she can't afford and refuses to have a cat, on principle.

Lin's next. Lindsay Corrigan, née Macleod. Where Georgie is gorgeous and glam, Lin's beautiful. Her makeup's haphazard and her clothes tend towards ethnic, but it doesn't matter. She's the real McCoy, an unearthly fairy creature who looks as if she's just stepped out of the hollow hills, all wispy body and flawless face and misty Pre-Raphaelite waves of red-gold hair. And underneath there's a nice girl from Edinburgh whose looks have taken her places she didn't really want to go, namely to single parenthood in a house in Kensington, a succession of nannies who never seem to work out, and no leisure for a life of her own. And looks like hers – unlike Georgie's – don't last. She's thirty-one and it's starting to show: there's a faint tarnish of time and stress on all that flawlessness, a hint of mortal wear-and-tear on immortal perfection. She isn't particularly vain, but we're vain for her, and we're afraid she'll wilt like a dehydrated flower before Mr Right comes along to pluck her.

I know, old-fashioned bollocks, unsuited to the Liberated Woman. But Lin's an old-fashioned girl. She thinks Women's Liberation still means burning your bra.

And then there's me. Twenty-nine (see above). Emma Jane Cook, known as Cookie, because everyone in publishing is called Emma these days. I've got all the things you're supposed to have: an Oxford degree and a good job (well, mostly) and my own flat and a boyfriend called Nigel – but that's his parents' fault and there are lots of nice men called Nigel. ('Only yours isn't one of them': Georgie.) I mean, it sounds good, doesn't it? But then there's the catch. The fly in the ointment. Me. A big fat fly – *really* fat, not Bridget

Jones Oh-God-I've-gone-over-nine-stone fat, not a-couple-of-inches-of-spare-tyre fat, not I-can't-get-into-my-size-10-jeans fat, but *fat* fat. FAT. Over two years' intermittent dieting I've just about got myself down from a twenty to a sixteen, if it's generous. And I'm only five foot four, so it isn't like the weight's spread out. My bust is vast, but it's balanced out by my hips, bum, thighs – you get the picture. My face is okay, but who cares? Hazel eyes, really good eyebrows (if anyone notices eyebrows), big lips that would look sexy on a thin face, but on mine, they just look – you've guessed it – fat. Hair dark, curling into a frizz. Big hair ought to counterbalance big body, but not in my case. I dream of slinky, sexy clothes with split skirts clinging to every lack of curve, but I wear loose, baggy, shapeless things to hide my loose, baggy, shapeless figure. I'm not really heroine material – unless there's a point in this story when I go on a miracle diet, and everyone suddenly discovers how beautiful I am. But I doubt it. I've tried every miracle diet there is, and only a very few pounds have oozed reluctantly away, like It girls forced to leave the party early. No, I'm just the narrator. Like Fanny in *The Pursuit of Love*, I just chug along comfortably while all the exciting things happen to my wonderful, glamorous friends.

Or so I thought that day at the Wyshing Well.

It was in a little arbour at the end of a gravel path so smooth it looked as if it had been ironed. Trellises arched over it, tangled with climbing plants, supposedly making it secretive and mysterious, but on that grey January day the effect was mostly rather dark. The well itself looked old, with green mossy stuff growing over the lip. There was no bucket, only the rusty chain wound round the winch. Chickenwire covered the top, presumably in case prospective wishers (well-wishers?) felt suicidal and tried to hurl themselves in. Or maybe they might want to retrieve the coins, a few of which could be seen glinting in the depths.

On a plaque nailed to the side of the well there was a verse in a Tolkienesque script:

> *Toss a penny in the welle*
> *Thynk on your hearte's desyre.*
> *The charm wille aid who aids himsel*
> *To wyshe is to aspyre.*

The sentiment seemed a bit pragmatic to me, a God-helps-them-who-help-themselves type thing, not what you'd expect from the fairy folk, but I paid it no attention at the time.

'Jerry Beauman to be rearrested, this time for indecent exposure, after flashing in front of a group of children and several gorillas in Regents Park Zoo,' Georgie said moodily. 'The gorillas will be permanently traumatised.'

'Your wish?' asked Lin. 'Okay. I'll add . . . the judge gives him ten years, in a cell with no laptop or writing paper. How's that?'

'Life,' I said. 'And then he wakes up one morning believing he's turning into a Tellytubby.'

There was a gloomy silence while we contemplated Jerry Beauman. I hope to God he isn't going to feature much in this story, but you may as well know (if you don't already) that he's good-looking in a ratty sort of way and has recently dumped a long-standing wife to be seen out with a designer bimbo of Oriental origins who looks inscrutable at a succession of book launches. His whole life has been embittered by the fact that, although he appeared at the launch party in *Bridget Jones' Diary,* after editing all you could see was the back of his head.

'We ought to have a real wish,' said Georgie. 'Toss a penny in for the fairy, or whatever it's called.'

'Might be a nix,' Lin said. She's into folklore. 'Or a minogue.'

'*Minogue*?' Georgie and I, in unison.

'It's a kind of fairy. Honest. And there are kelpies and selkies and—'

'Never mind,' Georgie interrupted. 'Let's just wish. I could do with a little fairy-luck right now. Or even a lot.'

'One big wish?' Lin asked. 'Or three small ones?'

'What's a big wish?' I was intrigued.

'Well . . . world peace, that sort of thing.'

'Let's keep it realistic,' said Georgie. 'Just untold wealth and happiness. We don't want the fairy to be overstretched.'

After some serious thought we each dropped a penny in – I had to give one to Lin, since she had no change – and wished. I wished hard, eyes shut tight, the way I did when I was a child, though I knew it was pointless. Afterwards, we all felt better. Like doing the lottery. Pointless, but fun. 'Besides,' Georgie said, 'we've got more chance of having our wishes come true than winning the lottery, any day.'

'I doubt it,' I said. 'You don't know what I wished for.'

'Can't be as impossible as mine,' said Georgie. 'I wished to clear my credit-card bill. Among other debts.'

Lin said: 'Aren't we supposed not to tell?'

'Why? I want to make sure the fairy – nixie – whatever it is – hears.'

'In that case,' said Lin, 'I wished to meet the Man in my Life.'

'You've had lots of men in your life,' I pointed out. 'At least – several.' Lin wasn't the promiscuous type.

'I mean *the* man,' Lin explained. 'You know. The One. When your eyes just meet across the room and you *know*.'

'My eyes just met Jerry Beauman's over the foie gras,' Georgie remarked. 'It was an accident. I happened to look up, and there he was, looking at *me*. Yuk.'

'Awful,' I said sympathetically.

'What did you wish for, Cookie?' Lin asked.

'Let's just say mine really will strain the fairy's magical powers,' I responded.

'Like world peace?'

'More.'

'Come on then,' said Georgie.

I didn't say 'no laughing' because they were my friends.

'I wished to become a sex goddess,' I told them. 'I thought that would give the fairy a real challenge.'

No one laughed. It might have been better if they had.

So that was how it all started. You wish for things – incredible, impossible things – and then you begin to want them, and wonder if they could ever happen. And from wanting and wondering it's only a short step to asking yourself what you can do to *make* them happen. A short but significant step. One of those 'All journeys start with but a single step' steps. Like it said in the verse: '*To wyshe is to aspyre*'. Not that we would have taken that step if it hadn't been for Georgie, of course. It's always Georgie who looks for the lever on the floodgates, rather than simply going with the flow. She's the sort of person who grabs life by the balls – and squeezes. Scary to be around, but never boring.

Anyway, she had the easy wish. Money. Quite a lot of money, true, but much easier than finding your One True Love or turning an overweight Ugly Duckling into a sex goddess.

'*You* don't know the size of my credit-card bill,' Georgie said darkly. 'Did you see that survey recently that said everyone in the country owed seventeen grand on their credit cards?'

'No,' I said.

'And there are lots of people who only owe about a thousand?' Her tone suggested this was profoundly unnatural.

'No.'

'Well, all those excess sixteen thousands are on *my* bill. Believe me.'

'*No!*'

'All of them?' Lin demanded, wide-eyed.

'*All* of them,' Georgie said firmly.

'Couldn't you remortgage your house?' I suggested. 'My aunt Jenny—'

'Dunnit. I just ran the bill up again.'

'Take in a lodger?'

Georgie shuddered. 'I know about lodgers. The fun ones have their music on full blast all night and leave unspeakable items of dirty washing in the bath and drink all your booze without telling you. And the nice, quiet ones who don't drink or smoke turn out to be axe-murderers.'

'A cat?'

'How would that help? Cats don't pay rent.'

'No, but . . . it's very soothing to stroke their fur. And they make nice purry noises. And catch mice. That might stop you worrying about your bill quite so much.' Just in case you haven't guessed, I *do* have a cat. A mog-standard tabby called Mandy, short for Mandelson, because he has this intense way of looking at you, as if to say: *I know where you live* . . .

'I don't worry about it *enough*,' Georgie said. 'That's why it keeps increasing. I only worry about not worrying about it.'

Lin and I gave up.

I think I should tell you something about the publisher for whom we work. (You can see I'm an editor, can't you? *For whom*, not *who we work for*.) It's called Ransome Harber, and for the benefit of any illiterates who haven't heard of it, the company is a big conglomerate owning lots of different imprints. About a year ago we acquired the small independent Cuckoo's Nest, in order to turn their MD into our Chairman.

'We liked the boss so much, we bought the company . . .' I work in Ransome hardbacks and the main paperback arm, Twocan, with the famous logo of a double-headed bird, twin profiles back to back. Other imprints we have swallowed or spawned include the vintage Angus McAngus, Sparrow children's books, the sci-fi/fantasy Phoenix (the company is very bird-minded, for some reason), and the tiny but wildly lucrative Eros, which produces pornography for women. Editors only do short-term placements on the Eros list ever since the tragic and very expensive case of someone who stayed there two years, developed a pathological horror of sex, and scooped a small fortune after suing the company for work-related trauma. Georgie runs the Publicity Department for all the imprints, with Lin as her main assistant and several others specialising in different areas. Eros doesn't need publicity, though Promotions will sometimes arrange to give away, for example, a leather G-string with each book (or vice versa). That evening Georgie had organised a launch party for someone at Porgy, a label publishing writers from ethnic minorities. I was going for the free booze, and because Nigel was away at a convention.

The writer was a bespectacled guy with beautiful manners called Vijay Ramsingh (his editor had changed it to VJ, to recall VS) who looked much younger than his thirty-one years. PR had suppressed his middle-class origins to imply an inner-city background and an authentic Voice of the People (in these circumstances, it's not the book that matters, it's the image of the writer). He looked faintly bewildered, as authors often do when caught up in the publicity machine. 'Congratulations,' I told him, over a glass of Château Plonque in the carefully chosen party venue, an Islamic wine bar off the Edgware Road. Well, maybe not actually Islamic, but it looked it, with frescoes of camel trains on the walls and nibbles consisting of pounded-up chickpea and things wrapped in other things. 'You must be very pleased,' I went on. The party was well attended by the literary press; Georgie always knew how to create a buzz.

'Will there be any other writers?' Vijay asked innocently.

'I shouldn't think so,' I said. 'This party's for you.' Excess writers aren't encouraged at launches, unless they happen to be critics as well, or so famous you can't turn them away. A stray writer can be a loose cannon, especially if there's booze available. With authors, two's a crowd.

'But . . . isn't that Todd Jarman over there?' A note of genuine excitement had crept into his voice.

'Of course not,' I insisted, looking round.

I was wrong.

My heart didn't exactly plummet, but it did slither down a few notches. Todd Jarman is a thriller writer whose books are so classy that broad-minded critics have been known to hail them as Littritcha. A couple of years ago his stuff was adapted for television with a rising star in the role of his main detective, and Jarman promptly went mega. For the first eight books, his hardbacks just managed four-figure sales; now, they go straight into the Top Ten. Always difficult, he became virtually impossible to deal with, but an editor who'd been there practically from the beginning managed to cope, if only by barely altering a word. Then the editor took a career change and switched to being an agent, hassling the publishers instead of the writer. Long-suffering Laurence Buckle took over, lasting less than a year before Jarman dug his heels in, saying he didn't want to be turned into another Jerry Beauman.

Guess who was co-opted next.

So far, we'd only spoken once, over the phone, when I'd been given the unenviable task of telling him his latest title was too long for the dust-jacket artwork. He'd expressed himself in the kind of language his hero reserved for the discovery of a particularly unpleasant corpse. I really, *really* didn't want to meet him face-to-face unless I was fortified with Prozac and a gallon of Rescue Remedy.

'What's *he* doing here?' I asked Lin in a panicked whisper.

'Dragged here by his girlfriend, I think. She's a human rights lawyer. Someone at Porgy sent her Vijay's book for a quote, and apparently she adored it.'

The girlfriend was much in evidence, a sleek blonde whose mere profile exhibited steely intelligence, effortless competence, and designer grooming. I loathed her on sight. Beside her, Jarman was inspecting the crowd with the sort of dark, probing gaze that would have bored holes in woodwork. He looked grimly handsome, tight-lipped, even saturnine – but perhaps that was my fault. Put on the spot by the Art Department, who had themed his jackets over several books and knew a change could damage sales, I'd finally got him to knock three words off the overlong title, but he hadn't been happy. Of course, it could have been sheer paranoia that made me imagine he was searching for me. Maybe he always looked murderous at launch parties.

'Nobody tell him I'm here!' I hissed.

I headed towards the bar for a refill, wishing I'd stayed at home. Mandy's ice-green stare was menacing, but at least I'd never had to edit him. And with Nigel away I could have watched *EastEnders* . . .

There are mysterious currents that circulate at parties, sweeping people inexorably together – or apart. Skilled socialites know how to ride them, borne round the room in the mainstream, talking to all the most interesting guests, while someone like me invariably gets stuck in the boring little eddies round the edge. On this occasion, however, I was hoping for a boring little eddy at the bar. But those same currents which always divide you from that really attractive man glimpsed about ten people away can be still more malevolent, casting you in the path of the one person you wish to avoid. I got my drink, stepped backwards – and collided with Todd Jarman.

Aiming for the bar was probably a mistake.

I gasped: 'Oh – er – hello.' That was a mistake, too. If I'd said nothing and moved on he wouldn't have spoken to me.

'Hello,' he said. 'Which is worse – the red or the white?'

I was drinking red. 'Don't know,' I said. 'I haven't tried the white.'

He took a glass of red and, instead of slipping back into the party mainstream, positioned himself beside me in conversational mode. Under other circumstances, I'd have been flattered. He's famous (for a writer) and, more important, quite good-looking, if your taste runs to tall, dark, saturnine men. At that moment, mine didn't. He has off-black hair and a rather long face with a hooky nose and the kind of lean cheeks that have a thin line running down from the jut of the cheekbone. Possibly a smile line, though most people who have them don't seem to smile much. Romantic novelists of the fifties would have called him lantern-jawed, though that's an image that has always baffled me. I've never seen anyone with a jaw that looked remotely like a lantern. I didn't register eye colour, but I noticed he hadn't bothered to shave.

'Have you read Vijay's book?' I asked, desperate to evade the subject of his own.

'God, no. Helen loved it.' The girlfriend. 'That was more than enough to put me off.'

'Why?' I said. He was annoying me already.

'She likes earnest, well-meaning fiction that says something significant about society, preferably without any excitement getting in the way. I like a good story.'

'*White Fang*,' I said promptly. 'Rattling good yarn. Never needed to read another.' I was thinking of Radlett Senior in *The Pursuit of Love*, but I didn't expect Jarman to recognise the allusion.

He did. I could see it in his face. His eyebrows went up at the outer edges, a good trick if you can do it. 'Exactly. Have you read it?'

'Well . . . yes.' Actually, I'd sobbed my way through half a box of tissues in the last bit, but I wasn't going to tell him that. 'I just don't think it's clever to sneer at your girlfriend, behind her back or to her face.' I didn't like her, but right now, I disliked him more. And I didn't care if he knew it. 'In fact, I think it's pretty cheap.'

'Ouch,' he said. 'Well done. The truth is, Helen cordially despises me for writing popular fiction, while I hugely admire her for defending the underdog in the courts of the overdog. My personality has become warped and bitter as a result. Sometimes it shows. I'm Todd Jarman, by the way. Will you introduce yourself, or do you want to leave it to our seconds?'

'You'll be much happier not knowing,' I said, mislaying some of my former bravado.

'*Will* I?'

'I'm Emma Cook. My friends call me Cookie, but I don't suppose you're going to be one of them.'

'Emma Cook . . .' He was frowning. My name had evidently made no impression, but I was sure my work had.

'I'm your . . . new . . . editor . . .'

This time, the inside edges of his eyebrows swooped abruptly down. Since they met already over the bridge of his nose (a sure sign of a werewolf, according to Angela Carter), this tangled them into a savage knot. Then they unknotted, soaring upward again. Irony. 'So *you*'re the individual who thinks *The Last Harlot of Lemontree Street* has – what was it? – too many words.' Why is it the term 'individual' can sound so offensive? 'Too many words for the title – too many words for the dust jacket – too many words for the limited attention span of the reading public. We don't want to distract from a pretty picture of a dismembered corpse, do we? We

13

don't want brain strain to set in before the morons who read me get to the first page. *The Last Harlot* is so much – snappier, didn't you say? All ready to *snap* up the roving reader. Thus spake the voice of wisdom and experience!'

Cravenly, I opened my mouth to pass the buck on to the Art Department, but Todd didn't give me the chance. Sarcasm, which had merely dripped before, now rushed over me in a torrent. He mocked my youth, my supposed arrogance, my literary talents, my artistic judgement. If I knew so much more about his job than he did, why wasn't I writing books instead of editing them? (I had every intention of writing books one day.) What qualifications did I have to pick holes in an accredited bestseller? Oh, a *degree*, a degree in *English*. He, of course, had learnt his English on the streets. (Since his background was relatively middle-class, I wondered which streets he meant.) He wrote for the people, not for the intellectual snobs in the literati.

'Exactly. Which is why the shorter title—'

The people weren't the braindead fuckwits that most publishers seemed to believe. His own success was proof of that. The people were acute and discerning. They could understand words of more than two syllables, titles of more than three words. They didn't judge a book by the blood-stains on the cover. I was a typical Oxbridge graduate, inflated with the conceit of education and privilege, hopelessly naïve about the real world. Who the hell did I think I was, teaching *him* how to write?

In a moment he would tell me my mother's milk was still dribbling down my chin.

Only the advent of Helen Aucham stemmed the flood. Close to, she had the lean, athletic body of a greyhound, if you could imagine a greyhound in Nicole Farhi. Her face resembled a computer animation: the features moved but everything else was frozen into smoothness. She had evidently overdone the Botox. She flicked me a wary glance which faded into disinterest when Todd, still in ironic mode, began to introduce me. 'This is the brilliant and talented Ms Cook, who believes she knows better than me what—'

'Todd darling, we're running late. We're supposed to be at the Granthams' for dinner, remember? God knows how long it'll take to get a taxi.'

She swept him off, willy-nilly, while he threw dagger-looks over his shoulder in my direction. If there had been genuine steel in them, I would have ended up like a pincushion. I took a deep breath as he left the room, and an even deeper swig of Plonque. The customer may be always right but the writer is always wrong, at least according to most publishers. However, editorial diplomacy decrees that you should never say so. Now the tirade was over and I seemed to be still in one piece I felt suddenly light-hearted. I turned back to the bar for another refill and determined to enjoy the rest of the party.

Back home, several pints of red later, I curled up with a packet of tortilla chips (I couldn't be bothered to cook), a tub of blue cheese dip, and the kind of romantic video on which Nigel would have poured scorn. In this case, *You've Got Mail*, which is all about booksellers, though I have never met one even a quarter – even an eighth – as charismatic as the hero, played by Tom Hanks.

In case you haven't guessed, Nigel is a bookseller, of sorts. He and a friend run a small shop specialising in Left-Wing political stuff – everything from *Das Kapital* to biographies of Che Guevara and Tony Benn – and ecobooks on the breakdown of the ozone layer, getting close to the earth, and even witchcraft, which he calls Wicca. (I always visualise the witches in basketwork hats.) The fiction section is dominated by futuristic gloom and environmental fantasy. He also campaigns for the Green Party and is currently immersed in complex schemes to oust the present candidate and replace him, which seems rather a wasted effort, since he only got about fifty votes at the last election. But Nigel is very passionate and idealistic and always believes the world is just about to wake up and see the light, or perhaps the dark, and vote accordingly. That week he had gone to a convention on globalism (Corporate Power and the Self-Destruct Society: that sort of thing) so I could relax and stop taking life seriously for a while.

There's a photo of us on the sideboard, his arm around my shoulders while I'm smiling up at him – though not far up because he isn't much taller than me – and he's smiling at the camera. He has about a tenth as much charisma as Tom Hanks, which is not bad for a real-life bookseller, particularly one with an ecoconscience. He's rather skinny – behind our backs I know people talk about thin men who fancy fat women – and pretty in a little-boy way, with one of those faces that invariably looks fifteen even though he's going on thirty. Women always want to cuddle and protect him: I know I did. At the same time, I saw courage in his high ideals, moral fibre in the warp and weft of his political convictions. I even tried to agree with them, sometimes. He hates football ('the new opiate of the people') and is never laddish or aggressively macho. Of course, on a scale of lamp to candle, if Todd Jarman is lantern-jawed, Nigel is pocket-torch-jawed, but then square jaws go with old-fashioned machismo, not New Age sensitivity. For the rest, he has beautiful blue-green eyes with very long eyelashes and dingy blond hair styled according to the Bob Geldof school of hairdressing. However, I have always held the unexpressed and probably sexist belief that straight men shouldn't care how they look: male elegance denotes gays or poseurs. I expect it's a reaction against my mother, who once dismissed a boyfriend of my sister's with a *sotto voce* murmur of 'polyester trousers'.

When I met him, Nigel was living in cramped conditions above the bookshop, with a single-bar radiator, camping gas, and a sleeping bag. Two weeks later he moved in with me. We'd been together nearly two years, and although he never mentioned marriage I hoped things were getting serious. After all, living together was halfway there, wasn't it? ('No,' Georgie always said when confronted with this argument. 'Living together just means one set of bills instead of two – and I'll bet you pay them.') I did love him, or so I told myself that night, mellow with wine and gazing at his beautiful eyes in the photograph, but it was rather pleasant to have an evening alone when I could love him from a distance without his high ideals getting in the way. I went to bed feeling sexy and tried to fantasise about him, but in the end I was forced to revert to Russell Crowe. It was my favourite fantasy of the time, where I was chained to a post in the arena in Ancient Rome, about to be devoured by slavering tigers. Sadistic handlers were slowly paying out their leashes, as they tore off my clothing without actually touching my flesh. Then Russell Crowe appeared, scantily clad in gladiator-grunge with ripped leather and rippling muscles. He fought off the tigers, wrenched my shackles free of the post, and we rolled over and over in the dust. I was all but naked, helpless and available, and he penetrated me immediately, casually, humping me like a tiger in front of a breathless audience and the cold gaze of the watching Caesar. To the resounding cheers of the entire Colosseum, I came.

You think that's weird? I read an article recently where a woman admitted fantasising about having sex with an octopus. Compared to that, Russell Crowe and thousands of cheering Romans is pretty mundane.

Enough of me for a bit, time to fill you in on the real heroines of this story. On how beautiful Lin left her native Scotland

and was swept down to the decadence and corruption of the south. There was a man in it, of course. She was nineteen, doing media studies at college, and a bewitched lecturer managed to get her placed on work experience at the local TV station. At that age she had the dewy, untouched look of an ethereal creature who has just crawled out of a new-opened flower and gazes in misty-eyed wonder at the big wide world. (I know: I've seen photographs.) Blasé TV executives were enchanted, and she was deputised to make coffee for special guests, where her mere appearance mellowed awkward stars into interview mode. Curiously, though, none of the visiting men asked for dates: she looked too pure to be the butt of sexy banter, or the other half of a quick roll in the hay.

And then along came Sean Corrigan. A soap-stud from the long-running, Liverpool-based *Mandela Street*, at that time his looks hadn't been raddled by drink and drugs and he was still the clean-cut, dark-featured Irish lad who had recently scrambled to stardom. His hair was as black as the crow's wing and his eyes as dark as peat and his moods as changeable as summer in Connaught – and all this despite the fact that he had grown up in Deptford and his English mother had named him Sean not because of his heritage but after her favourite film star. To him, Lin's aura of unearthly purity was merely a novelty, a challenge, a hurdle to be taken in his stride. He took her for a drink after the interview, called her 'acushla' in his carefully cultivated brogue, told her, with a certain lack of originality: 'I've never met anyone like you.' Lin, inexperienced, hadn't heard that line before, but she was instinctively wary.

'How do you know?' she said. 'We've barely talked.'

'I don't have to talk to you, mavourneen. Your face tells me everything. It's as open as the dawn. You couldn't lie, or cheat, or let a man down, not if you tried.'

'I haven't tried,' she admitted. And, with a glint of humour: 'Not yet, anyway.'

He laughed. 'You won't need to, I promise you. The man doesn't breathe who would deliberately do you harm. You are too young, too innocent . . .'

The thought just flickered through the back of Lin's mind: *What happens when I am not so young or so innocent?* Aloud she said, in an aggrieved tone: 'Of course I'm not *innocent*. Nowadays, nobody is.'

'You're so right,' Sean said warmly. 'The word has fallen into disuse because girls are just girls now, and there are few angels among them. You're the first I've ever met. You seem to glow like a rose in the moonlight.' There was no Blarney Stone in Deptford, but Sean claimed to have kissed it nonetheless. He had developed what he thought of as a poetic flair to complement his Irish image, borrowing freely from the scripts of his various shows. 'I want to pluck you and wear you against my heart forever.'

Lin was charmed, for all her Scottish common sense. Common sense, after all, is not strong in a teenager, and she was susceptible, and secretly romantic, and he had charm enough to impress the viewing millions, never mind her. And blarney was a rare commodity in Edinburgh, where the young men tended to be dour and earnest, or dour and yobbish, or just dour. She gazed deep into his eyes and sank into them as into an Irish bog.

Later that night, back at his hotel, after large quantities of champagne and assurances of love and prudence, he relieved her of her innocence. The condom split during the proceedings, but he assured her everything would be all right. 'Me sperm are very lazy: they won't go swimming off into the dark.' He was staying in the north for two weeks, and during that period she found herself borne off to nightclubs and restaurants, shrinking from the flash-bulbs of the

19

paparazzi, to other hotel rooms, even to a lochside castle where a friend took him grouse-shooting and Lin struggled to quell her compunction for the hapless birds, telling herself it was only Nature. Her studies and her job were brushed aside: Sean bore her along in his swath like a favoured pet. He didn't talk about the future but, naïve to a fault, she assumed that was because it was taken for granted they'd be together. She deplored her own sneaking doubts, and did her best to ignore them.

And then came the day when he told her he was returning, not to the relative proximity of Liverpool and *Mandela Street*, but to London. To the deep south with its pollution and corruption, its hot climate, its posh accents and overpriced cuisine. She knew he had been written out of the soap at his own request, to graduate on to Higher Things, and now he told her that he would be making a new series, to be filmed in the capital, in which he would be the principal star.

'Wish me luck, acushla,' he said.

'Of course, but . . . what about me?'

'You'll be doing fine. We'll meet again, one of these days; I can read it in the stars. When I've a Bafta or two to my name and you're a meedja sophisticate, we'll turn up at the same charity event and our eyes will meet and – POW! That'll be a moment to live for, won't it? Until then, you can always tell the Press how much fun we had. They'll be glad to run your picture under my name, though you don't photograph as good as you look.'

'I don't want my picture in the Press,' Lin said, feeling as if the bottom had dropped out of her world. 'I just want to be with you.'

'Ah, now, me darling, you've a deal of growing up to do, and you need to do it without me. Don't be crying now; it doesn't suit you. We'll be seeing each other, I promise you.'

And that was that.

What about my innocence? Lin might have asked, but she knew it had been used up and thrown away. Now, she was supposed to become a meedja sophisticate, just like all the rest. She returned to her studies, tried to concentrate, noticed belatedly that she had missed a period or two. She attempted two home pregnancy tests and got two different answers. Finally, she nerved herself to go to the doctor.

Once she knew the worst, she was flooded with a torrent of conflicting emotions. Shame at her easy acquiescence in her own seduction, remorse for both the pain and the problems she was going to cause her parents, panic at the premature onset of adulthood and responsibility – and a desperate, overwhelming love for that tiny seed that was growing unwanted inside her. She rejected abortion immediately, out of hand. When she told her Presbyterian father and conventional mother they did their best to suppress their disillusionment with their daughter and offered both moral and financial support, though Mr Macleod's meagre income would be strained to feed another mouth. Perhaps it was because of this that Lin decided she had to talk to Sean. Reeling from his effortless act of desertion, she still retained an unacknowledged optimism about the male sex, somewhere underneath her emotional numbness. Surely, if he knew the truth, he would help. She wanted to write to him, but had no address. So she packed a single holdall, and braved the long train journey south.

Sean had occasionally mentioned hanging out at a club called the Groucho and on reaching London, after lengthy inquiries, she found her way there. 'I'm a friend of Sean Corrigan's,' she explained. 'I know it's silly, but I lost his address.' She hated the lie, feeling it contaminated her, but circumstances had taught her a little worldly wisdom – if only a little. Staff inevitably wondered if she was an obsessive fan, but decided she looked relatively harmless and could not help being moved by her crystalline beauty. She waited the whole afternoon and evening, finding herself a B & B to stay in and returning the next day, and the next. Reception were impressed by her quiet manner, and the way she resolutely refused to enter the bar when male club members tried to pick her up. They fed her tea, soup, sandwiches. By the third day, they were beginning to have an inkling of the truth. 'Contact his agent,' they suggested; but she shook her head. She could hardly tell her story to an agent, and if she didn't give her reasons Sean might simply fail to contact her. (Or if she did.)

But that evening, he came. He might have been disconcerted at the sight of her, but only for a second or two, then the charm kicked in and he took her into the bar and appropriated a vacant sofa where they could talk. He hoped she would be impressed by the scattering of celebs, but she was too keyed up even to notice. He ordered champagne; she asked for mineral water. He said he was sorry, he couldn't stay with her long, he was meeting friends; she said it wouldn't take long. Then she told him.

She thought he would be horrified, but he seemed almost amused. 'Is *that* all? Have it out, me darling, have it out. We're not in the old country now.' He had never been in the old country. 'I'll pay, no problem. You don't want to be saddled with a baby at your age. You've got your life ahead of you.'

'I can't,' she said.

'It's not a big op, honest. Nothing to worry about. I've got two girlfriends up the spout before: they said it was a doddle. I must be fucking fertile.' So much for his lazy sperm.

'I can't.'

She tried to explain her feelings, but he wasn't listening. In the end, he gave her a pat on the shoulder, told her: 'You'll see it differently in the morning,' and went off to dine with

22

his friends, leaving her to return to her lonely B & B, defeated and desolate. On the way out she paused in Reception to thank the staff for their kindness (she was always polite). A fellow Scot in the process of retrieving his coat heard her accent and glanced round. Touched by her appearance – everyone was, except Sean – he asked her where she was from, and if she was all right. 'I don't mean to be nosy – actually, I suppose I do – but you look upset and a bit lost. Maybe you're new to London. It's a tough city if you don't know your way about. Can I help? We're fellow countrymen, after all.'

'I'm okay, really I am,' Lin mumbled.

'No you're not, anyone can see that. Look, my name's Andy, Andy Pearmain. The girls here'll give me a reference. I'm not trying to make a pass or anything: I'm much too old for you and anyway, my last girlfriend was such a disaster I'm going to convert to homosexuality. It should be easy: in Scotland, it's always been the men who wear the skirts. You're obviously in some kind of trouble. If you don't want me for a friend, at least let me be a stand-in.'

The receptionists, genuinely concerned about Lin, assured her Andy was to be trusted, and eventually, too devastated to resist, she let him take her out for a meal. He was thirty-two, which seemed incredibly old to her, and bearded, increasing his air of venerability – the aforesaid beard concealing a jaw which might or might not have resembled a lantern. His hair was unruly, his other features – well – ruly. He admitted to a family background in banking and to being involved in 'investment opportunities' in film and television, which were, he said, too boring to elucidate. He used words like 'elucidate' in normal conversation, with the air of someone who was accustomed to using four-syllable words. He had chosen an unremarkable Chinese restaurant because he guessed, quite correctly, that a more glamorous location would have daunted her, but his manner displayed the unobtrusive confidence that goes with wealth. He was gentle, thoughtful, neither coaxing nor pushing, and gradually, stammering at first, then in a rush, Lin poured out the whole story.

This was the point, of course, when she should have subsided gratefully into his arms and lived happily ever after. It's like that moment in *Sense and Sensibility* where Willoughby dumps Marianne to marry money and she is rescued by Colonel Brandon. But real life doesn't work that way. Andy was elderly and bearded, Lin was still hopelessly in love with Sean, he offered her the sofa in his Covent Garden flat in friendship only, then put her in the bed and slept on the sofa himself. He was kind and chivalrous, Sean was an arsehole. He didn't stand a chance – even if he had wanted a chance to stand, and there is little evidence that he did. An unhappy relationship with a sophisticated brunette three years his senior had left recent scars, and though he was touched by Lin's beauty and her plight, that was all. He was a responsible adult helping a desperate child: nothing more.

So much for romantic cliché.

Two days later Sean called Lin at Andy's flat after wheedling the number out of a mutual acquaintance. Evidently, he had had a change of heart. He insisted he had never meant to hurt her, she shouldn't take everything so seriously, she was so sweet and earnest, it was just that she had dropped a bit of a bombshell and he'd needed time to get used to the idea. He was coming along to fetch her right now.

A week later, in the full glare of the paparazzi, they got married.

To call Sean an arsehole isn't, I suppose, entirely fair. He's an actor. In some ways, that's worse. An arsehole is at least consistent: you know where you are with him. You can rely on the fact that under any set of circumstances he is going to lie, cheat, and let you down. But an actor, immersing himself in his current role, tends to take his colour from that, blending into the part like a chameleon. In *Mandela Street*, Sean had been the charming Irish ne'er-do-well who impregnated other men's wives and shed girlfriends in alternate episodes. In the new series (I forget what it was called) he played a tough cop torn between the pressures of the job and the pregnant young wife he adored. Inevitably, it went to his head. He adored Lin in a succession of minor interviews, in a piece in the *Radio Times* to promote the series – by then, the twins had arrived and could be included in his adoration – in a lengthy feature in *Hello!* After a brief, unremarkable appearance at Stratford-on-Avon he stated his aspirations in serious theatre, and, as a sideline, insisted on calling the babies Lysander and Demetrius. Lin, blinded by reciprocal adoration, acquiesced, despite a private preference for Fingal and Fergus. Lysander Fergus and Demetrius Fingal were non-identical, respectively reddish-fair and dark, silent Scot and sensitive Irish (or Deptford) in temperament. They looked amazingly endearing in all early photographs. By the time they had grown into tiresome toddlers vandalising their Notting Hill house, Dad's character had lost his wife to a terrorist bomb and was back playing the field, albeit with suitable undertones of brooding and tragedy. Since Lin had failed to meet a premature death, in real life Sean was forced to revert to a less gloomy promiscuity. While Lin was tied to house and family he would go out, returning late or not at all, always indignant if she ventured to object. 'These people are useful, acushla. I was meeting a producer/director/casting director' or 'You know I'm not the stay-at-home type. That isn't why you fell in love with me. You love me for my wicked, wicked ways.' But charm fades with proximity and the lies wore thin with overuse. Even before Sean's girlfriends and other misdeeds started to appear in the tabloids Lin had begun to see through him.

'You're supposed to be the angel, mavourneen,' he would tell her, in the course of what was less a row than the monotonous drip-drip of seeping domestic discord. 'I never pretended to match up, now did I? Don't turn into a nag: it makes you ugly. And you don't want to go believing everything you read in the papers – any fool knows that.'

'I don't need to read the papers,' Lin said. 'I've seen your address book.'

'What the fuck were you doing looking in my address book? That's private – my private property. HOW DARE YOU SNOOP IN MY THINGS?'

And so on.

But the marriage lasted, or at least malingered. Moving out would have been expensive for Sean, and he still enjoyed the occasional indulgence in domestic bliss, usually on a Sunday when there were no nightclubs or parties to go to. Once in a while, he even took Lin to parties with him, if they were the kind of social events where appearing with a wife might do him credit. It was at one such party that she met Garry Grimes.

The second series of *Dickheads* was just finishing, and Garry was *the* big name in post-eighties alternative comedy. He had a squashed up nose, a brown monkey face, and a smile that stretched out like an elastic band, twanging back into mock sorrow at the expiry of a punch line. His racial origins were reputed to include Afro-Caribbean, Chinese and Italian, though all of them via Soho. 'He made me laugh,' Lin always says, failing to add that she hadn't had much to laugh at for some time. She still remembers what she was wearing that night, a dress she had bought in an obscure backstreet boutique which ran to tie-dye patterns and embroidery and ragged hemlines; but that kind of thing suits her. She didn't have any mascara on since she had been crying before she came out. Afterwards, she wondered if Garry had guessed. He fetched her a cocktail, fed her canapés, noted with appreciation that she didn't recognise several of the celebrities. On the way home, Sean treated his attentions as something of a joke. Garry might be a rising star – rather more of a star than Sean Corrigan – but his monkey-faced appeal could not possibly compete with Gaelic good looks and Deptford blarney.

He was still treating the situation as a joke three months later, when Lin packed the children, her bags, and the new nanny, and moved them all into Garry's house in Kensington.

Not long afterwards she had dinner with Andy Pearmain to tell him all about it. Therapeutic dinner with Andy – for Lin, the equivalent of the psychiatrist's couch – had become a regular feature in her life, substituting for the family she had left behind in Edinburgh. This was probably just as well, since letters and phone calls from her parents and two sisters who remained obstinately married to the same husbands all conveyed reactions shading from disapproval to mere bewilderment. Andy was a far more sympathetic auditor. His beard had shortened and he had acquired an earnest Japanese girlfriend who deplored his personal wealth while expecting him to use it to put the world to rights. Lin, who had grown up enough to listen to his problems in exchange for airing her own, agreed that Mitsouko's position was very inconsistent. 'But people are like that, aren't they?' she said with a new element of maturity. 'Full of contradictions. Everyone thinks Garry is so funny all the time, but in private he gets these black fits of depression. You know – if a script isn't working out, or something. He writes most of his own stuff. And then he drinks, and gets even more depressed. But he's so *kind*, and so good with the boys. I'm afraid they don't miss Sean very much.'

27

'Do you?' Andy asked bluntly, noting, unsurprised, that they had reverted to her affairs.

'No,' she responded. 'I thought I loved him so much – he *hurt* me so badly I thought it had to be love – but when I came to go I found it had all evaporated. Like the smell of cigarettes when you plug in one of those air-freshening things. I don't know if it was Garry – I don't think so – Garry just made me see the truth. All the time Sean was playing around, staying out all night, seeing other women, lying or brazening it out or whatever, the love just sort of leaked away. It shouldn't do that, should it? Not if it's real.'

'You were infatuated,' Andy said. 'Hardly surprising. Sean's incredibly good-looking and oozes Irish charm, even if it is fake. And you were very young and totally inexperienced when he came your way.'

'I'm not so young any more,' Lin declared, at the ripe old age of twenty-two. 'I've learned about life now. I shan't make the same mistakes.'

'You'll make different ones,' Andy said cheerfully. 'We all do.'

'Garry isn't a mistake,' Lin assured him. 'He's difficult, but he's worth it. He really does love me.'

'Yes,' Andy said. 'I think he does.'

A few months later Lin had a daughter, christened Meredith Grimes, a name agreed on by both parties and without theatrical or folkloric pretensions. But although Lin had divorced Sean, she and Garry did not get married. He had a phobia about marriage, one of his many phobias: he was that kind of comic genius, Angst-ridden and manic depressive, the sad clown who alternately adored and abused his nearest and dearest. Nonetheless, Lin managed him well and was often happy if always slightly anxious. Garry could be cruel when the black mood was on him, not physically but verbally, though never with the children. Lin told herself that this was a penalty of living with the artistic temperament, and felt rather proud of her adult acceptance of the problem. She informed Andy that she was no longer a silly romantic girl, expecting love to be a bed of roses all the time; she was a grownup prepared to roll on the occasional thorns.

'Roses have thorns,' said Andy. 'You're still thinking in roses, even when the going gets prickly. I suspect you always will.'

'I won't. I'm not,' Lin insisted crossly. 'Garry and I are as happy as – as anyone can be.'

But Garry wasn't happy. Happiness probably wasn't part of his nature: he was born with an inbuilt tendency to gloom. His marital phobia dated back to a miserable childhood and a father who beat both his mother and himself. He was obsessive about cleanliness yet when drunk would wallow in slovenliness, wearing the same filthy sweatshirt on a three-day bender and falling asleep in his own vomit. His latest comic venture, *Bannerman*, a series in which he played a trendy-left politician whose ideals are corrupted once he gets into Parliament, misfired badly. Possibly it was before its time: it predated Labour's rise to power in 1997. Several subsequent ideas were turned down. A film won critical acclaim but fizzled at the box office. He was forced to accept a role he didn't like, in a laddish sitcom stereotyping the multi-racial divide in North London. *The Bhindi Boys* was an instant hit, and Garry was stuck with it, which depressed him even more. He was continuously evolving new plots which unimaginative producers dismissed as too far off the mainstream. By the third series of *The Bhindi Boys* his drinking had increased with his fame and he had begun to experiment with hard drugs, though Lin always maintains this was infrequent and never an addiction. One night he came home after bingeing on booze and heroin and passed out on the sofa. Lin couldn't rouse him, so she made him comfortable on his side – she swears it was on his side – and went upstairs to bed. In the small hours he turned over on his back, threw up, and drowned in his own vomit. According to the doctors, he died without waking up.

Eventually, Lin would get over his death. But she would never get over the guilt.

The Press had a field day. Columnists shelved their own drinking and cocaine habits to pontificate on the decadence of media idols and how role models like Garry were betraying the Youth of Today. It was generally felt that, by dying in such a way, he had set a bad example, particularly to the young working-class blacks who saw him as one of their own – or so various white middle-class hacks maintained. Those same hacks turned up at his memorial service to count celebrity heads and soar into tragic mode before lapsing back into self-righteousness. But the wave of hypocrisy washed over Lin. Her mother had come south to offer support, and she did her best to censor any newspapers which she thought her daughter might read. During that period, the only thing that bound Lin to reality was her children. For them, she made an effort, trying to see beyond the wall of grief into some kind of a future. She didn't know her troubles were just beginning.

Unfortunately, another of Garry's many phobias had been the regulation of his finances. A paranoid fear of the taxman combined with a misplaced faith in his own fiscal cunning had disastrous results for Lin. He had never made a will, and the house they were living in turned out – for some inscrutable reason – to be in the name of his mother. She decided to blame Lin for her son's death, and promptly turfed her out. There was no financial provision for Garry's partner or child. Lin had to fall back on Sean, whose career had taken a downturn since he had been travelling the same well-worn route, though in his case the main result was that his looks were going and he was having to switch to playing bad guys. When he was in funds he had often missed maintenance payments; now, they hardly ever came at all. Panic jerked Lin out of a state of numb despair into a state of – well, *feeling* despair. Her mother knew nothing about legal matters, but Andy Pearmain, slipping into his accustomed role of knight errant, produced a lawyer who happened to be his latest girlfriend. A prolonged battle ensued, at the end of which it was decided that Lin could have the house provided she paid Mrs Grimes half its current market value, while at the same time the estate (i.e. the Grimes family) was committed to pay a corresponding sum to her and Meredith. Under law the boys, though Garry had treated them as his own children, didn't get a look-in. In short, Lin was left with three kids and a place to live, but insufficient money to live *on*. She decided it was time to go back to work.

Being Lin, she registered at the nearest employment agency. Media friends already shocked by her predicament were even more horrified at such behaviour: you didn't get a job through an *agency*, that was for Other People, *ordinary* people. What happened was your friends made phone calls, and *their* friends made phone calls, and the right job would materialise without any filling in of forms or vulgar discussion of qualifications. With Lin's looks and connections, PR was inevitable. While the agency ummed and ahhed ('You've been out of the job market a long time, haven't you? . . . You don't seem to have much experience . . . How *are* your computer skills?'), she found herself pitchforked into the sort of glamorous position that most girls can only dream of, organising film premieres, attending press parties, fuel-injecting the careers of rising stars, repolishing the lustre of fading ones. It took her less than a week to discover she hated it, though she stuck it out for six months.

'I'm no good,' she told a girlfriend. 'I hate having to be pushy, and pester journalists to write about people, and I hate it even more when they pester back. And all these stupid parties! I can't afford a full-time nanny now; I have to be home with the kids. Besides, I've never been much good at the social scene. I can't think of any small talk. I just start boring on about the twins' school reports, or my broken washing machine, and people look blank, and I don't blame them. I wish there was something I could do where I could be polite. And no parties.'

'There's publishing,' said her friend thoughtfully. 'That's still fairly polite. On the surface.'

'What about the parties?'

'You needn't go if you don't want to. Most launches are just given to pretend to the writer you're doing something: they don't actually *matter*. Of course, the writers all think they're stars, which is a pain, but that doesn't matter either because no one else thinks so. And the important thing about publishing PR is that nobody expects you to be any good at it. It's always been *the* job for Sloanes, particularly those with literary connections. Serious PR types give it a miss.'

'I'm not a Sloane with literary connections.'

'Irrelevant. It's who-you-know, darling.'

'I don't know anyone in publishing,' Lin pointed out.

'I do.'

And so Lin came to Ransome Harber, sinking into the unglamorous background as into a haven. (On reflection, you shouldn't *sink* into a haven. Perhaps she just moored.) Georgie has enough push for the entire department, indeed for several departments, and she quickly learned to make use of Lin's admin skills. Lin is the sort of person who writes everything down, makes lists of every contact, never forgets an appointment, never loses a file. Nobody minded if she didn't attend most of the parties. And authors, she discovered, are far less demanding than *real* stars. They have to live in the everyday world in order to write about it (except for Jerry Beauman); film stars and their ilk can only afford their otherdimensional existence because they don't write the script. And while Lin settled comfortably into the world of publishing, juggling job and children, inevitably she lost touch with old friends of Garry's who had only ever considered her in the light of a supporting role and, as such, dispensable. Mind you, Lin's one of the few people I have ever met who genuinely *wants* to play supporting roles, and always shies away from the centre stage.

Chapter 2

I never nursed a dear gazelle
To glad me with its dappled hide,
But when it came to know me well
It fell upon the buttered side.

THOMAS HOOD Jr: *Muddled Metaphors*

Before I move on to Georgie, let's stand back from them both
for a minute. If this were a more serious kind of book, now
would be a good moment to make a point about life, and
destiny, and everything. If I had, as they say, the pen of
George Eliot, instead of the PC of Emma Jane Cook, I'd take
the opportunity for a quick moralise. Of course, modern
writers don't do that, moralising is out of fashion: they just
throw in another lavatory scene instead. Personally, when
I'm on the loo I read *Vogue*, possibly in the hope that the
sight of all those super-thin models might drop a hint to my
metabolism. Anyway, I shan't attempt to moralise, but let's
just take a second for a spot of philosophy. Getting me into
practice for the Great Novel I'm going to write one day.

What I'm trying to say is, Lin is the sort of person to
whom things just happen. She doesn't *make* them happen,
she doesn't necessarily *want* them to happen, but the current
of events picks her up and sweeps her along and she goes

with it. Whereas Georgie wants to be the one who does the happening, who jumps in the water and tells the current where she wants to go. So you would think that her life would be pretty different from Lin's, a controlled sort of life, a life that follows a plan. Fat chance. 'There is a tide in the affairs of women Which, taken at the flood, leads – God knows where.' (Byron, not Shakespeare.) The point is, life can't be controlled. Destiny, or whatever it is, carried Georgie along as helplessly as any of us. She made her own decisions, she jumped into the water instead of being pushed – but when you get it in perspective, her history is basically the same as Lin's. Life took over and swept her away. In the end, I suppose, we're all just mayflies who kick a little while the water clogs our wings, and then go under. It takes more than a fly's strength to swim against the tide.

Well, enough of that. Back to the story. Georgie grew up in the sixties and seventies; she remembers the mini-skirt, and first-time-around flares, Biba, the Beach Boys, John Travolta when he was young. If you ask her what she was doing when Kennedy was shot, she says: 'Potty training.' But she isn't like the generation before, who go all nostalgic and misty-eyed about their youth, as if the sixties were some kind of Golden Age. It was tough being a girl in the seventies, she maintains, because all the boys had very long hair and beards and it was impossible to tell what they really looked like. 'Of course nowadays, what with shaving and the ravages of time, you don't usually recognise old boyfriends, and that has to be a plus.' But despite the hairy condition of the menfolk, Georgie insists she had fun. Georgie could have fun anywhere, any time. Georgie could have fun in prison – especially if it was a men's prison. Georgie could have fun in *Milton Keynes*. She has a talent for it.

Anyway, she was bright and teachers thought she should study something serious, like law or medicine, but she decided that was too much like hard work and did English instead. She went to university in Bristol, where – you've guessed it – she had fun. She emerged after three years with a drink habit, a drugs habit, and a sex habit, and sailed naturally into PR, since it sounded like – hmm – fun. Not publishing PR but the really glamorous stuff, with models and film stars and parties, parties, parties. It was the eighties, Edina and Patsy were still young, the Bolly ranneth over. Everyone had money. 'Well, everyone who mattered,' Georgie amends. 'Except the poor people, of course. And me. I never *had* money, I just *spent* money. It's always been that way.' In those days, she spent other people's money, lots of it, launching everything from board games to blockbuster movies. She lived in a succession of increasingly beautiful flats and had affairs with a succession of increasingly beautiful men, including several celebs. Lin and I know names but I won't repeat them: Georgie doesn't want to join the kiss-and-tell brigade. She was living her life the way she wanted, even if it didn't feel too good the morning after. At the latter end of the decade she took up condoms to forestall AIDS, gave up coke before it eroded her nasal cavity, and moderated her alcohol intake to preserve some liver and brain cells. As far as anyone could be, she was in control. Or so she thought. Then along came Franco.

His full name was Francesco Michelangelo Cavari, Conte di Pappageno, though there were at least a dozen more middle names thrown in with which I won't bore you. Italian birth certificates used to get so overcrowded that a few years ago the government decided to slap a tax on excess names, ostensibly for the benefit of harassed form-fillers. The Italian system of taxation is highly creative, and would beggar the entire working populace if anyone ever bothered to pay. Anyhow, Franco was dark and handsome, if not actually tall, with the caramel complexion of the Mediterranean, black hair, and a wicked green glint in his eyes. Georgie met him in Venice, where she had gone for the carnival. The setting was a palazzo, lantern-lit, candle-lit, fairy-lit; reflections shimmered in the canal below; somewhere above the stars were keeping their end up. Music fought a running battle with conversation. Georgie wore gold silk in the style of the seventeenth century; Franco was dressed as a pirate. Through the slits in his mask, she saw that green glint. It was fatal. She had never yet completely lost her head over a man, and somewhere at the back of her mind she felt it was long overdue. He fulfilled all the clichés: the looks of a film star, the credentials of a Latin lover, even the title. 'It was so Mills and Boon,' Georgie sighs, 'that was the joke. I never could resist a good joke.' But the joke was on her.

As soon as she returned from Venice, she booked her next ticket out. By the third trip the ticket was one-way. She shacked up with him in an apartment in Rome and in due course they got married.

I've seen the pictures. Georgie's hair looks darker then, a more golden blonde, and long enough to put up, piled on her head and twined with white flowers and bits of silver leaf. She is wearing that reliable marital standby oyster silk, and a train. The pallor of the material sets off a perfect tan, and the sculpted bodice and skirt show her tiny waist and the slender curve of her hips. She looks unbelievably lovely in a totally different way from Lin, all assurance and warmth and sensuality. Beside her, the groom is wickedly handsome, glint and all, his tan deeper and greener than hers, with that olive tint that you get in southern Europe, his pointy smile and loose curls making him look slightly faun-like.

'Wasn't he a Catholic?' Lin asked.

Georgie made a face. 'Oh, yes. I was so besotted, I agreed to the whole package. It wasn't as if I had any religion – nor had he. It was just what you did in Italy. He had the guilt, of course. Fornication was a sin and all that. I expect that's what made him so good at it.'

'Do you regret it?' I inquired.

'No. I don't . . . really . . . think I regret anything. What's the point? I was madly in love, I got married. Some of the time it was magic. Some of the time it was hell. That was all right with me. Living happily ever after would be very boring.'

Georgie's a lot more down-to-earth than Lin, but in those days she had her romantic streak. She had traded in her glamorous London lifestyle for what she hoped would be the *dolce vita* in Rome, but it took time to make friends and her determination to get a job unnerved her husband. She didn't have the contacts for PR there, so she studied Italian and got work as a translator. She found herself drawn into a small community of ex-pat brides, women from colder climes who'd gone the Mills-and-Boon route, falling for heat, bougainvillaea, dark good looks, seductive accents, out-of-date titles. They would gather together and compare notes on their Italian stallions, on the dominant mothers-in-law, the masculine obsession with machismo and *bella figura*, the best ways of cooking pasta, their frustrated desire to repaint the *salone* blue, or green, or any colour except the standard creamy-white. They had secret feasts involving Marmite, Branston pickle, rice pudding and curry. Georgie, never at her best with too much female company, shocked both foreigners and natives by cultivating menfriends, not clandestine lovers but admirers and companions: a gay fashion designer, an artist who painted her, an American writer encountered in the course of work. When Franco objected she laughed at him. 'Jealousy is good,' she told him. 'I'm glad you're jealous. But you must know you have no cause.' When he tried to assert some authority she was not so much intractable as impervious. It amazed her that he – or any man – would even make the attempt to tell her what to do. But when he gave up she eventually realised that this was worse.

Franco had always been fond of women, gambling and drink, not necessarily in that order. He gave up other women when he married Georgie – she knew he was occasionally unfaithful but always maintains it was 'nothing serious' – but turned increasingly to gambling and drink to reassert his emasculated ego and deaden the smart to his self-esteem. He could not rule his wife; had she chosen to rule him, within the domestic domain, taking over from his mamma whose iron dominion had been curtailed rather than softened by chronic illness, he would have adjusted. But Georgie did not want to rule. It was her independence which defeated him, and when he protested, ranted, fumed, all he saw was that she didn't take him seriously. His male bravado and lust for mastery was a game to her, a game she won effortlessly, without even noticing the contest. He drank to give himself the courage to challenge her, to numb himself to her laughter and her charm. By the time she had begun to understand, it was too late.

They wanted children but, despite constant groundwork, nothing happened. Georgie went for tests, Franco wouldn't even consider it. Doctors attributed the problem to 'psychological barriers'. When she finally learned she was pregnant, after her mother-in-law's last stroke, she didn't tell him straight away, in case anything went wrong and the failure of his hopes proved too much for him. He was drinking now to blot out the dread of his mamma's approaching death, or for any reason, or just for the sake of drinking. He came back late one night barely able to stand; she was trying to help him up the stairs to their flat when he fell against her and sent her sprawling. She tumbled down the rest of the flight and lay still, bleeding copiously. Neighbours called an ambulance; Franco was too drunk to help. The next day, doctors told him she had lost the baby he hadn't known she was carrying; subsequent tests confirmed damage to the womb which meant she was unlikely to conceive again. He sobbed out his guilt on her hospital bed, promising to give up the drink and saying having children didn't matter. A week later, he was blaming her for not telling him, and drinking again to drown both his shame and his bitterness that he would never be a father.

And so it went on. Drink → penitence → abstention → awareness → guilt → drink. Garry Grimes had gone on benders lasting two or three days but in between he had periods of relative sobriety. It was depression he needed to fight, not alcoholism. But Franco was now a full-blown alcoholic. Ultimately, he drank because he drank. After his mother's death they moved into the family mansion, a decrepit villa full of nooks and crannies where bottles could be hidden. Georgie tried getting rid of them, but he only bought more. She sought medical advice, only to be told there was nothing to be done until he decided to do it himself. She took control of their finances, only to find they hadn't any: what remained of the Cavaris' ancestral wealth had mostly been gambled or drunk away. Franco borrowed money from her, and never repaid it. When she refused to lend, he stole. The tenor of their rows had changed: she no longer laughed or teased him. One day, he hit her.

That was when she knew she would have to leave. Not tomorrow, or the next day, but sometime, someday. She stood at the window looking out over the Eternal City and thinking that its roots were deeper than love and its towers higher, because a city was a strong thing, a work of skill and stone, and the edifices of the heart were as towers of mist, and like mist they blew away. She told herself she wasn't bitter – she swore she would never be bitter, because bitterness eats the soul – but cynicism had entered into her, hardening her mind if not her heart. She would have to leave, and return to London, and the *dolce vita* was gone for good. In fact, it had been gone for quite a while.

'Of course you had to leave,' said Lin. 'He might have hurt you.'

'Oh, I wasn't worried about that,' Georgie responded. 'He couldn't hurt me. Even when he hit me, I didn't feel it. What worried me was that *I* would hurt *him*. If he hit me again I might hit him back, or pick up a kitchen knife – and that would be that. I never wanted to hurt him, so I had to go. There was nothing I could do for him any more.'

It was a battle she couldn't win, and Georgie had always been used to winning. She could have stayed in Rome – she had been there nearly ten years, and had many friends – but she felt it was better to make a complete break. She sold her jewellery and put the money in a trust with anything else she could scrape together, and arranged for regular payment of basic bills and a small allowance for Franco. The American writer and a Cavari cousin were trustees. Then she packed her clothes and a few personal items and flew back to England. Everything she had in the world fitted into three suitcases and a flight bag.

In London, she moved in with the elderly aunt who would subsequently bequeath to Georgie both her house and her mortgage. She knew she wouldn't be able to pick up where she had left off and she was right: she was pushing forty and had been out of the game too long. But there was an opening at Ransome Harber and an old friend put in a word. The salary was mediocre, the social scene far from glittering, but it was a job. Georgie took it.

It must sound as if everyone in publishing gets their job through the machinations of a friend. Basically, this is true. But just for the record, I got in through an employment agency – which makes me almost as rare as an author who's been pulled out of the slush pile.

Georgie had been with the company about eight months when Lin joined, over a year when I came. She and Lin, though unlikely friends in terms of character and outlook, had enough similarities in their life histories to form an instant rapport; Georgie rapidly became Lin's chief confidante, mentor, and substitute elder sister (though a far more sympathetic and understanding version than the real thing). Since I was working in Editorial, not Publicity, it took me a little longer to form part of our trio. I was attracted to Georgie – everyone is, of both sexes – but it was only after a particularly disastrous launch at L'Escargot that we became close. The book in question was a classy legal thriller by a blonde barrister called Courtney Pryce (real name Davina). Her literary agent, a battleaxe of uncertain age and even more uncertain temperament, got extremely drunk at the party even by publishing standards and Courtney politely suggested it was time for her to go home. The agent, whom I won't name for reasons of tact, discretion, and libel laws, went berserk, attempted to sock her client, and had to be forcibly restrained. She was eventually sent home in a taxi, was subsequently dumped by Courtney, and a year or so later produced an inferior novel plagiarising much of her ex-client's plot which became a brief bestseller at the Walthamstow branch of Safeway. Meanwhile, back at L'Escargot, a furious Georgie repaired her smudged mascara – 'Thank God my blusher's okay: I haven't got it with me' – and thanked me warmly for leaping into the fray to assist her. We retired to the restaurant for dinner, lingering – with Lin – long after the author had fled, and bonded.

Most friendships formed at work happen because people are stuck in the same environment and getting along together is both pleasant and convenient. But I really hope the friend-ship between Lin and Georgie and me is the deep kind, the kind that lasts. We certainly worry about each other enough. But then, women always worry about their friends: it's so much more comfortable than worrying about yourself. For instance, Lin and I indulged in some serious worrying over Georgie after the office party two Christmases ago.

Office parties, as everyone knows, are an essential item in contemporary romance. What Almack's was to Georgette Heyer, what Cinderella's ball was to the fairytale, what the movie premiere is to the B-list celebrity, the office party is to chick fic. In the City, secretaries tart up to seduce their dishiest bosses while excluded wives rant down their mobiles, and So-and-So from Foreign Investments makes an exhib-ition of himself with That Blonde from Money-Laundering.

In publishing, contrary to Bridget Jones et al, there are very few dishy bosses: Peter Mayer at Penguin in the good old days of fun and *fatwas* was, I am told, the exception to all rules. But since it is perfectly true that us girls tart up more for ourselves than the opposite sex – if Nigel is anything to go by, men don't notice anyway – we duly tarted. That is, Lin wore something with ethnic embroidery and tatty hemlines, mascara too dark for her colouring and a smudge of lipstick; I did my best to cover the bulges in a loose silk shirt, daringly pink, which made me look like an oversized Christmas parcel; and Georgie wore an Armani suit, all slim-line trousers and stylish tailoring, which must have made a major contribution to her mounting credit-card debt. She looked sensational, with her tits looming from a wispy little top under the collarless jacket, her hair an exquisite blonde disorder, and a couple of face jewels (they were all the rage that year) on her cheekbones. And all for the massed might of Ransome Harber, including not only the resident imprints but also the Design Department, which, like Publicity, dealt with everyone, Contracts, who had turned procrastination into an art form, and the power-mad control-freaks from Sales, who, in the teeth of the evidence, still believed they knew How the Market Works.

From five-thirty, every ladies' loo was choc-a-block, while the men wandered around complaining because there was no one else to answer the phones, opening bottles, sampling their contents, pulling the odd premature cracker and, in extreme cases, wearing paper hats. Georgie, Lin and I finished our titivation in Georgie's office, where she had thoughtfully provided us with a portable mirror and desk lamp for makeup purposes. Then we emerged, headed for the drinks as usual, and several glasses later, when Lin had peeled off to discuss folklore with Graham from Phoenix, Georgie and I found ourselves talking to Calum McGregor, the Art Director.

Cal is the reason the Design Department can tell a writer like Todd Jarman that his title is too long. It is thanks to Cal that Ransome Harber has *never* been up for the Worst Dust Jacket award at the Frankfurt Book Fair. He claims he can turn a sleeper into a bestseller simply by changing the packaging, and has, on occasion, proved it, with a little help from Promotions. The fact that he's dyslexic and is said never to have read a book in his life is irrelevant. Colleagues complain he's a stroppy perfectionist who makes their lives hell, picks their work to bits, and always thinks he knows what's best – unhappily, he usually does – though if he's been particularly difficult he will sometimes compensate by buying them a beer later. At the time of that party he was still a year or so short of forty, with floppy dark brown hair that made him look much younger, designer specs, and a face which, without being classically handsome, was – is – definitely attractive in a rather boyish, half sad, half mischievous way. He plays killer squash and goes running most days on Streatham Common near his home, so what you can see of his muscles look more suited to the sports field than a publishing house. Perhaps to plug his artistic image, he shaves infrequently and never wears a tie.

He was also the office lech. In those days, anyway. He seduced all the prettiest temps and would then start on the plain ones, with little subtlety and a cheerful lack of discrimination. As a rule he avoided any entanglement with the permanent staff but was seen out from time to time with leggy models, pouting PAs, dashing advertising executives. None of his affairs ever lasted more than a few days, or at the most a few weeks, and male friends said that despite the philandering he was still in love with his wife, a former biochemist called Christine. His marriage was long-standing but reputedly sex-free since the birth of his second son, who was severely mentally and physically handicapped. His wife had given up her career and everything else to devote herself to her child, becoming immersed in related charity work and eventually rising to a directorship in the Williamson Trust, which specialises in the care of handicapped children. Cal, so he claimed, was forced to seek solace elsewhere.

I saw a distinct gleam in his eye as he studied Georgie's cleavage, but it didn't bother me unduly since such gleams were automatic with him, she was permanent staff, and his taste normally ran to girls of twenty-odd. I drifted away to talk to someone else and it was only when I glanced over, an hour or so later, and saw Georgie and Cal still nose to nose that I began to feel slightly anxious. Of course, Georgie was an older woman with aeons of experience under her belt: she could look after herself . . .

'Georgie and Cal seem to be getting on awfully well,' Lin said in my ear. 'Oh dear. You don't think they . . . ?'

'Not getting on,' I said. 'Getting off. What *is* she doing? She knows his reputation. Everyone does.'

'He's been dropping into our office quite a lot lately,'

Lin volunteered. 'He said it was about the posters for *Doomspinner* – but that isn't anything to do with us really. That's Promotions. I thought he was just being friendly. He tries to flirt with me sometimes.' Lin isn't the flirty type.

That, I knew, meant nothing. Cal would try to flirt with a lampstand if it looked vaguely female. It wasn't the possibility of flirtation that worried me.

If I'd known what I knew later, I'd have worried even more.

'I've fancied you for ages,' Cal was saying with a flash of his cheeky-schoolboy grin. 'I keep telling myself it's a bad idea, but I won't listen to me. I've always tried to avoid getting mixed up with anyone at work . . .'

'It *is* a bad idea,' Georgie agreed. 'What about Trudi Horn from Contracts? Was that another bad idea – or just a lapse of judgement?'

Cal made a face. 'Both. I was hoping you wouldn't have heard about that. Gossip travels at lightspeed in this place.'

'It didn't have far to travel,' Georgie pointed out. 'Besides, I gather Trudi mentioned it – discreetly, of course – to about half the world. She was pretty upset.'

'She wanted commitment. I told her, right from the start, I don't do commitment. I don't do the L-word. I'm a married man. I just want sex – and you're the sexiest woman I've seen in ages. You don't look the neurotic type – you're young enough to be gorgeous and old enough to be sensible – and I'm drunk enough to try it on. The question is, are you sober enough to slap my face?'

'Oh, I could do that drunk, too,' Georgie said sweetly. 'If you're so married, why all the extra-curricular activity?'

'Christy and I don't have sex. I thought everyone knew that. We're going through a bad patch.' He sounded slightly defensive. 'Lots of married couples do. We'll get over it, and when we do I'll go back on the straight and narrow. Until

46

then . . . I'm a man, I like women, I need sex. I suppose I ought to control it, but I've never been good at abstention. In any case, you've only got one life and you have to make the most of it. Someone or other once said it isn't the things you've done that you regret, it's the things you haven't done.'

'You wouldn't believe how often I've heard that one,' Georgie sighed. 'And you were getting points for honesty till then. How long has this bad patch lasted?'

'Since Jamie was born. My younger son.'

'And he is—?'

'Eight.'

Georgie didn't say anything more, not then. She was thinking: Eight years? That's more than a marital blip. Poor Cal. I wonder why? He's really very attractive . . .

She said: 'So you want us to have a little commitment-free sex? A quick roll in the hay – or the metropolitan equivalent? Even though we work for the same company, in the same building, so it's a really bad idea?' He shrugged, then grinned, an irrepressible sparkle of hope in his face. 'Why me?'

'I told you, I've been lusting after you for months. You're stunning, you could have any man, and I'm nothing special, but – I'm an optimist. I thought it was worth trying my luck. Nothing ventured and all that.'

'Try it, don't push it,' Georgie said with sudden hauteur. 'Take off your glasses. No – put them on again.'

'You wouldn't *believe* how often I've heard that one . . .'

She laughed, meeting smile with smile. 'No, really, take them off again. I want to see your eyes properly.' She saw they were grey, with a fleck of hazel at the centre. How can eyes be expressive? she wondered. It's lines and wrinkles, colour-change and muscle-movement, that create expression. Eyes are just balls of jelly with variegated circles on one side. How can a ball of jelly look sad? 'They're . . . sort of tweedy. Unusual.'

'*Your* eyes are lovely,' Cal said. 'Huge and deep and soft. I could fall into them.'

'That would be poetic,' said Georgie, 'if it was my eyes you were looking at.'

As the party fizzled out, Lin and I joined them and talked pointedly of departure. Cal bade us a cheerful goodbye and headed home first, leaving Georgie to wander along with us. Outside, she said: 'I can't be bothered with the tube. I'm going to look for a cab. Goodnight, guys.' She didn't tell us until some days later that the cab in question was waiting round the corner, by prearrangement, with Cal McGregor inside.

Lin and I wormed the truth out of her pretty quickly, but they managed to keep the affair secret from the rest of the company for quite some time. 'We're just having a little quiet fun,' Georgie said. 'It won't last more than a month or two. He's got a lovely body. I haven't been close to that much muscle in a long while. That's the trouble with this job: all the men I hang out with are middle-aged media types going flabby round the middle.'

'You should get yourself a toyboy,' I said. 'That's better than a married man.'

'I've never fancied very young guys,' Georgie responded. 'I don't want to wake up next to anyone prettier than me.' She extricated a small silver mobile phone from her handbag. 'Cal gave me this. He's taught me text-messaging. He says you can't have a clandestine affair without it.' She scrutinised her latest message in complete bewilderment. 'Can you read text?'

I gazed doubtfully at a jumble of letters and numbers.

'The dyslexia doesn't help,' Georgie conceded. 'Still, spelling doesn't matter in text.'

'He's never opened a book,' I said, unreasonably irritated. 'He only looks at the pictures.'

'We don't need books,' Georgie retorted. 'We've got Real Life.'

In bed, inevitably, they began to talk. You can't have sex all the time, and in between there are those moments when you stop, sip alcohol of some sort, and it's dangerously easy to open up. Cal isn't a verbal communicator: he expresses himself through images. But when Georgie wants to be sympathetic she could get a corkscrew to unwind or coax a confession from a hardened criminal. 'You're a terrific lover,' she told him, flattering with sincerity. 'I can't think why Christine doesn't appreciate it. It seems such a waste. I know you said the other day she had a medical problem after Jamie was born . . .'

'Sort of.'

'I don't believe you. That was years ago. If there was anything wrong, the doctors would've fixed it. Can't you tell me the truth now?' And, very gently: 'Is it so difficult?'

'Jamie . . . was premature. Things went wrong. That's why he – why he was handicapped. I didn't understand the technical details. They said it didn't have anything to do with. . . You see, Christy didn't want sex when she was very pregnant. She said she felt fat and ugly. I liked it – I liked stroking her stomach, feeling the baby in there. Our baby. I wanted to be close to her, inside her, part of it. I shouldn't have done it, I shouldn't have thrust so hard . . . She thought that started the contractions. Having sex. She thought that was why the baby came early. Why he was handicapped.'

'She blamed you?' Georgie whispered.

'No. Not *blamed*. She just wouldn't do it any more. She said she couldn't. She tried, but she hated it. More each time.'

'Has she had therapy?'

'She tried that too,' Cal said, 'but it didn't last.'

'It almost sounds as if she didn't *want* to get over the

problem,' Georgie mused cautiously, tiptoeing on eggshells. 'Did she like sex *before*, or—?'

'She seemed to like it,' Cal said. 'We did it enough.'

'What I'm saying,' said Georgie, 'is that if she didn't have a high sex drive, or if she saw sex simply as the necessary route to having children, maybe, subconsciously, she wanted an excuse to stop. Whatever. It wasn't your fault. You have to take some responsibility – maybe you should have given her more orgasms—'

'How do you know I didn't?'

'I know.' She snuggled up, kissing the hollow of his shoulder.

He softened. 'Okay. I was twenty-one when we started dating. I wasn't much good in bed then. Too inexperienced.'

'You've improved,' she said. 'We all start out young, ignorant if not innocent. When I was seventeen I thought I knew everything just because I'd read the right books. You don't need to feel—'

'Guilty? I don't feel guilty.'

'I was going to say inadequate.'

'Do *you* think I'm inadequate?'

Her hand moved down. 'Oh no. *Very* adequate . . .'

Some time later, coming up for air, he said: 'What about *your* marriage? You said he was an alcoholic. Was that what finished it?'

And so Georgie told him her story, and as their intimacy developed mentally, so their physical intimacy intensified. At the office, even the prettiest temps passed unmolested, and although Cal's flirtatious manner continued, it became more a matter of routine, with no real intention behind it. He began to discuss his work problems with Georgie, absorbing something of her attitudes, and colleagues declared he had mellowed. Lin and I watched with mixed feelings. 'You're going to get hurt,' Lin asserted with unwonted stringency.

'Married men are always a bad idea. Is he going to leave Christine?'

'I don't want him to,' Georgie said. 'Anyway, it's just casual.'

'What *do* you want?' I asked, but she didn't answer. Perhaps she didn't really know.

Georgie had been a *femme* mildly *fatale* for most of her adult life without ever doing any real damage. There was no trail in her wake of broken hearts and ruptured relationships; as she herself put it, no man ever died of unrequited lust. But when Cal assured her of his lack of intentions, when she set about unwinding the corkscrew – opening the oyster – coaxing from him the exposé of his most secret fears and feelings, a little demon at the back of her mind whispered: Go on. You can do it. *Make him care.* Whether born of vanity or devilry she didn't know, but she was ashamed of it, and doubtful of her power, and unable to take it seriously. Georgie had survived her various trials and tribulations largely by never taking them seriously. She played the game because it *was* just a game, always forgetting the catch. To take, you have to give. And because Georgie is warm and generous by nature she gave without thinking, without prudence or restraint. 'Of course I shan't fall in love with him,' she told us. 'I'm over forty. I'm sensible. I've only ever *been* in love once, and that was more than enough. Anyway, he's *Cal*.'

The night came, after a week of tension at home, when he went out with the lads, got horrendously drunk, and turned up on her doorstep in the wee small hours. He told her he loved her and was promptly sick in a basin which she had had the forethought to provide: intelligent anticipation is one of Georgie's many talents. Then he crashed out in her bed till morning. She looked down at him – he was lying on his stomach, his head half-turned, his profile very young and somehow vulnerable in sleep – and felt a sudden rush of tenderness, catching her off guard, an emotion so strong that it was physical, squeezing her insides, a wonderful deep twisty pain which scared her and made her happy both at once. 'You wouldn't understand,' she told Lin and me when she described it, long after. 'You're too young. You don't know what it's like to go through the years being *so* strong, and *so* independent, and all the while underneath there's the fearing – the knowing – that you'll never feel that way again. You'll never be that alive again. Then it comes, when you don't expect it, and you think that no price would be too high for that moment, that *feel.*'

I don't know about Lin but in my case she was right: I didn't understand. Love hurts, so the songs say. Well, we all know that. Because of the rejection, and betrayal, and all that part of the package. But I couldn't conceive of happiness hurting; I couldn't get my head around that one. I thought that the hurt was because of his marriage, and the hopelessness of it all.

'So you *do* want him to divorce Christine,' Lin said. 'Divorce her and marry you . . .'

'No,' said Georgie. 'If I marry again it's going to be to a millionaire. I've done romantic marriage; now I'm going to be practical. It's just . . . until then . . . it's wonderful to be a little in love. Just a little.'

She should have known better. There's no such thing as being just *a little* in love.

So there we were. At the time of the three wishes, when I started writing this, Georgie was still more or less involved with Cal, I was shacked up with Nigel, and Lin was sinking in a morass of domestic problems. Another nanny had bitten the dust, Sean had fallen behind with his maintenance payments, Sandy's school had accused him of bullying, and the only thing in the house that ever reached a climax was the washing machine. So much for the power of the Wyshing Well. A couple of weeks after Vijay Ramsingh's launch party, I got home to find Nigel had set up a candle-lit dinner for two.

I should have done a better build-up to that, shouldn't I? I should have described opening the door, and the waft of romantic music that greeted me (actually an obscure folk band performing their own eco-ballads, with a soloist on the lute, but that was Nigel's idea of romantic), and the alluring cooking smells, and the pop of a champagne cork (Cava). Somehow, it's much easier to write about Lin and Georgie than it is to write about me. When you get inside your own life there are so many feelings to contend with, guilt and embarrassment and wishing you hadn't made such a fool of yourself and the urge to edit and tidy it all up and make yourself look better. But it's no good. I thought it was lovely, the whole thing, even when I saw the takeaway cartons from a nearby Italian restaurant in the bin – Nigel claimed he had done the cooking himself – and especially when he apologised for the Cava, saying champagne was too expensive and anyway, you paid for the label, other fizz was just as good.

I was so touched, I kept the cork, pocketing it when he wasn't looking because I knew he would say I was being sentimental. I'd gone away the previous weekend to stay with my mother and Nigel hadn't come with me (he never did, always providing himself with a cast-iron excuse), and he said he wanted to make it up to me. We sat and talked, or rather he talked, about how Big Business was ruining the environment (I agreed), and how J. K. Rowling was indoctrinating the children of today with an outdated bourgeois value-system (not sure about that one), and other such stuff, and I was dazzled all over again by his high ideals, and charmed by his baby-faced looks (ignoring the pocket-torch jaw), and we went to bed and had sex and he enthused over my earth-mother figure, and I felt beautiful in his eyes.

Which just goes to show that beauty isn't in the eye of the beholder. It's in the mind of the beheld.

I went around in a glow for two days, undamped by Georgie, who nobly refrained from sneering at the Cava. On Wednesday evening I was putting the rubbish out when the bag split. Fortunately, it was a small split, and only a couple of things spilled from the bottom of the bag. One of them was a champagne cork. When I'd fixed the damage by the complicated process of inserting the full, slightly split bag into an intact one, I took the cork indoors, washed it, and went up to my room to check in my drawer. The cork from the Cava was still where I'd hidden it. That didn't mean anything, of course. Why shouldn't Nigel have had an earlier bottle of fizz while I was away, presumably to cheer himself up? Why should I assume he had shared it with someone? He couldn't do that – he *couldn't* – and then two nights later snuggle up to my earth-mother breasts, and make me feel beautiful.

I hid the second cork with the first like a detective hoarding the evidence, though I told myself no crime had been committed. I was over-reacting, over-imaginative, suspicious, neurotic, paranoid. Nigel loved me. After all, he lived with me. But my glow was tarnished, and that night we didn't have sex, and Nigel snuggled up to the pillow, and I didn't feel beautiful at all.

I told my friends about it eventually, over lunchtime sandwiches in the office.

'D'you really want to know what I think,' said Georgie, 'or would you rather I told you polite lies?'

'Lies,' I said. 'Definitely. I'm being paranoid. Please don't make it worse.'

'If you really thought that,' she said, 'you wouldn't have

told us. The duplicate cork is just the clincher. There's also the circumstantial evidence. You go away for the weekend, he refuses to accompany you, then when you come back he turns up the volume on your romance. Classic compensation behaviour. Motivated by guilt or simply the desire to keep you sweet. He's got himself a cushy number, living rent-free in your flat. You can bet he doesn't want to screw it up.'

'He pays me rent! I mean, he pays towards expenses – I can't ask him for rent, he's my boyfriend. That's – that would be crass . . .'

'How much?' Georgie demanded inexorably.

'As much as he can afford! Look, it varies. He doesn't earn a lot; idealists never do.'

'*How much*?'

'About fifty a week . . .'

'And how much is your mortgage?'

'Don't you criticise my financial management,' I retorted, rallying. 'You're the one with the monster credit-card debt.'

'It doesn't matter what he pays you,' Lin interceded. 'What matters is whether he's seeing someone else. I think Georgie's being awfully cynical, but—'

'But?'

'You're worried,' Lin said simply. 'And you're *not* paranoid. You need to know whether there's something worth worrying about.'

'In other words,' said Georgie, 'time to get sneaky.'

Lin demurred at this. For form's sake, so did I. I hated the idea of searching his drawers for love-letters (does anyone write them any more?), or stealing a look at his bills (probably uninstructive: he was too broke to be extravagant), or hacking into his PC to check his e-mail. I couldn't bear the vision of myself prying, and spying, and being jealous and pathetic and sad. At the same time, I *was* jealous, or at least twitchy, and only the truth would sort it out. If I really wanted the truth. And the phantom of a me who shrank from unpalatable facts and preferred to live in a dreamworld so I could keep my faithless boyfriend was even more pathetic than my paranoia. It was almost a relief to let Georgie, who has never had scruples about anything, ride rough-shod over mine.

'Get his mobile phone,' she suggested. 'Check for text messages. It won't take a minute.'

'He doesn't leave it lying about much.'

'You don't need much. Grab it when it's on recharge.'

So I turned sneak. He always left it charging up overnight, and I would creep into the living room when he was asleep and check it out. For several nights there was nothing. In desperation, I really did go through his drawers, but I only found the sort of things that you usually find in men's drawers – solitary socks, crusty underwear – and this, though unpleasant, was hardly incriminating. There wasn't even a porn mag: he had a soul above such things. I wanted to feel reassured, but I didn't.

I started to read hidden meanings into every nuance of Nigel's manner. If you've been there, you'll know how it feels. You look at the other person, and you tell yourself every-thing's all right: he's just been a bit grouchy lately, he's under pressure, work problems, he's too tired or too stressed for lots of sex, are you really going to write off the relationship because of a champagne cork which wasn't even real cham-pagne? He keeps getting back late, but that doesn't mean a thing. And then one night it's *very* late, and he crashes out without a word, and you tiptoe into the room next door and press the buttons on his mobile, feeling sly and slimy and suspicious and vile, and there it is. The evidence.

'2nite ws gr8. Luv u. xR'.

You stare at it, and stare at it. In the end you go back to bed, because what else is there to do, and you lie on your back, not touching him, not even with your hair, not sleeping, and your mind goes round in circles and your heart churns, and in the morning you act normal, in a robotic sort of way, and he seems normal, and when he's gone there's this awful snide temptation to put your head in the sand and pretend none of it has happened, and then maybe it will just go away.

I called the locksmith from the office. After work I went back with Georgie and a couple of bottles of wine (Lin had to get back to the children), packed his stuff into boxes and carrier bags and dumped them in the street. By the time Nigel put in an appearance I was pissed and floating in the air three feet above my emotions. I yelled out of the window; he yelled back. Neighbours peered out to watch the show.

'You're crazy,' he bawled. 'What've I done?'

'You've only been seeing someone else. You were with her when I was away. Don't bother to deny it. You were seen.'

Well, he must've been seen. By somebody.

'Look, I can explain. It doesn't mean what you think. She's a regular customer – she's keen on me – I can't help that.'

'You brought her *here*. To *my* flat.' I was guessing, guessing wildly, shooting arrows in the air and hitting the bull's eye every time. I wanted him to tell me it was all lies, but he didn't. 'She rang me,' I improvised. 'I know everything.'

'Oh God . . . Cookie, please. She's confused. She makes things up. I *had* to bring her here – she was suicidal – where else could I take her?'

'Her place?'

'Don't be silly. There's her husband.' Panic was making him careless. 'I couldn't turn away from her pain. I'm not that kind of person. You know I care for you—'

'You care for my flat! You care for having an easy life! So much for left-wing ideals. You're nothing but a – a *gigolo*!'

'Bullshit. It's those bitches at Ransome, isn't it? They've done this. They've been stirring shit for me, egging you on—'

Georgie swept towards the window, but I pushed her back and took a restorative slug of wine. 'I don't need egging. You've scrambled my life. Just get out. *Get out!*'

'Where am I to go?' He sounded pathetic now. 'You can't do this. It isn't civilised. Where can I sleep?'

'Park bench!'

Eventually, he went. I might have weakened and let him in, but Georgie kept me strong. I knew she would: that was why I'd asked her to come. The neighbours, show over, retreated back into their holes. Later, Nigel returned with a taxi and collected his stuff. I watched him from behind the curtain, but although he looked up at my window he didn't call out any more. By then, I'd put whisky on top of the wine and I felt as high as the stockmarket when it hits an all-time record, just before it's due to crash. I felt bold and decisive and in charge of my life. (And alone.) Later, I was sick. Georgie stayed over and put me to bed. The next night, I knew, I would have to deal with the emptiness, and the constant urge to phone him, and the feeling that if I could just find the right knob (no pun intended) and twist it, normal service would be resumed and I could be comfortable again. That, or turn to meths.

Nowadays we recognise the problem of addiction and do everything we can to help addicts kick their habit, whatever that may be. Alcoholics have AA and other support groups, junkies have methadone and support groups, smokers have Nicorette patches, hypnotism, and, no doubt, support groups. But there's no professional help if you're addicted to a person. No Ex-girlfriends Anonymous, no substitute drugs (except possibly chocolate), no Nigellette patches. I would have to struggle through on my own, trying not to dwell on the times when it had been good: the cuddles, the comfort of coming home to someone.

I'd never lived with a boyfriend before, and now there was a Nigel-shaped hole in my life and only time, or someone else, would fill it up. I missed his nagging principles, his sense-of-humour bypass, his little-boy petulance, his pocket-torch jaw. I missed all the things I shouldn't have missed. Georgie rated him so low I knew she wouldn't understand. But he had cared for me, or seemed to, and I missed that most of all.

I stuck it out for a week. A week of cold turkey – of sweaty panics, hot flushes, that feeling that there are insects crawling under your skin and only a phone call will make them go away. Eventually, I succumbed, and went to the bookshop. I knew it was a mistake – I had no intention of telling the others – but I couldn't help myself. I had to know – I had to know if there was any way I could put things back together, if he cared about me, if he cared about R, if the nightmare I was stuck in was all my future. He gave me a chilly unwelcoming look for which I didn't blame him. He looked tidier and more clean-shaven than usual and not at all as if he'd been sleeping on a park bench.

'I wanted to see if you were okay,' I said.

'I'm okay.'

'Sorry about the other night.' I was losing all the points I had scored, but I was beyond caring. 'I'm afraid I was awfully drunk.'

He shrugged. 'You did me a favour.'

'How . . . how come?' He seemed to be armoured in ice, and I couldn't make a dent.

'Rachel's booted her husband out. I've moved in with her. I don't know how to put this tactfully, and frankly, I don't see why I should try. You're a fat lump of bourgeois complacency with no sex appeal and a very limited outlook. I was compromising my integrity just spending time with you. You offered me the soft life and I took it – desperation makes the best of us prone to weakness – but now that I've left I feel like a chicken who's flown the golden coop. I'm myself again.

I'd like to pity you, but I'm not sure you deserve it. Go back to those superficial airheads you call friends. I wish you joy of them.'

I just stood there. I wanted to say: 'How is the soft life with Rachel?' but I couldn't. I couldn't say anything at all. After a moment – how long a moment I have no idea – I turned round and walked out. I felt lower than an earthworm. I shouldn't have gone there: I had courted humiliation, and humiliation was what I had been given, in spades. I'd thought I wanted the truth, and now I had it. This was worse than cold turkey – this was just cold. It was Claudio's vision of hell in *Measure for Measure*, being imprisoned 'in thrilling regions of thick-ribbèd ice'. When I got home I tried to eat, by way of comfort, but I felt sick. I couldn't drink. I didn't have the courage to call Georgie or Lin and tell them what had happened. There was only me, and my humiliation. I wanted to be angry – anger is good, anger is positive, it keeps you warm – but I was only empty.

In bed, I lay wakeful, re-enacting the scene with Nigel with various different endings, all better than the original, until sleep sneaked up and caught me unawares. Blissful oblivion. Then in the morning there was the business of waking up to being me, humiliation and all. I wondered how someone who was size sixteen could feel so small.

It was many nights before the only plus in the situation occurred to me. At least I could spend more time with Russell Crowe.

Chapter 3

The Moving Finger writes, and having writ
Moves on, nor all thy Piety nor Wit
Can call it back to cancel half a Line
Nor all thy tears wash out a Word of It.
EDWARD FITZGERALD: *The Rubaiyat of Omar Khayyam*

Tout pour un, un pour tout. (All for one, one for all.)
DUMAS: *The Three Musketeers*

When troubles come, they come not single spies, as someone once said. Probably Hamlet, because it usually is. I was Nigelless, boyfriendless, fat and unloved and likely to remain so. It was February, going on March, and spring seemed a long way off, in every sense. My sister rang and asked after Nigel, so I had to tell her we'd broken up, and she expressed her commiseration with just enough real pity in her voice to make me long to kill her. Sophie is ten years older, and slim, with a husband, two children, and three dogs, and she lives her life in a welter of love and laundry. She is frequently sorry for me, and I know it, and I could forgive her everything except that.

To cap it all, at the beginning of March Alistair Garnett (the Publishing Director) summoned me to his office. 'You're

61

doing well,' he told me. 'You handled the Mallory woman brilliantly: she thinks you're a star. Natural tact, obviously.'

A cold trickle ran down my spine. When your boss praises your tact, you know it's a preliminary to being asked to do something utterly horrendous.

'And you got Todd to cut the title: I can't believe that. He's generally about as flexible as the Rock of Gibraltar.'

'He didn't like it,' I ventured.

'Who cares? Keeping the author happy is, as we both know, a myth that we propound only to – well, the authors. Personally, I dream of the day when all books are written by computers.'

'They'd only develop a temperament,' I pointed out. 'And then you'd get one trying to destroy the world in a fit of pique after a couple of bad reviews.'

'There's always one,' Alistair sighed, presumably in agreement. 'Where were we? Todd Jarman. I've got the manuscript of his new book here. I've roughed out a few suggestions as to plot and so on – nothing major, but I think we could do with another body; it gets a bit slack towards the end. Oh, and it'll need line-editing afterwards. I haven't the time for that. You've hit it off so well with him I thought you could finish it off. You'll have to go round to his place and go through it with him: he prefers having editorial sessions at home. You won't mind that.'

'He hates me,' I said baldly, blank with horror. 'He said I was arrogant and ignorant and—'

'Nonsense. Just striking sparks off each other. The best kind of creative partnership.'

'*He hates me.*'

'I told you you'd be working on his stuff.'

'Yes, but – *with him?*'

Alistair fixed me with his sternest glare. 'There's no place for cowardice in this business, Cookie,' he said. 'We're in the front line here. We have to face the critics, we have to face the writers – we're the ones who must publish and be damned. The enemies of free speech may issue *fatwas* and plant bombs in our offices—'

'*Have* they ever?'

'Shut up: I'm holding forth. Our enemies may threaten, and bully, and intimidate, but we do not flinch. We point our Mont Blanc pens and say: "Come on, make my day."' ('Speak for yourself,' I muttered. I had a felt-tip.) 'We stiffen our sinews and march on in the cause of Literature. Arm yourself with commas, with colons, with little squiggles in the margin. As it says in the Bible, the Word is God, and we deal in words.'

I had no intention of listening to any more of this. He was starting to sound like Lord Kitchener's poster. No doubt he thought it was funny; I didn't. I really was the one in the firing line. 'All right,' I said. 'I give in.'

Todd's new book was good, perhaps one of his best, but it didn't cheer me up. His hero, D.I. Jake Hatchett, was alternately tight-lipped and foul-mouthed, possibly because he got hit on the head a lot, at least in this story. Under a stone-faced, flint-hearted exterior he had dark, brooding emotional depths which only the reader got to see: successive girlfriends in previous novels either got killed or did it, though here we had a new twist with a female lawyer who put herself beyond the pale at the end by agreeing to defend the murderer. Did Helen know? I wondered. Hatchett was invariably matey with prostitutes and down-and-outs, hostile to the rich and successful – in short, the kind of cop who only exists between the pages of a book or on TV. He was so clearly the sombre side of Todd Jarman's persona that as I read I found myself superimposing the author's face on the character, hearing the curt phrases uttered not in the tones of the actor who had been such a hit in the role, but in those of the man who had been so scathing about my editorial skills. Of course, most writers create their hero in their own image, or the image they would like to have, so this wasn't exactly new – but for some reason it made me feel uncomfortably close to Todd Jarman. There's nothing like a row for bringing down normal social barriers. Or professional ones. I hadn't felt that close to, say, Oonagh Mallory, that turner-out of historic soaps set invariably amidst the passions and potato-crops of the Emerald Isle.

I began the business of tinkering with the grammar, adding a comma here or removing one there, noting every alteration in the margin so Todd could object to it later on. In addition I marked – very tentatively – sections which I thought might need cutting or rewriting, and indicated places where Alistair's suggestions could be incorporated. By this time, the process was starting to go to my head, and I even came up with a shortlist of candidates for an extra murder, including a hooker who knew too much, a bent cop (Jarman always had lots of those), and a cab-driver who could have overheard a crucial conversation in the back of his taxi. (Something on the lines of: 'I had that Peter Sutcliffe in the back of me cab once . . .) I knew I'd overdone it, but I might as well be hung – or, more probably, strangled – for a sheep as for a lamb. It was nearly six before I finished. I reached for the receiver with a shaking hand and dialled Todd's number.

There's a natural antipathy between writers and editors – rather like that between the driver with nowhere to park the car and the ubiquitous traffic warden. Circumstances have made them enemies and there is no possibility of reconciliation without changing the basic structure of society. But in the literary world, at least, the association usually starts with courtesy. Todd and I seemed to have dispensed with this. Listening to the ring tone, I told myself the relationship had nowhere to go but up.

I got an answering machine. Relief had just begun to surge through me when an unrecorded voice cut in abruptly. 'Hello?'

'Is that Mr Jarman?' Instinctively, I went for formal courtesy.

'Could be. Who wants him?'

'It's Emma Cook,' I said. 'Your least favourite editor.' In the ensuing silence I could feel the attempt at humour going down like raw suet. 'Alistair and I have been working on your manuscript. It's terrific. I was wondering if I could come over and go through it with you.'

'If it's terrific what is there to go through?'

'Just a few minor points . . .' Editors always say that.

'I'd be happy to work with Alistair, but frankly, Miz Cook, I don't think there's anything *you* can do for me. Go teach your grandmother to fuck eggs. Sorry – suck. Printer's error.'

'Alistair's rather busy at the moment—'

A mistake.

'In that case, I'd better find a publisher who isn't too busy to work with me.'

'He thought we'd established a great rapport,' I said desperately. 'You and I, I mean. He said—'

'Didn't you disillusion him?' A note of surprise sneaked in under the sarcasm.

'I tried,' I said. 'He wouldn't listen. He thinks we were just "striking sparks" off each other. He called it a creative partnership. Then he made a speech about publishing and being damned.' This was wildly unprofessional, and I knew it, but I was past caring. 'I don't know if you know Alistair very well, but he has this crusading spirit.'

'I'll bet he does. In a bottle in the bottom drawer. Unfortunately, I know him well enough to believe you. You'd better come round on Friday. Two p.m. Or are you getting your hair done?'

'My hair does itself,' I retorted, but quietly. I had gained my point, but I didn't feel good about it. When I thought of my red ink on the manuscript, my knees turned to jelly. I contemplated Tippexing out some of the changes, but decided in the end I couldn't be bothered. What the hell.

Which only goes to show that indolence is a more powerful motive force than fear, though what that says about the human race God only knows.

On Friday, bundled into a large furry coat which made me look like an overgrown koala (not real fur: dead teddy), I arrived at Jarman's address, a slim, elegant house in Belsize Park several lightyears away from the mean streets of his novels. Urns flanked the front steps, sprouting exotic shrubs; a burglar alarm adorned the façade while a furtive satellite dish lurked round the side. I stiffened my sinews, imitated the action of the tiger, and pressed the bell. Nothing happened. I let my sinews relax a little, and pressed again.

Todd Jarman opened the door, clasping a portable phone to one ear, and threw me a look which said: 'How dare you interrupt my phone call?' as if I had done it deliberately. He was wearing a shabby grey sweatshirt, greying jeans, and a stony grey expression. His five o'clock shadow obviously dated from five o'clock the previous afternoon. He went on talking for what felt like an hour though it was probably only about ten minutes, retreating into an adjacent room at the same time to leave me standing in the hallway feeling like a lemon. Finally I heard him conclude the conversation; then he called out: 'Come on in.' The words were an invitation but the tone was brusque. Conscious of a sinking stomach somewhere below my tigerish sinews, I followed him.

I found myself in a room which looked like a study under invasion from a designer sitting room. At one end there was a desk with laptop, printer, and all the usual etceteras, while the wall beside it was stacked with crowded bookshelves and an old-fashioned lamp stood poised to fill in when the daylight ran out. The rest of the room had been taken over by a very long sofa with no cushions, a chair that resembled the satellite dish outside, and a glass-topped coffee table balanced on what seemed to be a hunk of natural granite. Here, the books were tidily arranged on black-painted shelves and interspersed with tasteful ornaments. A vast grey rug appeared to be advancing towards the work desk like a creeping tide.

Jarman evidently caught the bewilderment in my gaze. 'Helen's rearranging the place,' he offered unexpectedly. 'She thinks this is too nice a room to waste as a study: she wants me to move upstairs. As you can see, she's started re-doing it already, but I'm holding on. This is Custer's last stand over here – if you managed to fit in any history around your dedicated study of the English language.'

'Little Bighorn,' I said. 'I saw a movie. Wonderful how good their camerawork was in those days.'

He didn't smile, of course. 'Coffee?' he inquired, picking up the inevitable unwashed mug which probably features on every writer's desk in the universe.

'Tea,' I said, to be awkward. 'Please.'

He threw me a dark look but made no comment, merely inquiring my preferences in milk and sugar on his way to the kitchen.

'Just milk.'

He returned presently carrying two mugs, tea for me, coffee for himself, and wearing an expression suggestive of gritted teeth. 'Here you are.' He handed me the tea. 'Miss Cook – Emma—' (Have you noticed how men always say Miss when they're being polite, and Miz when they want to offend?) '– we seem to have got off on the wrong foot. Alistair assures me you're very good at your job. Under the circumstances, I think we should try to start over again.'

He wasn't being sincere, I told myself. Of course he wasn't. So I didn't have to be sincere either. 'All right,' I said, juggling with my mug to extend my right hand in a gesture that felt somewhat forced.

His grip was firm and strong. He would have made a good strangler.

'Have a seat,' he said, indicating the sofa. 'I'm afraid it isn't very comfortable.' I had already shed my coat on to the satellite-dish chair.

We sat down on the sofa, I produced the annotated manuscript, and we got to work.

Détente lasted until the first page.

Some writers work quickly and carelessly and need extensive editing to tidy up their prose. A few are dyslexic and make regular grammatical errors. (A lot can't spell, but spellchecks can deal with that.) An editor's nightmare is the perfectionist writer who thinks he/she never makes a mistake, whose command of language is faultless and who knows by instinct when even a comma has been misplaced. Todd Jarman was – of course – one of the latter. I knew bloody-mindedness had made me overenthusiastic, but by the time Todd had begun with the acid-tongued scorn, graduating through sarcasm and contempt to pure rage, I was determined to concede as little as possible. There was something about him that seemed to flip a switch inside me, cancelling out the tact and diplomacy with which I had handled Oonagh Mallory of the potato passions and turning me into the editorial equivalent of a virago.

I found myself saying whatever came into my head – and the remarks that came into my head were the sort you usually only think of after the event and, in a professional context, would have been better left unsaid. (Later, I thought how good it would have been if I had been able to come up with the same quickfire nastiness in my final scene with Nigel, instead of expending it on the far less appropriate target of Todd Jarman.) By the time we got to Alistair's suggestions for plot development we were in a state of total war and I knew in my gut I would be out of a job by the end of the week. I might get away with calling an author arrogant and pig-headed to his face but I had twice accused him of over-writing and once of lack of clarity. Jarman prided himself on his clarity and the raw simplicity of his style.

'You want *what*?' he said. '*Another body*? We've already got three.'

'You can never have too many bodies,' I said blithely. 'Look at *Taggart*. They have one before every ad break.'

'Of all the ludicrous comparisons – ! I don't intend to take my cue from some crap TV show named after a hero who died years ago – and can you blame him? My work is rooted in the stark realities of street crime—'

'There are over two hundred murders every year in London and the southeast,' I declared. 'You can do four of them.' It was utter rubbish – I hadn't the faintest idea of the annual murder rate – but I had noticed with Nigel the efficacy of statistics in any argument, and I was prepared to improvise. With a belated flicker of tact, I *didn't* point out that it was a crap TV show which had made Jarman's books a hit.

'A fourth murder would involve manipulating both my characters and plot. I don't intend to do that. I won't pander to the national appetite for gore.'

'Considering that your first body is a prostitute dressed as a nun with stigmata on her hands and feet and an upside-down cross cut into her forehead—'

'Every detail of that crime was psychologically significant.'

'And then there's the pimp found decapitated in an alleyway whose head turns up in the chilled section at Tesco, and the retired Chief Constable, also dressed as a nun—'

'I know what happens in my own novel: you don't need

to recap. I work out my plots very carefully beforehand. You can't just chuck in an extra corpse because you think the body count is too low. Stick to fiddling with semicolons and the state of the verb, Miz Cook—' the would-be friendly use of Emma had long gone out the window '– that suits your mentality. Literary criticism is way out of your league.'

I didn't mention that the whole extra-body thing was Alistair's idea. By then, I didn't care. 'If you re-read the book properly,' I snapped, implying that he hadn't, 'you'll notice that the pace slows up badly towards the end. You need something to wake the reader up. There's no point in having a perfect plot if no one can be bothered to stay the course.'

God knows what he might have said to that, but the sound of the front door and a quick, high-heeled step in the hall distracted him. Helen Aucham walked in, slender and power-suited, her hair as perfect as the ramifications of his plot. In daylight her Botoxed complexion looked smooth and flawless. 'Oh, are you working?' Her gaze skimmed over me without interest. As usual. 'God, I've had an awful day. They're going to deport Charlie Nguru even though the medical evidence of torture was conclusive. I've got three days to find a loophole. Be a darling and get me a drink.' I wondered how someone so superficial could be so caring. Or vice versa.

'We – we'd better give it a break,' I stammered, reverting to normal behaviour. 'We've got a month to sort out any changes . . .'

'A *month*? And you want *rewrites*?'

'You're in the catalogue for publication in the autumn,' I whispered. 'Sorry.' Alistair, a slow reader, had been sitting on the manuscript for some time. 'Anyway, not exactly rewrites. Just . . .'

'Another body. A corpse too far. Forget it. There's no way I'm going to fuck this up with an overdose of blood.'

'I thought that was the whole point,' Helen said with a careless smile. She had left the room to remove her coat and now wandered back in, flicking the sweep of blow-dried hair off her face. 'Darling, if you've finished—?' Her indifference daunted me. I got to my feet, gathering up my koala. Oddly, I felt a sudden rush of indignation at her dismissal of Todd's work. He might not be saving persecuted heroes, but his books entertained people, diverting them from the trouble and trauma of everyday life. That had to be a good thing. A friend of mine once declared that he was saved from suicide by the latest P. D. James. Todd Jarman's stories were quite capable of distracting any number of suicides.

'I'll call you next week,' I suggested.

'Whatever.'

He showed me to the door. As it closed behind me, I heard Helen's voice. 'Is that your latest editor? Poor thing. What a lump . . .'

Somewhere, according to modern scientific thinking, there was a universe where a reconstituted Tyrannosaurus Rex would smash through the window and devour her on the spot, tearing up the minimalist sofa in the process. Somewhere there was a universe where her corpse – dressed as a nun – would be found spread-eagled on the pale grey rug, rigor mortis completing the work Botox had begun. The main problem with the theory of parallel universes is that the one where all the good stuff is happening is *never the one you're in*. Have you noticed that?

It wasn't until I got back to my flat – my empty, Nigel-haunted flat – that it occurred to me that despite Todd's scorn and fury, for the whole afternoon the secret agony of rejection and humiliation had disappeared altogether. (At least until Helen came in.) It was as if Todd Jarman, of all people, had given me back something of myself. Maybe it was the job, restoring my sense of status. Or something. I ate an unhealthy supper consisting of a sandwich and a can of soup, watched a video of *X-Men*, and went to bed determined to dump Russell Crowe for Hugh Jackman.

I was a mutant known as Chameleon, since my skin reflected, or perhaps refracted, light in such a way that I could make myself invisible at will, provided I had no clothes on. (In fantasy novels invisibility spells invariably extend to clothing. I think this is cheating, so I decided to adopt the scientific approach.) Embittered by the cruelty of non-mutants – like Helen Aucham – I was working for supervillain Ian McKellen, and had been ordered to sneak into Patrick Stewart's college and spy on the so-called students. Caught short in his room by the entry of Wolverine (Jackman), I froze, fearful that a ripple in the air might betray my presence. He stripped and went into the shower, muscles flexing in his lean, pantheresque body, while I waited, motionless, knowing myself trapped. To open the door and slip out unnoticed would be impossible. When he re-emerged, water-droplets beading his bare torso, I found myself terrifyingly conscious of his maleness, of the fact that we were both naked, in close proximity, in his bedroom, though he was still unaware of me. Then he moved in my direction, and involuntarily I shrank back. He sensed something, his hand reached out – and touched my nipple. I stood rooted to the spot, half in fear, half in fascination, while he explored my body, discovering me by touch, murmuring my pseudonym: 'Chameleon. Chameleon.' His response was obvious: his organ lifted and stiffened into a pole so large and powerful that I flinched at the sight. Then suddenly he slammed me against the wall; I started to fight but knives sprang out of his hand; the tip of one blade pricked my throat. 'I know you,' he said. 'I know who you work for. Reveal yourself!'

'No!' I gasped, and then he was inside me, pounding and pounding at me, filling my unseen body, biting and kissing in the battle for my surrender. I struggled but in vain, unable to resist the pleasure, and visibility flooded through me like a giant blush, showing me in all my nakedness and vulnerability, and I came and came and came . . .

Afterwards, I lay panting and sated, relaxing towards sleep. I speculated idly on the mechanics of invisibility, wondering if in the foregoing scene my mutant powers could realistically be extended to cover hair, eyes, and teeth. J. K. Rowling, of course, had used a cloak.

But then, nothing like that had ever happened to Harry Potter.

On Saturday, Lin, Georgie and I had a girls' night out. We would see each other regularly every lunchtime and often for a quick drink after work, but a full evening together was rare since Lin's nanny problems meant she hardly ever had a babysitter, and even when she did chronic parental guilt usually sent her running back to assist with homework and listen to outpourings of childhood Angst. And until lately I had been preoccupied with Nigel, while Georgie was busy with Cal in the week and socialised with other friends at weekends. However, it was she who had declared a Saturday night session was long overdue, and Lin had persuaded Sean's mother to take Meredith as well as the twins. 'The house feels so empty without them,' she sighed. 'So quiet. Like a graveyard . . . It's heaven. I actually managed to tidy all the guff away this afternoon and hoover round. Bliss.'

'Life can hold no more,' Georgie said absently. 'How are we getting on with our wishes?'

'I'd forgotten all about that,' Lin admitted.

'Do I look like a sex goddess to you?' I snapped. I wanted to talk about Todd Jarman, and Helen Aucham, and alternate universes. I wanted to avoid talking about Nigel. The wishes were a side issue.

But Georgie was determined to stick with it. 'It's what we really want out of life,' she insisted. 'We ought to focus on that, instead of being sidetracked by everyday trivia. Achieving your goals is only a matter of determination.'

'Have you had a row with Cal?' I asked.

'N-no. But I have to dump him. Soon. He's never going to pay my credit-card bill. I'm still attractive enough to pull a millionaire – I *think* so, anyway – but it's going to get harder. In ten years' time I'll need a millionaire to pay for the plastic surgery so I can pull millionaires. I shouldn't be frittering away the last of my youth – or whatever – on a married man with no spare cash.'

Youth, I felt, was stretching a point, but I didn't argue. After all, I was heading for thirty, and the Bridget Jones years.

'So what have you done about meeting the Man of your Dreams?' Georgie demanded of Lin.

Lin looked blank. 'Well – nothing. I mean . . . it's up to Fate, isn't it? You just look across a room, and the magic happens. You can't make your own magic, can you? That's one you have to leave to the fairy in the Wyshing Well.'

Georgie clearly thought that you could make your own magic and was about to say so, but I interrupted. 'To meet the Man of your Dreams you must start by meeting men,' I pointed out. 'You should have more social life.'

'I can't. I have the children to think of. Even if I could find a decent nanny, they need me at home.'

'We'll babysit,' Georgie offered rashly. I mumbled something which might, or might not, have been agreement. Children make me nervous: they're a lot like animals, only not so well-behaved.

'Thanks, but . . . where would I go? No one asks me to parties any more. I was only invited as a kind of accessory to Garry, or Sean, never just because I was me.'

'Andy likes you 'cause you're you,' I said.

'He's getting married,' Lin said abruptly. 'I forgot to tell you. They're having a big do at the family castle in Scotland. I suppose I could go to that to meet men.'

'Weddings are great for romantic encounters,' I averred. 'All the books say so. Who's he marrying?'

'I'm not sure,' Lin said. 'I get them all mixed up. There was an environmental campaigner. He rescued her from a tree in the path of a new bypass. Then she went off to the Highlands to save the wildcat. He always goes for the idealistic type. But it might not be her – she was quite a while ago.' She didn't sound jealous, but she clearly wasn't enthusiastic.

What was it about these rampant idealists? I wondered. Andy Pearmain's fiancée, Helen Aucham . . . Nigel. In the twenty-first century principles are obviously sexy – but why do I always resent people who flaunt them in public?

'Pity it's too late to pair her off with Nigel,' I remarked.

'And what of Nigel?' asked Georgie. 'You haven't mentioned him for weeks. Well, days, anyway.'

'I haven't thought of him for weeks,' I lied. 'Or days.' But my face must have given me away.

'What have you done?' Georgie's voice was accusing. 'You'd better confess. You finished it on a high. Don't tell me you went crawling back.'

'Okay, I won't tell you,' I said obligingly. 'Happy now?'

So I told them. I couldn't look at them, even though they were my friends. The humiliation rushed over me tenfold, twentyfold, shrinking me inside myself, turning me to dust. I thought Georgie would rail at me but she didn't. She jumped up and came round the table, knocking over a glass, and hugged me, and Lin came and hugged me too, so we were all tangled up in one big hug, and suddenly I wanted to cry for all the right reasons. 'We'll get him,' Georgie said. 'He'll eat his words. We're going to turn you into the hottest sex goddess since Monroe's skirt blew up around her ears. We can do it, I promise. *You* can do it. Let's have some more wine.'

We ordered another bottle, and another, and the evening began to unravel comfortably like a roll of Andrex with a puppy on one end. I offloaded my feelings about Todd Jarman, and Horrible Helen, and designer sofas, and Georgie vowed repeatedly that she was going to drop Cal for an unmarried millionaire, and Lin, who had no head for drink, started rather unexpectedly to bemoan the fact that Andy Pearmain wasn't gay. 'Wives always get in the way,' she declared. 'He won't be there for me any more, and he's always been there for me. My best friend. 'Xcept you two, but that's different. Andy's a man – solid, strong—'

'Bearded,' Georgie interjected.

'Solid, strong, bearded . . . *reliable*. Someone to lean on. Why couldn't he have a boyfriend? He said ages ago he was going to be gay. He's so bad at women. He keeps falling for these earnest types who eat vegan food and spend his money on lost causes and . . . and take advantage of his kindness and solidity.'

'You mean – they lean on him?' I hazarded.

'Exactly! But not in a good way. They lean too – too heavily, they put pressure on him, they drain him. He never gets to laugh or make jokes. He needs to be leaned on gently, by someone who makes him feel good about it. These women, they blame him for being a rich capitalist and then when he feels guilty they suck him dry.' ('Does she mean a blow job?' whispered Georgie, who was becoming confused.) 'He needs a nice boyfriend who adores him, someone young and shy, with big eyes and long eyelashes.'

'Sounds like Bambi,' I said.

'If he had a nice boyfriend, I bet I'd get along with him

really well. I shan't get on with his wife, I know it. His girl-friends never like me. They despise my dress sense.'

'You haven't any,' Georgie said, shocked into bluntness. 'Not that it matters, of course. You're the only person I know who can make hippy-retro-cum-fashion-accident look like style.'

Fortunately – since that could have been more happily phrased – Lin wasn't attending. She had sunk into a state of rather wistful gloom, contemplating the fun she might have had with Andy and Bambi as they gave guilt-free, non-vegan dinner parties in the ancestral Scottish castle (which had only passed into Andy's family since his uncle bought it from its original set of ancestors). 'She definitely needs a man,' said Georgie.

'Food might be good,' I suggested.

'We'll go and have chips at the Soho House,' Georgie said. 'They do good chips there. But, mind, tomorrow you start the diet.'

'You mean the miracle diet that's going to turn me into a size eight sylph?' I said sceptically.

'No, I mean the realistic diet that's going to convert mere flesh into the voluptuous curves of a sex goddess,' Georgie retorted. 'Mae West wasn't thin. Monroe wasn't thin. Jean Harlow—'

'Bette Midler isn't thin,' I said, 'and guess what? I don't want to look like her.'

'Shut up,' said Georgie. 'All you need is a waist. Then we can get you some decent clothes.'

'I don't have a credit-card debt—'

'That's nothing to be proud of. It's because of people like you that I'm in my present financial mess.'

'How do you work that out?'

'I've got your share.'

At the Soho House they refused to admit us on Cal's

membership, pointing out, with some justification, that he wasn't there. We were saved from an ignominious exit by the arrival of a friend from Georgie's pre-Roman era, an elderly producer escorting a Young Thing who looked as dewily untouched as Lin ten years earlier. He agreed to sign us in and Georgie bought a drink for him and the Young Thing ('Milk?' I suggested) and champagne and chips for us.

'Are we celebrating?' Lin inquired.

'Yes,' said Georgie. 'We're going to make our wishes come true. We're going to have a solemn pact that all of us will do whatever it takes – *whatever* it takes, mind – to realise every single wish *in full*. No excuses, no get-out clauses, no small print. It's all for one, and one for all.' She thumped her fist on the small table we had appropriated, making the glasses rock perilously.

'The Three Musketeers!' Lin said, brightening at an allusion she recognised. She had been losing track of the conversation for some time. She slapped a wayward hand on top of Georgie's fist.

'Yup,' said Georgie. 'I'm obviously Athos, you'd better be Aramis, so Cookie—'

'Is Porthos.' I kept my hand to myself. 'Funny how I'm always the fat girl even when it's a guy.'

'Porthos had a good time,' Georgie protested. 'He pulled lots of birds.'

'I don't want to pull birds!'

'Look, are you going to do this pact or not?'

'Okay.' I put my hand on top of Lin's. 'But I refuse to be Porthos. It's against the spirit of the wishes.'

Georgie repeated her vow, added another 'All for one, and one for all' just for good measure, and we toasted ourselves in champagne. It was that kind of evening. Presently, the chips arrived.

'We don't have to be the Three Musketeers,' Lin said after

deep and alcoholic thought. 'I've got a better idea. We all begin with C – Cavari, Corrigan, Cook. We're . . . the Three Cs!'

'That's wet.' Georgie was scornful.

'We're Charlie's Angels,' I declared. 'And before anyone says anything, *I'm* Drew Barrymore.'

'Okay, but why was she the best?' Georgie demanded.

'Because she *was*. She defeated ten men – or maybe twelve – when she was tied to a chair. Cap that.'

'I think *I* should be Drew Barrymore. You can be Cameron Diaz.'

'No way. You're the blonde bimbo – in an older sort of way. I'm Drew Barrymore and that's that. She's sultry. That's what I'm going to be. I'm going to pout, and smoulder.'

'I'll get a fire extinguisher,' Georgie said tartly. Possibly she didn't like the reminder that she was older.

Lin – who only went to the cinema to see children's films and spent too much time stuck at home with the television – piped up suddenly: 'Can I be Farrah Fawcett?'

The level in the champagne bottle plummeted, to be followed by the level in another. Georgie turned down a proposition from a youthful would-be actor, Lin had a rather one-sided conversation (though no one knew which side) with a coked-up comic who used to know Garry, and I attempted to kick in the balls a drunken suit who tried to fondle my tits. (I was trying to emulate Drew Barrymore.) I missed, kneecapping him instead, but it made me feel good. We headed home in the small hours, quite how I'm not sure, but I must have been going the right way because when I woke up, much later in the day, I was in my own bed. I had a shattering headache and a vague feeling of a milestone passed, of my feet set upon a new path, though initially I couldn't recall why. I got up, made some coffee, and opened the fridge in search of restorative nourishment. Then the phone rang.

'Get out of that fridge!' Georgie.

'I'm hungry.'

'No, you're not. Famine victims in the Third World are hungry. You're overweight. Your body doesn't require food: it's just your mind leading you on.'

In future, she informed me, I would have to give her and Lin a complete list of everything I ate every day, 'and no cheating. It won't be for long. We're aiming for sex goddess, not supermodel. You want to do this, don't you?' I grunted, possibly in agreement. 'Think Nigel. Think stunning clothes. Think *loving* yourself.'

'Do *you* love yourself?' I inquired curiously.

'Only when there's no one else around to do it for me.'

That said it all, of course. Did I want to spend the rest of my life having invisible sex with the likes of Hugh Jackman, or did I want a Real Man?

To be honest, I wasn't quite sure.

It is likely that practically everyone reading this book has, at some time or other, been on a diet. According to one theory the entire female sex is always just about to diet, or just starting a diet – on the first day, or the second day, although, mysteriously, you hardly ever meet anybody who tells you they're on the sixth day, or in the third week. The beginning is easy: pounds drop off as your system clears itself, and major starvation pangs take a while to kick in. But by Day Four your weight stops going down – it may even creep up again – and it all seems pointless, and a packet of Hobnobs holds more allure than all the littleness of a little black dress. 'I diet regularly,' said Georgie surprisingly. 'It's the only way I can keep down to this size. The knack is to get your weight where you want it and then deal with any increase before it goes off the scale. Or scales. Don't worry, you won't crave chocolate indefinitely. It's like giving up cigarettes: after a bit, the mere taste nauseates you.'

I was silent. I wasn't certain I wanted to find chocolate nauseating. Without serotonin, what was there between me and suicide every month?

Besides, I knew she was talking bullshit.

'Eat little and often,' Georgie continued sententiously. 'Lots of fish and veg. And if I were you, I'd avoid all that low-calorie crap. You know: Diet Coke and Slimmachoc and stuff. Artificial sweetener tastes disgusting and anyway, I think it gives you cancer.'

'*Everything* gives you cancer,' I said. I didn't tell her I'd been on the low-calorie crap for years – on top of the high-calorie crap, of course.

In fact, I decided the best thing to do was to eat once a day, usually in the evening, and feel full. That gave me something to look forward to. Besides, the French only eat one main meal, or so I understand, and Paris is full of svelte, slender women in tiny Chanel suits, so they must be doing something right. I stopped buying tortilla chips and other lazy food and cooked properly: broccoli or cauliflower or courgettes, and portions of fish or steak or chicken (skin on: I like the skin). I bought polyunsaturated margarine, though I rarely ate it: it just made me feel good to have it in the fridge. And I wound up with the low-calorie drinking chocolate by way of dessert, despite the health risks. Georgie said I was doing it all wrong, but Lin said what did it matter as long as it was working, and, to my amazement, it did seem to work. Perhaps the real secret of dieting is to know you *can* lose weight. Deep in my subconscious I'd never really believed I *could* be any thinner. I'd been fat since I was fourteen, and the concept of a slimmer me had always seemed to belong to one of those other universes founded on fairytales – the one with the Tyrannosaurus Rex, for instance, or the one with Helen Aucham's corpse dressed as a nun. I was never going to be skinny, but the day came when I pulled my shirt tight around my body and found that I had a waist.

'I've got a waist!' I cried, at work the next morning. 'Look! I really have!'

'You're wasting away,' Laurence Buckle punned, predictably. He was partial to puns. Rumour had it he was secretly writing a chick lit-style novel for gay men which would out-pun Wendy Holden and even Jilly Cooper. It was variously said to be titled *Sore!*, *Bad Her Day*, and *Captain Corelli's Mannikin*.

'You're doing great,' said Georgie. 'A few more pounds, and we can go Shopping.' I could hear the capital S.

Meanwhile, she had launched her campaign to find herself a millionaire.

'You must have had lots of opportunities,' I said. 'The media is full of millionaires.'

'Wrong kind,' Georgie responded. 'They all have ex-wives and ex-children and Xpensive cocaine habits. And very often entourages and groupies as well. I don't want a glamorous celebrity millionaire: there's too much competition for those. I want a fat, boring millionaire from the City with stocks and shares and dividends and kickbacks and golden hand-shakes. I want the kind of millionaire who gives you diamonds and is too busy flying off somewhere on business to have sex. I want a millionaire with a *heart condition*.'

'We don't meet that kind,' Lin pointed out.

'I know,' said Georgie. 'So I'm going to advertise.'

'For a *millionaire*?' Lin demanded. I just stared.

'Uh-huh. In the personal columns. In *The Times* and the *Telegraph*, I think, *not* the tabloids. Possibly the *Guardian*: there are lots of rich guys in New Labour. I don't know if the *FT* has a personal column, or *The Economist*.'

'What will you say?' I inquired.

'I'm working on it.'

Two days after the triumphant flaunting of my waistline,

it was Georgie's turn to be gleeful. 'Eureka!' she announced by e-mail, unable to wait for lunchtime to bridge the gap between Publicity and Editorial. 'What do you think of this? "Penniless beauty – history of impoverished ne'er-do-wells – seeks philanthropic millionaire with cardiac condition who would like to die happy." I'm going to set up a special e-mail address for respondents, using the name of a famous gold-digger or celebrity courtesan. Mme de Pompadour? De Montespan? Ninon de Lenclos? Why is everyone I can think of French?'

'What about that blonde model who married the old boy of eighty-nine?' I e-mailed back. 'Can't remember her name, but she's not French.'

'I can't remember it either, so no good,' Georgie responded. 'Besides, too vulgar. I want to epitomise the poor girl/rich guy scenario in a classy way. What was the name of Cophetua's beggar maid?'

In the end it was Lin who came up with the answer. 'How about Cinderella?' she proposed, in the lunch hour. 'That says it all, doesn't it?'

So Georgie became Cinderella X, contacted the newspapers, and placed her ad. We all waited with slightly queasy anticipation for the results.

A few days before the ad appeared Georgie and I went on our shopping expedition. My diet had slackened off a bit but I was determined to maintain my newfound waistline and Georgie, looking me over with an experienced eye, declared: 'Fourteen. Maybe twelve in some things,' and decided I was ready to go for a change of image. 'We'll start with underwear,' she said, 'and work outwards. You're obviously wearing the wrong bra. What size do you think you take?'

'38DD?' I hazarded. Bras on me always rode up at the back and bunched into lumps at the front, but M&S hardly ever had a bigger cup size, except in something that looked like a straitjacket. As for the posh lingerie shops, with wispy bits of lace in the window clearly designed for women with wispy bosoms, they terrified me.

Georgie heaved a sigh. 'Rigby and Peller, here we come.'

I'd heard of Rigby and Peller, of course. I knew this was the Shangri-La among lingerie shops, as far above Marks and Spencer as Everest is above Highgate Hill. I'd heard women speak of it in accents varying from reverential to merely ecstatic – the way a Moslem speaks of Mecca or a cricketer of Lords. This was the place where the modern Cinderella took her pumpkins, where every transformation scene really began. I expected it to be grand and overpowering, but it wasn't. A friendly assistant weighed and measured the offending objects and announced that I was a mere 34EE, or possibly F, depending on the make, and bras appeared which cupped and lifted and decorated me, elevating my bust to undreamed-of heights. (I tried not to look at the price tags, and succeeded far too well.) For the first time in my life I had a Figure, instead of just a body. It was a heady sensation. I bought pale pink lace and ivory lace and black lace with little mauve flowers, all with matching briefs, and my credit card stoically withstood the shock.

'Much more of this,' I said, 'and I'm going to need a millionaire too.'

'Nonsense,' said Georgie. 'We've only just started.'

In the sixties, women thought it was liberating to burn their bras. The bra, they claimed, feminised and thus diminished them, pandering to male erotic whim, emphasising their harem status. Well, whoever came up with that garbage must have been as flat as a board. In fact, the two advances in the twentieth century that actually encouraged female emancipation were effective contraception and effective underwear. With the Pill, we no longer had to be pregnant all the time.

With the bra, we could come out of the corset and enjoy real physical freedom. The bra is lightweight, comfortable (when it fits), easy to wear, and enables someone like me to run for a bus without blacking my own eye. How many female athletes would have broken Olympic records if their tits had been bouncing around all the time? The right bra can transform your frontage from that look of a cow with too many udders to a streamlined superbust poised for action, breasts jutting like guided missiles. Looking at my reflection, I began to feel almost like a sex goddess, or at least a nymph with big ideas.

I hoped I had earned a coffee break, but Georgie was just warming up. 'Harrods,' she said. 'Then Harvey Nicks. Come on.'

'Georgie!' I screamed. 'They're too expensive! I don't go to places like that!'

'I do.'

In the end, we went to Harrods, but I baulked at Harvey Nicks. After that we headed east for lesser dives like Next, Principles, Wallis. I saw myself tapered by tapering skirts, heightened by short jackets. Nothing loose or baggy, Georgie decreed. 'The object is to take you out of the burkha and turn you into twenty-first-century woman.'

'I can't change my entire wardrobe,' I protested at last. 'I feel like a tatty drawing room in the hands of Laurence Llewellyn-Bowen. I want the fireplace left where it was or I'll be completely disorientated. Besides, I'm exhausted.'

'Okay, I suppose we could take a break,' Georgie conceded grudgingly. 'But after this, if I see you in one more case of baggy black I'll prosecute. Anyway, we still haven't done the hair.'

It had become *the* hair now, not my hair, please note. I had begun to suspect that as far as Georgie was concerned I'd ceased to be Emma Jane Cook and turned into something between a publicity exercise and a work of art – a drawing room to be rearranged, a Galatæa to be chiselled into shape. She was definitely getting carried away, my credit card was going to need absence-of-retail therapy, and although I had a reserve for emergencies (quite a lot, since I was no longer subsidising Nigel) I had never been accustomed to the Big Spend. I'd been brought up to be sensible about money, with an allowance from an early age and emphasis on responsibility. In addition, buying clothes when you're seriously overweight has far fewer charms than when the clothes start to look good on you. (Financially speaking, dieting is a potential disaster.) It was fatally easy to see how Georgie had run up her debts and I didn't intend to join her.

'I don't want anything done to my hair,' I said.

'Just a trim,' she almost pleaded. 'I've booked you in with Paolo next week. He'll know what products are best for you.'

Paolo was the genius who had evolved the blonde streaks, the tousling, that air of having been dragged through a hedge backwards at enormous cost which so suited Georgie. An appointment with him for someone who wasn't a regular was supposed to be as sought-after as tickets for the Cup Final. I wavered. Was this a man who knew how to de-frizz?

'All right,' I said. 'Just a trim.'

So my new image didn't burst on people all at once: it happened in stages, and at first I thought no one had noticed. Lin said immediately: 'You look terrific,' but then, she was so nice she always would. Then it was Cal, telling me in classic male fashion: 'I don't know what you've done to yourself, Cookie, but you're looking really great lately.' And Alistair: 'Lost a lot of weight, haven't you?' (I hadn't actually lost all that much.) 'Shaping up for action? Good girl.' Laurence Buckle, whose gayness was of the discreet, low-camp variety, was more perceptive. 'I gather Georgie's taken you in hand. Long overdue. You're so pretty, Cookie: it's time you learned to show it. Ravishing eyebrows.' I swung between elation and self-doubt. I wasn't yet the modern Venus, but I was making progress. And it wouldn't really be appropriate to go around being a sex goddess in a publishing company. It would be caviar to a pizza house – too exotic, too erotic, in mildly bad taste. But in my secret heart I dared to dream of stunning Nigel, of him crawling back to me, begging for the chance to unsay his cruel words, grovelling while I spurned him with contumely (whatever that is), until, in my weakest moments, I forgave him. I knew Georgie would condemn that part of the dream, but I couldn't help it. The emptiness in my flat, in my life, still ached for him, and the memory of the good times seared my soul. That's the hardest part, remembering happiness, that's the part you can't let go.

You must be bored with my going on about Nigel. You thought I'd had enough of him, didn't you? New clothes, new leaf, new fixations. But the worst aspect of pain, is that the sufferer never gets bored.

I went to see Paolo, an Eastender of Italian extraction with a down-to-earth manner who advised me never to blow-dry – 'We want big hair, love, but not Struwwelpeter' – and trimmed my hair with reassuring moderation. (I was privately terrified of being razed to the scalp.) Later, back at the office, I wandered into Publicity for coffee and approval.

'Looks brilliant,' said Georgie. 'See? The wish business is a cinch. I've had over fifty answers to my ad already. Cinderella X is going to the ball.'

'Lucky you,' sighed Lin. 'I haven't met a man for three months.' Work colleagues and traffic wardens didn't count.

'Get on the Internet,' Georgie said. 'That's the future of dating, take my word. Safe, anonymous, no commitment. Forget the singles bar. This way, you can find out in advance if he tells sick jokes, or is a rabid fan of Alan Titchmarsh. Then you can dump him on the compost heap before he's had a chance to take root at your side.'

'What about halitosis or a spotty back?' I said.

'The system's good; I didn't say it was loserproof. Anyhow, you wouldn't see a spotty back in a singles bar. Unless it was on the beach.'

'I couldn't do an ad like Georgie,' Lin said. 'I'd never be able to think of anything witty enough. Besides . . . well, I just couldn't.'

'Have you told Cal yet?' I inquired of Georgie.

'No.' She was unusually curt. 'It's none of his business. He's married. I'll tell him when there's a nine-carat diamond on my finger and I'm going up the aisle on the arm of a wheelchair.' She turned to Lin. 'Join a dating agency. You just type in your requirements and you get pages and pages of possibles. With photographs.'

'Bank details?' I asked. 'Back details? Spot checks?'

Georgie threw me a look that was intended to wither. 'Give it a try,' she said. 'What harm can it do?'

That, as it turned out, was the million-dollar question.

'I suppose I could,' Lin said. 'At least I don't need a babysitter to go online.'

Back at my desk, I took a phone call from Todd Jarman. I didn't want to, but it sneaked up on me: there was no variation in the ring tone to give me any warning. One day, they will come up with a telephone system that gives helpful advice before you answer: Do not take this call – salesperson; Anonymous caller – switch on Heavy Breathing tape; Very Bad Vibes – answer carefully. I'd been waiting for the Jarman bombshell to drop ever since our meeting, expecting a rocket from Alistair if not the sack, bracing myself to argue that I had taken the flak for major changes *he* had initiated (never mind all the minor ones). But curiously, nothing had happened. Whatever Jarman felt about me, he hadn't passed it on to my boss. (Maybe he was sorry for me? *Poor thing. What a lump* . . . The thought made me cringe.) Hearing his voice with the customary sinking of the stomach and stiffening of the sinews, I realised that his restraint owed nothing to acceptance or indifference, let alone pity. He was evidently determined to fight it out between the two of us. His words crackled with suppressed . . . well, suppressed something. Probably rage. He had found space for an extra body. Probably mine. Perhaps, since I was so good at his job, I would like to suggest a motive for the crime?

'Someone who Knew Too Much?' I volunteered flippantly. 'That's always a reliable old chestnut.'

Thanks. Were there any other clichés I would like him to insert?

Unable to resist, I said sweetly that I thought there were plenty of great clichés there already.

There was a short silence. Then: 'Of course there are,' Todd said. 'I put them in 'specially for readers like you. It's called dumbing down.'

It occurred to me that somehow we had crossed the borderline from overt hostility to mere banter. To my surprise, it was almost fun.

'The mass market, you know,' I said airily. 'D'you want the Man Booker or the Top Ten?'

'Both,' Jarman responded instantly. 'What writer doesn't? By the way, I've dealt with most of your lesser alterations: they're now back in their original form. Would you like to waste more space and time going over them again or shall we just clash over the big issues?'

I winced, but maintained my bravado. 'I'm game,' I said. 'Pistols at dawn?'

'A little later in the day would suit me – if suiting me is important to you.'

'Not really,' I said. 'But you're one of our top writers, so I have to be polite.'

'Fuck you, Miz Cook.'

Oddly, I ended the call with my stomach back in place and feeling strangely buoyant. Give Jarman his due, he hadn't pulled rank by complaining about me to Alistair – and as he's a bestseller, that would have done my career a power of no good – and no matter how sarcastic or insulting he might be, at least we quarrelled on an equal footing. It really was . . . *almost* fun.

During the afternoon I found myself speculating about how to practise my newfound sex-goddessness, and whether I too should go the Internet route. But it seemed an awful waste of a new haircut. Instead, I rang up one of those friends whom I like very much but don't see enough (this applies to almost any friend you don't work with) and we arranged a night out on the town. We met in a trendy Notting Hill bar, where she was gratifyingly stunned by my new look and insisted on a serious round of pubs and clubs to show it off. Amazingly, although admirers didn't exactly swoon and fall at my feet, I found myself resisting the advances of several men who could, in a bad light, be rated as attractive – even if one of them later proved to be gay. I hadn't been so sought-after since I was eleven years old and won a giant Easter Egg full of chocolate buttons at a children's raffle. I went home after three, subdued the urge to snack, and tumbled into sleep without pausing to dream of Nigel, or even Hugh Jackman.

Chapter 4

A single flow'r he sent me, since we met –
All tenderly his messenger he chose;
Deep-hearted, pure, with scented dew still wet –
One perfect rose . . .

Why is it no one ever sent me yet
One perfect limousine, do you suppose?
Ah no, it's always just my luck to get
One perfect rose.

DOROTHY PARKER: *One Perfect Rose*

O'er the rugged mountain's brow
Clara threw the twins she nursed,
And remarked: 'I wonder now
Which will reach the bottom first?'

HARRY GRAHAM: *Calculating Clara*

Time to take up my pen again, except this is the twenty-first century and so what I actually do is switch on my PC and get back to the action. In a certain type of old-fashioned novel – the kind written in the Victorian age for readers who couldn't deal with too much suspense – there would be chapter headings which told you what was coming in

91

advance. They always started *In Which. In Which Charles Fortescue Proposes to Miss Copeland, Freda Visits the Insane Asylum and Meets Horace's Wife, and Miss Morton Hears some Unexpected News.* That sort of thing. Anyhow, if this chapter had an *In Which*, without wishing to give too much away, it would go something like this: *In Which Georgina Meets a Selection of Millionaires, Lindsay Goes on a Date, and Emma Jane's Wish to Become a Sex Goddess Comes True.* And all I will add about *that* is that the fairy in the Bel Manoir Wyshing Well had a very nasty sense of humour.

Georgie's Cinderella X ad was producing phenomenal results, at least on screen. It occurred to me that we were all would-be Cinderellas really: that's what wishing is all about. Georgie wanted a wealthy prince, I wanted the transformation scene, and Lin just wanted to get out of the kitchen. 'Another couple of dozen last weekend,' Georgie told us on Monday. 'I can't possibly meet them all. I'm scrapping anyone who says they want a meaningful relationship or claims to have a gsoh.'

'A what?' I said.

'Good sense of humour, I think. The point is, how do they know? Everybody *thinks* they have a sense of humour, even people who haven't one – *especially* people who haven't one – but it might not be the same as mine. Anyway, I asked for dosh, not jokes. Gsohs get dumped.'

'What about serial killers?'

'Depends how rich they are,' said Georgie.

'You will be careful, won't you?' Lin said anxiously. 'If you're going to meet them . . .'

'Of course I'm going to meet them. Once I've whittled the list down to the most likely prospects. What really shocks me is how many of them insist they're frightfully healthy. I mean, with the high incidence of heart disease in this country, you'd think a fair proportion would be cardiac cases. It's supposed to be very stressful becoming a millionaire.'

'Not nearly as stressful as poverty,' Lin said.

'Never mind,' I told Georgie in consoling tones. 'If *you* can't give a man a coronary, no one can.'

She preened herself, not visibly, but in spirit. 'I should hope so,' she murmured. 'I tell you, this had better be worth it. Nobody mentions how time-consuming it is, doing an ad. I spent most of the weekend sorting my respondents into separate files, because otherwise I'm going to get them all mixed up. You send off so many answers, you forget what you've said to whom. I got so exhausted, one guy asked me what I *really really* wanted, and I couldn't be bothered to compose a proper reply, so I e-mailed one word: Diamonds.'

'What did he say?' Lin demanded, intrigued.

'He asked me what kind.'

'He must be mad,' Lin said in awe. 'I mean – *diamonds*. He doesn't even know you.'

'Mad is good,' said Georgie. 'Next to cardiac arrest, I'll take mad. I can have him looked after by a nice friendly nurse while I go out and spend all his money.'

'Makes it awfully easy for his relatives to contest the Will,' I pointed out.

'Some of my best friends are lawyers. Anyway, for the moment I want my millionaire alive. One thing at a time.'

'Shouldn't you have told Cal by now?' Lin whispered as he appeared beyond the glass partition, obviously heading our way.

'No,' Georgie hissed back. 'Project Cinderella X is Top Secret. For your ears only.' And, as Cal came in: 'Hi.'

The difficult part, I reflected, was that actually I rather liked him. In the past, having filed him under 'Office Lech', I'd only thought of him as a guy with a dirty grin who would make suggestive remarks to any woman, even me, if there was no one else available. But as his relationship with Georgie developed his attitude changed, and I'd found out there was a nice man behind the mock-Casanova exterior. As Georgie's special friends, Lin and I acquired a new status in his eyes, and he treated us accordingly. Georgie came first, of course, but I didn't like to think of him being left high and dry while she absconded with some ageing Croesus. There were times when I had to remind myself pretty sharply that he was, after all, a married man cheating on his wife – whatever the state of his marriage might be.

I tried to greet him without constraint and left the office feeling uncomfortable. Lin, who had launched into an unnatural flow of chat, was evidently having the same reaction.

Later that week, Georgie made a start on her shortlist. She had a dinner-date at the Bel Manoir – 'I thought it would be appropriate' – with a property tycoon who insisted he had never had time to meet Miss Right. She made an effort (Georgie always made an effort), wearing a tight black skirt split up the side, short black jacket, and a plunge blouse which frilled her cleavage like a ribbon round a wedding-cake. Her date looked duly appreciative. Hesitant and almost shy by e-mail, in the flesh he proved to be a stocky, blocky fifty-something with the kind of abrasive self-confidence that stumbles over its own feet every so often. His accent was Yorkshire, his face not so much lived-in as vandalised. Georgie gritted her teeth and determined to find him likeable.

'And he was,' she concluded the next day, 'in a blunt, northern sort of way. He talked about property all through the main course, which was boring, and his unhappy experiences with classifieds over dessert, which was sad. He kept telling me how wonderful and sympathetic I was, probably because no one had ever asked him about himself before. It won't do, though.'

'Why not?' said Lin. 'He sounds as if he might be nice. I mean, for a millionaire. He *is* a millionaire, isn't he?'

'Think so.'

'Did he have a ruddy complexion?' I said hopefully.

'Yes – why?'

'High blood pressure. Bound to be cardiac. He's the right age, too.'

'I daresay, but it won't do.'

'Why not?' Lin repeated.

'He lives in Huddersfield.' There was a depressed silence. 'What's the point of having lots of money, if you have to spend it in Huddersfield?'

'I thought you were going to clear your credit card,' I said. 'Not blue someone else's.'

'Just trying to plan ahead.'

'Anyhow, what's wrong with Huddersfield? Have you ever been there?'

'I don't need to.' Georgie shuddered. 'It's *up north*. It's cold and damp and the natives drink lots of beer and eat Yorkshire pudding and worship football.'

'Sounds a lot like the south to me,' I said. 'Bar the Yorkshire pud.' I like Yorkshire pudding, but I wasn't going to say so. It was against the spirit of my new diet.

'Shut up . . .'

On the Saturday, Georgie went to the Pont de la Tour to meet a City fatcat who said he had never answered a classified ad before. ('You wouldn't *believe* how many of them say that,' Georgie had remarked.) On arrival, the only unattended male she could see was a pink-faced young man of about twenty-five with fluffy blond hair and the beginnings of a gut framed rather unfortunately by a gaping bomber jacket. She requested James Wingrove with a feeling of trepidation which was fully justified. 'I say,' said the young man, 'you're a bit older than I expected.'

'How *is* your heart condition?' Georgie retorted frigidly.

By the end of dinner, James was waxing enthusiastic on relationships with mature women. 'I bet you know stuff the younger ones don't,' he said. 'Experience tells, right? A mate of mine got off with his girlfriend's mother: he said it was the best night of his life. Apparently, she totally blew him away. She handcuffed him to the chandelier, stuffed a courgette up his—'

'Courgettes are so yesterday,' said Georgie, who had decided to go with the flow. 'They went out with the gerbil. Which public school did you go to?'

'I didn't say I went to public school. How did you guess?'

On Sunday, she lunched with an Internet executive at a pub near Henley. 'I'm worth seven million at the latest computation. Well, yes, that's on paper, but the crash has hardly affected us. Boohoo.com is rock solid. The future of business is on the web.'

'Sounds like science fiction,' Georgie murmured unwarily, unable to think of anything else to say.

'That's exactly it. Science fiction is becoming business fact. Did you catch the last series of *Babylon 5*? It was brilliant . . .'

He moved on to *Star Trek: The Next Generation*, *Farscape*, and something called *Mutant X*, dabbled in *Buffy* and *Roswell High*, and wound up with *Blade Runner* (the director's cut), *Alien* (all of them), and *Terminator II* ('Far superior to *Terminator*, of course. The apocalyptic vision . . . the horror of the imagined holocaust . . . Linda Hamilton's outstanding performance . . .'). This, Georgie decided, is where I terminate. Time to return to Earth. And must make a note never to invest in the Internet – should I ever have something to invest.

Back at home, she collapsed in front of the TV, which was showing a nice soothing English country murder, and wondered if solvency was really worth all this trouble.

'So he was a nerd,' I said to her in the morning. 'We live in an age where nerds can make millions. Look at Bill Gates.'

'Millionaires are supposed to be interested in the Dow Jones and the Footsy – whatever they are,' Georgie said. 'Not Klingon foreign policy and Arnold Schwarzenegger's biceps. Or am I out-of-date?'

'You said it,' I grinned.

On Tuesday, she got the serial killer.

She knew he was a serial killer the moment she set eyes on him. Fortunately they were in a suitable venue for such meetings (a public place with other people), in this case an old-fashioned pub on Duke Street St James, although it did seem to be little frequented and there were rather too many dark corners. Her respondent looked elderly, though he must have been under fifty; he was the type who had probably looked elderly from thirty on. He had pale eyes set slightly too close together, in the accepted manner of serial killers, and a mouth drawn tight like a miser's purse from much primming in disapproval. His smile, when it came, was sudden and toothy, full of secret hunger. His clothes were so nondescript as to render him all but invisible and Georgie sensed immediately that he had a mother complex. (They always do.) Inwardly, she thanked Providence that she had only committed herself to having a drink with him. She ordered vodka and Coke, specifying non-diet.

'I'm glad you're not anorexic,' her companion said. 'One woman I met asked for Diet Coke. She was very thin. I knew at once she was anorexic, of course.'

Georgie wondered what he had done with the body. It seemed a little extreme to murder someone because they might have anorexia, but clearly any excuse would do. Possibly he had a mission to rid the world of anorexics.

'My mother doesn't approve of dieting. She says young

women nowadays are much too skinny. She says anyone who had lived through rationing would really appreciate good food. They don't know when they're lucky, she says.'

Aha! thought Georgie. The mother already. Knew it. Mother Knows Best. Anyone Mother doesn't approve, we eradicate. Bet my credit-card bill she wouldn't care for me.

'Do you like chocolate?'

Was this another test for suspected anorexia? 'Sometimes,' Georgie admitted cautiously.

'I could cover your naked body in molten chocolate, and then lick it all off,' he suggested, his tongue flickering in the toothy suddenness of his smile like that of a lizard. 'Or is that too daring for you?'

Georgie felt her skin crawl. Not only was he a serial killer, but he suffered from outmoded erotic fantasies which he obviously imagined were kinky. 'A bit much for a first date,' she said. 'Anyway, I did that when I was a teenager. It's frightfully passé. Tell me, are you really a millionaire?'

'You shouldn't be so mercenary. My mother doesn't like women who are mercenary. Your ad was all about money, when it should have been about finding a beautiful relationship.'

Georgie was temporarily staggered into speechlessness. *I don't want a beautiful relationship! I asked for a MILLIONAIRE! Of course I'm mercenary.*

'As it happens, Mother has a large house in Surbiton,' the psychopath continued.

'Do you share it with her?' Georgie asked.

'Oh no. But we'll get it when she dies, naturally.'

Georgie ignored the 'we'. His e-mails had clearly been misleading – or had she mixed them up? – but she had never given him her real name, so she would be relatively safe if she could only survive this date. She considered asking when his mother's death might occur, but curbed the impulse. In any case, the mothers of serial killers are notoriously long-lived (there may be some sort of compensation factor operating here).

'You know, you must get off the subject of money. You're not really that kind of person: I can tell. All through our correspondence I've felt we had a natural affinity. Do you know, we've exchanged over twenty e-mails?'

'I send twice that many every day,' Georgie said. 'I'm a compulsive e-mailer.'

'Yes, but that must be for work,' he responded, serene in his conviction of their affinity. 'Those don't count. I remember you said you work at a publisher's?'

'Yes,' Georgie conceded, increasingly wary. That might, she felt, have been a mistake. It was not the kind of information you should throw around.

Her worst fears were realised.

'Actually, I'm writing a book myself . . .'

'Why couldn't he have just tried to lure me away somewhere and strangle me?' Georgie lamented afterwards, on the phone to me. 'I told him I worked in the Accounts Department, but it didn't do any good. He said I didn't look like an accountant. Then he kept hinting I must be great friends with all the important editors, you know, sort of roguishly, only he didn't look roguish, he looked ghoulish. Then he produced his chunk of manuscript and sat over me while I read it.'

'I don't think you can *sit* over someone,' I remarked. 'You have to stand.'

'Stop being so bloody editorish.'

'Sorry. Go on.'

'I had to read a whole chapter of it, and there was this sex scene, involving – guess what? – molten chocolate, and he obviously thought it was terribly raunchy, poor sod, and then I started to feel sorry for him, he was so pathetic, even if he *was* a serial killer.'

'You didn't say you'd see him again?'

'Good God, no! I may be soft-hearted – on a bad day – but I'm not stupid. I got out as fast as I could.'

'It sounds awful.' My sympathy was sincere. I too have often been waylaid by acquaintances flourishing their literary efforts. People seem to think it's perfectly okay to impose on someone in publishing encountered on the social circuit, though they wouldn't dream of it with anybody else. I mean, you would hardly go up to a brain surgeon at a party and demand a lobotomy, would you?

In the silence that ensued I could feel Georgie unwinding like a broken spring. 'You know,' I resumed after a moment's reflection, 'wouldn't the molten chocolate solidify before you could lick it all off?'

'Coming to think of it,' she said, 'in my day we used chocolate spread. It made a fearful mess of the sheets . . .'

Shattered by her experiences in the millionaire market, Georgie decided to take the rest of the week off (from millionaires, not work) and have fun with Cal. On Friday lunchtime we all went to a nearby pub for a snack and a drink (I passed on the snack, nobly. At least I'd lost the habit of snacking). 'You really are looking gorgeous, Cookie,' Cal told me. Georgie had filled him in on the business of the wishes as regards Lin and I, but clearly not herself. 'Go easy on the weight-loss, though. It'd be a shame to shrink those tits any more.'

'You don't have to stare at them quite so much,' Georgie said somewhat coldly. 'They aren't going to go away. Not this week, at least.'

Cal grinned. 'If Georgie drops me,' he said, 'I'd like to land in your cleavage.'

'If I drop you—' Georgie's vocal temperature was plunging well below zero '– *when* I drop you – your life will be blighted, all other women will be as dust and ashes to you, you'll turn to drink—'

'I already have.'

'– and in the end you'll probably become a monk. Okay?'

Something in the way he smiled at her, a kind of warmth in his eyes, squeezed at my heart. I thought: He loves her. He truly loves her. What did she want with a millionaire and a debt-free credit card, when she had love? The price of a good man is above designer labels – as the Bible might have said had it been written rather more recently. On the other hand, Cal hardly qualified as a good man . . . did he? What is a 'good man', anyway? Does the woman of today want someone to offer her economic support and protect her from every wind that blows, or does she want a partner, an equal, a soulmate – an object of lust – a subject of love? Perhaps it's simpler just to have a checklist requesting male 25–45, interested in arts/sport/music, n/s, gsoh, looking for ltr with lots of tlc. Love is the spark which you don't find by adver- tisement or net-surfing, and what is a spark, in the end? A warmth in the eyes . . . a squeeze at the heart.

The price of love is not payable by credit card.

On which note . . .

'I've got a date,' Lin said abruptly, breaking into a conver- sation in which she had taken little part.

'That's wonderful,' I said.

'Who is he?' asked Georgie. 'How did you meet him?'

'I went on the Internet,' Lin said, with the air of one admit- ting to a secret vice. 'Like you suggested. I joined one of those dating sites. I gave a false name. I know it's silly, but I didn't want to – I thought someone might remember me. From magazines and stuff. I started e-mailing four or five guys, and it was fun, it was *easy*, chatting away, telling them what I wanted to tell, leaving out the bad bits. And they like me, they really *like* me. One of them proposed already, which was awfully sweet and romantic, but a bit quick.'

'Tell me about it,' said Georgie. 'I had a guy who wanted

to fly me to his villa in the South of France – and he hadn't even seen my picture.'

'*What*?' Cal snapped.

'Oh . . . I was just fooling around in a chatroom.' And, turning hastily to Lin: 'What about this date of yours? Is he the one who proposed to you?'

'No. We've just swapped e-mails. He's divorced – his wife went off with his best friend, but he isn't bitter. He says it was his fault for neglecting her. She wanted babies and all he did was work all the time. He's a systems analyst or something. He says he didn't realise what he'd lost until it was too late – it's really sad – and now he's prepared to work at a relationship, if he finds the right person. He wants kids, too.'

'Ready-made?' Cal queried sceptically.

'I told him about Meredith and the twins,' Lin said. 'He thinks they sound great.'

'The man's a fool,' I muttered, *sotto voce*.

'What's his name?' Georgie asked. 'Age? Vital statistics? Have you seen a photo?'

'He's thirty-six, and he sent me a picture. He's got a thin face with nice smile lines and he looks kind. Not drop-dead gorgeous, but definitely okay. Anyhow, I have to start somewhere.'

'That's the attitude,' said Georgie. 'Don't go falling in love across a room until you've seen the guy close up. What did you say his name was?'

'Derek,' said Lin, a shade defensively.

Georgie opened her mouth, presumably to say something unflattering, but was unexpectedly forestalled by Cal. 'I had a mate at school called Derek,' he offered. 'Great guy. Always backed me up in fights. I still see him from time to time.'

'Maybe that's a good omen,' I said. 'Where's he taking you?'

102

'Some place called Mean Cuisine,' Lin said. 'Brewer Street – or is it Beak Street? I'm meeting him there. I thought that was the right thing to do.'

'Mmm.' Georgie frowned. 'Never heard of it. Places with clever titles don't usually have brilliant food . . .'

It occurred to me that it might be the ideal restaurant to take Todd Jarman, for the name if nothing else. We had arranged another session at his house for the following week, but the obligatory editorial lunch would fall due sooner or later. And it had begun to seem very important that I strike the right note. An unpleasant one, of course.

'I don't mind about the food,' Lin was saying. 'Any food I'm not cooking tastes good. Particularly if I'm not doing the washing-up either. It's just . . . there's a problem.'

Why did I have a sudden feeling of impending doom?

'Clothes?' said Georgie, who could only visualise one kind of pre-date trauma. 'We'll sort you out. You could borrow my pink chiffon: it's a bit summery but you can put a coat over it and it's your kind of thing. Lots of floaty, drapey bits. It's short on me so it'll be fine on you.'

'It's not clothes,' Lin said hurriedly. 'The thing is, Vee Corrigan can't have the twins, let alone Meredith, and Sean's always too busy, and . . . and . . . you did say you might babysit, if I couldn't get anyone else . . .' She was looking at both of us, I noticed, though I had made no such offer. But friends stick together.

Doom.

Georgie blenched, then rallied. 'Of course,' she said. 'If you're really stuck . . . ?'

'I'm really stuck. Yes.'

'We'd love to.'

We? Oh, well . . .

'It's not like they're babies,' Lin said. 'They amuse themselves most of the time.' (My blood did not run cold at this remark, but it should have done.) 'I'll organise food for them, burgers or chicken takeaway which you can reheat. Don't let Meredith touch the mint-choc-chip ice cream, it – it doesn't agree with her. And don't let them watch anything unsuitable on TV. They watch it on their computers, mind you, but at least the definition isn't so good.'

'Don't worry,' said Georgie. 'I'm great with kids.'

'How do you know?' I said. 'You've never had any.'

Cal was looking decidedly amused.

'Some of my friends have them,' Georgie replied. 'They all adore me. Lin's lot will too.' Nothing like positive thinking.

'Bound to,' Cal murmured.

'Anyway,' Georgie continued, 'if the worst comes to the worst, I'm bigger than they are. When it comes to children, I believe might is right.'

'Actually,' Lin said tentatively, 'the twins are eleven now. They're getting very tall . . .'

'Doesn't matter,' Georgie attested. 'I have natural authority.'

'I hope so,' I said, ''cause I bloody haven't.'

'Cookie the realist,' Cal commented. 'Always the practical one.'

'Am I?'

'Yeah. Out of this trio, anyway. Lin's a real girly romantic, no matter how many men she meets whose minds are below-the-belt. Georgie still thinks the world is her oyster, though she's old enough to know better – she even fools it into oystering back, some of the time. You may be the youngest, but you're – oh, I don't know. Cynical. Pragmatic – is that the word I want?'

'Yes,' I said, 'but I'm *not* cynical. Cynics don't believe in anything. I do. I really do.'

'She really does,' Georgie corroborated. 'Anyhow, *I'm* the cynical one.'

104

'No – you just try to be. Sorry, Cookie. I didn't want to upset you. I meant to pay you a compliment – on your maturity.'

'A compliment,' said Georgie, 'is when you go on about her tits – but that doesn't mean I want you to get back to that, okay?'

He left me feeling vaguely unsettled, though it was hard to analyse why. Was I a down-to-earth cynic? On the surface, maybe. But underneath I was bubbling with secret romanticism and a yen to prove that the world could be my oyster too – with a pearl in it. The trouble is, when you've always been fat and not very attractive romantic ideals and world-oysterishness don't have much chance to grow. Maybe my newfound sex appeal would colour my whole outlook, melting the hard outer crust of my personality and releasing a gush of dreamy-eyed optimism and total impracticality . . .

'You're looking a bit wistful,' Lin said. 'Are you all right?'

'Fine. I was just thinking about . . . about Saturday night.'

'I understand.' Lin squeezed my hand. 'The biological clock's got a lot of tick left in it, Cookie. You'll have kids one day. I know you will.'

My mouth dropped open.

'In the meantime,' Lin concluded, 'it would be wonderful if you could develop a relationship with mine. I'd love that.'

'Absolutely,' said Georgie.

I didn't look forward to Saturday evening with a sinking heart, principally because I didn't look forward to it at all. It crept up on me like an end-of-term exam which you have convinced yourself can't possibly be as bad as you feared. Granted you've done no preparation, let alone revision, you missed the lectures and you know bugger-all about the subject, but a little common sense will get you through.

105

Children, I told myself, were just adults in the larval stage. The knack was to treat them as such. (I tried not to think about my nephew and niece, Raphael and Hermione, who definitely belong to another species.) Besides, any children with Lin's genes were bound to be basically decent. Of course, the twins also had Sean's genes, and Meredith had Garry Grimes' genes, but . . . I abandoned that train of thought as discouraging, called Georgie on her mobile to synchronise watches, and set off for the rendezvous point.

Despite being close friends with Lin, we had seen little of the kids. They were all bigger than we remembered, especially the boys. Sandy was – well, sandy, with a collection of freckles that should have been endearing but weren't and a taciturn manner which would have defeated a professional interrogator. I was not at all surprised he had been in trouble for bullying and felt he needed only a can and a couple of tattoos to turn him into a lager-lout. (He later showed us a tattoo on his arm, but it transpired he had done it himself with indelible ink.) Demmy was dark-haired and sallow, slighter in build than his brother, the taciturnity here mutated into swift sulks and occasional smiles where the ghost of Sean's charm danced unawares. Probing questions revealed that Sandy despised Harry Potter ('kids' stuff') but Demmy thought well of Pullman, Sandy grudgingly admitted to liking pizza, Demmy preferred pasta, both had PlayStations and skateboards, played football and/or rugger, supported Manchester United, Arsenal, and, failing that, any other British team, and seemed to have no ambitions beyond the soccer field. This information was elicited with some difficulty while Lin rushed around doing last-minute things to her face. When she finally appeared, mascara'd, lipsticked, and jacketed, Georgie asked: 'Where's Meredith?'

'In her room,' Lin said, trying not to look anxious, and failing. 'She'll be down in a minute. I bought you this.' She thrust a bottle of wine into my hands. 'I'm sure they'll be fine. Do I look okay?'

'Fine,' we said in chorus.

'Take care of them, boys. Try to remember your manners. Is that the taxi?'

It was. We pushed her through the door with a last 'good luck' and turned back to the bottle of wine, which was clearly all that stood between us and tedium. Or so we hoped.

Meredith still didn't appear, and the boys immersed themselves in a DVD in which a supernatural villain specialised in lopping off the heads of random victims, evidently in order to replace his own, which had gone missing some time previously. (Why he needed so many was not clear: he'd only lost the one.) At one stage, Sandy remarked sapiently of one of the female roles: 'She done it.'

'She can't have,' I said, lured into dispute against my better judgement. 'It's a ghost story. The ghost done it.'

'She done it,' Sandy repeated obstinately.

'How d'you work that out?' asked Georgie.

'She's that actress who always plays the villainess. I've seen her in lots of things. Of course she done it.'

'But she's just been killed herself!' I objected.

'It's a fix. She done it.'

(Amazingly, he was perfectly right.)

'I'm hungry,' said Demmy. 'Can we have supper now?'

We reheated chicken nuggets as per instructions. Sandy demanded pizza. 'There isn't any,' said Georgie.

'Yes there is,' he said. 'In the fridge. I don't like chicken. I told you: Mum always has pizza for me.'

'Perhaps you'd like something different too,' Georgie said sarcastically, turning to Demmy.

'Yes please. There's pasta in the cupboard.'

I grinned, left her to it, and went upstairs to locate Meredith. Like a fool, I thought that was the soft job. When

my tap on her door produced no answer, I opened it slowly
and went in.

It was clear that at some time in the remote past the room
had been decorated to suit the supposed tastes of a little girl:
butter-yellow walls, curtains patterned with sunflowers, pale
blue carpet. But the walls were smothered in posters, not
S-Club 7 or Gareth Gates but an assortment of far from
cuddly monsters, an old-fashioned Dracula, *Lord of the
Rings*, and prints of Max Ernst, Escher, and Warhol's Coke
bottles. Clothes, books, and CDs littered the floor; in the
middle there was a mock-bearskin rug with pink furry mouth
agape and an array of white furry teeth. It was wearing
sunglasses. Meredith herself sat at a desk watching something on her PC. There were earphones clamped to her head
connected to a Walkman on her lap, and a carton of ice
cream, nearly empty, beside the keyboard. When she turned
round my worst fears were realised (not for the last time,
except the truth was to prove worse than my worst fears).
A smudge darkened her cheek and a pale green moustache
rimmed her upper lip. It was mint-choc-chip. She studied me
with a jet-black gaze that was completely impenetrable.

'Hi,' I said. 'I'm Cookie.'

No response. Presently, by gesture, I got her to remove the
earphones, though I was perfectly sure she could hear me
even with them on.

'Why Cookie?' she asked. 'Because you eat so many
biscuits?'

So much for my diet. 'No,' I responded, suppressing infanti-
cidal urges. 'My surname's Cook. That's why they call me
Cookie. Should I call you Merry?'

'Not if you want to live,' she said, deadpan. Meredith, it
was plain, was good at deadpan. She had her father's monkey
face without the humour, squashed under an unnaturally
domed forehead, the small features set into tight little lines.

Her hair was braided against her scalp and twisted into curious-shaped nodules on either side, like the head-pieces on a cartoon robot. Her eyes were so black it was impossible to distinguish iris from pupil: they looked like little round holes into nothingness. Most nine-year-old girls have some spurious charm – the bloom of childhood and all that – but Meredith Grimes appeared uniquely and determinedly charmless. Her monkey-face was at once unreadable and alarmingly intelligent.

'You shouldn't be eating mint-choc-chip,' I said, picking up the ice-cream carton. There was clearly no point in trying to make friends. 'Your mummy says it disagrees with you.'

'Does she?' Meredith said. 'I like it.'

'Would you like to come downstairs and have some chicken?'

Rather to my surprise, she got up, discarding the Walkman and switching off the computer. As it went into shutdown mode, I caught a quick glimpse of the vanishing picture. 'That was a porn site!' I gasped in horror.

'I know.'

'You shouldn't be watching that stuff. You're *nine*. You shouldn't be able to log on to those sites.'

'Oh, it isn't for me. I was checking it out for the twins. I'm better with computers than they are: I know how to bypass the anti-child system. I don't like porn much, it's boring. I don't think they do either really, they just watch it so they can talk about it to impress their friends. They pay me to get past the censorship device. They get more pocket money than me, 'cos they're older. Grandma Vee gives them money too.'

'Does your mother know?' I found myself asking, mesmerised.

'Of course not.' She gave me what, in another child, would have been a winning smile. 'Don't tell her, will you?'

'Why not?' I rallied.

The smile faded to a black glare, latent with menace, but she said nothing. She didn't need to. Her expression said it all.

Downstairs, she ate her way through most of the chicken while the supernatural villain bagged a few more heads. 'I don't think we should let her watch this,' Georgie hissed, *sotto voce*.

'It's better than what she was watching in her room,' I replied, out of the corner of my mouth. This is what children do to you. I had never spoken out of the corner of my mouth in my life – for one thing, it's extremely difficult – but five minutes with Meredith had turned me into a mutterer of furtive asides.

'It might give her nightmares.'

'Chance would be a fine thing.'

'I beg your pardon?'

When both the chicken and the head collection were finished, the boys switched to a sports channel showing something which, from the massive padding and frequent bouts of inactivity, appeared to be American football. 'I don't get this game at all,' I remarked. Astonishingly, Meredith proceeded to give me a comprehensive explanation that left me none the wiser, but impressed. 'Do you enjoy it?' I asked her.

'Not really: it's very slow. I don't like any sport much.'

'But you understand it?'

This time, all I got was a sort of shrug. Understanding things, evidently, came naturally and meant nothing.

'What kind of games do you like?' I persisted.

'Chess. Bridge. World Domination.'

'I play chess,' I volunteered bravely.

'Are you any good?'

My turn to shrug.

'I play on the Internet with a man in New Zealand. He's a maths professor. I've won our last two games.' So much for that.

Georgie, who had been distracted by the array of muscular male buttocks on screen, remarked: 'I think we need the wine now,' and went into the kitchen.

'Do you want to see my party piece?' Meredith said unexpectedly.

I couldn't imagine her having a party piece, and for a few seconds my stare must have been as blank as hers. 'All right,' I said.

I should have been warned by the way the twins lost interest in the TV and turned to look at me. Meredith stood up, facing the armchair where I was sitting. Her eyes squeezed shut and an expression of intense concentration convulsed her features. She pressed her hands to her stomach, which made a horrible glooping noise. 'Are you okay?' I demanded in idiotic concern.

The jet of vomit – pale green with chicken lumps – caught me full in the chest, dousing my sweater, bra, breasts. I must have screamed, because Georgie came rushing in, a half-corked wine bottle in one hand. 'My God!' she gasped. '*Cookie!*' And, to Meredith: 'You poor child—'

Meredith was panting slightly, possibly with triumph. 'My party piece,' she announced.

'Your *what*?' said Georgie.

'Her party piece.' The vomit was starting to ooze down my cleavage. I got to my feet, white with fury. I know I was white because I could *feel* it – the blood draining from my cheeks as my face went hard and cold. In that instant, I wondered how anyone could object to corporal punishment for children. Or capital punishment. I spoke to Meredith in a voice I had never heard myself use to anyone, let alone a child. 'Take me upstairs to the bathroom. *Now.*'

'Why on earth did she do this?' Georgie demanded, dumping the bottle on a convenient sideboard.

'God knows. She's probably a budding psychopath. Can you find me something of Lin's to wear?'

'Mummy's things won't fit you,' Meredith said.

'Something *loose*. You. Bathroom.'

We trooped upstairs, Georgie to Lin's bedroom, Meredith and I to the bathroom. I stripped off my sweater and bra – my beautiful Rigby and Peller bra. The first thing was to wash me, then my clothes. 'You'd better find some soap for clothing,' I told Meredith. 'You made this mess: you're going to clean it up. You can wash my things.'

'But I don't know how!' For once, Miss Smartarse admitted to something she didn't understand.

'It's like chess. You can learn.'

Meredith backed away towards the door, which we'd left ajar. I could see her in the mirror. Suddenly, she stuck two fingers in her mouth and gave vent to an ear-splitting whistle. There was a pounding of feet, and the door was flung open. I wheeled instinctively, bare-bosomed, my nipples erect from the cold (I hadn't waited for the water to run hot), to find myself face to face with the twins. There was a moment of frozen silence . . .

'Wow!' breathed Demmy.

Sandy said nothing. He was too busy staring.

Then I exploded. I can't recall what I said except that, amazingly, it contained no four-letter words. Modesty went out the window: I was Venus Enraged, and I didn't give a damn about my absent draperies. At one point Meredith tried to slip away, but I grabbed her by the scruff of the neck – or at any rate, the scruff of something – deposited her by the basin, and ordered her to get scrubbing. 'And don't forget to pick the chicken bits out of the plughole: you can flush them down the loo.' Georgie came pelting along the passageway, assimilated the situation at a glance, and disappeared, returning with one hand behind her back. By this time, my tirade was running out.

'Go to your room,' Georgie told the boys. 'Sit down, and write letters of apology to Cookie. And they'd better be good.'

'Why?' Sandy demanded truculently.

The hand emerged from behind her back. 'Because I've got your PlayStations,' she said, 'and they go to the charity shop in the morning.'

I was lost in admiration. Georgie would have made some poor child a wonderful mother – or, failing that, a pretty good drill sergeant.

'Mummy won't let you,' Sandy said, but some of the toughness had ebbed from his voice.

'Want to put money on that?'

There was a thoughtful pause. Lin's children might (possibly) respect her as a parent, but they could see she would be no match for Georgie, and Sandy was doubtless smart enough to realise that Mummy might not feel Right was on his side. With a last, yearning look at my heaving bosom, they filed out. Georgie and I exchanged the satisfied glances of generals who have got the enemy on the run, and I turned back to Meredith. Something in Georgie's last line had rung a bell in my head. *Want to put money on that*? Money. Of course.

'So how much did the twins pay you for that little stunt?'

'*Pay* me?' Meredith endeavoured to look innocent, but her face wasn't cut out for it. Deadpan, yes. Malevolent, yes. Innocent, no.

'How much did they pay you to throw up over me, so I would take my top and bra off, so they could see my tits?' I elucidated.

'They didn't pay—'

'*How much*?'

'Fiver . . .' she whispered.

I studied her narrowly. 'I'm guessing ten. Each. When you've finished washing my clothes, you're going to give it to me. Then I'm going to give it to a suitable good cause. The NSPCG.'

'NSPCC,' Meredith corrected quietly.

'Nope. I mean the National Society for the Prevention of Cruelty to Grownups. Are you done?' I would have to wash everything myself afterwards, naturally, but it's the principle that counts. 'Don't forget to scoop all those yukky bits of chicken out and chuck them in the loo, will you?' (She didn't like that part at all.) 'Good. Now you're going to bed.'

'But—'

'*Bed.*'

No doubt about it, authority was beginning to go to my head. It was a wonderful sensation. Maybe I could find a vacancy as a mad dictator somewhere.

Some time later, Georgie and I were sitting in the living room over restorative glasses of Shiraz. The children were in bed, or at least in their bedrooms. I was wearing a floppy blouse of Lin's, all embroidery and mirror chips, while my sweater and bra were drying on the radiator. There were two new ten-pound notes in my wallet, retrieved from the drawer of Meredith's desk, and two letters of apology reposed on the table in front of me. 'Let me see,' Georgie said, picking them up.

'*Dear Cookie,*' Demmy had written, '*we are very sorry we got Meredith to do a sicky so you would take your clothes off and we could see your boobs. I know this was wrong and must have been embarassing for you. Please forgive us and don't tell Mummy as she would be very angry. We promise not to do it again.* Well, that's something, I suppose!

114

What about Sandy's letter? *Dear Emma Jane* – more formal, I see – *I am very sorry—*'

'He's the dominant twin,' I commented. 'Demmy says *we*, he says *I*.'

'*I am very sorry for what we did. We didn't mean you to be upset. It's very hard when you are adullessent* – is he trying to be cute? – *and want to know what naked women look like but you aren't allowed. It was very educational seeing you.* Cheeky! *Please don't tell Mummy. Yours sincerely, Lysander Corrigan. P.S. Fantastic tits.* Bloody hell! That boy will go far – though God knows in what direction. Well, you wanted to be a sex goddess . . .'

'Not funny.'

Suddenly she glanced down at her own not inconsiderable bust. 'I wonder why they picked you, not me?'

'Size *is* everything,' I suggested.

'I suppose so.' Georgie still looked faintly peeved.

'Do you *want* projectile vomiting on your designer gear?'

'No, but – am I getting old?'

'You'll never be old,' I assured her, 'even when you're older.'

'I'll drink to that. In fact, I'll drink to anything.' Georgie refilled our glasses. 'Now, what shall we watch? Football – cricket – horror?'

'I've had enough horror for one night . . .'

Lin came home around one, without Derek. By that time my bra had dried out, though not my sweater. 'How did it go?' Georgie inquired.

Lin sat down, looking slightly mournful. 'All right really. He was nice. He seemed to like me, too, but—'

'No vital spark?' Georgie said.

'Vital spark?'

'The vital spark of attraction. You didn't feel tempted to meet his eyes across a crowded room.'

'Definitely not. Maybe I'm just out of practice with the dating thing. Or else I should stop being romantic and settle for a relationship that's just comfortable and friendly . . .'

'No,' Georgie and I said in unison.

'Living with a man is hard enough,' Georgie concluded. 'Without love, why put yourself through it?'

'Being on your own is worse,' Lin said.

'You're not on your own.' I jerked a thumb towards the ceiling.

'Children aren't the same,' Lin said unanswerably. 'Were they – were they good? Why are you wearing my blouse?'

'I spilt some wine on my sweater,' I said, avoiding Georgie's eye. 'I hope you don't mind my borrowing this?'

''Course not. I was afraid – never mind. Were the kids okay?'

'Fine,' I said.

'Practically angelic,' said Georgie. The PlayStations lay on a nearby bookshelf.

Lin gave her a startled look. '*Really*? The thing is, Meredith can be . . . a bit of a problem.' *Now* she tells us. 'She was so young when Garry died – I feel you have to make allowances.' Absently, she drank from Georgie's glass. 'She gets sick sometimes. I mean – she makes herself sick.'

'Bulimia?' I hazarded, looking shocked. 'Isn't she rather young for that?'

'N-not bulimia. More – sort of – temper. Or temperament. She says she just screws up her stomach and thinks sick thoughts and it comes out. The doctors say she'll grow out of it. She's awfully clever, you know. Brilliant at maths and computers and things. Prodigies tend to have these problems. I was pretty sure she wouldn't do it with you, of course. Kids always behave better with strangers, don't they?'

No comment. 'Where does the mint-choc-chip ice cream come in?' I asked.

Lin turned pale. 'How—?'

'You mentioned it before.'

'Did – did I? Oh . . . Well, she likes to have it when she's planning a sicky. She says it makes the vomit a nice green colour.'

'She should try pistachio,' I suggested.

'Or pea soup,' said Georgie.

Lin stared doubtfully at us, but we both did a better job than Meredith of looking innocent. 'They must have liked you,' she said at last. 'I'm so glad. Perhaps, another time – if I was stuck—?'

'Are you seeing Derek again?' I said hastily, changing the subject.

'I'll call us a cab,' Georgie chimed in.

'It was great fun,' I perjured myself, as we left.

'Your children are unbelievable,' Georgie added, choosing her adjective with care.

Lin smiled mistily. 'I know,' she said. 'I hate them sometimes, but then, I'm their mother. You wouldn't understand. You've only seen them at their best.' She turned to me. 'When you've got kids of your own, you'll see what I mean. The whole parent thing – it's amazing. You'll see.'

For an instant, something flickered across Georgie's face and was gone. 'Okay?' I murmured, in the cab.

'If I ever have any regrets about motherhood,' she said, 'just say to me: mint-choc-chip ice cream. Promise?'

'I promise,' I said. 'Personally, I'm getting sterilised in the morning.'

My biological clock, I decided, was ticking because it was a time bomb. I was in no hurry for it to go off.

Chapter 5

The breeze is chasing the zephyr,
The moon is chasing the sea,
The bull is chasing the heifer,
But nobody's chasing me . . .

Ravel is chasing Debussy,
The aphis chases the pea,
The gander's chasing the goosey,
But nobody's goosing me.

COLE PORTER: *Nobody's Chasing Me*

'Too late!' she cried, as aloft she waved her wooden leg.

Source unknown

A few days later I was having a meeting about the PR campaign for one of our long-standing authors with Laurence Buckle, Georgie and Lin. We were playing Twin Titles, a game where you have to roll two well-known book titles into one, usually via a common word. Everyone was cheating.

'*The Sun Also Rises on my Undoing*,' Georgie offered. (*Fiesta: the Sun Also Rises* and *The Sun is my Undoing* . . . get the idea?)

'*Captain Corelli's Mandarin Is Not the Only Fruit*,' I said.

'*The Woman with White Teeth*,' said Laurence. 'I only changed a preposition.' You can tell an editor because he will use words like 'preposition' in normal conversation.

'*The Woman with White Fangs*,' Georgie riposted.

'*The Murder of Peter Ackroyd*,' Lin suggested. 'I know it's a book and an author, but . . .'

'Good idea,' said Laurence. It was not clear whether he was referring to the title or the concept.

'Gerald Durrell: *Captain Corelli's Pangolin*,' I said. 'I'm sure there was a Gerald Durrell about a pangolin. My mum had them all.'

'No more Captain Corelli,' Georgie decreed. 'You're fixated.'

'Headache? *Nausée*? Use *Captain Corelli's Anadin*!'

We were interrupted by the ringing of the nearest phone and the advent of Alistair Garnett, looking portentous. It's impossible to get any work done in a publishing house. Alistair had been in a bad state ever since his PA broke her arm on a climbing holiday in Wales: the temp who was covering for her had proved dauntingly efficient and mildly contemptuous of all things editorial. He liked to find fault from time to time: we all knew that, and catered accordingly. Perfection in a subordinate frustrated him, particularly if it was in his own office. He also liked to radiate enthusiasm where others doubted and decried, but he wasn't used to dealing with the underlying scorn of someone who had honed her skills in the frenetic atmosphere of the City. 'I even find myself sticking up for the bloody writers!' he had complained recently.

That day, he didn't look in a mood to stick up for anyone. 'Break up the party,' he snapped. 'Laurence, in my office.'

'What's the matter?'

'Shit-fan collision course. *In my office*.'

Laurence made a face and trailed off in his wake. The rest of us abandoned our game and, as a last resort, resumed discussions on the PR campaign. Since the writer's sales had been flagging the Accounts Department, with their usual logic, had lopped the budget, which meant we were going to have to get creative. 'Creative' is the word PR people always use when there isn't enough money available for real promotion. I had often wondered about illegal stickers on the Underground and overnight graffiti, but although this is okay for a gig by some obscure band I don't suppose it would do for a mainstream novel. Georgie began talking about pressing the flesh with her contacts on the literary pages and trying to find a slot in an upcoming festival. Once she got going, she sounded energetic and positive. Budget or no budget, Georgie always gives her all.

'Has Warbeck any contacts of his own?' Lin asked. (Emlyn Warbeck was the writer.)

'Of course not. He's a recluse who's lived for the past thirty years in a remote Welsh village with no railway station. He's only just traded in his typewriter for a laptop.' Unless they do regular journalism, writers very rarely have 'contacts'. Which is why publishers are always signing up C-list celebs – the kind who've spent their lives networking – to produce novels, only to discover, invariably too late, that they can't actually write. You'd think the senior executives would know better by now, but they never learn. One Dirk Bogarde does not a literary stable make.

Anyone contemplating writing a book, pay attention. You think it's easy? All you need is a hazy knowledge of grammar and the ability to put one word after another – right? And you've got this great idea for a plot which no one has ever done before? (Forget it. *Everything* has been done before. There really are only seven plots in the world – though I wish someone would list what they are. Then writers could simply pick and choose.) Take a look at the bestseller shelves. They are dominated by maybe a couple of hundred names

– and that's *internationally*. Beyond that, perhaps a few thousand make a decent living from their books, if that many. This is *not fluke*. If it were as easy as you think it is, there would be a lot more stars in the literary firmament. Most people can't even tell a story straight. They go off into these rambling digressions . . .

Laurence reappeared after about twenty minutes looking pale – or as pale as someone with a naturally pink complexion *could* look.

'What's the flap?' Georgie asked.

We offered him a chair but he preferred to pace up and down, fuming. Metaphorically, steam was coming from his ears. We could almost see it. None of us had ever seen Laurence angry – he was the type who became irritable and occasionally peevish but didn't seem to have a temper to lose. We were all rather shocked.

'Beauman,' he said. 'Fucking Beauman.' He didn't use four-letter words either. 'Fucking arsehole Beauman. Fuck fuck fuck.'

And so on.

'What's he done?' Georgie asked. Lin and I were too alarmed to pose home questions.

'He's *heard* I'm gay,' Laurence said, tight-lipped – a difficult attitude for someone whose mouth was of the soft-and-sensitive brand, 'and he thinks my editorial touch would detract from the machismo of his prose.'

We stared at him, staggered. 'I bet he didn't put it as well as that,' I muttered, voicing the second thought that came to mind.

Laurence wasn't listening. 'I did his last book, for God's sake! Number one on every bestseller list! Well, except where it was number two. I've been wasting half my evenings on this one – and it isn't like I get overtime. No complaints before. I don't know who told him—'

'Probably no one *told* him,' Georgie said. 'I expect someone just said something because they thought he knew.'

'Who cares? It doesn't matter now. Look, I've never made an issue of being gay. It isn't a political thing for me, just a sexual preference. I don't do the clichés. I still like football and beer – I don't collect Princess Di memorabilia – I don't wear a lilac suit and march for Gay Pride. I don't even do guilt any more.'

'Your gayness and your guilt are *not* besmirched With rainy marching in the painful field,' I was unable to resist paraphrasing.

Laurence, cooling down, managed a short laugh. 'Nice one, Cookie. The point is, gay isn't who I am, it's just who I fuck. What difference does it make to my work? None. We just have to pander to the whims of that bigoted cretinous little ex-con—'

'At least it's a nasty job you don't have to do any more,' I said.

'Don't be naïve,' said Laurence. 'It was my job security. My road to promotion. Without it, I'm just another editor, back on the bottom rung.'

'Like me,' I said.

'Not quite. I forgot to tell you, Alistair wants you in his office. I suspect you're taking over.'

'*What?*'

Georgie, unforgivably, gave a shout of laughter. Even Lin giggled. I could see nothing funny in the situation.

'Don't knock it,' Laurence said, with a generosity which I should've appreciated more. 'It's a real chance to show what you can do. Beauman needs so much work – it's a hell of a job, and beyond the portals of Ransome Harber no one will know, but in the company your stock could skyrocket. Besides, tactful handling of impossible bastards seems to be your forte. You did well with Todd Jarman.'

Unaccountably, I was annoyed. 'You can't possibly compare Todd with Jerry Beauman! Anyway, I – I wasn't tactful. We . . .' We struck sparks off each other?

In Alistair's office, my worst fears were realised. (It's funny how often worst fears are realised – and not just in this book. You never read of worst fears *not* being realised, do you? You'd think we'd learn from experience, and tone down our fears – but then perhaps the unpleasant future would just creep up on us unawares, which could be far nastier.)

'Sit down,' Alistair said with an expansive smile. It reminded me of Lewis Carroll's crocodile – it was smug, it was laid back, and it said: You're dinner.

I sat.

Alistair launched into his spiel about the publisher's mission, winding down when he inferred, possibly from my expression, that I'd heard it before. Then came the doom-laden words.

'I've got a wonderful opportunity for you.'

Later that same evening . . .

The three musketeers were sitting in a nearby wine bar with a bottle of celebratory champagne, though I for one was not at all sure what we were celebrating. Cal had gone straight home due to family commitments and Laurence had declined to join us. 'We're celebrating your freedom, not Cookie's enslavement,' Lin had claimed.

'Pah!' said Laurence, or something that sounded like that. Which was interesting, because I couldn't recall ever hearing anyone say 'Pah!' before; it's the kind of thing people said in novels of the mid-twentieth century, when writers weren't allowed to go for anything stronger. Possibly Laurence was more camp than he pretended. 'Sorry – thanks for the invite – but "Pah!" just the same. What's the point of being one of the lads when you're categorised solely by what you do in bed?'

'Ladettes,' said Georgie. And, as he walked away: 'Where are you going?'

'To start a collection of Princess Di teacups!'

So it was just the three of us, and the champagne. Lin had called in her latest emergency babysitter, the teenage daughter of a neighbour who was anxious to earn some extra cash. 'How tough is she?' Georgie had inquired doubtfully.

'Well, she's got multiple lip-piercings, a nasal stud, and her hair dyed black with purple streaks, so she *looks* tough enough,' Lin said, not pretending to misunderstand.

'Does she wear vomit-proof clothing?' I asked, adding, delicately: 'You told us about Meredith's little problem . . .'

'Oh – yes. She wears leather. At least, fake leather. Anyway, I'm sure they'll think she's cool. Though they were really taken with you two . . .'

'Kids always appreciate natural authority,' Georgie declared airily.

We drank to my new role as Jerry Beauman's editor, dissuaded Lin from phoning home in a panic (more worst fears could've been realised there), and fished for other things to drink to.

'There's always the wishes,' Lin said. 'I've had a date, even if it wasn't a big success, and Cookie's become a sex goddess.'

'Not yet,' said Georgie, forestalling my protest. 'We've still got to find a suitable event where she can shine in all her goddessly glory. The Christmas party's way too far off. It may have to be a book launch.'

'Launches aren't really sex-goddess territory,' I said hastily. I could see a certain gleam in Georgie's eye which was making me nervous. Something told me another transformation scene could be in the offing, and I wasn't sure my credit card could stand it. 'How about you? Met any good millionaires lately?'

'Yes. Sort of.' Georgie looked tragic. 'I'm supposed to be going out with a glamorous doctor at the weekend. The Harley Street kind. He sounds glamorous by e-mail, anyway. He's taking me to the opera.'

'Why're you looking so gloomy about it?' Lin asked. 'I should think that would be wonderful. Andy took me to Glyndebourne once: *The Marriage of Figaro*. It was out of this world. Is this Glyndebourne?'

'Covent Garden.'

'You do fall on your feet,' I said, a little enviously. 'What's the opera?'

Georgie was still looking tragic. 'Wagner.'

'Oh.' I thought I understood her gloom. 'Can be heavy going.' Years ago, I had attempted to sit through a video of the Ring Cycle, in order to impress an operatically minded young man with my musical knowledge. I had tried to absorb it piecemeal, over several days, frequently leaving the room to make coffee and fortifying myself with a book on the side, but it had still been hard work and very unrewarding. The young man had preferred a fan of Bananarama. Now, all I could remember of the production, bar its length, was the opulent black diva who had been singing Frigga – a particularly unlikely Nordic goddess. 'Which Wagner?'

'*Lohengrin*,' said Georgie. 'Slow and grim.'

'That's not too long, is it?' I said, hearteningly.

'About four hours,' Georgie responded. Her gloom was unalleviated.

'Could be worse. The Ring goes on practically forever.'

'It'll be fun,' Lin insisted. 'Opera's amazing, isn't it? You must have been to lots when you were in Italy. Italy's the home of opera. The Italians are all mad about it.'

'No,' Georgie said baldly. 'They ain't. Italy may be the home of Rossini and Puccini and other composers ending in –ini, but most Italians don't give a damn. There's a small clique at La Scala who reminisce about Callas and throw tomatoes at singers they don't like; everyone else just goes for the party. Opening night there is the biggest social event of the season. It's all about dressing up like a Christmas tree and being photographed in a whirl of celebs; no one listens to the music.'

'I should've thought that would be your scene,' I said. 'I mean the dressing up and the celebs.'

'Only when I'm part of it. During my marriage, I wasn't. We went once, after – after things started to go wrong with me and Franco.' A quick smile chased the shadow from her face. 'It was something called *La Vestale* – unbelievably dreary. Vestal Virgins, Ancient Rome, large men in togas. I don't think the toga does anything for anyone; it just makes you look as if you're wearing your bath towel. And there weren't any hit songs. I took a small torch and a book.'

'How did you get away with that?' Lin asked.

'We were in a box. I sat at the back.'

'Maybe your doctor will get you a box,' I said.

'Bit iffy,' said Georgie. 'Too secluded. He might try to make a pass at me in the sex scenes.'

'*Sex scenes?*' Lin and I stared. 'In *Wagner*?'

And: 'What's this doctor's name, anyway?' I inquired.

His name, apparently, was Neville Fancot. It didn't sound promising, but when they met in the foyer, locating each other by mobile phone and a series of passwords, Georgie found herself thinking with surprise that he looked presentable, even attractive. Her previous experiences had not engendered optimism, and she checked hastily to see if his eyes were too close together or there were signs of a latent mother-complex. In fact, he had a thin, rather brown face with folded lines in his cheeks that unfolded when he smiled and a respectable distance between his eyes. His hair was brown-going-grey (or possibly, Georgie speculated, grey-going-brown), his voice

126

plummy, with an upper-class accent that belonged more to British films of the forties and fifties than the present day. His suit bore the hallmarks of Savile Row tailoring, with a carnation in the buttonhole for recognition purposes. (Georgie's suggestion: 'Let's say it with clichés.') After considerable research, Georgie had abandoned any idea of full evening dress and wore her slinky black skirt and a top with the inevitable plunge neckline, draped in a pashmina for subtlety. If Dr Fancot was impressed, he managed not to show it.

'I've arranged dinner in the restaurant in the intervals,' he explained. 'I think we should go and order now.'

'So what's someone like you doing using the classifieds?' Georgie inquired while they awaited the maître d', hiding blunt interrogation behind a dazzling smile. At least, she hoped he was dazzled. 'You don't look the type.' If there was a type – after her previous dates she wasn't sure.

'Nor do you.'

'The ad says it all.' Georgie grimaced. 'I need a millionaire in my life. *Do* you have a cardiac condition?'

''Fraid not. I'm forty-eight, pretty comfortably off, and my back plays up from time to time, especially after too much tennis. Will that do?'

'I'm not sure,' Georgie said cautiously.

The maître d' materialised to take their orders: both went for the smoked salmon, followed by rare steak. 'Couldn't you order something with more cholesterol?' Georgie demanded.

Neville started, then grinned. 'Sorry. If we have coffee afterwards, I'll eat all the chocolate mints.'

'You still haven't answered my question,' she resumed, over champagne at the bar. 'Why the classifieds? Are you married?'

'Divorced. The usual story: I have a busy life, limited time for socialising, I wanted to meet someone outside my everyday circle. Not for any sinister reasons, just for the fun of it. Your ad made me laugh.'

'It wasn't a joke,' Georgie said darkly.

'Well, I may not be rich enough, but at least let me give you a good time this evening.' Her eyes widened. 'Unfortunate choice of words. I mean—'

'You call Wagner a *good time*?'

'Actually, I've never done Wagner before. I've always played safe with Verdi and Mozart. I was hoping all this would impress you. Are you keen on opera?'

'I lived in Italy for years,' Georgie said.

'So you're an expert.'

'So I know nothing about it.' She began to explain the popular misconception about Italians and opera.

'Then this is a first for both of us,' he said bracingly.

He's nice, she thought, determined to be positive. Probably a good doctor. Quietly competent, reassuring, not too charming. She had a hazy idea doctors shouldn't be charming: there was something deeply suspect about anyone in a position of trust exuding even the subtlest form of sex appeal. Besides, Georgie liked to be the one with the charm. It gave her an edge – yet at the same time it was a quality she despised, since it came to her so easily, and she used it so lightly, and it meant so little. I read in an old Margery Allingham that charm is 'the ability to make people think you like them', which sums it up nicely. Georgie – who is only superficially superficial – had enough discernment to place little value on hers, even though she would exercise it without scruple.

A bell summoned them, and they polished off their champagne and headed for the auditorium.

Afterwards, Georgie said she was ready for what she called the Herrenvolk bit, in which some king or other pushed the theme of Germany for the Germans. I'd rung an opera buff the previous day who looked *Lohengrin* up in Grove, so I'd been able to inform her that the writer George Eliot had described the music as resembling 'the wind whistling through the keyholes in a cathedral'. But Georgie paid little attention to the lack of good tunes. Even before the (relatively brief) Nazi propaganda was over, it dawned on her that the militant monarch was dressed exactly like Queen Amidala in *The Phantom Menace*. The villain appeared, in a vast black cloak which swirled as he strode across the stage – though curiously, several of the characters failed to detect his villainy, despite that giveaway cloak. Then came the heroine, in white with earphones. ('It was just like *Star Wars*,' Georgie assured us on Monday, 'only the music wasn't as good.') A red-haired villainess added spice, someone called Waltraud singing Ortrud, or possibly vice versa. Lohengrin, the hero knight, arrived floating on a swan, causing Georgie to wonder if they'd switched to the ballet by mistake. He was operatically fat – about .4 on the Pavarotti scale – which was disappointing, since the rest of the cast were of normal proportions. If he had been covered in armour he might have passed for merely hefty, but the costume designer had put him in a sort of flowing tunic, full-length, which made him look like a pregnant woman in eveningwear. He and the heroine married, on condition that she never asked him his real name, so of course you knew she would. After a long wedding-night scene she put the fatal question ('If he'd given her an orgasm she'd have gone to sleep perfectly happy': Georgie). He revealed that he was Lohengrin, son of Parsifal (see prequel), and now she had broken her promise he would have to return to the otherworldly Eden where he lived forever under the 'fluence of the Holy Grail. The swan reappeared, and turned into the heroine's long-lost brother, a character so unimportant the audience had forgotten all about him. The villain had bitten the dust in a skirmish with light sabres some scenes earlier and Lohengrin departed, leaving the heroine to collapse in a swoon or die of a broken heart, depending on interpretation and her state of cardiac health. In the stalls, Georgie found herself applauding with the rest.

'It was wonderful,' she told Neville, to her own surprise. '*Star Wars* and Indiana Jones and everything. I loved it.'

During the intervals, they had sprinted up to the restaurant and wolfed down their dinner with undignified haste. 'I should have booked somewhere afterwards,' Neville said. 'But Wagner goes on so long it would have been much too late.'

They went to a wine bar for more champagne and Georgie allowed him to drive her home, feeling fairly confident he was neither stalker nor axe-murderer. He kissed her on the cheek by way of goodnight and didn't suggest another meeting. Damn, Georgie thought.

If Georgie's Saturday was a qualified success, mine was definitely a failure. My sister Sophie had rung on Friday, announcing her intention of coming up to London for a day's shopping and appropriating my company on her usual careless assumption that I could have nothing better to do. I didn't, which didn't make me feel any happier about it. I love Sophie: as big sisters go, she has been kind, protective, not unduly bossy and only intermittently patronising. But she has also, always, been the pretty one. She has the sort of naturally slim figure that ignores calories – quick metabolism or some other injustice of Nature – and even after two children her waistline has hardly thickened. Her face is heart-shaped, her hair a glossy bob, straighter than mine and blow-dried into sleekness. That weekend she arrived wearing the kind of trousers that show off slender thighs, her casual tan enhanced by a pink top with judicious gaps. Somehow, even with my new image and hour-glass proportions, she managed to make me feel like a lump. A short lump. She's only an inch or two taller than me, but it feels like a yard.

'You've lost weight,' she greeted me, accusingly. 'Looks good, but be careful you don't get anorexia. I had a friend years ago, desperate to lose a stone. She tried every diet going and ended up living off black coffee and pickled walnuts. She got addicted to them – couldn't stop – wound up in hospital weighing the same as an eight-year-old child. And it wasn't like she was ever really fat. If you ask me, we shouldn't try to conform to fashion: it's dangerous. Much better to just go with whatever Nature intended.'

Easy to say, when Nature intended you to be a size 10.

And a bit later, suspiciously: 'You've got an awful lot of pickles in that cupboard. Are you *sure* you're okay?'

'Nigel liked them,' I said.

'Well, at least you're rid of him; that's one good thing. Sorry, darling, but he *was* awful. All that phoney left ideology went out with the seventies. Nobody goes in for that stuff any more.'

'It wasn't phoney,' I said defensively. 'Anyway, he didn't want to conform to political fashion.'

'What? Oh – clever little sis. But he did conform: you know he did. There's no one as conventional as an extremist.'

And the annoying thing about that, I reflected, was that it was probably true.

At school, Sophie had been very bright in an idle, don't-give-a-damn way in which minimum effort produced maximum results. But by the time she got to university (Bristol), indolence or indifference began to take hold. She flunked her degree and instead landed a job on a Paris-based fashion magazine, where she shacked up with a photographer some ten years older and enjoyed what seemed to me, then still a child, a wildly glamorous lifestyle. When I was thirteen she invited me to visit, but my parents wouldn't allow it, so I *knew* she had to be having fun, moving in a world of unimaginable glitz and decadence. (Though of course I imagined a good deal, undoubtedly exaggerating in a mist of envy and awe.) At seventeen, I was just about to leave on the longed-for trip when the relationship foundered and Sophie returned home. She didn't stay long, going to see a friend in New York and falling on her feet as usual with another magazine job and an offered flat-share in a brownstone. While she was there she met an English banker based in Wall Street – the kind with looks and money, an apartment in the Village, a house in the Hamptons. In due course she came back to England with a huge diamond and a date for the wedding. I don't think I'll ever forget my embarrassment and horror when, co-opted as chief bridesmaid, I waddled up the aisle behind her in stilettos and lilac chiffon, feeling like something that maiden aunts put on top of a loo roll. Relocated back to London, Gareth retired from banking at thirty-five, bought a garden centre near Oxford, and moved to an idyllic country house from which to run his idyllic country business. Needless to say, he made money. Sophie junked the world of magazines, had children and a maid, and frequently declared, with a certain smugness, that she was turning into a vegetable.

'Why London?' I asked, when the subject of Nigel had been brushed under the carpet. Sophie always said the boutiques in Oxford were second to none.

'I felt like a change. Anyway, I thought I might as well give you a bell. It's been a while.'

'Mum been at you?' Some things needed little explanation.

'Mmm. You know how it is. You never brought the dreaded Nigel to meet them, you're looking peaky, your job at Ransome has bad pay and no prospects. The usual.'

'All jobs in publishing have bad pay and no prospects. As it happens, I've had promotion – in a way.'

'In what way?'

'I'm editing Jerry Beauman's next book. Apparently, it's a

privilege. He's supposed to be the biggest bastard in the business – but that's top secret.'

'Good,' said Sophie. 'Who can I tell?'

'Whom,' said the editor in me, but Sophie didn't notice.

We went to Harrods in quest of an outfit for Sophie to wear to someone's wedding, but my sister, easily sidetracked, wandered into departments of designer children's clothes and scooped up frilled and beaded miniatures of teenage gear – 'Hermione will look *so* sweet in that!' – and diminutive macho jackets and sweatshirts for Raphael. From our last meeting I remembered him as one of those boys who manages to be grubby no matter how often you wash him, while Hermione, not surprisingly in view of her mother's attitude, was a proper little madam. 'She's so fashion-conscious already,' Sophie cooed. 'Mind you, they all are nowadays. I bought her a new party dress last month – the loveliest thing, yellow with sequined appliqués – and she looked at it and said: "Mummy, I can't wear that! It's so *yesterday*!" Wasn't that sweet?'

Personally, I felt Hermione's dress sense might benefit from a good spanking, and on an impulse I said so.

'Spanking?' Sophie laughed. 'Darling, nobody spanks any more. It's *Victorian*. Besides, she'd probably get hold of the school lawyer and prosecute us for child abuse.'

School lawyer???

In due course, we went to lunch. I ordered salad, and Sophie reverted to the subject of my supposed anorexia, nagging me to have the cannelloni. 'It's summer,' I pointed out. 'Everyone eats salad in the summer.'

'Nonsense. You don't *like* salad; no one does. People only eat it to look healthy. You've *never* lost weight, Em, it can't be good for you. You're not one of Nature's dieters.'

And so on.

By the time she went, not long after tea, when I resisted her Marie Antoinette-like urging to eat cake, I felt worn out, both mentally and physically. Who was it who said you choose your friends but your family you're stuck with? Back home I rang Georgie, who agonised at length about her outfit for the opera that night, and Lin, who inquired in beseeching accents if I and/or Georgie might consider another stint of babysitting, as Andy Pearmain was in town next week. The multi-pierced teenage tough-girl had apparently retired from the lists in an advanced state of trauma. I hedged, wavered, and finally succumbed, wondering where I could get a Kalashnikov. When I eventually hung up I found myself revising my reaction to that line about choosing your friends. The work environment cultivates an unnatural intimacy, and friendships are forced along like hothouse plants. Either that, or I was a very bad chooser.

In the evening I went out with a selection from my wider social circle, but it didn't offer much relief. We went to an Indian restaurant where I ordered very hot curry on the grounds that I don't like it much, and therefore wouldn't eat a lot. Unfortunately it was even hotter than I thought, my tongue began to blister at the excess of chilli, and I had to sit with a mouthful of milk for about ten minutes to cool it down. Then we went to a downmarket wine bar, where the first person I saw was Nigel with a couple of friends.

I hadn't seen him since that terrible confrontation in the bookshop, and my stomach quailed, my knees turned to water, my voice stuck in my throat and my heart shrank. All the standard symptoms, in fact. I hated myself for my weakness, for the horrible mixture of excitement and terror and returning shame that battered my nervous system. I was supposed to be a sex goddess, with an undulating hour-glass figure worthy of Jessica Rabbit, but the sheer panic I felt was more reminiscent of Roger. I told myself I wasn't ready for this, I didn't want him to see me, I would have my drink and leave, unnoticed, unrecognised, unacknowledged. We went to a table some distance from him and I sat down in a corner, where I could see him and hopefully remain unseen. But there was a part of me that wanted to catch his eye, wanted him to look at me, see my change of image, speak to me – that treacherous part of me that said: *This time, it will be different. This time, he'll appreciate you. This time . . . this time . . . this time . . .*

We ordered a bottle, and I drank. I couldn't have said if it was white or red.

'What's the matter, Cookie?' asked one of my companions, seeing my rigid attitude and glazed eye.

'Nigel,' I said. 'Over there.'

'Oh, Lord . . .'

It was a mistake to say anything. The nudging and whispering of my friends seemed to me more noticeable than a shout. I sank back into what shadows there were, trying to change colour, like a chameleon, against the cushions of the bench. Nigel didn't seem to be with a girlfriend – an omission guaranteed to give me false hope – but was leaning forward, talking to two guys whom I'd met occasionally, a long-haired vegetarian called Rom (whatever that was short for) and a thin Asian with overlarge specs. At a guess they were rearranging the world – that, or discussing the shortcomings of absent fellow ideologues. I watched them, hawk-like, feeling queasy. Drank more wine. Ate a handful of something (crisps? peanuts?). Then back to the wine. Any minute, I thought, he'll look round and see me. Maybe it would be better to attract his attention, to have the advantage of making the opening gambit . . .

God knows how long this went on. Belatedly, I was aware of being drunk. Not too drunk, but drunk enough. Dutch courage stiffened my sinews, put the joints back in my knees. I got up, went to the loo, retouched my face. On the way back, I stopped at his table.

'Hello, Nige.' Not a good opening line, not remarkable for cutting-edge wit, but I was sufficiently pissed not to care.

'Cookie. Hi.'

'How are you?'

I was conscious of him looking me over, of the other two surveying me with deadly unenthusiasm. Sobriety seeped coldly into my head.

'You've lost weight,' he said, in a curiously similar tone to Sophie's. Accusatory. Critical. 'You should be careful. You don't want to—'

'Get anorexia? Yes, I know. I'm a long way off the twiglet figure just yet.'

'You're looking pale, too. Poor Cookie. Been having a bad time?'

I stared at him, slightly baffled. He didn't look cruel or scornful, the way he had at our previous meeting. In fact he was looking gentle, lightly teasing, an expression I remembered too well. I muttered something about work pressure.

'I'm sorry I was a bit hard on you last time. But you were pretty vile, booting me out like that. It was that harpy Georgie, wasn't it? Awful old slag. For God's sake, don't end up like her.'

'She's not a slag,' I said. 'She's—'

Nigel wasn't listening – a habit of his. 'Poor old girl. You must have been pretty down, wasting away like that. I should've known it would hit you hard.'

Wasting away? *Wasting* . . . ?!

'You think I've been pining for you?' The surge of indignation that rushed through me was so violent I could feel the heat of it in my face. 'Pining – for *you*? I've been on a diet. Not anorexia, not a green and yellow melancholy – a DIET. People do that. And now I feel good, and I'm told I look good, and I miss you like – like a pain in the gut. Goodnight!'

It wasn't a great exit-line, but I was pleased with it. In

that moment, I thought I was well rid of him. How dare he – how *dare* he – assume I had been pining away, missing him, going into a decline? The fact that I had was immaterial. That wasn't why I'd lost weight – was it? I strode back to my table, plumped myself down and demanded more wine.

Someone said: 'Perhaps we should move on.'

'I don't care,' I said, 'as long as there's alcohol at the end of the move.'

'What did he say?'

I think I ground my teeth. There's nothing like anger to give you a lift. 'Don't ask.'

Several wine bars later, the anger had worn off or been forgotten and I knew I'd blown it. Not that I wanted Nigel back – or if I did, it was only out of pride, nothing else – but I wanted to behave with dignity, to be coolly unattainable (while at the same time being a sizzling sex goddess), to see him torn by vain lust, racked by might-have-beens. What I didn't want was pity, sympathy, *kindness*. I couldn't decide which was more humiliating, kindness or cruelty – not that it mattered. Neither had shown me to advantage. Sunday morning found me hungover and depressed. I thought about eating, just for comfort, the way I used to, and found I had no inclination. Maybe I was becoming anorexic after all.

'I *don't* want him back,' I told the bathroom mirror, spluttering toothpaste. But by evening, alone in front of the television, I was lapsing into fantasies about his abject return.

In desperation I put on a video, and went to bed with Hugh Jackman.

The following week Todd Jarman returned his manuscript, with most of my corrections re-corrected. I considered altering them again, sneakily, but decided that would be underhand. Besides, he had – as requested – added a new body. Surprisingly, instead of being a cab driver who Knew

Too Much or another prostitute it turned out to be the gang-sters' legal adviser, an ultra-smoothie who, in the previous version, had oozed out of the narrative like cream from a plastic tube. Of course he, too, Knew Too Much, mainly under the heading of client confidentiality, and his gory demise was particularly satisfying. As he was a lawyer, it would have been tempting to probe the incident for sub-conscious motives, but I guessed the truth was probably more straightforward. Ten-to-one Helen's social circle included a few slimy solicitors from the opposition team. I rang him up, feeling a strange uprush of confidence, to suggest a session to finalise disputed details.

'It's really good you killed that guy off,' I said. 'I loathed him.'

'I aim to please.'

We fixed a date and I hung up, turning my attention to the rather more slapdash offering from Jerry Beauman. It was very much as expected. Upright hero, slightly naïve, inveigled into a criminal involvement by evil associates. He himself does nothing wrong, but is left to carry the can for their misdeeds. Sent to prison, a sort of *Shawshank Redemption* scenario ensues, as he becomes the confidant of the crooked governor and a role model for fellow inmates. Finally released, he sets out to prove his innocence and wreak revenge on the crooks who framed him and the corrupt judge who misdirected the jury and doled out his sentence. In a succession of action-packed chapters, he gathers together a band of ex-cons and other unlikely allies to entrap and expose the bad guys. It was a good story – or rather an all-too familiar medley of good stories – the only problem was the way it was written. There were gaps in the narrative, grammar and punctuation were both erratic, and many scenes needed extensive re-working. My heart sank. (It had done that a lot lately.) My editorial input was going to be a long, long job.

I went to find Laurence.

'This is a nightmare,' I said. 'Have you been through any of it yet?'

'A few chapters. I'll e-mail my notes to you.' He was looking grumpy and drinking coffee from a mug with a cartoon nude of Princess Diana on the side. 'Remember, you'll have to polish his style.'

'Has he got one?'

'Okay, you'll have to polish his lack of style. Good luck.'

'I've set up a meeting for you,' Alistair told me later. 'Thursday week, at his flat.'

Venturing into the lion's den *chez* Jarman looked, in retrospect, like a stroll in the park. Oh, for the safety of publishers' offices!

I escaped to lunch and exchanged confidences with Georgie and Lin, only to fall alive into the babysitting trap.

Georgie and I went on Wednesday (Cal was coaching his son Allan's football team). Lin departed for her dinner-date looking sunnier than she had in a long while and the two of us, without prior discussion, adopted a Camp-Kommandant stance which worked very well. When the twins demanded suppers that were not on the menu, we told them flatly to eat what was on offer or starve. Sandy protested he was a growing boy; I assured him I would be only too happy to stunt his growth. Demmy, looking like a famine victim, said he wasn't hungry; Georgie said, '*Good.*' In the end, they both ate what was available. Meredith said: 'Look what I can do,' and Georgie and I both ducked, but it transpired she only wanted to demonstrate a headstand. I pointed out that turning upside down was bad for the digestion, and once all three children were more or less the right way up Georgie rewarded them with a packet of chocolate brownies with which she had thoughtfully provided herself. Later, all we had to do was switch over from *Sex and the City*; I threatened them

139

with a video of *Thomas the Tank Engine*, as a result of which they sat fairly contentedly through some unsuitable reality TV before being dispatched to bed. Georgie and I recuperated with a bottle of wine, feeling like the villains in a Dickens novel – the kind who refused to give Oliver Twist seconds of gruel. (I can't recall their names: I'm not a big Dickens fan.) We were very pleased with ourselves.

Lin, meanwhile, was sitting in Zilli's with Andy Pearmain eating bruschetta and wondering why she couldn't chat away to him as easily as in the past. After all, he was just the same as always. The beard was very short these days, little more than a shadow-line emphasising his jaw; there was a hint of grey in his hair; his habitual expression of sympathetic interest was enhanced by a myriad of tiny lines, smile-lines, thought-lines, furtive etchings of anxiety and stress. Unreasonably, she found herself blaming his fiancée for the latter. He really should have been gay. All the gay couples she knew (Laurence and partner) were in incredibly stable, comfortable relationships with no anxiety factors at all.

Of course, he could be stressed out by the problems of high-powered banking, but Lin's a romantic: despite experience, she thinks the only significant strain in life comes from love and family.

She began to ask him, rather awkwardly, about his bride-to-be: how and where they met, what she did, whether she was another of his otherworldly idealists. What campaigns she would be spending his money on.

'Actually, Cat's a bit different from the others. She's into hunting and the Countryside Alliance. I know you won't approve, but you're not a country girl. They seem to believe hunting is pretty necessary. Foxes *are* vermin, apparently.'

'Cat?'

'Catriona. Her parents are friends of my mother's. All very cosy, you see. When it comes to really getting hitched at last,

I return to my roots. She's not a glamour girl, just sort of clean and glowing. The outdoor type.'

'She looks good in tweeds?' Lin queried. Her heart was sinking, though she wasn't quite sure why. Perhaps it was just chronic pessimism about all Andy's women.

'She looks good. Wholesome – no makeup – like fresh fruit and wild flowers. Sorry: I'm not much good at the poetic stuff. She reminds me of the way you used to look, when I first knew you.' Lin stared at him, suddenly stricken. 'Shit! I didn't mean that to come out that way. Cat isn't beautiful like you, but she has that untouched aura. She's only twenty-four; life hasn't done anything bad to her yet. I hope it never will. You know, you always reminded me of a wild flower, transported to the big city and stifling in the fumes.'

'Wilting,' Lin said. The sinking feeling had become a pain, sharper than regret. Twenty-four, she thought. Untouched. *Innocent* . . . Why did it hurt so much?

'Just – drooping a bit. Stuck in a formal bed by a busy street when it should have been growing on a mountainside in the fresh air.'

'You never said.'

'It wasn't my business to say,' he responded. 'First there was Sean, then Garry. You chose your own life. I just wanted to be there for you, when you needed a friend. Sometimes, I wanted to say to you: "I'll take you away from all this. I'll take you home" . . . but you wouldn't have listened.' Lin's eyes filled with treacherous tears. One escaped down her cheek, and splashed on to the bruschetta. 'Never mind. Maybe you'll go back one day. Who's the latest unsuitable man?'

'Oh – umm – he's – he's not unsuitable . . .' She couldn't tell him there was no one – not when he had wholesome Catriona, who looked good in tweeds.

'Sorry, didn't mean to sound cynical. Bring him to the wedding: I'd like to meet him. I really want you to be happy, Lin. You deserve to be. You're a very special kind of person.'

He was looking at her with an expression of tenderness which hurt her somehow. She thought it must have been there before, only she hadn't seen it, hadn't cared, and now it was too late. Too late . . .

'You're getting weepy,' he said gently. 'No need for that. Save it till I go up the aisle. There's nothing to cry for now.'

'I'm not weepy,' Lin said. 'It's – it's the garlic.'

'At least you've got good friends here. It was nice of your mates to babysit. What're their names? Georgina and—'

'Cookie.'

'The thing is, they belong here. You don't. To continue the horticultural analogy, Georgina's clearly an orchid, something out of a hothouse anyway, Cookie – maybe a rose. One with *lots* of petals. But you're just a little Scottish flower which misses the wind off the loch.'

Lin had been born in a village nowhere near a loch and moved thence to Edinburgh, but she wasn't going to argue with his imagery. Groping for something to say, for a way out of the emotional morass, she returned to the standard questions. 'What does Catriona – Cat – what does she do?'

'She's in publishing. Coincidence, isn't it? But she's going to give up work after we're married.'

'Oh?'

'She wants to concentrate on having babies.'

'How lovely,' sighed Lin.

'How was it?' we asked her when she came in. 'Did you have a good time?'

'Fine.' In the full glare of the living-room light she looked almost ravaged.

'Did he tell you any more about the environmentalist?'

'The—? Oh, it isn't her. This is another one. Her name's Cat.'

'As in Saving the Wildcat?' I asked.

'Catriona.' Lin ignored the pun, which was probably what it deserved. 'She wants to Save the Hunt instead. Countryside Alliance. She's twenty-four and wholesome and glows.'

'In the dark?' said Georgie, at sea.

But Lin wasn't registering our side of the conversation. 'Like me,' she said. 'Like I used to. He said I was a wilting flower.'

'He can't have done!' I was horrified.

'Not wilting, drooping. He was very poetic – and Andy's never poetic. He said I missed the wind off the loch.'

'I should bloody well think so,' said Georgie, shuddering. 'I went to Scotland once. Awful climate.'

I poured Lin a glass of wine. So successfully had we bullied the children, we hadn't even needed to finish the bottle. 'You'd better start at the beginning,' I told her.

Fortified by the wine, she related the conversation in a more coherent form.

'Oh *shit*,' Georgie said when she'd finished. 'You haven't decided you're in love with him, have you? After all these years? After several million missed opportunities?'

'Of course not,' Lin said hastily. 'It was just – he talked as if he'd cared for me, though he never mentioned it before. And he said Cat reminded him of me, only . . . younger, cleaner. Sean once talked about my purity, but it's gone. He took it. They all took it. And now I'm old, and – and soiled, and used up. A drooping flower, missing—'

'The wind off the loch,' Georgie concluded. 'Yes, we know. Bugger.'

'He was *sorry* for me,' Lin went on. 'I can't bear that. He thinks I'm washed up, rejected by everybody. He didn't exactly say so, but that's what he thinks. He said he wished

143

I could find someone to make me happy, as if – as if he knew it was hopeless. He was – pitying me. I can't bear it – do you understand? Not *pity*.'

We understood.

'I *have* to have a date for the wedding.' Lin's teeth appeared to be gritted. 'I told him – I let him think I was seeing someone, but I'm not sure he believed me. Even if he did, he thinks it'll be another loser: he said so. So you see, I *have* to find somebody – even if it means working my way through every date on the Internet. There's got to be a guy out there who'll do. After all, I've always found it easy to like people.'

In fact, I reflected, she had found it easy to fall in love with people – the wrong people. Don't we all. And Andy Pearmain, who might have been the right person, was marrying someone else, bemoaning the loss of her flower-like purity. (Stupid fart.) Why couldn't he have done a Colonel Brandon when he rescued her from Reception at the Groucho all those years ago? But no, he had been platonic, protective, disinterested – cretin! – and now he was marrying into the Countryside Alliance. Briefly, I wondered if we could shanghai the unknown Catriona, who was obviously hearty as well as wholesome and liked to kill foxes. But Georgie was already starting on the Great Manhunt with ruthless practicality.

'We'll get going on the files tomorrow,' she said. 'We'll weed out anyone who sounds eligible and then you'll have to meet them all. Just a quiet coffee or a snack at lunch to begin with; you don't want to waste an evening on someone unless you're sure he might do. I warn you, this is going to be pretty tiring.'

'I know,' Lin said. She didn't look happy at the prospect. 'But I have to do it. There has to be somebody.' Her voice was breaking up. 'I can't be that much of a dead loss, can I?'

We squeezed her hands, and topped up her wine, and dabbed at her with tissues.

How much babysitting will we have to do? I mouthed at Georgie.

Georgie scowled back.

When Lin was calmer, we shared a taxi homewards. I thought of the Wyshing Well, and how Lin had dreamed of meeting Mr Right, eyes locking across a crowded room. Only she'd been so busy looking for that eyelock she hadn't seen the Mr Right standing just beside her. He'd swept her up, that first evening, just like all the clichés, but she hadn't seen, hadn't wanted to see, until it was too late. And now there was nothing to do but salvage her pride, and try to move on . . .

'Don't be so gloomy,' said Georgie. 'Lin's the type who can fall in love with almost anyone, given a little encouragement. She's just been shut up with those kids for too long. We'll sort her out.'

'I hope you're right,' I said.

Chapter 6

My heart is like a singing bird
Whose nest is in a watered shoot;
My heart is like an apple tree
Whose boughs are bent with thickest fruit;
My heart is like a rainbow shell
That paddles in a halcyon sea;
My heart is gladder than all these
Because my love is come to me.

Raise me a dais of silk and down;
Hang it with vair and purple dyes;
Carve it in doves and pomegranates,
And peacocks with a hundred eyes;
Work it in gold and silver grapes,
In leaves and silver fleur-de-lys;
Because the birthday of my life
Is come, my love is come to me.

CHRISTINA ROSSETTI: *A Birthday*

I know no person so perfectly disagreeable and
even dangerous as an author.

WILLIAM IV

I returned to Todd Jarman's house the following Tuesday for our wind-up meeting on the manuscript. Since my first session *chez* Beauman was due on Friday I was feeling secretly rather grouchy about all these authors who demanded home visits. Like the doctor, I thought, called out unnecessarily to a patient who was quite capable of coming to the surgery. Editing should happen in publishing houses – although I knew really this was unreasonable of me, since the legendary days of old-fashioned premises with characterful panelled offices were long gone. (I had never seen any, but rumour swore they had once existed. Like green-and-white Penguins, and tooled leather hardbacks, and publishing companies run by publishers.) Ransome Harber was a huge modern hive, air-conditioned and pot-planted, humming with computers, honey-combed with book-cases, where desk backed on desk, and phones shrilled constantly, and the privileged few who had any office space were so hemmed in by novels, proofs and paperwork there was certainly no room for character, let alone panelling. Working with an author at home was far more congenial, provided he didn't live too far away. But I was unenthused by my putative association with Beauman, and determined to stay out of charity with Jarman – if only because it was so much fun.

In his front room, the study was fighting back. Books and files spilled over the glass-topped table, a couple of shabby cushions had found their way on to the sofa, and even the grey rug seemed to be in retreat, though that might have been my imagination. I sat down, much heartened.

'Tea?' he offered.

'Coffee.' Start as you mean to go on.

I thought he looked amused, but I wasn't sure. When you have a long, dark, saturnine sort of face an expression of mockery can easily be mistaken for mere amusement. Nonetheless, I decided to be positive. 'Are you winning?' I asked.

'I beg your pardon?'

'The room.'

He glanced round, then allowed himself a faint smile. A saturnine smile, of course. 'Ah, yes. It's stalemate if not checkmate. Helen's determined; I'm obstinate. The irresistible force and the immoveable object.'

'Something's got to give?' I hazarded doubtfully, remembering the old song.

'Possibly. There's always the hope of a diversion. At the moment, she's absorbed in the tribulations of an illegal Balkan refugee accused of gun-running who she claims will have no chance of a fair trial in his own country. I'm not convinced he's a worthy cause, but Helen thinks every client is a hero *in potentia*. It's one of her strengths. In spare moments from the fight for justice, she's having a go at the second bathroom. It doesn't leave her much time for this room.'

'Good,' I said. 'I mean, I like the study part.'

He gave me a quizzical look – that's another one a saturnine face does well, particularly with mobile eyebrows – and went to get the coffee.

We worked our way through the manuscript in a state of armed truce, disagreeing to differ but holding our fire. I even let myself wax enthusiastic on the new murder. 'I think lawyers should get murdered much more often,' I said, realising too late I had put my foot in my mouth. 'In books, that is. Shady lawyers. Not – not like your Helen; she's one of the good guys.' Curse her.

'She thinks so,' he said obliquely. 'But I'm not sure upholding the law is about good and bad. It's about the fairness of the system. Every crook has the right to a decent defence, no matter what he's done. Without that, justice means nothing. And someone has to do the defending. It's only on TV that the lawyer-hero believes his client is always innocent.'

148

'I know,' I said, feeling belittled. 'I just wanted to say . . . I approve of your latest murder.'

'Makes a change,' said Todd. 'Your approval.'

'I didn't realise you wanted it,' I retorted.

'You know how it is with writers. We're such sensitive souls, we're always desperate for praise. Doesn't much matter where it comes from.'

'Don't you have a fan club for all that?'

'Good God, no. My hero has a fan club. Any adulation goes to Dick Lancer.' (The actor who played Hatchett on TV.) 'Not much of it gets back to me.'

'It's a tough job,' I said. I could do mockery too.

'I'm glad you appreciate that,' he said, with an edge in his voice.

We broke for lunch, and he produced some rather squashy sandwiches: cheese and pickle where the pickle had soaked through the bread, and ham and egg with oozy mayonnaise. 'Here's one I prepared earlier,' he said. They weren't the sort of thing a figure-conscious girl should eat, but I accepted one, not wanting to be impolite. Besides, I like cheese and pickle.

'Is that all you're having?'

'I'm supposed to be on a diet.'

'Stand up.'

I stood, realising too late that it was the response of a subordinate woman, and anyway, why should I stand up, just because he said so? He looked me over dispassionately. Horse dealers and fillies came to mind.

'You look fine to me,' he concluded. 'Why bother?'

'Helen's got a lovely figure,' I found myself saying, to my shame. I didn't want him to see that Helen turned me green, Botox or no.

'Too thin,' he responded unexpectedly. 'When I first knew her she had tits, but she kept shaving off a pound here and there, worrying about her bottom, or her thighs. She says it's a girl thing.' He added: 'I can see you've lost a bit and it looks good, but don't lose any more. Stay the way you are – if you want my opinion.'

'Not really,' I said. But I said it quite amicably.

The tag-end of the working day found me in Publicity, where Georgie was short-listing prospective dates for Lin.

'I can't go out with *him*,' she was saying wretchedly. 'His hobbies include macramé and tropical fish.'

'He sounds very sensitive and caring,' Georgie said. 'I thought you would like that.'

'Don't be nasty,' said Laurence, who'd come to join the fun.

'What about this one?' Georgie resumed. 'Malcolm Radford. He's really quite a hunk. Look at those muscles.'

'He's wearing a sleeveless vest,' Lin pointed out with unusual acerbity, 'and he says he works out six times a week. It's revolting. Muscles like that probably go from ear to ear.'

'I know someone who does *The Times* crossword while on his exercise bike,' Laurence volunteered. Nobody paid any attention.

'This one looks sweet,' Georgie went on. 'Like you'd want to mother him.'

'I've done motherhood,' Lin retorted. 'Three times. I don't want the man in my life to be another child. I want *him* to do the mothering – fathering – whatever. I want him to be big and strong and protective and take care of me.'

'Don't we all, ducky?' Laurence sighed theatrically.

'What century is she living in?' Georgie demanded of no one in particular. '*All* men are children who need looking after by their womenfolk. It's just that we have to be subtle about it. We have to let them think *they* look after *us*.'

'Glad to hear it,' said Cal, making a timely entrance. Or

untimely, depending on your point of view. 'So when you got pissed out of your brain at the House the other week, and refused to come out of the loo for an hour because you were sulking, and had to be taken home in a rickshaw – you were just being subtle.'

Georgie didn't even falter. 'Absolutely,' she averred. 'I do subtlety in a big way. I believe in being obvious about it.'

'We're supposed to be sorting out potential dates for Lin,' I said, feeling it was time everyone got back to the matter in hand. 'This guy looks okay.'

'He's got glowing red eyes!' Lin.

'You know perfectly well that's the flash. At least, I *think* so.'

'His chin is too long.'

'He's lantern-jawed,' I said, grasping thankfully at the familiar metaphor.

'I couldn't possibly go to Andy's wedding with a chin like that. I'd be a laughing stock.'

'Andy's got a beard,' Georgie said. 'Who's he to make fun of people's chins?'

Lin, normally easy-going and open-hearted to a fault, was being uncharacteristically difficult, but it would have been tactless – and counter-productive – to make an issue of it. Eventually we sorted out a couple of candidates for tentative e-mail correspondence and headed for the pub to recuperate.

Over the next few days we scrutinised Lin's e-mail regularly. Results were not encouraging. One guy sent her several jokes which managed to score in every area of political incorrectness including sexism, racism, homophobia, and even, if you counted the one about the sheep, cruelty to animals. Another contributed some embarrassingly bad poetry. A third complained at length about his previous girl-friend and said he hoped Lin would never expect him to do the washing up, or gossip to him while the football was on, or object to him leaving his dirty socks in the sink. A fourth said he was witty, clever, attractive, making good money selling (dubious) pension plans, and he was sure Lin would find it a privilege to go out with him. 'This is hopeless,' said Lin, the tolerant. 'These guys aren't even sad and lonely. They're just . . . yuk.'

'Maybe they're sad and lonely *underneath*,' Georgie said, trying to stir her compassion. 'Nobody could be as repulsively overconfident as that last one pretended. I expect he's just shy.'

But since her dinner with Andy, Lin's compassion was working to rule.

'I don't care,' she said. 'I don't want someone shy. Or sad and lonely. I just want a nice ordinary bloke who'll adore me to bits. Like Dad adores Mum. Why've all the men in my life been bastards? Don't they do nice guys any more?'

'You never called Garry a bastard before,' I said.

'I loved him,' Lin said sadly. 'But you have to face things. He could be horribly cruel when he was drunk or drugged and he left me high and dry financially. I don't call that very caring. I've felt guilty about his death for years, but I've had enough of it. I hope wherever he is now he feels guilty about me.'

From Lin, that was a nasty speech. She was definitely undergoing an apostasy lately.

'Sean stole my purity,' she continued, her Presbyterian background emerging in her terminology, 'but Garry took my self-respect. He loved me, but he always made me feel I failed him. No matter how hard I worked at the relationship – no matter what I did – it was never quite right. It's awful to know that you've failed the person you love. The thing is, love ought to be enough for happiness, but

152

Garry wanted more. He wanted success – on his own terms. He wanted audience adulation, even though he said he despised it. He wanted publicity and privacy – things that contradicted each other – things that would never work. Fame without the price. Hangers-on who were really friends. Shallow people who cared deeply about him. He *wanted* to be happy, but he was *determined* to be unhappy. I used to feel his muddle was all to do with creativity and genius, but I think it was selfish too. If he'd thought less about his own problems and more about the children and me we'd have been fine. So you see,' she concluded, 'he was a bastard too, in a way. Not like Sean, but still bastardly. I only seem to attract bastards.' She gazed again at the final communication from the pension salesman before deleting it. 'Even by e-mail.'

Georgie and I were temporarily silenced, slightly stunned by the adjustment in her thinking.

Lin stared gloomily at the computer screen. 'I had no idea there were so many awful men in the world,' she said. 'I hate this Internet dating lark. All it does is show you how isolated you are.'

'Don't say that!' Georgie, ever optimistic, was shocked. 'What about Derek? I know you didn't fancy him, but at least he was nice.'

'What's the point of being nice if you're not fanciable?' Lin mourned. 'There could be heaps of nice men out there whom I won't fancy. I might have to date them all to find out – the same date, over and over, like *Groundhog Day*. Endless conversations about what he does, and what I do, and his divorce, and mine, and his children, and mine, and how we both want a meaningful relationship, and all the while I'm thinking: *Not with you.* I can't face it.'

'You've only had one date so far,' Georgie said, becoming pragmatic. 'Don't give up yet. You're too young to despair.'

'No, I'm not,' Lin insisted. 'I'm thirty-two next week. That's practically middle-aged.'

'Bollocks!' said Georgie with understandable indignation.

'I think you should just go home and contemplate suicide,' I said. 'We can start again in the morning. Tomorrow *is* another day.'

'There you are,' said Lin. 'Rhett Butler. Another bastard. Besides, where on earth did he get a stupid name like Rhett?'

'Short for retro,' Georgie said.

On Friday, armed with careful directions, I went to see Jerry Beauman. He lived in a flat off Berkeley Square, the kind with a sub-tropical roof garden and rooms so large there were whole areas of floor with nothing to do. I was admitted by a Filipino maid whom I mistook – briefly – for the Oriental girlfriend. Shown into a vast living room, I stayed close to the wall in case I got lost. I had been expecting a designer interior worthy of the colour supplements, but instead I was confronted with a sort of sumptuous banality, a bland taste-lessness without the flourish of vulgarity or the style of natural elegance. The furniture was antique, presumably genuine, but so lustrously polished, so artfully restored that it appeared fake. There were acres of gleaming parquet scat-tered with Persian rugs, chandeliers adorned with electric candles, swags of brocade curtain tied back with tasselled cords. The paintings included several big landscapes (one, I guessed, might be identifiable as a Constable, had I known anything about art), a simpering Venus clutching a hand-kerchief to her crotch amid trailing *putti*, and a couple of conscientiously modern abstracts. I was sure Beauman was a Collector: the pictures looked Collected, somehow, rather than simply bought for fun. There was also a portrait of a gentleman called the Sieur de Beaumont whom I learned later Jerry claimed as an ancestor, on no grounds whatsoever. The

nearest bookshelves to catch the visitor's eye were packed
with his own oeuvres in a variety of languages, side by side
with Shakespeare and translations of Horace. Optimist, I
thought. I was studying a *Lorna Doone* vista of gloomy rocks
and tumbling water topped off with a windswept tree and
some pretty foul weather when Beauman came in.

To my surprise he was both genial and friendly, turning
on something that might have passed for charm in the
Klingon world. He had barely noticed me when we met at
the Bel Manoir, but then I had been of no use to him; now,
I was going to tidy up his book. Or rather, as he put it,
'assist the creative process'. He showed me round the flat
in an expansive spirit, possibly with the object of adding me
to the exclusive ranks of his admirers, told me the value of
every picture (the Constable *was* a Constable), even demon-
strated the workings of the alarm system. Not for the last
time, as I was to discover, I experienced a sudden impulse
to become a professional burglar. He made me stand respect-
fully in front of the inevitable photos of him with various
iconic figures, including Nelson Mandela. (I do feel the Hero
of our Time could be more selective about the company he
keeps.) 'I call that one Old Lags Together,' Jerry joked. I
blenched. Mandela had been a prisoner of conscience on
Devil's Island, or some such island; Jerry had done time for
fraud, mostly in a cosy open prison. Did they *really* have
anything in common? Besides, the photos obviously predated
Jerry's stint as a guest of Her Maj. Other pix showed him
pally with politicians, ageing popstars, and all-purpose celebs
like Peter Stringfellow and Neil Hamilton. You'd have
thought he would have removed the last one, but he seemed
oblivious to its impact on visitors. In fact, he seemed
oblivious to a lot of things. His self-assurance was absolute,
turning his seedy little crime into a dashing adventure, trans-
forming inconvenient truth with the light of fantasy. In a

warmer personality, it might have been endearing. But there was coldness and calculation underneath the buoyancy, and an expression in his eyes – or lack of one – which gave him away. They were narrow, beady, ratty orbs without depth or soul, unaware of anything beyond his own appetite and need. This, I thought, is a man with no real friends – but he doesn't know, he doesn't care. He's perfectly happy with pretend ones.

When the tour was over we retired to his study, a slightly smaller room with a panoramic view of the backs of expensive houses. He had all the accoutrements of a successful writer: teak desk with wafer-thin laptop, wodge of manuscript, Mont Blanc pen for hand-written alterations, telephone, Dictaphone, printer, reference books. Everything but the blackened coffee mug – and that could have been cleared away by the maid. But it all looked faintly like a stage set. I got the feeling he wasn't so much writing as Being a Writer. Listening to him talk about his current book I realised that here, again, his blinkered vision enabled him to take an idealised – if narrow – view of himself. He held forth on his creative genius as if he expected to make the Booker shortlist. The fact that the end result needed to be revised, re-punctuated and partially re-structured by someone else seemed to bypass him. He *believed* he was a great writer. His self-belief was like armour-plating. Other people's perceptions, doubts, criticisms, bounced off it. He was the best thing since Shakespeare, and he knew it. After all, every book with his name on it had sold at least a million.

It was a daunting thought.

'Hope you'll enjoy working with me,' he said, with a smile that stopped short of his eyes. (They always did.) 'Nice to have an attractive female colleague after poor old Buckle. Came across as quite a he-man; just goes to show, you can't be too careful these days. Not that I've got anything against pansies – I just wouldn't want to live with one.' This was clearly meant for a joke. I looked blank. 'Never been that way inclined, even at public school.' I was sure he hadn't been to public school. 'How about some coffee?'

I didn't ask for tea; there was no point. Beauman wouldn't have noticed.

We had coffee. Jerry talked about himself, moving from his chair to perch on the edge of the desk where he could have gazed down my cleavage, had I been showing any. Actually, I was covered to the clavicle, but my bosom tends to obtrusive at all times and there was nothing I could do about it. He suggested that on these long hot summer days I could always do my editing up on the roof terrace. 'Bring a bikini. Have a sunbathe. I really wouldn't mind.'

A few pounds off, I thought, and now Jerry Beauman, of all people, wants to see me in a bikini. The Wyshing Well fairy had certainly picked her moment to endow me with sex-goddessness. No doubt about it, she had a *very* nasty sense of humour.

'Thanks,' I said noncommittally. 'Er – don't you think we should talk about the book now? We do have a pretty tight deadline.'

He grinned and went back to his chair. 'I thrive on deadlines. Never missed one yet. They call me Mister Deadline. We'll make it, you'll see.'

We?

'Of course we will,' I said.

We discussed plot and character exhaustively for a while – at least, I was exhausted. Like many writers, Jerry threw out half a dozen new ideas at every turn, though his were more far-fetched and implausible than most. I did my best to discourage them, diplomatically, and insinuate a couple of my own, while making him believe they were his. Laurence had told me this was the standard procedure. By the end of the session Jerry was beaming. 'I can see we're going to work well together,' he declared. 'You're a lot brighter than old Buckle. You can help to give me that feminine slant which, I must admit, has often eluded me. I've always been more of a man's man.'

So's Laurence, I felt like saying, but resisted the temptation. Jerry evidently hadn't registered that many of my suggestions were those which Laurence had kindly passed on to me – suggestions which Beauman had previously rejected out of hand when he realised they came from a poofter.

'Got to go now,' Jerry said, skirting the desk to grasp my hand and plant a kiss on my cheek. 'Lunch with Jonathan Aitken. A good chap – much misunderstood.'

He was gone, leaving me temporarily speechless. Anyone in his position ought to be anxious to rehabilitate himself, avoiding other notorious ex-crooks like the plague. But not Jerry Beauman. Clinton might apologise, David Mellor resign, George Galloway deny and sue, but Beauman remained brash and unashamed. He was right, he was wronged, he was the comeback kid who'd never been away, the star who could outshine all the mud that stuck to his image. I really, *really* didn't want him to get away with it.

'He will, you know,' Georgie said, back at the office. 'Everyone knows he's a liar and a cheat and a thief – everyone except him – but it doesn't matter. His sheer arrogance will carry it. Did you see the latest *Private Eye*, or that sketch on *Dead Ringers*? Talk about savage – but it's all grist to his mill. It wouldn't work if he was a politician, or anything in public life – it would finish him in TV and probably as an actor – but no one cares what writers do. Any publicity is good publicity. It may be bloody hard to get coverage for some people but, believe me, this is the one business where the adage really does apply. His book will come out in a furore of indignation, criticism and contempt, and *everyone* will buy it, just to see what the fuss is all about.'

'*His* book?' I said. 'It's totally derivative.'

'So what?' said Georgie. 'All writers do that.'

There was only one thing to be said, and I said it. 'Fuck.'

Jerry Beauman has that effect on everyone's vocabulary.

While Lin's Internet dating exchanges were driving her to contemplate suicide, Georgie's quest for a millionaire seemed to have come to a full stop. After her night at the opera she had allowed herself to hope that Neville would call again: he had been attractive enough, and amusing enough, for her to consider taking things further, and when, after more than a week, she had had no word, she was conscious of disappointment. Her marriage might have been a long-term catastrophe, but Georgie wasn't used to failure in the short-term, and it left her feeling rather damped. She knew looks and charm alone wouldn't inspire every passing male – or any passing male – with true love, but she did expect the combination to engender lust, particularly after an evening's exposure. 'I must be getting old,' she said. 'Over the hill. I just can't do the *femme fatale* thing any more.'

'Of course you can,' I assured her. 'You're not at all old.' First Lin feeling middle-aged, now Georgie old. It was getting to be too much.

'Don't be kind. I know I am. I looked in the mirror and counted the lines.'

'We've all got lines,' said Lin, on the strength of her one or two.

'How many?' I asked Georgie with curiosity.

'Fifteen. And that's *before* I smile. Maybe I should give up smiling.'

'*I* can't see fifteen.'

'You aren't looking as closely as I was,' Georgie retorted.

'There's a couple on your forehead which your fringe hides, and the hint of a smile line . . .'

'See? No more smiles.'

'Then you'll just be old and miserable,' Lin pointed out with a gleam of mischief. 'No one's going to fancy you if you're gloomy.'

'You're right,' Georgie agreed, stricken. 'It's no good, I'm finished. My career as an attractive woman is over. I shall just have to decline into someone's aunt, or an elderly eccentric who bores people by reminiscing about her beautiful youth. I shall carry a stack of photographs to show them how lovely I once was.'

'How about a wedding cake?' I said. 'With cobwebs.'

'You're just not taking me seriously. Hi, Cal.' It was ten to six and nearly time for close of play, and he had drifted into the office looking like a man in need of a drink.

'Georgie's worried she's getting old,' said Lin.

'Ain't we all. Ten years ago I could shag six times a night, and not necessarily with the same woman. Nowadays, I don't have the stamina.'

'Good thing too,' said Georgie, reviving. 'One, I want all the energy you've got, and two, I don't share. Let's go to the pub.'

Lin went home to relieve the child-minder, cook for the brats and swap e-mails with her would-be admirers, and I headed pubwards with the other two. Georgie, forgetful of her advanced years, eyed up the new barman in an automatic way and managed to infuse a request for dry-roasted peanuts with come-hither overtones. The barman – inevitably – was an Aussie, with bleached-blond hair and a skimpy T-shirt revealing his six-pack. 'Behave yourself,' Cal ordered, hauling her away and depositing her at a table. 'I think I'll put you on a lead.'

'Kinky.'

160

With Jerry Beauman's book to work on, I left early. Cal was staying the night with Georgie; he did so on a fairly regular basis these days, telling Christy he was with one of his mates, an explanation she accepted without question or interest. After I'd gone they wandered off to a small Italian restaurant, ate seafood linguine, splashed out on a bottle of Barolo.

'Would you ever leave Christy?' Georgie asked suddenly. 'Not for me particularly. Just – leave. Because the marriage doesn't work.'

'God knows. I live in the moment – don't look ahead very far. I can't plan things. Who knows how I'll feel next year, or the year after? But . . . I couldn't fail the kids. You know that. 'Specially Allan. Christy's always so absorbed in Jamie – well, I've told you how it is. Allan needs me; they both do. I want to be a good dad. I couldn't bear to let them down.'

'Your dad left, didn't he?' Georgie said.

'Mmm.'

'So . . . you don't want to be like him, right?'

'Mmm.'

'So this is all just temporary, you and me. A casual affair.' She looked down at her plate, toying with a strand of pasta. '"Since there's no help, come, let us kiss and part."'

Cal, the dyslexic, had little acquaintance with poetry. 'No need to rush it. Anyway, it's not casual: you know that.'

'Isn't it? These things don't last. D'you know of one single relationship between a married man and an unmarried woman that has ever been permanent? I don't. Sooner or later I'll meet some guy with less baggage – an ex instead of a wife, kids only on Sunday, double bed with a vacancy – and I'll succumb to the lure of security and a wedding band. It always happens that way. Will you mind?'

'Of course I will.' The trace of sadness in his face, so often

161

erased by his smile, was suddenly very plain. 'Why're you talking like this? I thought I made you happy. I didn't know you had this craving for security.'

'Doesn't everybody?'

'You aren't everybody. Please – let's just enjoy now. I told you, I don't like to look ahead. Typical male, I guess; I don't want to face unpleasant things. I prefer to put them off.'

Georgie grinned wryly. 'Typical male.'

It was Cal's turn to focus on his plate. Then he looked up at her, his expression intent and very serious. 'I love you,' he said. The L-word, the word he never said – or never when he was sober. But he wasn't drunk this time, and she knew it was true, it was deep and real, and now it was out there it couldn't be brushed aside. It hung in the air between them like a musical note that would never die away. 'I don't know where we're going, or what will happen next. I can't make promises. There are the children, and Christy needs my support. But I do love you.'

She found there were tears in her eyes, and blinked furiously, knowing they would smudge her mascara. 'I suppose . . . I love you too. Damn. This is getting like *Brief Encounter*.'

'What's that?'

'Movie classic. Black-and-white. Rachmaninov in the background.'

'Sounds bloody depressing.'

'It's meant to be moving and tragic,' Georgie explained. 'She's married, and they meet, and fall in love, on a railway station, and part, never to meet again. On the same railway station. They don't even have sex.'

'Bloody unrealistic too.'

Georgie managed a watery laugh. 'Too right!'

'This is us, not some vintage film,' Cal said. 'It's like books and things. You read too many books. Life's different. Books have endings: happy endings, sad endings, but the writer has to stop somewhere, so he makes the characters stop, the story stop. I'm not saying this very well – I don't say things well – but you know what I mean. Life doesn't have endings, until you die. At least, it doesn't have to. I love you – you're part of me. That won't have an ending. If there's another man, if you marry, and you're secure, and happy, I'll still love you. You'll still be part of me. Even if there's someone else for me, I'll love you. We'll be friends, we'll go out to dinner, and I'll listen to your problems, try to help, do what I can. I'll always be there. I'll be your – your faithful admirer, hopelessly adoring you. Like a puppy. Whatever happens. This is – always. Whatever happens.'

Georgie blinked again. 'It isn't like that,' she said. 'Lovers don't become friends. I'll never stop caring for you, even if I marry – women don't – but you'll forget me, or I'll dwindle to a pleasant memory, a pang of nostalgia. That's how it goes.'

'You don't understand, do you?' Cal said. 'You really don't understand.'

I'm afraid to, Georgie thought. I'm afraid to believe in it. I'm afraid to believe in *us*.

And: It's never been like this before . . .

'Well,' she said, changing gear with an effort, 'since the wine bottle's empty, and this isn't a black-and-white movie with Rachmaninov, let's go home and have sex.'

'Good idea,' Cal said.

He paid the bill, refusing to split, and they walked some way in search of a taxi, feeling shaken, and sad, and happy, and intensely alive. Back at Georgie's, they made love with a depth of emotion that hadn't been there before, falling asleep at last still welded together, as if they could never bear to part.

During the following week I had a couple more sessions with Jerry Beauman, or rather, at his flat. He put in only brief appearances, but he preferred me to work in his study, on his personal computer, instead of at the office – he said that made collaboration easier. I wasn't offered any food, even though I worked through lunch one day; just coffee and mineral water. As he wasn't around much, I decided to take advantage of his invitation to use the roof garden. I rolled my vest-top down to expose my shoulders and hitched my skirt up to my bum to tan my thighs – doing something useful while reading through the manuscript and scribbling comments in the margin. The second time I did it, I was startled to hear his voice behind me. He must have approached very quietly; I hadn't heard a thing.

'How's it going?'

'Getting there,' I said. Damn, damn, damn. He was standing over me, dark against the sky, looking arrogant and sure of himself, exuding the aura of an aggressively dominant male. I didn't need this.

Visions of sexual harassment suits flickered through my head.

'Too hot?' he said. Shit. I was blushing.

'A bit. I think I'll come in.'

He backed off, a complacent little smirk playing around his mouth, undoubtedly pleased to have disturbed my equilibrium. Oh no you haven't, I swore to myself. I'm perfectly equilibrious. Just . . . *irritated*.

To my further embarrassment, he insisted on watching while I attempted to pull my skirt down – it got twisted, and I had to wriggle to straighten it out – and resumed my shoulder-straps. Then he drew my attention to the view from the terrace – posh houses interspersed with posh streets, sky on top – steered me downstairs, and offered me a gin and tonic 'to cool off'. Weakly, I accepted. I needed one. He had whisky and water, lecturing me on how good Scotch shouldn't be ruined with ice or mixers. While we were drinking, the phone rang. The maid answered, somewhere in the further reaches of the living room, and called out: 'Is Mr Weed, from Switzerland.'

'Wahid,' Jerry corrected her. 'Put it through to my study.' He never used pleases or thank yous, with her or me. I got a quick, tight smile. 'Won't be a minute.' He went into the study and shut the door. I was left contemplating my G & T.

He'd taken calls in front of me before without a qualm, chatting away to his pseudo-friends, occasionally dropping a Name, as though keen to show even me, an editor of little importance, how chummy he was with everybody. He'd never shut me out. Inevitably, the imagination of someone who makes a living in fiction came into play. Perhaps he was being blackmailed by a former cellmate, or threatened, or – no. Not from Switzerland. Switzerland where the Swiss bank accounts come from . . .

The maid had gone. I sidled towards the study door, leant casually against the panels. Jerry's voice carried faintly to my ears.

'—can't do anything with it right now. Much too chancy – Never mind where I've got it. It's in a safe place – No, not the *safe*: I said a safe place – It's all right for you, you're not a British citizen. They can get warrants to poke their nose in anywhere these days. Bloody New Labour are turning the country into a police state – There's been too much about it in the Press lately. I can't take the risk – Acme City, they're calling it. Those bastards at Dryden must've scooped eighteen or twenty mil – Makes our 500K each look pretty paltry – Yes, I know it's a bugger – Some old dodderer on the Board's been asking questions – Nothing'll come out – We made peanuts; Dryden are the ones who – Okay, Pierre. I'll be in touch.'

I heard him hang up and moved quickly away, my tiptoeing

footsteps noiseless on a convenient rug. Well, well. Sounded like Jerry was involved in another shady deal. I made a mental note of the names – Acme City, Dryden – and wondered vaguely how to go about checking up on them. The prospect of leafing through the financial pages was very daunting. It wasn't as if it was my business. And in the unlikely event that I found out something, I couldn't imagine myself turning supergrass to Scotland Yard or the Serious Fraud Office. Nonetheless, a tingle of investigative excitement made its way down my spine.

'How's the drink?' Jerry again, emerging from the study with smile in place, back in charmer mode. 'Need freshening up yet?'

'No thanks,' I said.

'Couldn't you ask Andy?' Georgie said to Lin. 'He's a banker. He must know about these things.'

Lin looked unhappy. 'I can't. Not *now*.'

'Don't push it,' I murmured. 'Haven't you got a spare banker left over from your clutch of millionaires?'

'Not one I'd like to call.'

Lin had a brainwave. 'Why not ask at your own bank? There's bound to be some nice helpful person there who could fill you in. You could say it was research for someone's book.'

'I'm online,' I said.

'I daren't go near mine,' Georgie said, shuddering. 'I keep hoping if they don't see me they'll forget I exist. It's your idea – how about you?'

'I'm online too,' Lin admitted. 'Perhaps Laurence . . .'

'No,' I said. 'This is just between us. I don't want half of Ransome to know I'm gunning for one of their star authors.'

'*Are* you?' Lin queried, wide-eyed. 'Gunning, I mean.'

'Not exactly. I suppose I'm just being inquisitive. He's such a creep . . .'

'How much money did he say he pocketed on this mystery deal?' Georgie asked.

'Half a million.'

'And it's hidden in the flat somewhere?'

'He didn't say that. He said it was in a safe place. Then he said *not* the safe. It could be *any*where.'

'But it's probably in the flat,' Georgie persisted. 'After all, if you had half a million, you wouldn't want to risk stashing it away in someone else's house, would you? It isn't exactly peanuts – even to Jerry Beauman.'

'Actually, he said it *was*. Peanuts.'

'He owns a big house in the country,' Lin volunteered. 'Gloucestershire, I think. I've seen pictures.'

'His wife's got that,' Georgie said knowledgeably.

'What about the girlfriend?' I inquired. 'Where does he keep her? She's not resident with him.'

'It doesn't matter. He wouldn't trust her with a large sum of money; he's not the trusting kind,' Georgie declared. 'It's bound to be at the flat. You could start having a look for it – in your spare moments.'

'Georgie!' Lin and I exclaimed, almost simultaneously.

'What are you suggesting?' I pursued.

'Well, he evidently got this money illegally, so it isn't really his. And ill-gotten gains are anyone's for the taking, aren't they?'

'*Georgie!*'

'Half a million would pay my credit-card bill – keep Lin in nannies for the next ten years—'

'GEORGIE!'

'It's just a thought,' she protested. 'Maybe – maybe the Wyshing Well fairy *meant* you to overhear that phone call. Maybe it was Fate. Maybe we're fated to have half a million pounds.'

'Fate isn't like that,' I said, taking a Hardyesque view of

life. 'Fate's a sadistic deity playing Monopoly with the destinies of men. And women. Do not pass Go and collect five hundred grand. Go to Gaol.' Those whom the gods wish to destroy, I reflected, they first cause to run up large credit-card debts.

'Have a little faith,' Georgie said. 'Cultivate optimism. When you're older, you'll learn that's the only way to get by. You just have to keep hoping life will get better – usually in the teeth of the evidence. Anyhow, wishes don't always work out the way you expect.'

'If you ask me,' I said, 'that damn fairy's been nothing but trouble.'

I didn't know it, but there was a lot more trouble yet to come.

I didn't get time to check up on Jerry's deal, of course; I was too busy working on his novel. The hero was a self-portrait – weren't they always? – with all the bad bits left out, a sort of cartoon Beauman. Not the Simpsons: Disney. In prison, he palled up with other convicts, bluff, gruff, tuff guys, ex-blaggers with 'earts of gold who respected him for his man-to-man approach and standing up to the nastier screws. Once out and struggling to clear his name, the old lags were there to help. A few friends had remained true, braving public opprobrium and social ostracism; the untrue were exposed as treacherous and shallow, fellow travellers in the wake of the tabloid press. After elaborate plot and counter-plot, the Danglars who had set him up and the de Villefort who had sent him down both got their comeuppance. Carried away on the tide of Jerry's creativity, I even persuaded Beauman to insert a Fernand de Morcerf who swiped the hero's wife while he was behind bars, thus allowing him to wind up with his post-porridge girlfriend who had assisted him in proving his innocence. (In the original version, he dumped his wife from motives of misguided nobility after his conviction, but no one was going to go for that.) Sorting out the plot to both my satisfaction and Jerry's cost me several nights' sleep, and the whole business filled my mind to the exclusion of all else. Much as I loathed him, tailoring his book was an opportunity – a challenge – it was even fun.

The next time I saw Nigel, I had hardly thought about him for days. It was at an event for independent booksellers, where they would all get together and complain about the big chains, occasionally issuing edicts which would be reported briefly in the trade press and then ignored. I was putting in a courtesy appearance on behalf of Ransome, to show that we were sensitive and caring and wanted small bookshops to stock our writers. It hadn't occurred to me Nigel would be there. He had often deplored the market control exercised by the big book chains, but in the past he would have considered this kind of event too cosy and middle-class for his taste. But there he was, drinking cheap wine and eating bits of things on sticks, his pocket-torch jaw designer-stubbled, his dirty-blond hair looking – well, dirty. My heart didn't leap, but it twinged a little, like a pulled muscle that hasn't quite healed. He was talking to a lanky individual with an even lankier beard and a woman whose proportions would have made me look slender *before* my diet. She was dressed in several tiers of brocaded chiffon and resembled a well-upholstered sofa surmounted by an expensive haircut. Her face, I noticed, was very pretty.

Once again, I was smitten with the dilemma of whether to go over and say hello. I procrastinated, talking to a man from the wilds of Buckinghamshire who apparently specialised in poetry. A fool or a madman, I concluded, but it was impossible not to admire his resolution. When the conversation wore out I let the natural currents in circulation carry me towards Nigel.

'Hello, Cookie.' He broke off whatever he was saying to greet me, but he didn't look particularly thrilled. 'Still on the diet?'

'No,' I said. 'I'm comfortable the way I am.'

'You aren't eating the nibbles.'

'I don't like plastic cheese.' I'd never been much of a party nibbler, even when I was tubby. For one thing, you can't always tell what canapés contain until you've bitten into them, and then you can get a nasty shock. For another, the kind of comfort food which was my main weakness meant curling up with a book or video, chocs on the side. Eating on the hoof is much too hazardous. I still recall a regrettable incident at a publisher's Christmas party, involving a paper plate, a fork, and a pickled onion. The onion shot across the room at unbelievable speed and hit Clive James on the ear. His TV career declined shortly afterwards, but I'm sure that was just a coincidence.

Nigel introduced me to the lanky beard, whose name was Terry, and went on to explain how he was struggling to compete with an especially malevolent branch of Waterstone's, somewhere in the outer reaches of North London. He was soon well away on a tirade which expanded to condemn the big publishing conglomerates, as represented by me, and how we were hand-in-glove with the major booksellers, and it was all a conspiracy to wipe out the gallant independent and crush the voice of literary protest crying out to the people. While he had some good points, I knew this last was garbage. Ransome would happily publish the voice of protest, if the people wanted to buy it. But most of the time, they don't. As an older and wiser (independent) bookseller once put it to me: 'Everyday life is full of ugly realities. When you open a book, you want to get away from them.' Or, in the words of a successful fantasy writer: 'Writing isn't about life as it *is*, it's about life the way it *should* be. That's why the good guys always have to win in the end – because in real life they don't, and people need encouragement to keep fighting. Fiction is there to encourage them.' Although I couldn't help wondering what sort of encouragement readers were going to get from the fictional redemption of Jerry Beauman, unrepentant fraudster and ex-con.

When Nigel finally ran out of steam Terry interceded, rather shyly, evidently feeling I was getting a raw deal. 'I'm sure Cookie here does her best for – for any writer she likes,' he stammered.

'I try,' I said. 'But it's pretty difficult. I don't have much influence yet. I'm just a novice among editors.'

Terry then launched into a hesitant appeal for me to look at something he was working on, 'just for an opinion'. My heart quailing, I asked what it was about, expecting neo-ante-modernism extending the parameters of the contemporary subculture – or something like that. Instead, Terry confessed, with an air of guilt, that it was a children's story.

'Harry Potter?' I queried doubtfully.

Apparently not. It was about a boy and his cat, and his father marries again, and his stepmother may be a witch and wants to turn the cat into her familiar, but secretly the cat can talk and helps the boy, and . . . Terry petered out, looking embarrassed.

'It sounds really interesting,' I said, with sincerity. 'I don't do children's books, but I'd be happy to have a look and pass it on to the right person, if I think it's any good. I'll give you my address—' I didn't have cards; I'd never felt important enough '– and you can send me a copy, if you like.'

Terry blushed violently under his beard and Nigel – even though the manuscript was clearly not a voice of protest – cast me a look of approval. To my horror, I found it warmed me. I didn't want it to – I wanted to be over him, as indifferent to his approbation as I was to his political ideology – but it did. Absent-mindedly, I took a cube of plastic cheese with a cherry on the top from a passing plate and turned to the chiffon sofa. We hadn't yet been introduced, and Nigel's jeremiad had effectively excluded her from the conversation. It wasn't my fault, but I felt I'd been impolite.

'Are you a bookseller?' I inquired predictably.

'Oh no. I'm an estate agent.'

I stared, at a loss for the right response. You can hardly say: 'How interesting' to an estate agent. Or can you?

Think of all those property programmes on TV . . .

'This is Rachel,' Nigel said.

It is rare to be at a loss for words twice within a matter of seconds. My jaw didn't drop – contrary to popular cliché, jaws hardly ever do – but it may have locked. Thoughts whirled madly through my brain, zipping after one another at lightspeed. *Nigel* was going out with an estate agent – he was going out with a fat estate agent – he really was a thin man who liked fat women – no wonder he was anti-dieting – talked of earth-mother breasts – Nigel was *living* with a FAT ESTATE AGENT . . .

Standard courtesy deserted me, social graces went west. I think I said: 'Oh.' That was all I could manage for the next five minutes.

Lots of things can leave you speechless, but few compare with the impact of genuine surprise. I wasn't heartbroken; I think the last of my affection withered away in the shock of that moment. If I'd been hurt – if I'd been bleeding inside – I'd have found the words to hide it, the necessary phrases to conceal my secret wound and uphold my pride. Instead, I was merely stunned. I stood there as if I had been stuffed.

Nigel, unbelievably, was looking faintly pleased with himself, as if nabbing Rachel was a major coup. Possibly it was. It could hardly be a minor one.

(There you are. A few pounds down and I make fattist jokes.)

'Nigel said you were terribly upset when he dumped you,' she said. 'You threw him out, didn't you?'

I threw him out when he dumped me? What was she saying?

'It was a really good thing for me,' she went on. 'It made me get rid of Trevor. Our marriage had been going wrong for ages, but I just couldn't make the break. Then you and Nigel split, and that did it. Nige and I are very happy now. I hope you don't mind too much?'

Was she for real, or just being smug?

I didn't care. 'Not at all,' I found myself gabbling, idiotically. 'Glad to have helped. Any time.' I turned away, grabbed Terry, demanding to hear more about the children's story, and tottered off to find a refill. Several refills. Once the shock had worn off a bit, I discovered my main reaction wasn't exactly what I would've expected.

I couldn't wait to tell them all at work.

'Nigel's going out with a *fat estate agent*?' Georgie and Lin echoed, like a Greek chorus.

'It's too good to be true,' Georgie continued. 'If it was fiction, nobody would believe it.'

'Are you sure you aren't upset?' Lin asked anxiously. 'I mean, you have been missing him a bit, haven't you?'

'Not lately,' I said. 'I hadn't really thought about it, but I just haven't had time. It's one good thing about doing this book of Jerry's: it's taken up every moment. I haven't had the *energy* to miss Nigel, either.' Or to spend the night with Hugh Jackman. I must do something about that soon.

'I went out with an estate agent once,' remarked Cal, who was propping up the desk in Georgie's office. As PR chief, she merited an office of her own, though Lin, as her assistant, generally shared it.

'When was that?' Georgie asked.

'Last time we moved house. About five or six years ago. She was trying to sell me a four-bedroom semi in Cockfosters.'

'Must've been something about the name,' I murmured.

Cal flicked me a Look. Georgie said: 'What was she like? Was she fat too?'

'Nah. Curvy, not fat. I remember noticing her nipples jutted through her sweater, sort of outlined by the knit. It was when she was showing me the master bedroom.' He sighed reminiscently. 'The owners were away, so we had it off on the bed.'

'A meaningful relationship,' Georgie said. 'How long did it last?'

'Till I told her I didn't want to buy the house.'

'When was that?'

'Well . . . after we had it off on the bed, actually.'

We all laughed, though Lin cried out in protest.

'They don't do that on *Location Location Location*,' I said.

'They will,' Georgie opined. 'They just haven't thought of it yet. Fantasy property-buying plus sex: it's an ideal formula. Before you know where you are, *Big Brother* will be out there, picking themselves a castle in Scotland in which to be incarcerated.'

It was an unfortunate allusion. 'Don't mention Scottish castles,' Lin said. 'I'm getting nowhere with this dating lark.'

'How does your shortlist look?' Georgie asked.

'A would-be comedy writer and stand-up performer with a day job in a laundrette. A member of the chorus in *The Lion King* with gluten allergy. A computer technician who does bellringing on the side.' She tried not to look depressed, but we did it for her.

'Keep at it,' Georgie said. 'There are millions of guys on those lists. Some of them must be nice.'

'These *are* the nice ones,' Lin responded. 'I told you. Nice isn't enough.'

'We can see that from your record.' Georgie spoke without thinking.

'What about yours?' Lin retorted, with a flash of rancour. It's one thing to admit yourself, at an emotional low point, that the men in your life were all bastards; it's quite another to have someone else say it.

'Stop it,' I said. 'None of us have done well in the past. It's awfully easy to criticise other people's choice of men but, let's face it, we all make mistakes when it comes to choosing for ourselves.'

'Hrrm!' coughed Cal. 'Still here. In case you girls have forgotten. I'm nice. Well, quite nice.'

'A guy who got off with an estate agent in the master bedroom of a house over which she was showing him, and then dropped her immediately afterwards?' Georgie riposted.

'No point in continuing. I told you, I didn't like the house.'

We booted him out of the office till drink time and I returned to my desk and the further adventures of Jerry Beauman, who was to the prison system what Biggles was to the RAF.

I was distracted by a summons from Alistair.

'I've just had a call from Todd Jarman,' he said critically.

I perfectly understood the critical tone. Todd was a successful writer and Alistair appreciated him as such – and was quite happy to meet him under carefully orchestrated circumstances – but he didn't want any author to get into the habit of telephoning him at random as if he was, say, a lesser editor. Like me. Alistair was the Boss: he was far too important to be telephoned with trivial demands and queries. I and other minions were supposed to insulate him from the creative temperament.

'I thought you'd established a good working relationship,' he went on.

'Well,' I temporised, 'working, anyway.'

'Thing is, he's been asked to guest at some bookstore event in Manchester. Bit last minute: they were going to have Ian Rankin, but he had to drop out. Evidently it's a big deal, local TV and all that. Think he should have someone to look after him. Should be Publicity, but Georgie's busy and Lin can't get a babysitter. Best be you.'

'But I – Manchester?'

'They read books up north, or so I'm told. Nothing else to do.'

'When is it?' I asked, with that familiar sinking feeling.

'Saturday.'

I objected, but it did no good. If you're young and single you can't plead family commitments, and as I'm far more junior than Georgie I couldn't claim my social engagements took precedence. I said Todd was an adult who certainly didn't require a minder, but Alistair brushed that aside. All writers, in his view, needed looking after, if only to ensure that they didn't say the wrong thing. 'You won't have to spend much time with him,' Alistair offered by way of palliative. 'He's driving. We'll send you by train.' Oddly enough, that didn't make me feel any better about it.

I travelled up on Intercity, sitting in a bay with a table so I could work on Jerry's manuscript. I had mixed feelings about spending more time with Todd Jarman. There was no denying that working with him had given me a buzz, there had been moments of something like camaraderie; but I definitely didn't like him. I didn't like his twitchy werewolf eyebrows and his been-there know-that superior manner and his snooty girlfriend and his mock-streetsmart façade. On the other hand, I didn't like him in a stimulating way which was sometimes more fun than mere liking . . . I found my thought zigzagging erratically from one extreme to another (and back again), and put Jarman from my mind for the rest of the journey. In Manchester, I hailed a taxi to the hotel where Lin had booked me a room, dumped my bag, and headed for Waterstone's in Deansgate.

I found Todd in the manager's office, drinking whisky and giving an interview to the *Manchester Guardian*. Contrary to Alistair's claim there was no TV, but plenty of regional press and apparently he'd already done a radio show. 'Nice to see you,' he said with more politeness than sincerity. 'Alistair said he was sending someone, but I really don't need my hand held.'

'You *don't* think it's nice,' I said baldly. 'If it comes to that, nor do I. I have other things to do with my Saturdays.' Well, actually Jerry's rewrites and a cosy evening with the television, but I wasn't going to tell him that.

He grinned and offered me a whisky, having appropriated the bottle from the manager.

'No thanks,' I said. 'I hate it. I'd rather have wine.' I'd seen a few glasses of red on a tray.

'Somehow I knew you would. Whatever I offer, you always want something else.'

'It's a matter of principle,' I said, feeling gratified that he'd noticed. Provocative behaviour is wasted if it doesn't provoke.

'You do your best to annoy me, don't you?' he responded. 'Whether it's removing my commas or refusing my coffee. It's what they call bad chemistry.'

'Striking sparks off each other,' I reiterated. (Bloody Alistair. Why did he always let me in for this?) '*I* wasn't the one who started it.'

'Of course you were.' There was a glint in his eye. 'Cutting my title like that.'

'That was my *job*,' I protested. 'Anyway, it's better short. More eye-catching.'

'I like long titles. *The Murder of Roger Ackroyd. A Portrait of the Artist as a Young Man. À La Recherche de Temps Perdu.*'

'None of them made it to number One,' I stated, hoping I was right. 'It was *you*. You said I was too young to edit your books, you – you poured scorn on my efforts, you said my mother's milk was still wet on my lips!'

'Did I? It seems very unlikely.'

'Well no, but you might've done.'

'It doesn't appear to have discouraged you.' The glint had reached his teeth, which showed in the sort of smile you give an enemy, knife-edged and short on humour.

'I put on a bold front,' I said.

'A front, anyhow,' he remarked, with a flicker of the assessing look he had given me when he'd told me not to lose more weight.

I was disconcerted, and temporarily at a loss for a retort, but the manager joined us and conversation became general, and there were no further opportunities for argument.

The store was crowded – always a novelty at a literary event. Todd read an extract from his previous book (rather well) and answered questions from fans and novel-in-the-bottom-drawer literary aspirants to well beyond the allotted time.

'Don't worry,' he said when the session finally ended. 'You don't have to take me out to dinner. I'm driving into the country to stay with friends – and I'm going to be bloody late.'

I was conscious of a needle of disappointment, but I didn't intend to show anything. 'I could've borne it,' I said stoically. 'It's my duty. You're still owed an editorial lunch, after all.'

'I'll look forward to that.' Obvious sarcasm.

'Me too,' I responded in kind. I wished him a dulcet goodnight, and departed in search of a taxi to my hotel.

For the others, it was an eventful weekend. Lin, driven by desperation, daring the perils of the Internet from the safety of her own home, had decided to venture into a chatroom. And Georgie, with mixed feelings, took a message on her phone from Neville Fancot, asking her for another date.

Chapter 7

For woman's face was never formed in vain
For Juan, so that even when he prayed
He turned from grisly saints, and martyrs hairy,
To the sweet portraits of the Virgin Mary.

BYRON: *Juan and Haidée*

It is always the best policy to speak the truth – unless, of course, you are an exceptionally good liar.

JEROME K. JEROME

I had to finish sorting out Jerry Beauman's manuscript in a ludicrously short time since my holiday had been booked six months earlier and I had no intention of taking work away with me. 'Watch out when you get the proofs,' Laurence said. 'He'll want to do more rewrites: he always does.' Strictly speaking, proofs are supposed to be corrected but not altered, since major changes at that stage are expensive. But cost wouldn't bother Jerry Beauman, and so – perforce – it wasn't allowed to bother us. I sighed, shrugged, and thrust the problem from my mind. I had two weeks on Crete, at a lay-back, strip-down resort called Plakias (pronounced, appropriately enough, Plucky Arse), and all I intended to think about was my tan. I was going with a friend from college days. We don't see much of each other under normal circumstances since she lives in Leeds, but we had fallen into the habit of taking our summer holiday together. This worked quite well since, having a year in each other's lives to catch up on, we always had plenty to talk about. Sinead is very dynamic and runs her own business (some sort of mail order) and is always having broken engagements. I reflected quite cheerfully that at least this year I could keep my end up, with the disintegration of the Nigel affair.

Georgie and I went on a shopping expedition to find me the kind of bikini where the top comes in proper bra sizes and you can buy the bottom separately. 'We can't have you lying about in a one-piece with your tummy staying white,' Georgie said. 'You'll have to spend serious money.' But somehow I got the feeling her heart wasn't in it.

'Where are *you* going?' I asked. 'Have you booked anything yet?' She'd got just a week off, overlapping my slot.

'No. I thought I'd pick up a cheap deal at the last minute.'

'It really *will* be the last minute if you don't do something soon.'

'I might just stay home and enjoy the heatwave.'

'But you've always been into exotic foreign travel!' I protested.

'I'm economising.'

We were walking down the street as we talked, and I stopped abruptly, staring at her. 'Are you quite well?'

'No need to be funny. I have to economise. You know I do. When they refer to the debt mountain, they mean me. I'm a mountain all by myself.'

'How much did that Dolce & Gabbana T-shirt cost you last week?'

'A lot less than a holiday.' She sounded curiously listless. But listlessness had always been alien to Georgie's nature.

'This has to do with Cal, doesn't it?' I deduced. She had

already told us about the conversation over the linguine.

'I'm in love,' she said sadly. 'It's really coming home to me. The big L. Head over ears, arse over tit. With Cal McGregor, former office lech, married, unavailable, a man so illiterate he never opens a book – he's only interested in what goes on the cover. How the hell did it happen?'

'Don't say we didn't warn you.'

'I know, I know. I thought I was immune. With Franco . . . it was different. It was Romance with a capital R. We met in Venice, and he was wildly handsome, and a *conte*, and mad about me: I think I fell for the aura more than the man. So I guess I got what I deserved, in the end. And before that, there were a couple of celebs with whom I was sort of infatuated – until it fizzled out. An actor, a TV presenter. I could've understood if I'd fallen big time for someone like that: fame and sex appeal is a hot combination. But Cal's not famous; he wouldn't want to be. He's attractive, but not a pin-up. He's *ordinary* . . . How could I fall for someone ordinary?'

'You said it was fun to have that feeling again,' I reminded her. 'You said that ages ago.'

'It's fun to be a *little* in love. It's an emotional romp – a roll in the hay – your heart goes on holiday, and then it comes back, intact, with a few nice memories to keep it warm. That was the idea. This is – deeper. So deep it hurts. I don't do deep, Cookie. I don't do hurt. I'm a lightweight in love – I flutter through life like a butterfly – a butterfly with painted wings – drifting from flower to flower.' She paused, evidently dwelling on the image.

'Butterflies start storms,' I said. 'That's physics.'

'Fine,' said Georgie, 'as long as they aren't in my teacup. I don't feel like myself any more. I don't want to spend money all the time. I had to force myself to buy that Dolce & Gabbana T-shirt – you know? And it didn't even cost very much.'

'This is serious.'

'I'm losing my sparkle, aren't I? Just when I need to be utterly gorgeous, it's all fading away. I've got fifteen lines going on sixteen, and no one will ever take care of me . . .'

'You don't look very faded to me.'

'Damn Cal. Perhaps I should build me a willow-cabin at his gate . . .'

'You'll never get planning permission, and anyway, he'd be embarrassed. Bad move. Book a holiday. At least it would give you a break.'

There was a short silence. Then she said in a different voice – a voice that was carefully noncommittal: 'Did I tell you Neville rang?'

'Neville?' I'd forgotten who he was.

'Neville Fancot. The doctor who took me to Wagner. My most promising cardiac millionaire. Not cardiac and probably not a millionaire but definitely promising.' She went on: 'He left a message on my machine. I haven't rung back yet.'

'And you're in love with Cal,' I said.

'I told you,' Georgie said with grim wretchedness, 'I'm a lightweight.'

We found my bikini in the end, one that offered support without upholstery and actually made me look curvy rather than bulgy. I hadn't worn a bikini since I was thirteen and the purchase gave me a thrill that was well worth the dent in my finances. I chose a floaty thigh-length shirt to wear over it with the same sea-shell pattern as the bikini and remarked with a grin that I was buying an awful lot of clothes to wear on a predominantly nudist beach.

'Nudism is unsubtle,' Georgie declared. 'No mystery. Besides, men like making love to women with bikini marks. It gives them the illusion you've still got your underwear on.'

'I bet Cal said that.'

Georgie didn't comment. 'You must have a holiday romance,' she said. 'There's nothing like it. You pick some guy on looks alone – usually a waiter or barman – 'cos you won't be with him long enough to discover he has no brains or personality. You're crazy about him for a few nights and then you leave before it all goes sour on you with a great story to tell your friends. Everything's fine until you get the pictures developed . . . Make sure you chuck out the awkward ones. You don't want to look back ten years later and think: My God, that's Stefano – or Jean-Yves – or Angelos. Was I really at it with *him*?' She checked herself, and sighed. 'That didn't come out quite the way I intended. I meant to encourage, not put you off. Bugger. Nothing's coming out the way I intend any more.'

All the same, I liked the idea of a commitment-free fling. It was just what I needed, post-Nigel – an antidote, an ego-boost, a dash of fantasy sex in the real world. There hadn't been many flings in my life; I hadn't been the sort of girl men wanted to get flung with. Maybe I could find an Angelos who looked a little like Hugh Jackman, in a bad light . . .

Lin hadn't booked a holiday either. With three kids and no backup, Abroad was too expensive and much too much like hard work. Later in the summer Vee Corrigan was taking the twins to the Isle of Wight for a week, whether they liked it or not, and Lin had fixed some time off after Georgie got back to ram some culture down her offspring's throats, in the form of museums, art galleries, and theatre trips. 'What're you taking them to see?' I asked. 'Shakespeare at the National?' I could visualise the boys quite enjoying the tragedies, if there was enough blood.

'*The Lion King*,' Lin said. 'And *Chitty Chitty Bang Bang*. I needed to play safe.'

'The kids are bound to find them awfully slow,' Georgie said.

(In fact, despite affecting to despise musicals, Sandy and Demmy adored both shows. 'I *like* musicals,' Meredith declared. 'It's just the songs I can't stand.' She was sick in the foyer at *Lion King* and in the auditorium at *Chitty Chitty*. Lin couldn't get tickets for anything else and now suspects she's on a blacklist.)

Meanwhile, on the Friday, Cal stood Georgie up after Christy, who had to attend a fund-raising dinner, commanded his services as a babysitter. As they had been planning to go to the cinema to see the latest summer blockbuster Georgie was very pissed off.

'It isn't Cal's fault,' I said.

'I know,' said Georgie. 'It never is.'

She rang Neville from her mobile, making a date for Saturday: cocktails and a restaurant.

'You're doing this for all the wrong reasons,' I pointed out.

'I know,' Georgie said again.

At Monday lunchtime, we all dived into the nearest pub to get the details. 'Why didn't he call for so long?' Lin wanted to know.

'Apparently he had a family crisis. His father's been ill for a while, and he collapsed suddenly and had to be rushed to hospital. He was in Intensive Care. Neville's parents retired to one of the remoter parts of Wales, so he had a long way to go to be in attendance.'

'Was it heart?' I asked. 'I don't want to be over-optimistic, but these things can be genetic, can't they?'

'As it happens, it was,' Georgie said. 'I did ask Neville if he'd inherited the condition, but he just laughed. I think he was a bit shocked at my asking, though. Why is it nobody ever takes my ad seriously?'

Lin and I were silent, feeling comment would be superfluous.

'So where did he take you?' I resumed presently.

And: 'Is he as nice as you thought?' from Lin.

'We had cocktails at The Savoy and dinner at Quo Vadis,' Georgie related. 'And, yes, he's very nice.'

'Nice and fanciable or nice and unfanciable?' Lin demanded.

'Fanciable,' Georgie insisted. 'The impossible combination. He's got a palatial flat in Cadogan Gardens, he's going to buy a house in the Dordogne, and he drives a Saab with a Jaguar on the side. You don't get more fanciable than that.'

'How do you know his flat's palatial?' I said suspiciously.

'I went back for a nightcap,' Georgie confessed.

'And bedsocks?'

'Not funny. We had a kiss and cuddle, that was all; then I got a taxi home. Anyway, why're you fighting Cal's corner? You're supposed to be on my side. You're supposed to tell me that married men are a bad idea, and I should get myself a decent single guy. You're supposed to tell me I'm being had for a sucker.'

'Cal loves you,' Lin said unhappily.

'You love him,' I averred.

'He's married,' Georgie retorted. 'Married, *married*. He's not planning to leave his wife. He doesn't even bother to lie about it. All I'll ever get is all I've got – crumbs of his time and attention. What happens when I'm older, and my looks start to go, and he doesn't lust after me so much? I'll become someone he feels he must visit because he always has, a habit, a chore, and then there'll be nothing left.' She was clutching her glass so hard I could see the whites of her knuckles. 'I won't wait around for that. I'm not going to be suckered all my life. I married Franco in a whirl of romantic folly; I'm not letting Cupid make a fool of me again. Besides,' she added, relaxing a little, 'I might fall in love with Neville.

186

He wants to take me for a week in Mallorca. Mountains, olive groves, de luxe hotel. Sounds like a good place for falling in love.'

'Majorca?' I said sceptically, pronouncing the J.

'Mallorca,' corrected Georgie, not pronouncing the Ls. 'They spell it differently now. You're behind the times, Cookie. These days, they've changed the image as well as the spelling. The lager-louts have all gone to Cyprus; Mallorca's very upmarket now. Neville was telling me all about it. He's been several years running.'

'Who's Neville?' said a voice. A flat, hard voice, familiar and unfamiliar.

Cal.

Lin and I looked at each other and then, with one accord, down into our glasses.

I heard Georgie say: 'He's a man I'm seeing.'

'You didn't mention it.'

I nudged Lin's leg with my foot. 'This is where we get off.' We vacated our seats, moving towards the bar. Cal slid along the empty bench without a word of thanks or a glance in our direction. I don't think he even registered we'd been there. His face had a tight look, as if someone had wound up a spring inside him, tensing his muscles, pulling flesh against bone. His features were compressed, even the eyes and eyebrows, all thin and taut. The same tightness was evident in the scrunch of his shoulders.

We didn't watch.

Georgie told us about it afterwards.

'How long have you been seeing this bloke?' Cal asked, in a carefully level tone.

'Does it matter?' He made an impatient gesture. 'Not long.'

'Are you sleeping with him?'

'Not yet.'

'Not *yet*?'

'He wants to take me on holiday,' Georgie repeated.

'So I heard.'

'That usually includes sex.' She paused, fishing for the right words to say what she meant; but there weren't any right words. Only wrong ones. 'He's attractive . . . and attracted to me . . . and unattached. You've got a wife – children – responsibilities – commitments. I don't fit in. I'm not part of the long-term picture. You've said some nice things to me, but ultimately, they're not worth a damn.'

'D'you think I didn't *mean* what I said?'

'It isn't relevant.' Her voice was light, brittle. You could have cracked it with a feather. 'Words don't count. Actions count. Your most consistent action is to go home to your wife. It's easy to say you love someone. It's much harder to act it.'

'You really don't get it, do you? I act it every moment – every moment that I can – but I can't walk away from everything. My responsibilities – my commitments – my children. I can't just . . . *leave*.'

'The boy stood on the burning deck,' she said. 'Bully for you.' He flinched from her sudden flippancy, as if she had struck him. 'You're married, I'm single. That's the way you want it. I'm a single woman, free to go out with other men. Neville offers me—'

'Security?'

'Maybe. Maybe just . . . fun.' She knew that would hurt him, and it did. She saw the hurt in his eyes.

She wanted to hurt.

'This is it, then,' he said.

'Yes.'

They sat staring at each other, unmoving. Their discussion wound down like an old-fashioned gramophone.

'This. Is. It.'

'Um.'

At two o'clock they walked back to work, side by side, not touching, not speaking. They parted on a monosyllable, without a kiss, diverging to their separate offices, where neither got anything done for the rest of the day.

It wasn't that simple, of course. They kept bumping into each other, talking, arguing, covering the same ground, again and again, over coffee at Ransome, over drinks in pub and wine bar. Cal was by turns angry, hurt, bitter, desperate, contrite. Georgie was contrite, desperate, bitter, hurt, angry. It seemed to get them nowhere, and it drove the rest of us to despair. We wanted to help, but they were beyond human aid, and all we could do was to watch them grinding away at each other's self-control until one of them snapped, usually Georgie. She would rage at him with the fury of someone who's trying to blot out her own inner voice, while he wrapped himself in an icy, brooding quiet which kept everyone at a distance. He vented his feelings on the Design Department – who rapidly succumbed to something resembling Gulf War Syndrome – and anyone else rash enough to put their head above the parapet. One hapless writer, calling to complain about the background colour for his dust jacket, was crushed without finesse. (Mind you, any input from writers on dust-jacket artwork is invariably crushed, usually at editorial level, but finesse is supposed to be involved.)

'Why does it have to be green?'

'Because I say so.'

'But look—' the writer clearly had a death-wish '– I just don't see my whole literary concept as being best represented in green.'

'Fuck the fucking concept. It's fucking green and it's staying fucking green and that's that.'

'Ah.'

Most people gave the Design Department a wide berth.

Even Alistair, wandering in to demand something tasteful for one of his pet protégés at Porgy, re-emerged wearing the stunned expression of a man who has just strolled inadvertently into a tiger's cage. In Publicity, Georgie remained charming, injecting extra husk into her huskiest tones and flashing dazzling smiles down the telephone at people who couldn't see them, but her surface glitter was unnatural and she would lose her thread in mid-sentence, or listen for five minutes with apparent attention before murmuring vaguely: 'What?' However, any suggestion that she should abandon her prospective trip with Neville evoked a violent response. 'Why?' she would say, her voice rising. 'I'm single, he's single – why shouldn't I go with him? Why shouldn't I have some *fun?*'

'You have fun with Cal,' Lin said unwisely.

'When he has the time,' Georgie retorted, with a savagery out of all proportion to the words.

It didn't look good.

On Friday, I left, adjuring Lin to keep the peace.

'What peace?' she sighed.

'Well . . . keep the pieces, then. We'll stick them together when I get back.'

I was trying to sound upbeat, but it didn't come out right. There are few things more distressing, in an everyday context, than the sight of two people you like, who you know love each other, wantonly tearing their relationship apart. But there was nothing I could do to stop it, and I was off on holiday, and utterly determined to leave all my worries behind. Ransome Harber and its denizens were a long way from the Isles of Greece, and I was going to take advantage of that distance. No more agonising over Georgie and Cal, no more babysitting, no more bumping into Nigel on the social circuit, no more Jerry Beauman. (Especially no more Jerry Beauman.) At least for a fortnight. At home I packed my new bikini, clothes, books, suntan oil. I left my upstairs neighbour several tins of cat food and comprehensive instructions on feeding Mandy. I refused to look Mandy in the eye. (I never can when I'm going away.) There are times when I wonder if going on holiday is more trouble than it's worth.

At an unearthly hour on Saturday morning I set off for the airport, too sleepy even to fantasise about the possibilities of a Cretan romance.

I noted earlier that everyone who is reading this book has probably been on a diet at some time in their life. The same can be said for going to Greece. It's one of those things that most people do, sooner or later. When I was a child I dreamed of visiting the haunts of legend and history: the Athens of Theseus and Themistocles, Odysseus' Ithaca, the Oracle at Delphi (although in those days I thought this was in India). But somehow, as I got older, my priorities deteriorated. Now – like most people – I want sun, sand, sea, and lots of booze. The Isles of Greece offer, relatively cheaply, picturesque beaches, a relaxed attitude to nudity, and bars that stay open most of the night, with bronzed, god-like natives as an added extra. While some of those amenities must have been available in the classical era – no wonder Jason and Odysseus spent so much time island-hopping instead of getting on with the job – both the wildness and the grandeur of the mythical world seem to have somehow been lost. And, as a tourist, I know it's my fault. Sinead and I did visit Knossos, nursing the kind of hangovers that made the bull-paintings quiver on the walls, but there was little atmosphere left in the sun-baked ruins: the visitors had driven it away.

In any case, it was much too hot for sight-seeing. Back on the beach at Plakias, we concentrated on the important issues: the careful build-up of a tan, no pink, no peeling, dipping in the Med to cool off, eying up the talent and hopefully being eyed up in our turn. 'You've lost weight,' Sinead commented inevitably, early in the proceedings. She didn't sound critical, she sounded envious. My heart warmed. I had forgotten how much I liked her. 'You look terrific.'

I'd been to Greece before, naturally, but I'd never taken so many clothes off. On the beach, I'd worn a one-piece which wrapped itself around my spare tyres (like Michelin Man, I'd had more than one) like skin round a sausage. Off it, I'd covered up in loose floppy garments which hid both my bulges and my assets. Now, I felt voluptuous. I didn't even have acres of pallor to put on view: Jerry Beauman's roof terrace had given me a base coat. I don't tan very dark, but, I reminded myself, dark tans are out of vogue: they give you wrinkles and skin cancer. I topped up at night with fake and went a beautiful golden colour. And for the first time in my life I was conscious of men looking at me, not because I took up space in the landscape but because they wanted to. It was a heavenly sensation. In London, even though, lately, some guys had looked at me with admiration, the climate of fevered work and frantic socialising left little time for the mating game. Relationships, too, tend to be fevered and frantic: the chat-ups, the let-downs, speed-dating, affairs (like Georgie's) squeezed into the corners between other commitments. But in Greece, it's all about sex. The beach, the booze, the body-pampering. Even if you don't do it, that's still what it's about. You put yourself on show, you lure and allure, you sun yourself in reflected desire. There's no work to get in the way, no frenzied pressures of urban life. In the past, I'd always been an onlooker on the scene, but now I was part of it, I was doing some of the alluring, feeling myself desired, and I blossomed. Who wouldn't?

It was easy – even amusing – telling Sinead about Nigel, including the bad bits. She laughed and laughed over the dénouement with Rachel.

'Thank God you're rid of him,' she said. 'It's transformed you. I always knew you'd be beautiful if you gave yourself the chance.'

I'm not beautiful, I know that, but it was nice of her to say it.

It was the second week when my Achilles turned up. He didn't resemble Hugh Jackman or Colin Firth, but still, Nature had done a good job. His jaw fell somewhere between the pocket torch and the lantern, his hair was dark and gelled into uplift, his eyes – actually, I didn't really notice his eyes. He had the sort of tan that, if he made a habit of it, would turn his skin to leather in ten years' time, but who cared? This was now. He looked particularly good in swimming trunks. On introduction, he turned out to be English and resident in Nottingham. ('That's okay,' Sinead said. 'Far enough away so you won't be bothered with him when you get back home.') His name was Mike. I asked him about Robin Hood, which was all I knew about Nottingham. He asked me about Dick Whittington, which (he said) was *almost* all he knew about London. It was a promising beginning. We drank long cocktails in assorted colours with even more assorted contents and shared the inevitable speculation as to what the little umbrella was really *for*.

'To keep the flies out,' Mike suggested brilliantly.

'It's not doing a very good job,' I said, pointing to something black floating in my drink. On closer inspection, however, it proved to be half a grape.

After an hour or more of this sort of conversation we naturally felt we knew each other frightfully well, though the cocktails may have had something to do with that. We strolled down to the beach, swam under the stars (the sea was decidedly chilly), and then sprawled on the sand at the water's edge, embracing passionately, like Burt Lancaster and Deborah Kerr in *From Here to Eternity*. Rolling around on

193

the beach is an overrated activity: the sand gets into every crevice in your body, and there are few things more disagreeable than gritty buttocks. I was relieved when we headed back to the bar, and still more relieved when I realised the presence of Sinead meant I couldn't invite him back to our room.

('D'you want to invite him back to our room?' Sinead hissed. 'I could stay out for an hour or two.')

The next evening we went to the local disco, and he grabbed me from behind, his body swaying in rhythm with mine, at least in theory, his hands cupping my breasts. I could feel his barely suppressed erection pushing against my bottom. It should have been wildly exciting, but somehow it wasn't. The thing about fantasy sex was that Russell Crowe, Hugh Jackman et al were familiar, and imaginary; this was real, and unfamiliar, and I wasn't comfortable with it. Even without the sandy bum. I began to wonder if the core problem with my career as a sex goddess was that I simply didn't have the temperament for it. Georgie, I thought, would've been dancing crotch to crotch by now.

'My mate's shagging that flat-chested blonde in the blue T-shirt, so I've got the room to myself tonight,' Mike murmured in my ear. Not exactly my idea of sweet nothings, but no matter.

'But what about *her* friend?' I asked.

'The brunette with the eyebrow stud? She's at it with one of the local boys. He's got his own place.'

I'd forgotten Greece was like that. It's different when you're not part of the chain.

I escaped somehow, clutching at Sinead for succour. She told me I was a fool, and we needed to make the most of life before we hit thirty and creeping eld did whatever it is creeping eld does. (It sounded like a relative of ground elder, but I think it's a Shakespearian term for old age.) I said I would rather be thirty than in bed with Mike, which she couldn't understand. 'You're looking gorgeous,' she said, 'and it's all going to waste.'

The night after I saw him chatting up another bosom, evidently also from the big city. 'All I know about London is Dick Whittington,' I heard him say.

The bosom quivered responsively.

So much for holiday romance, I thought.

While I was in Greece Georgie had finally taken the plunge and flown to Mallorca with Neville. They were staying in the west of the island on the edge of Deia, a location more than a cut above Plucky Arse. The Hotel Es Moli was stacked in layers against the mountainside, with several tiers of garden, restaurant terrace, bar terrace and pool terrace rising one above the other. The bedroom had French windows opening on to a crumbly stone balcony – at least, it looked crumbly, though Georgie hoped that was merely artistic effect – with a view of steep slopes intersecting in a V, enclosing a blue triangle of sea. The village rambled picturesquely down one slope; olive groves plumed the other. It all resembled a rather tasteful postcard. 'It's beautiful,' Georgie said, with genuine approval. Privately, she was wondering about the sleeping arrangements. The room was twin-bedded, and she had never shared a twin-bedded room with a man before. What was the etiquette? Would he expect to leap from his bed into hers without so much as a by-your-leave? Would he want to push the beds together? (Fatal: he or she was bound to slip down the gap.) Would he want her to do the leaping?

Neville asked her which bed she would like, and she chose the one nearest the window, and then wished she'd picked the bathroom side as it would be easier to get to the loo without being waylaid. But she was here to be waylaid, wasn't she? Or at any rate, laid . . .

195

They unpacked, and found there was nowhere near enough hanging space in the wardrobe for Georgie's clothes. Neville chivalrously gave up a couple of hangers. (He's chivalrous, thought Georgie. Maybe he won't try to leap at all.)

He went into the shower and emerged with a towel round his hips. His chest was on the thin side, his arms wirily muscular, his legs rather skinny. But then most men look better with their clothes on, Georgie reflected, and whoever came up with the kilt must have been blind to the impact of Scotsmen's knees. Of course Cal, who was slightly more solid, always looked good to her . . . But she mustn't think of Cal. That was history. Neville – despite his legs – was attractive, and available, and rich; she couldn't possibly have a problem with that. When she was at college she had once had three members of the rugger team on successive nights – or perhaps two of them on the same night; she couldn't remember precisely. She had always maintained she liked sex, lots of sex, with lots of men. Now wasn't the moment to become choosy.

(What was that song? *Something about you've got a nice face but not the right face . . .*)

She went into the shower in her turn, and came out in a bathrobe, covered from neck to calf.

Neville was dressed, a state of affairs which showed him at his best. 'If you like, I'll wait for you in the bar,' he said. 'Give you a bit of privacy. I want to catch up with some friends. We all know each other here. We come back year after year: it's like a club.'

'Who did you bring last year?' Georgie asked with a smile.

'All you need to know,' he said, 'is that she wasn't as attractive as you.'

The smile faded. Neville gave her directions to the bar, which she immediately forgot, and left her alone.

I'm here for a week, she thought. Seven nights. I'm going to have fun. I *always* have fun: it's what I'm good at.

196

She dressed in cropped trousers, a skimpy top, and an embroidered cardigan which wasn't really necessary, but she didn't intend to expose her legs and arms in the evening until they were considerably browner. Outside the room, the corridor stretched unhelpfully to right and left. She couldn't even recall where the lift was. She turned right at random, and presently found some stairs. Down a flight there was another, almost identical corridor, and a door leading on to a terrace with tables and chairs and panoramic view. It was early for drinks but several people were already there, sipping tall glasses of this and that. Congratulating herself on her unerring instinct Georgie looked round for Neville, and found another door opening on to a panelled room: the bar itself. It was empty except for a young man mixing drinks who glanced up and gave her a Puckish grin. He was, she guessed, about thirty, with eyes all sparkle and mischief and black hair that appeared to have been recently rumpled. Georgie cheered up immediately.

'Can I help you?' the young man said. 'I am Juan.'

You would be, Georgie thought. She perched on a bar stool. 'I'm looking for a friend,' she said, 'but he doesn't seem to be around.'

'You stay here,' Juan said. 'I find him for you. But first, I make you a drink.'

A waitress came in, and removed the tray he had just loaded. Georgie accepted a lavish gin-and-tonic and fished for her purse.

'Is on me.' Juan waved payment aside. 'Who is your friend?'

'Neville Fancot. Do you know him?'

'Señor Fancot? Of course. He is a nice man. Every year, he brings a pretty girl.' He leaned forward, lowering his voice. 'But you are prettiest.'

'I bet you said that to the girl last year,' Georgie teased.

The grin again. 'Maybe.'

197

By the time Neville arrived, unsought by Juan, Georgie was two G & Ts to the good and feeling much happier. They went to dinner with another couple and she was at her most animated, assisted by a quantity of wine and a large digestif. Going up to bed she swayed a little on the stairs and complained of tiredness, and once in the room she slipped into the ensuite and changed into unusually demure pyjamas bought especially for the trip. Then she climbed into bed and fell instantly into something resembling sleep.

It wasn't that Georgie made a decision; instead, she put off the moment of decision-making, pushing it away from her, telling herself, in the native lingo: *mañana*. The problem could wait, the choice could wait, Neville could wait. *Mañana*. During the day they went to the beach, or lay by the pool, and Georgie hid herself in a book. Fortunately, since she had only brought a couple, the hotel had a good library. She allowed Neville to oil her back but declined his services for any other part of her anatomy. He went out for walks with fellow guests but Georgie didn't accompany them; it was, she said, far too hot. He also played tennis, but Georgie had never been sporty. She worked out regularly at a gym, and was in consequence fairly fit, but as far as she was concerned tennis was something that happened to other people, preferably on the Centre Court at Wimbledon while she consumed champagne and strawberries. (She had once been skiing, but had sprained her thumb on the first day, apparently by holding the strap of the pole incorrectly, and the doctor had told her that further activity would be inadvisable.) I hardly know him, she thought, with regard to Neville. Of course, she *would* have sex with him, that was why she had come on holiday, but not immediately. She needed a little time, that was all.

On the first afternoon, she retrieved her emergency Lil-lets from her suitcase, began to carry them about with her, and explained to Neville that she had her period. During the course of the evening he grew friendly, putting his arm around her and drawing her attention to the stars, telling her, *sotto voce*, that he really didn't mind a little blood. 'I do,' Georgie said, accepting the arm and duly admiring the heavens.

'You're still taking your pills,' Neville said. He must have noticed her keeping the packet in her bag. 'You shouldn't be bleeding now.'

He would be a sodding doctor, Georgie cursed silently. 'I'm changing to a new one,' she said. 'My monthly cycle seems to have got scrambled.' She was wondering how long she could stretch the phantom menstruation out. Maybe three nights . . .

While he was out walking, she took the opportunity to wander into Deia. It was, as has been said, picturesque. The main road – such as it was – wound its way through the middle, with a twisty street and various flights of steps zig-zagging up the hill to the church. There was much golden stonework overhung with vines and bougainvillaea, funny little cul-de-sacs ending in tiny courtyards and terraces, gnarly olive trees sprouting from negligible patches of soil. Small boutiques displayed stylish versions of the usual holiday clothing: T-shirts, caftans, embroidered silky things. Cafés offered coffee; restaurants flaunted menus. Off to the right she found the Residency, Deia's grandest hotel, former owner Richard Branson. There was an exhibition of splodgy abstract paintings in reception and a green lawn lapped at the verandah, but Neville had told her the pool was inferior to the Es Moli's. Georgie contemplated having a drink there – it was supposed to be a good hunting ground for millionaires – but decided she was in enough trouble. Anyway, she didn't like the paintings.

Instead, she climbed up to the church, perched on the

hilltop like Georgie on a bar stool, with a cemetery which boasted amazing views of the country round even if the residents couldn't appreciate them. Robert Graves was meant to be buried there, but although the cemetery was small she couldn't find him. Perhaps, she thought, he was buried under a *nom de tomb*. Back in the village, she found a pharmacy and made various purchases.

'Surely you not need this?' the woman at the counter insisted. 'Eat much olives. Put more oil on salad. Then these tablets not necessary.'

'I'm allergic to olives,' Georgie improvised.

Her fictional period had run out, and somehow, though she had every intention of sleeping with Neville, it wasn't going to be tonight. Alone in the bedroom, she shook out a couple of senna tablets on to a plate and attempted to pound them up with the base of a tumbler. They were much harder than expected, and in the end she had to cut them into pieces with a knife, which wasn't at all satisfactory. In films, when people wanted to administer a sneaky dose of laxative, they simply tipped some fluid into a drink or added it to food, but the pharmacy hadn't offered a liquid option and anyway, Georgie suspected that in real life a *lot* of liquid would be required. And then there was the taste factor. She sniffed doubtfully at the pills and sampled one on her tongue, with the wary approach of a TV detective checking for heroin. It had the flavour of All-Bran cut with natural compost. Even in highly spiced food, it would add a certain sort of something which Neville would be bound to notice. And how was she to introduce the tablets (chopped, not ground) into his meal? How many would she need? The recommended dosage was two, so an overdose must mean at least eight. Finally, how long would they take to work?

It was no good. These things were all very well in books, but reality threw up so many complications. Writers do all that research when it comes to explosions and poisons and guns, Georgie thought, but no one ever bothers to check up on something like this. She flushed the two chopped-up tablets down the loo and returned to the table, tipping eight more on to the plate.

'What can I do?' she demanded of an unhelpful providence. 'There's no way I can get him to take them.' She tried dissolving one in water, but the particles settled on the bottom of the glass, leaving an obdurate lump of tablet in the middle. It went the way of the first two. Morosely, she shook another one on to the plate. Then she sat staring at them in search of inspiration which didn't come.

There was only one thing to be done, and Georgie did it. She took them herself.

Let's take a break from the holiday sagas. Back in England, Cal's tension had reached snapping point: he had virtually stopped drinking and communicated only in monosyllables and the occasional snarl. Lin tried to talk to him, with the true kindness that had rarely failed to elicit a response – until now. 'Don't want to discuss it,' Cal said brusquely. 'Leave me alone. I said, leave – me – alone.'

In her lunch hour, Lin resorted to her friend from the chatroom. She had been exchanging e-mails with him for a couple of weeks, telling neither Georgie nor me, on the spurious grounds that we had other things to think about. Georgie was suspicious of chatrooms, saying that with Internet dating people had to register formally, but in a chatroom you could be talking to anyone. (There were plenty of loopholes in this argument, but Lin hadn't ventured to probe them.) So the correspondence was clandestine, with accompanying guilt and all the pleasure of secrecy. Lin signed off with her own name, thinking it was brief enough and common enough for relative anonymity. Her correspondent called himself Ivor, claiming that this, too, was his real name. Getting the bad news out there first, she had told him from the beginning that she was a single parent with three children, one father dead, the other too busy to take an interest. Being stuck at home most evenings she had a limited social life, but now she was starting to discover how the computer could widen her horizons. Ivor said he was amazingly lucky to have stumbled across her, and he felt instinctively they were going to have a great deal in common. He sent her no jokes, non-PC or otherwise, and no poetry. He didn't complain about his previous girlfriend, saying merely that it hadn't worked out; he was looking for a serious relationship but she just hadn't been the one. He didn't claim to be especially attractive or clever, sending instead a brief summary: 'Thirty-six, five eleven, own hair, own teeth, no distinguishing marks. How about you?'

'Thirty-two, five five, no hair, no teeth,' Lin replied, and then, panicking that he might believe her, filled in the description with a few more details. Ivor said he loved red-gold hair, it reminded him of that painting, the Madonna, you know the one, he couldn't remember which artist it was. He went on to tell her that he was a teacher in South London, he hoped she wouldn't be put off: teachers didn't have a great image, people thought of them as a necessary evil. Lin confessed she was in publishing, and waited for him to tell her about the novel in his bottom drawer. When he didn't she expressed her relief, and he said he'd always wanted to have a novel in his bottom drawer but there wasn't room for it: the drawer in question was full of old socks. In any case, the world of inner-city education – or attempted education – was far too scary for any genre but horror. Maybe some day he would get around to writing about it; he had several pupils eligible to star in *The Blob*, or *The Teenager from the Black Lagoon*. Lin said her children were pre-teens, but they could be just a tiny bit horrifying at times, while also being completely wonderful, of course.

Ivor encouraged her to elaborate, and Lin told him about the twins, and how they were doing (or not doing) at school, and how their father was a fairly successful actor who didn't have leisure to be with them, and how she worried that they needed an authority figure in their life. Then she moved on to Meredith, avoiding details of her more extreme behaviour, simply talking about her exceptional intelligence, and her difficult moods, and the tragedy of *her* father's death. Ivor said Lin had obviously had a bad time, and was incredibly brave to try and cope alone, and clearly needed someone to take care of her. Lin, responding instantly to these magic words, insisted valiantly that she could manage, she really could, only it was so difficult to have a Life, and sometimes she was lonely, in spite of the children. Could he understand that?

He could. 'I know all about loneliness. You can be in the middle of a crowd, but if there isn't someone you can touch, not just physically but emotionally, someone with whom you can share your thoughts and feelings, little jokes, everyday details of your life – then you're as isolated as if you were in the heart of a desert.'

Lin was deeply moved, although a typing error meant that he had actually said 'in the heart of a dessert', and she couldn't help a brief fantasy about how it would feel to be immersed in raspberry Pavlova. She thought of mentioning this, but didn't want to spoil the tenor of their exchanges. She said that was *exactly* what she meant, and he replied that since he had been e-mailing her he didn't feel alone any more. Did she know they'd already swapped over thirty thousand words since they started their correspondence?

Lin said a few more weeks and they'd have a novel of their own. She didn't think anyone had done a novel entirely in e-mail yet, although it was plainly the literary format of the future.

Ivor said could she send him a photograph. He knew she was someone special, what she looked like wasn't important, but he would like to be able to picture her. A photo of him was attached.

Lin brought up the image on her screen and saw a thatch of dark-blond hair, a normal-sized chin, a smile that cut dimples in his cheek. Even the inevitable red-eye of the flash didn't make him look demonic. She studied the picture for a long, long time.

In Mallorca Georgie sat by the pool in her bathrobe, looking pale under her tan. The effect of this was unfortunate, since it turned her face from warm brown to washed out yellow. Even now, she had to bolt to the bedroom every so often in search of the loo. A gallant Juan was on hand to pamper her with cups of tea, expressions of sympathy, and the occasional pat on her towelling shoulder.

The pool was indeed superior, being very large, very blue, cool though not cold in the heat, and surrounded by enough sun loungers to accommodate a small army, with a choice of sunshine and shade to lie in. This time, Georgie was in the shade. Having wanly declined Neville's offer of moral support, she had insisted that he go off and enjoy himself (walking, the beach) while she recovered on her own. She had picked out a thriller at random from the hotel library, yet another tale of multiple corpses where the heroine was a pathologist. In modern fiction, she reflected, there seemed to be some kind of rule that all top pathologists must be women. Georgie was darkly suspicious of this trend, probing it for connotations of sexism. Was it that female pathologists were supposed to be more sensitive and caring in their attitude to the dead than male ones? Of course, it was undeniably true that women were generally less squeamish than men, far better at mopping up sick and dealing with bodily functions and malfunctions – aeons of bringing up children and nursing war-wounded husbands had seen to that. But the real motivation for these writers, Georgie decided, was to show their masculine rivals that they too could produce lengthy descriptions of rotting, burned or blood-boltered bodies, thus seizing control of a readership with an appetite for gore. The yuk factor. In the past, that market had been dominated by men; lady novelists had only written restrained murders with lots of little grey cells and not much blood. Now, with the advent of the female pathologist in a starring role, authoresses could demonstrate that Woman was caring and superior while simultaneously outdoing the blokes in graphic detail of the body count. We too can churn your stomach, they were saying. Georgie's stomach had churned more than enough in the last twelve hours. She closed the book on a comprehensive analysis of dismembered limbs retrieved from a sewage tank and turned thankfully to her cup of tea.

The question was, what was she to do next? 'Face it,' she told herself. 'You don't want to sleep with him; you never wanted to sleep with him. You just *wanted* to want to sleep with him, and that won't work. Now you've got two nights left in which not to sleep with him, and you're running out of ideas.' She contemplated painting her genitalia with lurid spots to fake a sexually transmitted disease, or going mad, or going home, but knew none of it was any good. He was a doctor: he wouldn't be fooled by the spots, and putting underpants on her head would ruin her hair, and she couldn't afford the air-ticket home. Her stomach had ceased churning, and she had a dip and went to her room, in order to dress for dinner before Neville returned. She didn't feel much like eating, so at least she could pick at her food, look pale (or rather, yellow), and say she was still unwell. There didn't seem to be any other options left.

Neville got back early, catching her in her bra and briefs. She snatched a cushion to her bosom, and then realised she was being silly and put it down.

'How are you feeling?' he asked her.

'So-so.'

'You haven't had a great trip, have you? One thing after another.'

'I'm sorry,' Georgie said with sudden sincerity. 'I've been awful company, I know that. I wish . . .'

'Never mind. Not your fault. Maybe you'll be better when you've eaten. Give the wine a miss, I think, don't you?'

Shit. She was dying for a drink.

'Oh yes,' she said.

She was downstairs before Neville and happily ensconced at the bar when he joined her. 'What's that?' he inquired, indicating the glass of cloudy yellow liquid at her elbow.

'Pina colada.' She flourished the bottle. 'Just coconut and pineapple juice.'

Behind Neville's back, Juan winked at her. He had topped it up lavishly with rum.

Over dinner she duly ate little and avoided the wine. The rum kept her going. By bedtime she was starving. She went up early, followed, to her alarm, by Neville. When she retreated on to the balcony he pursued her, wrapping his arms around her, telling her he was worried she might take cold (it was twenty-five degrees). She couldn't evade a long, lingering kiss. Panic set in, and she dived into the bathroom, pleading an urgent need to clean her teeth. She ran the tap, flushed the loo, ran the tap again, scrubbed, gargled, spat. When she eventually reappeared, swathed in a bathrobe, he was lounging on top of his bed in his boxer shorts, looking hopeful. Even the boxers looked hopeful.

'I need – some milk,' Georgie said, inventing wildly. 'For my stomach. To – to settle it. I'll just pop down and get some.' She grabbed the card for the door off the table.

'But you can order room service—'

She mumbled something about it taking too long, and fled.

The bar was nearly empty, though there were still several people sitting on the terrace enjoying the warm darkness. Large sparkly stars twinkled happily in a blue velvet sky. Scattered lights across the valley showed the houses of Deia climbing up the ridge to the church, where Robert Graves might or might not be buried. It's beautiful here, Georgie thought. I should be having a wonderful time. Bugger.

She sat on her usual bar stool and Juan mixed her a drink containing several kinds of alcohol, slightly diluted with a slice of lemon, a couple of ice cubes, and a splash of some exotic juice. For safety's sake she ordered a glass of milk on the side, in case Neville put in an appearance. But time passed, and gradually she felt more secure. 'This is a great hotel,' she told Juan. 'I could sit here all night in my bathrobe and nobody cares. If Neville comes, can I hide behind the bar?'

'Of course. But why don't you want to be with him? He is a good man. He is a doctor. Is good to be a doctor.'

'He's a very good man,' Georgie sighed. 'He's rich and successful and attractive. That's as good as it gets. I'm a cow. I should never have come.'

'So what is wrong with him?'

'Nothing. It's me. I'm in love with someone else.' There. She had said it. Not in the heat of the moment, with Cal in front of her, and that look in his eyes which was always a little sad even behind his specs – not to a girlfriend, a confidante, which didn't count – she had said it when Cal was far away, and their relationship in ruins, to someone who knew nothing of either of them.

'Then why are you with Señor Fancot? This other man, he is in love with you? He must be: you are so pretty.'

Always responsive to flattery, Georgie managed a smile. 'Oh yes, he's in love with me – or so he says. But he's married. He won't leave because of the kids; one of them's severely handicapped. He and his wife don't have sex any more.'

'I understand,' said Juan, leaning on the counter in front of her. 'I too am married. We have ten children. Now, we cannot have sex. My wife is Catholic, very religious, she will not use contraception, so I am forced to sleep with other women. It is very sad.'

'That,' said Georgie pensively, 'is the biggest load of bull-shit I have heard in a long time.'

'Yes,' Juan admitted. 'It is. But many women believe me!'

'I'll bet.'

Gradually, the terrace emptied. So did Georgie's glass. The remaining staff trickled away and Juan, on late shift, produced a bottle of the local speciality, which was dark in colour, extremely potent and probably poisonous. He poured a lavish measure for both of them.

'It's no good, you know,' Georgie said mournfully. 'No point trying to seduce me. A few years ago, I'd have been your man – sorry, woman – but not now. I'm reformed. It's awful. Anyhow, I'm old enough to be your—' she was going to say *mother*, but changed it '– sister. Older sister.'

'Incest is fun,' said Juan with a commendable command of English.

'What is this stuff?' Georgie demanded, taking a large gulp of her drink.

'*Palo.*'

'It's disgusting. Give me some more.'

By three o'clock the level in the bottle of *palo* had sunk out of sight and Georgie decided it was safe to go to bed. She tottered upstairs, draped over Juan for support. 'Tonight

I sleep in hotel,' he explained, not for the first time. 'You can share my room. I do nothing you don't want.'

'I believe you,' said Georgie. 'That's the trouble. I'd be leaping out of the proverbial frying pan into the fire. I told you, it's no good. Even when I want to, I *don't* want to any more. This love business is destroying my sex life. *And* it's very bad for my credit card.'

Juan looked puzzled, but Georgie couldn't be bothered to go into details. Outside her room, they kissed – not long and lingeringly, but with passionate if brief enthusiasm. Georgie felt better for it. At least it was an honest kiss, if slightly disloyal to Cal. There were no pound signs involved. She said goodnight, swiped her card through the lock, and tiptoed through the gloom to her bed.

Lin was rifling through her most recent photographs – there were none less than two years old – trying to decide which was most appropriate. There were whole albums full of shots of her with Garry or Sean, which obviously wouldn't do, and an ancient studio portrait from the days when she still looked misty-eyed and wholesome, even though her purity had already been lost. It was all shiny with youth and beauty, so she couldn't possibly use it: Ivor would be dreadfully disappointed in the reality, should they ever meet. Maybe she should send him an ugly picture, and give him a pleasant surprise. There was one of her with the twins, making a face because Demmy was waving a dead beetle at her. No: that would put him off the boys as well as her. There was another with Meredith, in which she looked anxious (her usual expression when with her daughter), and a third at a party, in which she looked tired. In the end she settled for one in profile, even though it showed little of her appearance, since at least there were no visible circles under her eyes and the tie-dyed lettuce-leaf outfit she was wearing was still one of her favourites. She scanned it into the computer and typed an accompanying e-mail. '. . . taken a couple of years ago, and not me at my best, but I don't seem to have anything more up-to-date. The furry white cat I'm holding didn't belong to a Bond villain but to one of the boys—' an aspiring Bond villain '– and was run over shortly after. Sandy spent the next few months taking down car numbers and trying to pin the crime on someone in the area.' She didn't mention that, having deduced one of their neighbours was the guilty party, he let the man's tyres down. She didn't feel Ivor needed to know that – or not yet, at any rate.

'The picture mystifies me,' Ivor responded. 'I stare at it and will you to turn towards me. I think you're beautiful, but it's a shy, secret beauty, like a flower that hides its face from the sun. Which, of course, is not what flowers do, as I'm sure you'll tell me. I'm not much of a poet, and less of a botanist.' Like Andy, she thought. I miss the wind off the loch. 'Sorry about the cat. I sometimes think we give children pets in order to introduce them to the concept of grief and loss at an early age. That way, they can make a start on the grownup emotions, and how to deal with them, before the trials of adulthood arrive.' How *wise* he is, thought Lin. He'd make a good father. 'I don't want to press you, but couldn't you bring yourself to send me a full-face shot? Even if it's years old, it'll tell me something about who you were, which is a part of who you are now. I want to know everything about you.'

'All the early pictures of me are with other men,' Lin typed in, and then thought that made her sound like a tart, and deleted it. Finally, she sent him the studio portrait. 'I don't look a millionth that good now,' she told him. 'I don't want you to get the wrong idea. I haven't got fat or anything but I've got older and lived through some difficult times and the gloss has worn off. In those days I was still innocent, but life does things to you, and innocence goes, and you can't get it back.'

'I can see you were beautiful,' Ivor replied. 'I know you still are. Not because of the way you look, but because of who you are. The person I've got to know through our correspondence is beautiful, beautiful inside, and I know it shines out. Innocence is just ignorance with a halo. In children, it's precious, but in a grown woman it would be out of place. As if you still drew stick figures or believed in Father Christmas.'

'Actually,' Lin admitted, 'I do still draw stick figures. I'm not much of an artist. And I write to Santa every year; he just doesn't answer any more. I can't think why.'

'Next Christmas,' Ivor said, 'there'll be a full stocking at the end of your bed, even if I have to climb down the chimney.'

Lin hugged herself at that one, feeling a sudden wonderful glow inside.

Georgie woke late and rolled over, cautiously, to find she was alone. She had missed breakfast (she usually did), the sun was struggling to get round the curtains, and her stomach, once again, was wobbling if not actually churning. She groped for water on the bedside table and in due course found a folded note from Neville. 'Gone for a walk. Back twelve-ish. I think we should talk.' Her heart plummeted, which did her innards no good at all. But there was no point in losing her nerve – if she had any nerve left to lose. After all, what could he do to her? Sue her for coming on holiday under false pretences? Tear up her air-ticket home and leave her to moulder in Mallorca forever? (There could be worse fates.) The truth is, Georgie acknowledged to herself, I've been deceitful, and wrong, and I don't like it. But I *meant* to have sex with him, I truly did. (Didn't she?) The problem was Cal.

And she didn't really like the feeling of being paid for her services. Like a prostitute . . . Before her marriage men had occasionally taken her away for the weekend, but it hadn't made her feel cheap. She'd been madly in lust, and when they picked up the tab it was a plus, not a reason for being there. I shouldn't have come, she thought, six days too late. How do I get out of this one?

'Why did you come here with me?' Neville asked over cold drinks in a secluded corner of the terrace. 'It can't have been for a free holiday. You don't seem to be having much fun. Except,' he added, in a barbed voice, 'with Juan.'

'Oh no,' Georgie said, glad to find one area in which she could plead Not Guilty. 'I didn't – I mean, I haven't – I don't want to be with him any more than with you.' Well, not *much* more. 'That's not it at all.'

'What is it then?' His tone was gentler. 'After all, I'm not exactly repulsive. At least, most women don't think so. This is a first for me.'

The male ego, Georgie thought, suppressing the recollection of his legs. 'I'm sorry,' she said. 'I've behaved very badly. I *wanted* to come away with you – I mean, I thought I did – but when I got here . . . You see, there's someone. Back in England. I thought – I hoped – if I could get away from him, be with a nice guy, like you, then I would get over it; but it didn't work. There isn't any excuse for me. I should've known . . .'

'He dumped you?' Neville inquired.

'No!' Georgie said with a flicker of indignation. 'He loves me. So he says.'

'He's just not a millionaire with a cardiac condition?'

'Married,' Georgie explained, taking conversational short-cuts.

'And he won't leave his wife? Doesn't sound like a good prospect to me.'

She gave him a resumé of the situation, feeling she owed him that much.

'Are you *sure* he loves you?' Neville pursued. 'It's easy to say.'

'Not for him. He isn't some smooth-talking part-time Casanova; I've met plenty of those, I know the type. He's a bad liar. And . . . I'm not young and credulous. No man's ever fooled me – or not for long.' She gave him a look at once beseeching, and regretful, and hopefully just pathetic enough but not too pathetic. 'Anyway, that doesn't matter now. I've used you – deceived you – I didn't mean to, but I did, and now I feel cheap and tacky. I'm sorry: you're a nice guy, you don't deserve it.'

'Isn't being used and let down the usual fate of nice guys?'

'I don't think so. You said most women don't find you repulsive – *I* don't find you repulsive –' except for the legs '– so you don't have to worry. Hell, eligible single men are at a premium nowadays. You could pick and choose.'

'Right now,' he said ruefully, 'I feel like an eligible single mug.'

'Please don't. I'll pay you back.'

'Forget it. You're broke. No need to make matters worse.'

'Oh, I'm used to being broke,' Georgie said. 'If I was out of debt I'd panic.'

'Well,' he said with an effort, 'at least we should be able to get along tonight without any more subterfuge. You won't need to flee into the arms of the barman or indulge in further self-harm.'

'*Self-harm?*'

He produced the packet of senna.

'Oh shit,' said Georgie.

'Appropriate. Were you thinking of giving them to me?'

'Sort of, but I couldn't. So I took them myself.'

'For that at least I'm grateful. Nice to know you have some principles.' He wasn't quite joking.

None, thought Georgie. You just don't understand the practical difficulties.

'I'm going to spend the rest of the day with my friends. I'll see you in the evening. Suit you?'

'Thanks,' Georgie said.

Chapter 8

Love is the fart
Of every heart:
It pains a man when 'tis kept close,
And others doth offend, when 'tis let loose.

JOHN SUCKLING: Love's Offence

I got back from Greece feeling brown and glowing despite
– or perhaps because of – my aborted romance. Georgie,
returning from Mallorca, was brown but didn't seem to glow.
'How did it go?' I asked her, at the first available opportunity. She told me – at length. Lin was absent now
endeavouring to broaden her children's minds (*do* musicals
broaden the mind?) and the two of us had dived into the
usual pub after work to swap holiday sagas.

'Have you told Cal?' I asked.

'That I'm back? He knows.'

'That you didn't sleep with Neville.'

'Why should I?' Georgie said. 'That's like saying I want
to be faithful to him. I *don't* want to. I just can't help it.
Besides, I think we've split up. All he said to me this morning
was *hello*.'

'*Hello* is a start.'

'Not the way he said it,' she retorted.

'Anyway,' I said, 'if you've split up, you can't be faithful to him.'

'Then I'm becoming frigid,' Georgie said miserably. 'That's worse.'

At that juncture Cal himself walked in with another member of the Design Department, who was looking harassed. However, all the Design Department were looking harassed these days. He greeted me politely and Georgie coldly, and headed for the bar.

'You could try talking to him,' I suggested. 'You don't have to tell him about not shagging Neville.'

After a couple of drinks Georgie duly went over to join him. Ten minutes later she was back, her eyes more spark than sparkle. 'He answered me in monosyllables!' she said. '*Me*! How dare he? And he's giving off enough bad vibes for a pneumatic drill.'

'What did you say to him?' I demanded.

'I said I'd had a great holiday.'

'Georgie! Deliberate provocation. No wonder he was a bit abrupt.'

'He doesn't care any more,' she insisted. 'If he did, he'd try to get me back. He wouldn't just go all taciturn and brooding. That doesn't get you anywhere.'

'You're always telling me men aren't logical,' I said. I was facing the bar; Georgie had her back to it. 'If Cal doesn't care,' I went on, 'how come he's just walked out, leaving half a pint of beer undrunk?'

'*Has* he?' Georgie perked up.

'Don't look round.'

'Why not?'

'It's too late: he's already gone. It would have been uncool if you *had* looked.'

'I didn't,' Georgie said. 'Still, I would've liked to see the expression on his face. Did he look heartbroken?'

'No,' I said baldly. 'He looked . . . bitter and angry and sort of cold, as if his face was a frozen crust on top of the bubbling depths of his emotions.'

'You've been overdoing it,' said Georgie. 'With imagery like that, even Jerry Beauman will never make number one.'

'You just don't appreciate real talent,' I said.

Meanwhile, between museums and musicals, Lin was spending every available moment on her computer. Towards the end of the week she telephoned Georgie at work, asking for backup. Since she had yet to patch things up with Cal her Friday night was free, so we picked up bottles and take-away and headed for Kensington. We found Lin looking lit up, as if the sheen of her youth and much-mourned purity had returned. 'You're using a new shine spray,' said Georgie, gazing at the long ripples of her red-gold hair. '*And* light-reflecting foundation.'

'I was experimenting,' Lin admitted. 'But that isn't it. I've met someone.'

We asked the standard questions – *Quis? Quid? Quomodo? Quibus auxiliis?* etc. – and received more than usually vague answers. At intervals the children came in, interrupted, and were dispatched back to the distractions of computer and television. At length the truth came out.

'I haven't exactly *met* him. We've been corresponding by e-mail. He's different from the others – special. You know, normal, definitely not weird, but special. He sent me a photo.'

She conjured the picture on screen, and we studied it accordingly. Even allowing for the fact that it was an obviously flattering snapshot, he looked far too attractive for Internet dating. 'I don't remember him from the website,' Georgie said.

'I didn't find him on the website. We met in a chatroom.'

'I don't like that.' Georgie frowned. 'On the websites people

have to register, you can check back if there's anything suspect
– at least I think so. But in a chatroom you could run into
anyone. He could be an axe-murderer—'

'*You* had the axe-murderer,' I said. 'Anyway, his eyes seem
quite far apart, and his mother-complex isn't showing.'

'I thought you'd be pleased for me,' Lin said.

'We are,' I assured her, nudging Georgie unseen. 'We just
want you to be a bit careful.'

'Georgie wasn't particularly careful with her cardiac
millionaires.'

'Of course I—'

This time, I trod on her foot. 'Where are you meeting him?'
I asked Lin.

'I haven't decided yet. I wanted your advice. He suggested
dinner, but I thought that was too much, too soon. I don't
want to rush into anything. Maybe lunch . . .'

'Coffee,' Georgie said. 'Somewhere *very* public. And we're
coming with you.'

'Don't be silly!' Lin almost snapped. 'I can't turn up with
a couple of bodyguards. That would look ridiculous.'

'We'll be at an adjacent table,' Georgie said, warming to
her theme. 'In disguise.'

'Hiding behind newspapers,' I embellished. 'With eyeholes
cut in them.'

'You'll be *several* tables away,' Lin said. 'I've got to decide
on a location quickly. We're meeting tomorrow – Vee's taking
the twins away, and Meredith's at a friend's house, so it's a
good opportunity. I have to send Ivor an e-mail tonight.'

We settled on a coffee-shop near Harvey Nicks, and sat
down to the takeaway, the wine, and a video of Lin's choice.
Inevitably, it was *You've Got Mail*, which so disgusted the
children they retreated to their rooms, if not to bed, disappearing into a world of virtual reality. 'I don't like it,' Georgie
reiterated, when Lin went out of the room.

'I think it's sweet,' I said.

'Not the film. Lin's fella. For one thing, he's got dimples.'

'What's wrong with that?'

'I hate men with dimples. They're like lifeboats on the *Titanic*, fine for women and children but only dishonourable men would go for them.'

'He probably can't help having dimples,' I pointed out. 'Anyhow, he's not your date.'

Lin's return put paid to the discussion, but Georgie's doubts were such that the next day, at her insistence, we arrived at the rendezvous fully three-quarters of an hour in advance. 'It gives us time to check out the terrain,' Georgie said. 'Like the SAS.'

'Case the joint,' I retorted. 'Like a burglar.'

About twenty minutes later my mobile rang. It was Lin. 'I've changed my mind,' she said, in the hurried tone of someone who wants to give unpopular news as quickly as possible. 'I e-mailed Ivor again this morning. I didn't think the atmosphere in the café was quite right. The tables are too close together.'

Like axe-murderer's eyes, I thought. 'Where are you meeting him?'

'Waitrose.'

'*Waitrose*? The cafeteria? – If there is one.'

'The fish counter.'

'But *Lin*—'

'It's a public place,' she said defensively. 'Very public. I feel safe there. And you two won't be so obvious.'

'We'll never get there,' I said.

'I put it back till two.'

We fled the café, almost forgetting to pay the bill, and arrived at the nearest Waitrose at a sprint, three minutes before zero hour. I seized a trolley and threw in a few items at random in order to look like a shopper. Georgie, meanwhile, was asking the way to the fish counter. We did our best to set off at speed, but in the Saturday crowd it was impossible. 'She did this deliberately!' Georgie hissed. I wasn't sure. Lin's motives, I suspected, had been mixed. She had evidently been discouraged by her unsuccessful evening with Derek. Here, if there was no instant rapport between her and Ivor, she could make a quick getaway without being trapped at a table for the duration of coffee. Equally, I thought – like Georgie – that she didn't really want us two trailing along. Perhaps she feared she might be making a fool of herself, and wanted to do so without an audience – even an audience of her friends. I could sympathise with that. I tried to explain this, but Georgie was too busy panicking. 'She met him in a chatroom!' she kept repeating. 'Everyone knows they're frequented solely by paedophiles—'

'Lin's grown up.'

'– and psychos and—'

'There she is!'

Lin was standing beside a montage of whole salmon and tiger prawns, an unconvincingly empty basket on her arm. She seemed to be very still, as if frozen in a moment of time. A couple of yards away was the man in the photograph. Ivor. He was instantly recognisable although the dimples weren't in evidence, dark blond hair recently shorn, his gaze fixed on Lin. He, too, had an empty basket. In a film, the whole super-market would have gone quiet, and the air between them would be glimmering with fairy dust. I remember thinking: Oh my God . . . It was the classic eyemeet across a crowded room. The bodyguards were redundant or forgotten. Presently, they moved a little closer. He spoke; she answered. Then he took her arm, leading her away. We tracked them to a nearby coffee-shop, saw them seated at a table, clearly absorbed in each other, oblivious to the rest of the universe. He smiled at something she said; the dimples danced and vanished.

'I don't like him!' Georgie whispered.

'Shut up,' I said. 'Spoilsport. Just because we aren't having any luck with men doesn't mean Lin can't have any either.'

'I'm *not* unlucky with men,' Georgie protested, punctured in the ego. 'Things are just a little confused right now.'

We left them to it. Later that afternoon Lin telephoned, bubbled, sparkled – the verbal equivalent of champagne. She didn't want to get carried away, but he was wonderful. They were totally on the same wavelength. She'd got worried at the last minute – hence the change of venue – but her apprehension had been unnecessary. Their eyes had met and she'd known, somehow, deep inside, that this was her soulmate. It hadn't been that way with Sean, or even Garry – that miraculous instant magic. The pangs she had experienced for Andy, love or nostalgia or regret, were gone without trace. This was the Real Thing. 'You promised you weren't going to rush it!' Georgie wailed from over my shoulder. 'You met him in a *chatroom*.' You said the future of dating was on the Internet, Lin reminded her. Be happy for me – please. Don't rain on my parade.

'Of course we're happy for you,' I said. 'But . . . don't go too fast. Good relationships take time.' I'd rushed into things with Nigel, and learned my mistake the hard way.

Lin assured us that she had no intention of going too fast. They'd gone to lunch after Waitrose, then tea, but she wasn't seeing him on Sunday. They would merely swap e-mails every half-hour. He was going to print out all their correspondence for her; someday they might publish it. Like the epistolary romances written in the Victorian age. They would be having dinner together on Thursday: the twins were in the Isle of Wight and Meredith would be at a sleep-over (an invitation plainly issued by parents who didn't know her well).

'How does he feel about the kids?' I asked.

He was a teacher, he was great with kids, it went with his job.

When she rang off, I said to Georgie: 'It does happen, you know. A friend of my sister's e-mailed some guy in Canada for six months, then she flew over, married him, and lived happily ever after.'

'How long for?'

'Nearly a year so far. Anyway . . .'

'All right,' said Georgie. 'I expect it's just sour grapes on my part. I want Lin to be happy – of course I do. I suppose – I'm not much of a believer in romance. I did it myself: remember? Me and Franco, that was romance. Our eyes met across a crowded ball – *and* we were masked, so it wasn't easy. I told you, I fell for him *because* it was romantic – Venice, the carnival, his panto-title, his amazing looks – and I'm afraid Lin's doing the same. Falling for the romance, not the man.'

'In *Waitrose*?' I said.

'Oh, yes. It's very trendy to start a relationship in a super-market nowadays. Don't you see the ads? Mind you, I don't think it would work if it was Asda.'

We had returned to her house and, by unspoken consent, I went in for further confabulation. Over Earl Grey tea and lemon Georgie grew increasingly despondent.

'I was mean about Lin and her Ivor,' she declared. 'Mean and jealous and vile. Just because he's got dimples and she met him in a chatroom . . . I should be so lucky. He did look nice – and attractive – and genuine. I didn't meet anyone a millionth that dishy through my ad. He'd better have some faults or it really will be unbearable.'

'Maybe he sucks his tea through his teeth,' I said, thinking of one of Nigel's less appealing habits. 'Or tries to endear himself to his pupils by being into Eminem. Or eats brown rice and farts a lot.'

'You can see he doesn't do that,' Georgie objected, and, lowering the tone as ever: 'Perhaps he's just got a small dick.'

'Lin might not mind. After all, Size Isn't Everything.' I managed to speak in capital letters.

'Hmm. I've always thought she had a soul above such things.' We considered Lin's soul for a minute.

'It's time you told Cal about not sleeping with Neville,' I said. 'Then you'd be happy too. Broke, but happy. Right now you're unhappy *and* broke.'

'I *did* tell him,' Georgie said. 'He didn't believe me.'

There was a depressed silence. 'Are you sure it's the Real Thing with Cal,' I asked, invoking more capitals, 'or is it just romance?'

'It ain't romance,' Georgie said. 'He was the office lech, for Christ's sake. He had a sexy smile and a great body. It was just a fun way of passing the time. I never thought he could get under my skin – until it was too late.' She took a mouthful of cold tea, and resumed unexpectedly: 'I used to be a starfucker, before Franco. I try to make a joke of it now, but in those days I *really* went for the fame thing. I had an affair with a TV presenter for years – he said we had to keep it quiet, he didn't want the paparazzi pursuing us. I thought he was serious about me – one day we'd go public – get married. I fantasised about doing the stuff Lin hated: *Hello!* mag and the tabloids. Basking in his reflected glory. Well, he went public, but not with me. She was an up-and-coming actress, not even pretty but she added gravitas to his image. They were a golden couple – for fifteen minutes. He still wanted to go on seeing me, though. But I ended it. I felt such a fool. I was disillusioned with the world of the glitterati – I wanted something *sincere*. Ha. So I went to Italy, and fell for Romance. Trading one fantasy for another. I was still a fool.' She concluded, bleakly: '*J'accuse* . . . me. A fool forever.'

'What happened to the TV presenter?' I inquired.

'The actress divorced him and went on to higher things, and he fell from grace and ended up in digital radio. So it's just as well I didn't marry him, really. I'd have been awfully disappointed.'

'In fact, you'd be perfectly fine now,' I said, 'if you weren't in debt. And if Cal wasn't married.'

'Too many ifs. I always said my wish was the most difficult. Lin seems to have got hers, and you look sensational—'

'I could use a man to prove it.'

'What you need is an occasion at which to shine,' Georgie maintained. 'It's high time we gave it some thought. That's better than moping or gnawing my liver – in any case, gloom and envy don't suit me. We want a major event – an awards ceremony or something. A chance for you to wear a posh dress that shows off your curves.'

'I don't have one,' I said.

'You will, Oscar, you will. What's coming up on the party front? There's the Mallory launch – but that's not glam enough. A Sci-Fi do at Waterstone's – no. That'll be all geeks and nerds. What about the Ultraphone Poetry Awards? They're being televised this year.'

'*Are* they?' I said, impressed. Poetry rarely made TV.

'It's only BBC4, so it doesn't really count, but everyone will dress up for the cameras. They're holding the do at the Reform Club. That's a cool location since it featured in the Bond movie. I was going to get something new myself.'

'No,' I said. 'Think *debt load*.'

'I tell you what,' Georgie said, grinning like a Cheshire cat, 'if you get a new dress, and I go with you, that'll do instead. How about it?'

I gave in, not too reluctantly. 'As long as I don't end up contributing to the debt mountain as well.'

Georgie didn't comment.

* * *

At work next week we had to spend far too much time being bored by interminable details of Lin's meeting with Ivor, his many perfections, and all the amazing things he had said to her, by phone, text, and e-mail, since then. As Georgie was in the office with her, she got the worst of it. But of course, this is what friendship is all about. You suffer the ongoing saga of your friends' joys and sorrows so you can impose on them in your turn. And, while a trouble shared is, if not precisely halved, at least spread around, happiness should be communicable. Which was why it bothered me that, although I was happy for Lin, it took a bit of an effort. Unlike Georgie, I didn't have any major reservations about chatrooms, or even dimples. My doubts, I feared, were rooted in a sort of cynicism which filled me with secret shame. I couldn't really believe in that eyes-across-the-room thing. Lust at first sight, yes, but the L-word Lin kept using wasn't lust. It was fine in books – you could get away with anything in books – but reality was always somehow more mundane, short on glitter-dust, and much harder work. In my admittedly limited experience, it still seemed vaguely wrong to me that love could just *happen*. You should have to slog at it, to build it up brick by brick, fill in the cracks, putty the window-frames, install central heating. You couldn't just buy the whole edifice ready-made. Lin was opting for instant love, which is rather like instant coffee, a distant cousin of the real thing with much less flavour.

(Sorry about the mixed metaphors.)

Maybe – like Georgie – I was trying to justify feelings based on envy, because Lin's wish had been fulfilled and she was floating on a pink cloud of bliss. I half hoped, half feared that – at least jealousy was commonplace.

Maybe my relationship with Nigel had soured me, leaving me bitter and twisted, unwilling to believe in anything good.

I told Lin how pleased I was for her, I agreed that Ivor

sounded wonderful, that the lightning-strike of true love had come to her at last. But behind my words the niggle persisted, an ugly little worm of doubt. 'We need to meet him,' said Georgie. 'Then we'll know if he's okay.' She had every confidence in her own judgement, but I wasn't so sure. I had failed to suss out Nigel, after all. 'Go slow,' we advised Lin – Lin with fairy-dust in her eyes, and a radiance about her of youth renewed.

'I know,' she said. 'I'm going to be sensible. I'm too old to be swept off my feet again.'

But she didn't look sensible.

On Thursday, they had their first dinner date. Lin, who never agonised over what to wear, agonised over what to wear. Her wardrobe consisted mainly of skirts and dresses with tie-dyed or batik patterns, curly embroidery and ragged hemlines, but she wondered if she ought to borrow something off Georgie. Should she look more sophisticated? 'Look the way you want to look,' Georgie said. 'Look like yourself.' Evidently it went down well with Ivor. He told her she was beautiful – which was true, but no man had said it to her for some time – and that he didn't like women in lots of makeup or over-priced designer clothes. He had always dreamed of finding a woman like a Pre-Raphaelite painting, pale and pure and untouched by whatever trials and tribulations life had thrown in her way.

Pure, thought Lin. I'm pure again. I've rediscovered my innocence . . .

When they went to bed together, on the Saturday, she confided that she had felt like a virgin.

'Ugh!' said Georgie, but only to me.

On the Wednesday, he came to Ransome and met us all for lunch.

He was definitely attractive, I decided, though slightly too boyish for my taste. Not that he was in any way like

Nigel: it was a manly boyishness, as if maturity and assurance were overlaid by a patina of youthful enthusiasm, possibly an essential in dealing with teenagers and pre-teens – though another teacher that I knew said he preferred a machine gun. Georgie encouraged him to talk about his job and he responded initially with flippancy ('Try reading Milton to a chimpanzee'), then with flashes of something more earnest. 'I know it's a cliché, but children are the future. If I can broaden one tiny mind – eradicate one prejudice passed on by the parents – open the window of opportunity an inch or two for someone who can't spell *window*, let alone *opportunity* – Well, anyway, that's the aim. You can't do more than that. I'll be lucky to achieve as much.' He taught in a school in South London, with pupils from mixed social backgrounds with assorted religious and ethnic origins. His subjects were English, History and Current Events. I couldn't help being impressed.

When Lin went to the Ladies, he said: 'I'm glad of the chance to have a word with you two on our own. I know you're Lin's best friends: she's told me a lot about you. You must feel very protective towards her—'

'No,' said Georgie, showing hackle.

Ivor looked nonplussed, for the first time thrown off his stride.

'She's an adult,' Georgie said. 'Why should we feel protective? She can look after herself.' Bullshit, of course, but at least Ivor was disconcerted.

He struggled to pick up his thread again. 'Anyway, you care about her a great deal. Everybody must: she's so gentle, so lovely . . . I want to tell you that I would never hurt her. I really do love her. This must seem very quick to you – though we got to know each other by e-mail over several weeks—'

'Three,' Georgie said. 'Not exactly several. Three weeks.'

'I'm not sure. It seemed longer. We had so much to say, swapped so many ideas . . . When we met, it was the same for both of us. A sort of recognition . . . I don't know if it's ever happened to you.'

'No.' Georgie again.

'From now on, I'm going to take care of her,' Ivor persisted. 'Nothing and no one's going to hurt her again. You don't have to worry about her any more.'

'We weren't worried,' Georgie snapped.

Afterwards, when we had left Lin alone with him, she declared sweepingly: 'He's a phoney.'

'He sounded okay when he talked about teaching,' I said. 'Anyhow, it's always hard for a guy to explain his – his intentions to family and friends. Think of the prospective groom in *Father of the Bride*. Sincerity is difficult to do when you really mean it.'

'I've never tried,' Georgie admitted.

'English isn't a good language for expressing genuine feelings,' I asserted, profoundly. 'We're too reserved – too ironic – the stiff upper lip – the floppy lower lip – all that stuff. It works better in French.'

'*Merde*,' said Georgie.

Two days later, Ivor and Lin had their second dinner date, and he moved in.

I'm running ahead of myself here. Lin's new romance wasn't the only thing happening in our lives at that time, but once you pick up a story-line, it's simpler to run with it until you reach a convenient place to stop, regardless of any action on the side. I know that's not how it's done, of course. I managed better in the previous chapter, jumping about from scene to scene, following everyone at once. Modern writers usually do it that way, and if they don't, editors are supposed to

228

correct them. Today's reader – so we are told – has a short attention span and is easily confused. The book is competing with other distractions: the portable CD player, the computer screen with all its charms, the conversation of fellow travellers on train or tube. So the reader needs to be able to dip in and out of a book without getting lost. Zooming to and fro in time is therefore discouraged (except in fantasy and SF, where you can get away with anything, on the assumption that your readers are sad freaks who have few distractions in their lives and, as a result, phenomenal powers of concentration). However . . .

Going back a few days, I took Todd Jarman to lunch. This is traditional after intensive editorial effort and an equally strenuous response from the author: in theory, it's a treat for the latter, but in practice it should be a treat for both. Of course, a few editors disdain tradition, and some authors don't want to see any more of their colleagues than is strictly necessary (this is called being a recluse, and is generally popular with publishers), but overall the custom has survived, unlike the defunct wood-panelling and gentlemanly contracts of yore. The literary lunch remains a staple of doing business in the publishing world.

I looked forward to my date with Jarman (if you could call it that) with mixed feelings. I didn't like him, naturally I didn't, he was arrogant and difficult and a pain to work with. But I'd enjoyed editing his book, being difficult back – I'd been exhilarated by the sense of freedom I experienced, so far only with him, the freedom to be spiky, provocative, even offensive. With anyone else, the smart remarks – if they occurred to me – stayed in my head. And at a previous meeting, he'd been almost complimentary about my figure, though Helen Aucham would doubtless still consider me a lump. More than almost. Of course, perhaps he was merely being kind, perish the thought – but saturnine types aren't usually given to that sort of kindness. It doesn't go with saturnity. Anyhow, rejecting the charms of Mean Cuisine, I hovered indecisively over several possibilities before consulting Georgie. Like all the best PR people, she knows every restaurant worth knowing and can get a table at short notice even in the most sought-after venues. 'The Gay Hussar,' she said promptly, when I had explained my requirements. 'Leave it to me.'

She was looking a little happier that day, almost back to normal levels of vivacity. Apparently, she and Cal had had a brief but polysyllabic exchange that morning, which indicated the ice might be about to thaw.

'Don't push it,' I advised. 'Let him come to you.' As if I would've done any such thing. It's so easy to know the right moves – for other people.

'It's okay,' she said. 'I'm older than you: remember?' When not bewailing her advanced years, she makes use of them. 'I've been around the block – much too often. I can be patient.'

I didn't comment. Patience is *not* one of Georgie's virtues.

However, she sent me an e-mail shortly after confirming the booking at the restaurant and I met Todd Jarman there later that week.

On the way, I found myself thinking about his hero, D.I. Jake Hatchett – a far more complex piece of self-portraiture than Jerry Beauman's Disneyfied alter ego. The Beauman character resembled the original only in the most superficial, rose-tinted way, Jerry as he wished to be seen, or possibly as he saw himself: trusting, wronged, oozing noble qualities, yet intelligent and capable of outwitting his enemies. Having worked with Jerry, I was quite prepared to believe that he suppressed any awareness of his own cunning, manipulative, criminal nature, or any of the defects which had earned him public derision and private disdain. He saw himself as a one-dimensional, cardboard figure, and wrote (or tried to write) accordingly. But Todd had penned his own likeness with perception, some depth, a glimmering of artistic truth. That's a quality you can't define, but you always know when it's there. Hatchett was mean and moody, difficult to get along with, a pain to colleagues who failed to understand the ragged principles to which he clung. Those in authority rarely praised him, even when he got his man – which, of course, he usually did. In some ways the classic hero-cop, he was a survivor rather than a success, cast in a mould that has actually varied little from Dirty Harry to Inspector Morse. But he was also self-doubting, occasionally wrong-headed, a failure in his relationships, above all, a man who made mistakes. And Hatchett, beneath his gritty exterior, was capable of the odd act of kindness, though only to homeless alkies or junkies, a rent-boy dying of AIDS, a whore whose 'eart of gold had been transformed into lead by the touch-stone of life. (He would have had no time to be kind to a dumpy bourgeoise with an Oxford degree who presumed to tell him how to be a good cop.) Jarman saw the world as a dark, violent, grubby place where Hatchett walked alone, trying to change some small thing for the better, and gener-ally failing.

On which thought I reached the restaurant, and there he was, not looking mean and moody but actually quite welcoming, in a saturnine sort of way. I apologised for my lateness (five minutes), pleading a meeting which had overrun, though in fact I'd simply miscalculated how long it would take me to get there. I don't normally drink at lunchtime – it makes me sleepy for the whole afternoon – but Todd was already nursing a whisky and when we came to order I decided, rashly, to share a bottle of wine.

'Good,' Todd said. 'I hate drinking alone. It makes me feel like an alcoholic.'

D.I. Hatchett, I recalled, *did* drink alone, often. There were frequent scenes of gloomy introspection over a solitary glass of something or other. 'Your character does,' I said. 'Are you like him?' I'd never ventured to comment on the parallels before.

He made a wry face. 'I suppose most authors resemble their main characters,' he said. 'But Hatchett drinks more than me. The stress of his job. Being a writer isn't nearly so stressful – or at least, it wasn't until I started to work with you.' But his tone was light, mocking; he even smiled. 'Mind you, I'd like to drink more heavily, only my body won't let me. Getting to middle age, I'm afraid. Heavy drinking means heavy hangovers. I don't fancy that.'

'You're not middle-aged,' I found myself saying, confusedly. 'Middle age starts at fifty . . . or more.'

'What am I then?' he asked, looking quizzical.

I fished for a word, and found one. 'Mature,' I declared. 'Like – like Stilton.'

'I see. Improved flavour, but smelly. Sounds appropriate. Anyway, Hatchett's younger and tougher than me, though he's probably ruining his liver. Fortunately, political correctness hasn't caught up with him yet.'

'How much like you is he?' I pursued, feeling daring.

'Much better in a fight. I keep fairly fit, but it's years since I was involved in a punch-up. On the other hand, I've got more brains. I always know who-dunnit and why. I give him the clues, but he can be bloody obtuse. It usually takes him a whole book to catch on.'

'Good thing too,' I said. 'Otherwise we'd both be out of business.'

'Am I too obvious?' He sounded almost diffident, a trace of Hatchett's self-doubt creeping in. 'I can't tell. How quickly do you get it?'

I hesitated before answering, realising he was genuinely

worried. 'Fairly quickly. But I'm supposed to. I read differently from other people – more analytically – I have to, I'm an editor. I started reading Agatha Christie when I was twelve, and after I'd got through a couple and sussed out her style I *always* guessed the murderer. If you haven't cheated, if you've given the reader all the info, the final twist shouldn't really be a surprise, more a revelation. Only most readers get caught up in the story, and so they race through without stopping to think. That's how it's done. The quickness of the pen deceives the brain. Judging by your sales, you do it very well.'

'You're paying me compliments,' he said lightly. 'Now I *know* this is a special occasion.' But he looked pleased.

'Hatchett has a very sombre view of life,' I went on. 'It's all poverty, and deprivation, and despair, and rich people who are indifferent or corrupt or both, and people in power who abuse their position. Is that how you see things?'

'Now, the difficult questions,' he said. 'Yes. And no. It's . . . how I feel I *ought* to see things, because I suspect that's how they are. I'm privileged – insulated – I go to dinner parties in Hampstead and Islington with other privileged, insulated people – when I feel I should lead a more useful life, I should try to change things. So I lead the life I *should* be leading in fantasy, and make money out of it. Sounds pretty contemptible, doesn't it? I even let myself like people, sometimes. Hatchett's a morose sort of bastard – he doesn't like anyone much. Especially writers.'

'Books can change things,' I insisted. 'They help people to see . . .'

'That's the sop I throw to my conscience,' he said. 'When it needs sops.'

'And you *should* let yourself like people. There are good guys out there. Your Helen . . .'

'You don't care for her much, do you?' he said with

disconcerting acuity. 'Don't bother to deny it: I can hear the effort in your voice whenever you mention her. She does good, yes, but . . . she knows it. In recent years I think she's become a little too sure of her own rectitude. Like a pillar of the church in the Victorian age. She disregards people who don't need her help or whom she feels don't deserve her attention. Now I'm doing it again – criticising my girlfriend – you'll be down on me like a ton of bricks. But I noticed she was offhand with you: she does that sometimes. Don't let it upset you. She cares desperately about her clients, and I think, on a subconscious level, she feels that fulfils her quota of caring. She wasn't like that when I first knew her, but since she became successful . . .'

'You've been with her a long time, haven't you?' I said, thinking it was rather a waste. 'You're obviously much better at relationships than Hatchett.'

'Don't you believe it. I was married at twenty-two: we were madly in love, or what we thought was love, and rushed in where angels fear to tread. It came apart because I wanted to write and wasn't making enough money. My wife left me, but she said it was my fault, and she was probably right. I have a teenage son who's only just got around to forgiving me.'

'Do you see him?' I asked, tentatively. 'On a regular basis, I mean.'

'Yes, of course. But it hasn't been easy. My ex imbued him with the idea that I'd failed both of them. I was supposed to be a solicitor, you see, but I chucked it before I'd done my articles. Maybe that's why I started dating Helen. A latent attraction to the Law.'

I remembered what he'd said about the importance of justice. 'You think you were wrong to give it up,' I said. 'You think you should have been more like her, fighting for human rights. But you can influence more people with books, really you can. And you're a good writer. You mightn't have been a good lawyer.'

He laughed suddenly, his face lightening. 'What a sensible girl you are! All right, enough of me. You've asked all the questions so far. Now it's my turn.'

As lunch progressed, I remember feeling vaguely disturbed that we weren't arguing. After all, it was the arguing which had been fun – wasn't it? But he was unexpectedly easy to talk to. And since he'd been so open about himself, I felt it was only fair to tell him a little about me. More than a little, in the end. I told him about my childhood, about being fat, the diet, my job at Ransome, and my secret ambition to be a writer too.

'When you've done something,' he said, 'let me criticise it. Then I can get my own back.'

But I didn't tell him about the three wishes – that was girl stuff – or the story I'm trying to write, this story: it wouldn't be his sort of thing.

We worked our way through fish balls and creamed spinach (me) and veal with red cabbage (him), avoiding the inevitable jokes about fish and balls. I didn't eat much; I was too busy talking. Or listening.

'I like this place,' he said. (Clever Georgie.) 'I haven't been here in ages. Helen says Eastern European food's too fattening.'

'She's right,' I said guiltily.

'Don't you lose any more weight. I meant what I said the other week. You look fine as you are.'

'Men always say that,' I retorted. 'And then they go out with very thin women.'

'Touché! But she wasn't so thin when I—'

'You said.'

Suddenly, we were both silent. One of those silences that sneaks up on you and takes over, more forceful than words.

But it didn't feel awkward, more – expectant. A tingly kind of silence. We stared at each other until embarrassment kicked in, and I felt myself starting to blush. I *hate* blushing.

'I must be getting back,' I said hastily, hoping the blush hadn't yet made itself visible.

And Todd, at the same moment: 'Time I made a move.'

We chatted in a desultory way while Ransome took care of the bill, and said goodbye on a handshake. Maybe it was my imagination that he held my hand just a little too long.

That weekend, something awful happened. So awful that I blush to remember it, even worse than I blushed in the restaurant, the kind of blush that makes you hot all over and goes right down between your legs. When I started writing this book (if it ever becomes a book) I knew there would have to be spicy bits: you can't have this type of novel without spicy bits nowadays. But I didn't want to write about *real* sex – it's too personal, too special; putting it on public view feels like a betrayal of your partner. (Georgie said that was nonsense, and she was happy to give me all the graphic details of her sessions with Cal, but I refused.) So I've written about fantasy sex instead – I don't have any inhibitions about that. I can't imagine Hugh Jackman etc. would mind: it's all pure fiction, even to the roles they play. I would never imagine having sex with an actor as *himself*; that wouldn't be any fun at all. I'd never fantasised about real people, on screen or off, though once or twice I'd tried. Which is why it was such a shock when . . .

Let's start again. Nigel's friend Terry Carver had sent me his children's story just before I went to Crete, but I didn't want to take it with me and I hadn't made time for it until now. I'd e-mailed him confirming receipt and said I would get back to him asap, so on the Saturday afternoon I decided to tackle it. I'm not much of a judge of the genre, but I

thought it was good, and should be passed on to the relevant imprint with a vote of confidence from me. But for all
the merits of the story, I found it hard to concentrate. My
mind kept wandering off at vague tangents and having to be
hauled ruthlessly back on track. In the evening I went to a
barbecue in Hampstead (I thought of Todd and his dinner
parties) which promised a selection of single men, but I left
early. It was too hot to go near the brazier, too hot for hot
food, and the men seemed immature and dull – or mature
and dull – or just dull.

The flat, too, was sweltering. Mandy was restless and
whiny, evidently wanting to get out of his fur, but short of
a shave there was little I could do about that. I lay in a luke-
warm bath to cool down, offering to lift him in with me,
but even the worst heatwave won't drive a cat to water. He
quietened down later, once he had turned up his nose at
dinner and put me in my place to his own satisfaction. I lit
some candles – they don't give out any significant heat – and
lay on the sofa since the bedroom, under the roof, was
horribly stuffy. I was thinking about Todd, re-running
extracts from our lunch-date. Gradually, I found my fancy
roaming down unknown avenues. Supposing he'd come to
the barbecue . . . Or we might meet at a dinner party, on an
evening when Helen couldn't make it, and we'd be seated
together, talking exclusively to each other, unaware of the
people around us. My imagination fabricated various conversations, all of which, like tributaries, flowed naturally into
the same stream of thought. In due course, he would take
me home. (By taxi: we'd been drinking.)

Back at my flat, he came in for coffee. I didn't offer; he
didn't ask; it just happened. I was moving round the kitchen
doing the usual things with a cafetière when I found he was
studying me the way he had once before, the time he said:
'Stand up'; that dispassionate, assessing gaze, as if I was a

237

horse for sale. Yet somehow it *wasn't* dispassionate, and I didn't feel at all like a horse. 'You have a great body,' he said. 'Really great. Don't diet any more. Leave everything . . . just . . . the way it is.' His eyes rested a fraction too long on my breasts. I wasn't wearing anything particularly revealing, but it felt like it. Hastily, I returned to coffee-making.

'Black, no sugar, isn't it?' I said.

It was.

I poured him a drink (in my fantasy, there was whisky in the flat) and he took it from me, standing very close, looking down at me – he's much taller – in a strange, unsaturnine fashion, his face set, focused, as I had seen it sometimes bent over the manuscript. It was curious how much I'd noticed his expressions when we'd been together, how clearly I could re-create them in my mind. When he accepted the glass his hand touched mine, a touch that made me warm all over, in fancy and in fact.

In the living room we sat down on the sofa, side by side. Mandelson checked Todd out with his customary scornful air; I apologised for his haughty manners and explained the origin of his name. Todd laughed. (That was another expression I'd learned: how the lines in his cheeks deepened and crooked around his mouth.) We talked about writing, and life, and how, like Jake Hatchett, relationships had never worked out for him. 'Maybe the real problem,' he said, 'is that I've never found the right woman.'

'Not even Helen?' I asked, daringly. It's easy to be daring in your imagination.

'Helen and I aren't great together any more. I fell for her because she was a lawyer – because I admired her high ideals – she represented the route I thought I should have taken, the career I should have had. I always feel I copped out, being a writer.'

'No you didn't,' I objected, passionately. 'You write wonderful books. You mightn't have had wonderful court cases. Anyhow, in books they always get the right guy. As I understand it, it doesn't always happen that way in court.'

He laughed again – I was good at making him laugh – and put down his drink, and then his arm was around me, and he was coming closer, closer, and I couldn't escape, I didn't want to, and his mouth reached mine, and we were kissing and kissing, tongues entwined, his free hand exploring my breast. In a tiny corner of my brain I was horrified at myself, because this was a real person, not a boyfriend or casual lover but someone I *worked* with, and at some future stage I would have to face him (hopefully not for ages), with the guilty memory of this moment lingering in my head. But I couldn't stop. He was undressing me, slowly, exploring my body with unhurried skill, but behind the restraint I sensed a growing urgency, akin to desperation. And then he was on top of me, and I felt his crotch jutting against me, the hard ridge of his erection straining at his flies. Now was the time to call a halt, before it was too late – but it was already too late.

'We mustn't,' I whispered, in fantasy. 'We work together. How will I be able to look you in the face after this?'

'The usual way.' A hint of saturnity came and went. 'With your eyes. You have beautiful eyes, did you know?'

(No. Surely he wouldn't have said that.)

But what he said didn't matter any more. He was unfastening his jeans, and his cock stood up like a great tower – probably Pisa, from the angle – impossibly massive, the swollen helmet with its cleft like a ripe red fruit, and then he was opening me with his finger, melting me, turning me into cream, until at last I felt him nudging at me for entry, pushing into me, and into me, and *into* me . . . I came with a violence and intensity that left me gasping and shattered, and emerged from the lost world of my imagination to find I was lying half on, half off the sofa, and the candles were guttering, and Mandy was sitting bolt upright staring at me with chilly disapproval.

'All right,' I said when I had got my breath back. (I said it out loud because I do talk to my cat, confident that he will never repeat anything.) 'It was a mistake, okay? A – a one-night stand.' Except I was the only person who had stood, unless you counted the massive organ of my fevered invention. 'At least, when we meet again, he won't know why I'm cringing with embarrassment. And I *can* control my blushing, if I practise.' How do you practise blush control?

It was the heat, that was the trouble. It might have been too darned hot for Marilyn Monroe, but it was never too hot for me. I went into the kitchen and got myself a cooling glass of water, daubing some more between my legs, an agreeable sensation. 'Anyway,' I said to myself, 'ten-to-one you exaggerated the size of his cock. A hundred-to-one. Nobody could possibly be that big.' I had a dim recollection of hearing something about big noses indicating bigness elsewhere. I visualised Todd's nose, which was undeniably aquiline. Hmm . . . Or was it big feet?

I resolved not to dwell on the subject, and lay down again on the sofa, unable to sleep, dwelling on it for some time.

The great thing about Lin's love-life, I reflected when I was back at work, was that it distracted me from my own. I seemed to have drifted further into the realms of fantasy than usual – after all, there was no concrete alternative – with added complications too hideous to contemplate. What I needed was something else to get really worked up about.

'What is she *doing*?' Georgie demanded after we'd heard

the news about Ivor moving in. 'She's only known him a few minutes. He could be a complete psycho. Talk to her.'

'Why me?' I said, startled. 'You're much better at talking to people about things. It's your job.'

'This isn't work, it's personal,' Georgie said unarguably. 'You're tactful. Anyhow, she keeps begging me not to piss on her parade.'

'Rain,' I said. '*Rain* on her parade. Look, I know they're moving a bit fast, but it could work out all right. Just because he's got dimples—'

'Never trust a man with dimples,' Georgie reiterated. 'Not on his face, at least. She said she wasn't going to rush into anything, and now look at her.'

'Even if I *did* talk to her,' I said, 'd'you think she'd listen?'

That one was unanswerable.

'He was living in this crummy little flat,' Lin said. 'Peely wallpaper, and brown stains in the bath. He'd sold his last place and was going to buy somewhere new, but the deal fell through. So he had lots of money in the bank but nowhere to live, and he had to rent something quickly. I was horrified when I saw it, the flat was so scuzzy, and the landlady was like a caricature, all tight lips and curlers. So when he stayed with me on Saturday we talked about it, and decided he should move in with me. He's given her a month's notice, but he's bringing his stuff over this week.'

'How do the children feel about it?' I said guardedly.

'You know how kids are.' Lin looked faintly discomfited. 'They're not good at changes. Ivor's great with them, though. He says they'll get used to him in no time. He bought the boys a new computer game, so they're starting to think he's okay.'

'He's a con man,' Georgie confided later. 'Cheap rented flat, *pretends* he's got money in the bank, plausible cover story. Pretty soon, he's going to be after her to invest.'

'Lin hasn't anything to invest *with*,' I said.

'Ivor doesn't know that,' Georgie argued. 'He sees her living in a big house in Kensington – celebrity exes – all the trimmings. You can bet he thinks she's rolling in it.'

'Then when he finds out the truth, he'll be off,' I said. It didn't cheer us up.

Georgie was propping herself against my desk during this exchange, and straightened up quickly at the approach of Cal. He was showing signs of emerging from the Ice Age, though slowly, coming to talk to me from time to time presumably because I was Georgie's friend. He would ask about her in an offhand sort of way, or tiptoe round the subject without ever quite knocking up against it. Now, seeing her with me, he stopped – then came over. They swapped nonchalant hellos, and tried to pretend they weren't looking at each other when they were. 'You're having girl talk,' Cal said, perceptively. 'I'd better leave you to it.'

'Stick around.' I was casual. 'We were discussing Lin.'

'Is she all right?'

We told him about the situation with Ivor. Perhaps out of perversity, he determined to be tolerant. 'He wants to shag her every night so of course he'll move in if he can. It's natural. It doesn't mean he's a bad lot. He's probably nuts about her. Why not? She's very pretty.'

'You're so predictable,' Georgie snapped. 'It's not that you've got a one-track mind: it just doesn't play any of the other tracks. You may not care about Lin, but we do. We don't want her to be hurt.'

'I do care about her,' Cal protested. 'I think she's a lovely person who deserves to be happy. Looks like this bloke's doing the trick. Why're you so set on spoiling sport?'

I intervened hastily, trying to calm things down, but after weeks of tension they had finally got into a good quarrel and weren't about to walk away from it. Maybe, I thought, when they had finished, the last ice-sheet would disintegrate and they could get back on their old terms. I made an excuse which neither noticed, temporarily vacated my desk, and left them to it.

Chapter 9

'Who knows this damsel, burning bright,'
Quoth Launcelot, 'like a northern light?'
Quoth Sir Gauwaine: '*I* know her not!'
'Who quoth you *did*?' quoth Launcelot.
''Tis Braunighrindas!' quoth Sir Bors
(Just then returning from the wars).
Then quoth the pure Sir Galahad:
'She seems, methinks, but lightly clad!
The winds blow somewhat chill today;
Moreover, what would Arthur say?'

GEORGE du MAURIER: *A Legend of Camelot*

It was the beginning of September, the heatwave had cooled down a few degrees, and the Ultraphone Poetry Awards loomed. (Picture of a man trying to make a phone call with a large dahlia. 'Why say it with flowers when you can say it with Ultraphone?') Jerry Beauman's proofs had materialised in record time – publishers can produce a book very quickly if there's a lot of money at stake. 'Jerry's news right now,' Alistair said. 'In a year the public will have forgotten him and we'll have to pack him off to prison again to get him back in the headlines.'

'Sounds good to me,' I said.

244

As predicted, Jerry wanted to make last-minute alterations and I was summoned to Berkeley Square to discuss them. 'Be diplomatic,' Alistair said. 'Let him shift a comma or two. You've done a great job. We don't want him buggering it up at this stage. He's a total prick but he'll sell millions.'

'On the telephone,' I said in a carefully noncommittal voice, 'he said he wasn't happy about the fate of de Villefort. Jerry thinks he should be killed off in an incredibly gory manner instead of simply disgraced.'

'De Villefort?'

'The judge.'

'Oh. Oh, I see. Actually, I think the original de Villefort was the prosecuting counsel – but never mind that. What you must remember, Cookie, is that all authors pinch their plots – that's perfectly okay, as long as they pinch good ones – and we know they do, but we must *never let them know we know*. Writers are very sensitive about accusations of plagiarism. You know Pamela Winters? Feminist thrillers – one of them was televised recently.' I nodded. 'She's very upmarket now, but she started her career with a bodice-ripper. Shocking stuff – anti-heroine who should've been played by Faye Dunaway in her younger days, wallowing in incest and murder and so on. No, of course I didn't read it, never read anything of ours if I can help it, but Twocan did the paperback. Anyhow, Pamela was at a lit party here when some bright spark of a junior editor pointed out the story-line was cribbed virtually intact from a famous children's classic. Winters was so upset she tore up the contract with us and gave her next book to Hodder.'

'What happened to the junior editor?' I asked.

'Last heard of selling double glazing.'

I didn't believe that part, but it was a good story.

(Out of curiosity, I subsequently picked up an old copy of the bodice-ripper and read it. The junior editor was perfectly right – the children's classic had been a staple of my youthful library, so I recognised it at once.)

None of this assisted me in managing Jerry Beauman.

On my arrival he greeted me with a preoccupied air, oozing rather less Klingon charm than usual. There was a faint frown between his brows that never quite vanished, deepening when the phone rang, but after the maid had given the identity of the caller he seemed to relax. 'Tell him I'm working,' he said. 'Take a message.' Then he turned back to me, and the fate of the doomed judge. 'I think it falls a bit flat, having him merely lose face. I know he's defrocked –' ('That's bishops,' I muttered) '– and has to live in seclusion in the heart of the country and is socially ostracised, but we need something a bit stronger. If he were to have a fatal car crash, with the imputation that it was a little more than an Act of God . . .'

'If your hero orders – or even condones – a murder by one of his ex-con pals,' I said, 'I think he would run the risk of losing the readers' sympathy.'

'But my God, the judge is corrupt, he's greedy, he's an evil bastard – any intelligent reader would feel he deserves to die!'

'Maybe,' I said (diplomatically), 'but they wouldn't want the hero involved.'

'What if we showed he has an unnatural relationship with his daughter? Perhaps if he raped her—'

'He's already driven her to drink and drugs. We really mustn't overdo it. The changes we can make at this stage are rather limited . . .'

'Look, Emma, this book has to be *right*. You may not know, but I'm a perfectionist. My public expect certain things from me: a great story, gripping narrative, but above all, literary integrity.' *What?* 'They want to see justice being done. It may not always happen in real life, but they know that in immortal print I'll give them the proper ending.' In a strange way, it was an echo of the fantasy writer's sentiment: *Fiction is there to encourage people.* Only when the writer was Jerry Beauman, I wasn't sure what people were being encouraged to do.

'Supposing his wife leaves him?' I suggested desperately. 'They've been married thirty – forty years, she's stood by him through everything. And now at last she sees what he's really like, and she walks out. He's utterly alone. There's no one left for him . . .'

'He kills himself! Brilliant. Brilliant.' The phone rang again, and he got to his feet. 'That's exactly what I was looking for. You and I really are a great team. Hang on: I won't be long.'

I sighed, but faintly. The maid had announced: 'Sir Harold Chorley,' and Jerry's frown snapped back into place. We'd been sitting on one of the sofas in order to pore over the proofs together; now, he retired into the study, closing the door. When the maid disappeared I tried to listen, but I didn't dare go too far from the sofa in case she came back, and I could hear very little. 'Yes, Sir Harold – No, Sir Harold – I can assure you, Sir Harold, I discharged my obligations to Dryden with absolute integrity – I had no foreknowledge of the position at all . . .' That was the second time he'd used the word *integrity* in the space of ten minutes. Curious how people who don't have any always feel compelled to talk about it. And he'd mentioned Dryden again. I have a good memory for names, even without writing them down: I knew it was one he'd used during his last phone conversation *in camera*. I really should check up on it some time.

I think he made another call himself but I was feeling nervous, hovering near the door, and returned to my station on the sofa. When Jerry re-emerged he was curt, saying he had to go out and would see me tomorrow; I could remain in the flat and work for a while (whether I wanted to or not). A chauffeur was summoned who looked more like a minder, a bulky six foot three with the sort of lumpy, battered face that seemed to have been on the receiving end of too many punches. I wasn't sure what a cauliflower ear was, but I suspected he had two. He wore no uniform and answered Jerry in a Scots accent as thick as porridge. Beauman called him MacMurdo.

When they had gone I took the initiative, requesting tea from the maid. When she brought the tray she explained, rather timidly, that she had to go to the shops. Would I be all right on my own? (I would.) It was not necessary to answer the telephone because there was a machine.

'Fine,' I said.

And then I was alone in Jerry's flat.

I could almost hear Georgie's voice whispering in my ear, like a devil sent to tempt me. I stared resolutely down at the proofs, roughing out a few sample sentences for Jerry's approval, in which I attempted to condense the departure of the judge's wife and his consequent suicide into so few words that it wouldn't throw out the entire section. Fortunately, we were at the end of a chapter. There was a fair-sized blank space over the page. I reduced the required passage into five sentences, crossed my fingers that Jerry wouldn't change them too much, pocketed my felt-tip, and set off to explore the flat. The money was in a safe place, Jerry had said. Not *the* safe – a safe place. What would be a safe place for half a million pounds?

Ordinary drawers and cupboards were obviously out: it wasn't a sum you could hide under your knickers. There might be a secret drawer or concealed compartment in the study desk, but even if there was, surely it wouldn't be big enough. After glancing round the vast acreage of the living room, I followed my instinct and went into the master bedroom. Anything of value, I reasoned, you want hidden somewhere close to you, in your personal space. Overnight guests might occupy other bedrooms, visitors colonise the sofas or meander across the parquet, but the study and the master bedroom were Jerry's exclusive territory. There was a huge four-poster bed, with scalloped drapery above and a pleated flounce below. Any hint of femininity was counteracted by the colour-scheme, which was predominantly red. There were whole walls of built-in wardrobes, walnut doors polished to a mirror gloss. Other doors were panelled with actual mirrors, so the entire room gleamed, the lighting (there was lots) glancing from door to door, reflections and bright shadows flickering around you with every movement. A large unit beside the bed (more walnut) opened to reveal a widescreen TV with video and DVD, and a complex sound system. Remotes were on the bedside table, along with a humidor of cigars and an enormous modern silver ashtray which, I thought privately, was the nicest thing in the room.

I looked in the wardrobes, rifling through racks of suits, shirts, ties, but there was nothing behind them but the wall, solid and unyielding. No sign of magical countries with fauns and witches and snow, let alone half a million quid. I climbed on a chair to study the canopy over the bed more closely, thinking it would be clever to have a hiding place on the top. I couldn't see above the rim but I managed to feel along it, and there was definitely nothing there. I peered round the headboard, moved the pillows, looked under the flounce, all without result. I even lifted the corners of the Oriental carpet and shifted every piece of furniture that I could. The room, though large, wasn't cluttered, and I didn't think I'd missed anything. The money wasn't there.

I went into the ensuite, the centrepiece of which was a circular Jacuzzi bath big enough for a spa, encased in what looked like marble and reached by a flight of steps. I adore luxury baths, and my mouth all but watered at the sight of it. Inside, there were numerous buttons for the different pressure-jets, fuel-injection bubble bath, something that might have been a temperature control. I toyed with the idea that one of the buttons might open a secret cavity somewhere nearby, but of course Jerry wouldn't always use the bath alone, and it would be too easy for a girlfriend to press the appropriate button by mistake. Exploring the rest of the room, I noted the grouting between the tiles showed no chinks or cracks and the walls were seamless. The cupboards were filled with the usual things: mounds of towels, spare loo rolls, men's beauty products (plenty of those), soap, shampoo, Just For Men hair colorant. I giggled at this last item, which was unfair of me, since no one thinks it funny if women tint their hair. I don't – an unhappy home experiment in my teens put me off – but most do. We have streaks and bleaches and rinses and dyes, and it's all part of the fun of being female. (I must try again some time.) Men have cringe-making advertisements – 'My daddy looks younger than your daddy' – and products that don't seem quite so successful, possibly because their heart isn't in it. Still, I giggled. Jerry Beauman would be embarrassed if the world knew he coloured his hair. No woman would give a damn. When it comes to vanity, we have the edge.

Dismissing the rest of the bathroom, I turned back to the Jacuzzi for a final yearn. Then I noticed something. Though the bath was round, the casing formed a square, presumably to accommodate the intricate plumbing underneath. Each section was separate: a hairline crack marked the join. And one side, I discovered, was subdivided into two, the shorter piece being only a couple of feet in length. Of course, maybe they'd been running out of marble – but this was a no-expense-spared apartment, and I didn't believe that. I remembered when I was a student sharing a house where the casing round the bath had been broken. Through the gap, you could see a tangle of pipes and the lair of a gigantic spider whom we christened Ernestine. When we had parties, we used to tuck any drink we wanted to save in there, safe from the predations of thirsty guests. There must be quite a lot of space behind the surround of Jerry Beauman's bath . . .

I dropped to my knees and inserted my finger-nails into the crack, trying to lever the section free. (By the feel, it wasn't marble, just a lookalike.) No luck. But I was still sure I was right. Somewhere, there would be a button to press or knob to twist. I pushed all the buttons in the bath without success, turned the taps on and off, scanned the steps and surround for anything button-like and pressable. Fleetingly, my mind jumped to the collection of remotes on the bedside table – but no, too risky, the bimbo girlfriend would be bound to try them all when watching porno films in bed. I would just have to go through all the bathroom cupboards again, looking for a button this time. I was just about to make a start when I heard a noise. Not footsteps: the carpet deadened those. The click of a handle turning, the shush of an opening door – I was too busy panicking to be sure. Relief surged when only the maid walked in, carrying a multipack of Andrex and evidently surprised to see me.

'Just nosy,' I said, making what I hoped was a conspiratorial face. 'I needed the loo, and I wanted another look at the bath. Jerry showed me round when I first came, but we were only in here a moment. Isn't it sumptuous? Have you ever used it?' It was a shockingly naïve question, and I knew it, because even if she had it would have been on the sly, and she would never admit to it. I definitely couldn't visualise Jerry Beauman inviting his maid to use his private bathroom. However, I hoped it would distract her from wondering what I was really doing there.

She shook her head violently, clearly as embarrassed as if

it was she who had been caught snooping. We almost collided in the doorway as each attempted to leave the other in possession of the field. But I was too nervous to resume my search; right now, all I wanted was to get out in one piece. I really wasn't cut out for a life of crime. In the living room I gathered up the proofs, complete with amendments, and escaped.

I don't know what I'd been planning to do if I found the money: I hadn't looked that far ahead. I certainly wasn't going to steal it, or start a new career as a supergrass to the SFO. I just wanted to find out where it was – to see what half a million pounds looked like (on TV, it's always neat wads of banknotes in suitcases) – to go away, leaving it there, *knowing*. And then, Plan B.

At that stage, there was no Plan B.

At the weekend, Georgie and I traipsed round a range of stores in quest of my posh dress. This isn't meant to be a shopping novel, so I won't go into details. You've already had plenty of retail therapy, and I don't want to get repetitive. Suffice to say we found a dress that fulfilled all requirements, at the cost of a staggering debit on my Mastercard, very sore feet, and the kind of exhaustion normally experienced by top athletes after a particularly gruelling decathlon. We finished in Liberty's, where we dived into the coffee shop to recuperate. Georgie had been meeting Cal on Friday night, 'just to talk', and I asked her how it had gone.

'Good and bad,' she said, making what the French call a *moue*, which is a kind of foreign pout.

'Explain.'

'We got along fine to begin with, until the subject of Neville came up. He said had I really not slept with him, and I said no I hadn't, but I would have if I'd wanted to, because Cal's married – and he said he doesn't sleep with Christy or shag around any more, so I should be faithful too – and I said that wasn't fair because he *lives* with Christy, which is a kind of infidelity – and we started quarrelling all over again. And then some people from Ransome came in and joined us, so we couldn't sort it out, and one of them was going Cal's way home and offered to share a cab, so I didn't get to see him later, and I think we're back at stalemate.'

'He loves you,' I said. 'You love him. You'll sort it out.'

'Do I want to?' said Georgie. 'Maybe I'll get over him, and meet another Neville, and live happily ever after. I just wish the idea didn't depress me so much.'

By way of diversion, I told her about further developments *chez* Beauman, and my search of the flat.

'A secret compartment under the bath?' Georgie said, impressed. 'By George, I think you've got it! My aunt – the one who left me the house – kept all her jewellery in a plastic bag in the lavatory cistern. Actually, it was a hell of a pain. The house has one of those old-fashioned loos with the tank right up near the ceiling. She had to climb up a stepladder every time she wanted to wear ear-rings. But it was a great hiding-place; she had a burglary once but they never thought to look there.' And, reverting to Jerry's bathroom stash: 'The question is, how do we open it?'

'We're only looking out of curiosity, remember,' I said.

'Absolutely.'

'Well, I tried to lever it open but couldn't. I reckon there has to be a button somewhere which does it automatically, but the maid came in and I didn't get much of a chance to look.'

'When are you going to the flat again?'

'I don't know,' I said. 'Anyway, I think we should do some background research first. On the phone to this Sir Harold person, Jerry mentioned Dryden – it was one of the names I heard him use before. Sounds like a company, not an individual. And the other time he talked about something called

Acme City, which rings a faint bell. It's time we found out what's going on.'

'How?'

'Perhaps Lin wouldn't mind asking Andy, now she's got Ivor,' I suggested.

'Worth a try.'

Possibly because she was restless after her inconclusive evening with Cal, Georgie wanted instant action. She called Lin on her mobile – to be hailed with a sort of gushing relief which I could hear from across the table.

'Georgie! How wonderful! I was just thinking of calling you. Are you – are you busy?'

Yes, I mouthed, immediately apprehensive.

'I'm in Liberty's,' Georgie said. 'With Cookie.' In her dialect, anything to do with shopping meant she was busy.

'The thing is, Ivor's parents are in town, and he wants me to meet them, but I don't think it's a great idea to take the children. The twins are playing cricket this afternoon, but there's Meredith . . .'

Georgie rolled her eyes, grimaced, sighed. 'I've got to go to a dinner party this evening,' she said. 'In Chiswick.'

'It wouldn't be for the evening,' I heard Lin say. 'Just tea-time for a couple of hours. I'm so sorry to ask you, but I'm desperate.'

I made various gestures signifying resignation and surrender. Your place or mine? Georgie asked me, in sign language.

We settled on my flat, in the outer reaches of Notting Hill, since it was nearer to Lin's place. 'When she gets there with the brat,' Georgie said, as she hung up, 'I'll ask her about Andy.'

Back at home we made basic preparations – checking my supply of videos and soft drinks, locking up the silver, trying to teach Mandy to respond to the command 'Kill!' Lin arrived on a flood of gratitude, depositing Meredith on the doorstep;

Ivor, hovering at her side, provided a more moderate echo to her sentiments.

'Actually,' Georgie said, 'there *is* something you can do in return. Cookie's back on the track of Jerry Beauman's financial shenanigans. We really need your chum Andy to give us some inside information.'

'Who's Andy?' Ivor asked. (Odd that Lin hadn't mentioned him.)

'Just an old friend,' Lin said carelessly. At least, I *thought* she sounded careless. 'From Scotland. I hardly see him. He's got a beard.'

I detected relief in Ivor's expression. No serious rival would have a beard.

'He's a banker,' Georgie was saying. 'We need his expertise.'

'We'll talk about it on Monday,' Lin said. 'We must dash now. See you about six-thirty.'

Meredith, meanwhile, was gazing critically round my flat. Her eyes met Mandy's, matt black stare fixing cold green one. They approached each other warily.

'Is that your cat?' Meredith asked. I said it was. 'What's its name?'

'It's a he. Mandy.'

'Mandy's a girl's name.'

'Short for Mandelson.'

'That's a funny name for a cat.' She sat down on the floor in front of Mandy, reaching out to stroke him. He tossed his head disdainfully and mewed, but didn't move away. 'Sandy had a cat called Snowball because it was white, but it got run over. That was ages ago, when I was very little. After that Mummy said we couldn't have any more cats, because there are so many cars on the road and they would always get killed. The twins had a pair of gerbils – that's a kind of rat – but they escaped. I helped them. I didn't think they were happy in a cage.'

'How did Mummy feel about that?' I asked.

'She never knew. She thought the boys left the cage open.'

'Have you ever had a pet?'

'I wanted a tarantula, but they wouldn't let me. Your cat isn't very friendly, is he?'

'I always think he's like the cat in the *Just So Stories*,' I said. 'You know: I am the Cat that Walks by Itself, and all places are alike to me.'

Meredith didn't know, so I fished out the book and read her the story, while she succeeded in coaxing Mandy to climb on to her lap, where he kneaded her legs with his claws in customary cat fashion before condescending to sit down. (I keep all my favourite children's books and re-read them regularly.) Georgie went into the kitchen and produced pineapple squash and chocolate digestives, bought on the way home. After the story, Meredith chose an unsuitable video. *Die Hard*. 'That's the one where he walks on broken glass and his feet bleed,' she said. 'I like that.'

'Because of the bleeding feet?' said Georgie.

'I like the villain. He's funny. I wish he didn't get killed. Why do villains always get killed? They're often much more fun than heroes. Heroes are boring.'

'That's fiction for you,' I said.

'Talking of heroes,' said Georgie, 'how do you get on with Ivor?'

'Ivor's not a hero!' Meredith retorted, with an unexpected grin.

'Depends,' said Georgie. 'How boring is he?'

I stretched out to give her a dig in the arm.

'He's not boring,' Meredith said decidedly. 'He bought me a dress from Monsoon, with pink fluffy bits on, and glitter. I don't like pink, but Mummy says it's really cerise. That's French for cherry – only the cherries I had last summer were purpley-black.' The jury was clearly still out on Ivor. 'I might wear it, though. The twins didn't like him at first, but they do now. Just because he's into football, and when he found them looking at porno pictures on the computer he laughed. Boys are stupid. They like anyone who likes football.'

'Does Ivor play chess?' I inquired.

'Yes,' said Meredith. 'He's pretty good. He nearly beat me, but I won in the end.' Tactful Ivor. 'Mum says he's only staying for a bit, but I think he wants to stay forever. She wants it too. He goes all soppy and romantic over her, and she likes it.' Her voice was dark with disapproval.

'Your mummy was bound to get another boyfriend sooner or later,' Georgie said.

'Why?' Meredith demanded.

'She's young, and pretty, and she wants to be loved. All women do.'

'I shan't. I don't want boyfriends. I'm going to be a Lesbian when I grow up.'

I choked.

'Do you know what that means?' Georgie asked, temporarily distracted.

'It's a woman who wants to marry another woman, so she doesn't have to do all that yukky sex stuff with a man.'

'Mmm. Good definition. Anyway,' Georgie got back to the point, 'your mummy doesn't love you any less, just because she's got Ivor. You and the twins will always come first with her. I know that.'

'That's what Ivor said. Your mummy loves you, and I want to love you too. I asked if he was going to be my daddy, but he said no, my daddy's dead, and he wouldn't want to replace him. At least he was sensible about that.' Conflicting expressions glanced over her face: a disconcerting intensity, a regression into childishness. 'It isn't Ivor, exactly. But I liked it best when it was just us. Why do things have to change?'

'That's life,' said Georgie. 'Things change all the time. You didn't do a sicky on him, did you?'

'I was going to.' Meredith's monkey-face looked doleful. 'But Mummy said she would *kill* me if I did. She looked all pale and tense, as if she meant it. That wasn't very loving of her, was it?'

'Of course she didn't mean it,' I said mendaciously.

'*And* she hid the mint-choc-chip ice cream. It's much harder without ice cream. I have to have runny stuff inside me.'

'Do we really need the technical details?' Georgie murmured. 'On balance, I think it's a good idea *not* to be sick over people – unless they deserve it. Like mass murderers and bank managers and traffic wardens.'

Meredith's face brightened. 'There's a traffic warden in our street sometimes,' she said. 'Mummy doesn't like him.'

I decided it was time to switch on the video.

On Monday we reminded Lin about contacting Andy Pearmain. 'You've got a date for the wedding now,' Georgie said. 'You don't have to feel – uncomfortable – with him any more.'

'I know,' Lin said. 'I told Ivor about it. He said he's looking forward to going – visiting a castle in Scotland and everything. And Vee Corrigan said she'll have Meredith as well as the boys. I thought I'd call Andy tomorrow. You'd better write down all the stuff I have to ask him – I'll never remember the names.'

'So that's sorted,' Georgie commented afterwards.

'The research problem?'

'The Andy problem. Lin seems to have forgotten her desperate yearning for might-have-beens. The dimples beat the beard any day of the week.'

'Hyperion to a satyr,' I said. 'Frailty, thy name is woman.'

'In the theatre,' Georgie remarked, 'quoting *Macbeth* is considered unlucky.'

'It was *Hamlet*.'

'Shit. So it was. I don't know what's wrong with me. My brain's gone on hold.'

'Have you talked to Cal lately?' I said.

Georgie threw me a dagger-look, and reverted to considerations of publicity.

On Wednesday, Lin reported her conversation with Andy. 'Acme City's a new shopping centre they're building in Birmingham,' she said. 'Andy's going to find out about the other names and call me back. He said he was really pleased to hear about Ivor. He wants to come down to London before the wedding to meet him. He might bring Cat, if she can get away.'

'You can have a cosy foursome,' I said, a little too drily.

'I could take her round the shops,' Lin pursued. 'Andy said she'd like to go to Harrods and all the glamorous boutiques.'

'You never shop in Harrods!' Georgie objected.

'I know. That's why you'd have to come with me.' Lin's voice was pleading. She's good at pleading.

'Georgie isn't safe in Harrods,' I said. 'Unless you lock up her credit card first.'

On Thursday, we went to the Ultraphone Poetry Awards.

Before the advent of the gramophone, poetry was a big deal. In the eighteenth and nineteenth centuries great poets were like rock stars, idolised by the masses, or at least the masses who could read, their verses quoted by all and sundry, their celebrity lifestyles the subject of envy and scandal. Drink, drugs, sex – they had it all. Where Sting went off to save the rainforest, Byron fought for the freedom of Greece and died of fever in the process. Where Mick Jagger was arrested for possession of cannabis, Coleridge swigged a quart of laudanum a day. Hutchence hanged himself, possibly by mistake in the course of hazardous sexual practices; Chatterton took arsenic at the age of seventeen. In those days, poetry had rhyme and rhythm, it was catchy and memorable, the words made a tune in your head. For music in the home you needed an instrument, a musician and a singer, and while many families had a piano the level of talent available was limited to your immediate circle. Then along came His Master's Voice – the wind-up, hi-fi, sound system – 78s, LPs, tapes, CDs – the Sony Walkman and portable CD player. Pop had arrived. Like painting on the invention of the camera, poetry shot off down a side-street. Rhyme went out of vogue, metre vanished. The parameters of language were breached, whether they liked it or not. The poet gradually became an obscure figure, celebrated only in his own field. Even if he *did* take drugs or have sex, no one cared any more.

Now, poetry is struggling to get back on the scene. We have rock poets, performance poets, post-modern poets, protest poets. Larkin epitomised a sort of grey northern dullness and Betjeman was a rather camp character from P. G. Wodehouse, but the new generation of poets are starting to be glamorous again. Televising the Ultraphone ceremony – even on BBC4 – meant there would be as many egos on show as at the Brit Awards, but without the millions of fans, the multi-million-dollar incomes, or the multiple minders. Georgie marked the occasion with the floating chiffon dress she had once offered to lend to Lin; it was far more frilly and feminine than her usual style, and I couldn't help feeling she didn't look quite like herself. But then, nor did I. The posh dress clung and scooped and plunged, its angled skirt going for a little flutter down one side, its blood-orange tones enhancing my topped-up tan and newly trimmed, anti-frizzed cloud of hair.

'This dress isn't me,' Georgie said, surveying herself critically in the mirror in the Ladies' loo. 'I think I'll give it away. But it doesn't matter. You're the star tonight; I'm just your sidekick.'

'That's rubbish,' I said. 'You always look stunning.' Which was true, but I couldn't help feeling a tiny thrill of anticipation. My dress *was* something special, a centre-stage kind of dress, and I'd never been centre-stage in my life. For once, I really did feel like a sex goddess, exotic and voluptuous . . .

Beware the day your wishes come true.

Lin joined us, in a two-piece of crinkly rainbow silk which wouldn't have worked on anyone else and probably didn't work on her, but no one would notice. Even without Ivor, who was babysitting, she glowed with inner bliss. I still found it slightly scary, but I wasn't in the mood to worry any more.

We took a taxi to the Reform Club, Georgie gave her name to the doorman, and we went in to mingle with the throng. Throngs are rare at poetry events, but the lure of the TV cameras had done the trick. The usual accoutrements of television were in evidence: tripwire cables, very bright lights, and young men balancing chunks of expensive technology on their shoulders. We looked round for any of 'our' poets. Mainstream publishers won't normally touch poetry, but in the last couple of years Ransome had produced an annual anthology of work by first-timers. It had a print run of about fifty copies and made no money whatsoever, but it was good for our lit cred, and our presence at the Ultraphone Awards was the result of it. At least two contributors who had started with us had gone on to higher things: protest songs for the more intellectual rock bands, or prize-winning verse for upmarket ad campaigns. To survive, the modern poet has to be versatile.

'D'you know what our guys look like?' Lin asked.

'No,' said Georgie. 'But it doesn't matter. They'll have labels like everyone else.'

It was the kind of occasion where you were given a badge with your name on it as you came in, but only Lin was wearing hers. Georgie and I, not wanting to mar the impact of our dresses, had pinned ours to our shoulder bags. In any case, name tags at a party aren't as helpful as you'd think. People peer at your shoulder when speaking to you instead of looking you in the face, and even when they've deciphered your name they still have to ask if you are animal, vegetable, or mineral, and precisely what you're doing there. I did a good deal of shoulder-peering, but never found a poet who belonged to us. Not that it was relevant: we'd come for the party, not the poetry.

Poets are even rarer than writers at any literary function, even a poetic one. I did recognise a few of the more glamorous variety: Angus Dudgeon, the only poet whose very name sounds depressive, his bony good looks now going to seed (he would have been craggy, but Ted Hughes had the monopoly on cragginess); Philip Wells, whom I'd once seen perform, resembling a rather dishy footballer, prowling the stage and throwing out rhymes in all directions; Aidan Dun, with long black hair and the face of a Burne-Jones knight, who writes the way Keats might have done if he had been a latter-day hippy with Coleridge's opium habit and *no doorbell*. Around them, writers posing as journalists, journalists posing as writers, critics, publishers, publicists – the usual mob. There were even a couple of those rent-a-celebs who will turn up at any event just because it's an Event. I exchanged a few words with a children's TV presenter who was producing a book of verse for kids, possibly to counteract the stories of sex-and-cocaine binges in the tabloids, and nearly collided with an ex-Olympic runner who was talking earnestly to someone from Faber and Faber, last bastion of poetry publishing.

Just as everyone tends to believe they could write a book

if only they had the time, so far too many people nowadays think they can write poetry. It doesn't have to rhyme or scan any more: how difficult can it be? All you have to do is remember to stop the lines before you reach the edge of the page. If it sounds like gibberish, that's because it's inscrutable, and the meaning is beyond the ken of ordinary readers. Sentimentalists may claim we are all poets at heart, but they forget to mention that we are not all poets at brain. 'There won't be readings, will there?' I whispered to Georgie in sudden horror, as the tapping of microphones and the turning of heads prefaced a pause for speeches.

'God, I hope not.'

I was experiencing worst fears again, but on this occasion they weren't realised. There were five awards: Promising Newcomer, Comic Verse, Lifetime Achievement, Publisher Who Has Contributed Most to Poetry, and Ultraphone Poet of the Year. The winners, three of whom I hadn't heard of, were selected by a panel of rather more famous judges, including a popular scientist and even a celebrity chef. Philip Wells won Comic Verse for a selection of nonsense poetry, Aidan Dun Poet of the Year. I didn't recognise the Lifetime Achiever, and the Publisher Who Contributed emerged from obscurity to make a robust acceptance speech and then vanished again. When it was over everyone applauded enthusiastically, probably out of relief that there had been no readings, and went back to guzzling champagne. (Not real champagne, of course, but whatever substitute they were serving was suitably fizzy, reasonably dry, and went down easily.) I began to be aware, rather mistily, that my flame-coloured dress and Page 3 cleavage were attracting a good deal of attention. Poetry, unlike prose, is male-dominated, and suddenly a lot of them seemed to be eddying round me. At one point Angus Dudgeon was hovering over me ('Watch out,' Georgie whispered. 'Love rat.'); at another Aidan Dun, looking too otherworldly to notice anything as carnal as a pair of tits, was explaining in his deep, musical voice how the Holy Grail was hidden in King's Cross. By then, such was my state of intoxication, I believed him.

'I have this terrible problem with women,' he informed me with a heart-shattering smile. 'I simply can't say no.'

In view of his extreme physical beauty, I reflected, that really *would* be a problem. (I was only surprised he found time to write poetry.) However, I had no intention of putting it to the test. I waited till his notice was claimed by a gushing magazine editor, and moved away. I'd seen a familiar face.

'Hi, Cal. What're you doing here?' Designers don't normally attend these affairs.

'I came for the booze.' He raised his glass. 'And the scenery.' His gaze travelled over the visible portions of my anatomy – both of them.

'Georgie get you in?' His name would have had to be on the door for him to gain admission.

'Mmm. Where is she?'

'Don't know. She was with me a moment ago.' Scanning the room, I saw her standing a dozen yards away with Angus Dudgeon, who had evidently switched his leer to her bosom. She appeared her usual sparkling self, but in view of her comment earlier I guessed she was on autopilot.

'Who's that git?' Cal demanded, following my gaze.

'A very famous poet.'

'I'm not much of a one for poetry,' he confessed, unnecessarily. 'It all sounds silly to me. Like those poems in greetings cards.

Roses are red,
violets are blue,
let's go to bed
and – have a good screw.

'That the sort of stuff he writes?'

I giggled. There's something irresistible about a total philistine on the literary scene. 'Pretty much,' I said.

Seeing us, Georgie extricated herself gracefully from Angus' dudgeon and came over. 'Are we talking,' she asked Cal, in a flippant tone, 'or just arguing?'

'Up to you.'

I left them to it, hoping that at last they would sort themselves out and normal service would be resumed. Heading towards Lin, I was waylaid by a broad Yorkshire accent who thrust a book of his verse into my unresisting hands – always a hazard at these events – and proceeded to tell me he saw himself as the Emily Brontë of the twenty-first century. Glancing through the book, I found it difficult to agree. He had a sobering effect on me, and I hastily grabbed some passing champagne. In the main, I was enjoying myself – anyone can be sought-after in Greece, but it takes rather more effort at an Awards ceremony in London. However, despite the feedback from the dress I didn't feel my success matched up to Cinderella's. It would have been fun if – say – Todd Jarman had been there . . .

No. Mustn't think like that. I had promised myself no further fantasies, erotic or otherwise. That way lay embarrassment and potential humiliation. After all, he was still with Helen Aucham – Helen the high-minded, Helen of the Inns of Court. Was this the face that launched a thousand briefs, And burned the topless towers of lawyerdom? Damn: all these poets were going to my head.

The New Brontë was holding forth on the need for a Romantic Revival and required little prompting from me, which was just as well, since I gave none. He was a large man with a sagging gut (unusual for a poet, since most of them tend to be worn thin from starving in garrets on inadequate Arts Council grants). A Brontësaurus, I thought. I let my gaze wander, and saw Lin in earnest conversation with the Publisher Who Contributed and Georgie and Cal separating abruptly. Georgie looked stormy, Cal merely bleak. He put down his glass and strode towards the exit. On an impulse I excused myself from Yorkshire Romanticism and ran after him.

(Well, not exactly *ran*. Not in that dress – plus the three-inch spike heels I had chosen to go with it. More like walked very quickly.)

'Cal . . .'

He stopped, the bleak look softening a little when he saw me.

'Please stay,' I said. 'If you keep stalking out, and Georgie keeps storming off, you'll never make it up. Give it another go. You want to; she wants to. You just have to try.'

'I'm not sure she does want to,' Cal said. 'She resents my being married. I can't blame her for that; but she knew the deal when we got started. I've told her, I can't leave the kids. That's it. And now she wants to see other men . . .'

'No she doesn't,' I said. 'She just talks about it. I think – I think she's scared of what she feels.'

'You're a nice girl, Cookie,' he said with a tired smile. 'Kind. You say kind things. And you've got fabulous tits.'

'Come and have another drink.'

We found more champagne and Cal produced a hip flask of brandy to make it more interesting. 'Never enough booze at these affairs,' he said. 'I always come prepared.' The brief flicker of sobriety induced by twenty-first-century Brontë had faded, and I advanced into second-stage inebriation, which is even mellower and more comfortable than the first stage, but without the disagreeable side effects of the third and fourth stages. Unfortunately, it does tend to cloud your thought processes, as I realised when it was too late. At one point, the Yorkshire brogue came over with the obvious intention of cornering me again, but Cal wrapped a possessive arm around me and gave him a fuck-off smile, which did the trick.

'Thanks,' I said, unwrapping the arm. 'This was supposed to be my evening to pull, but somehow, he wasn't my type.'

'Don't give up yet,' said Cal. 'Georgie said I should go back to shagging around. Perhaps I could start with you.' His tone was half teasing, half serious; but I turned it off as a joke.

'One of the crowd, huh? Boy, you really know how to make a girl feel special!'

'Sorry. I never was much of a smooth talker. But I mean it. You've got so gorgeous lately – I expect you always were, underneath, but you've really blossomed. That dress is sensational.'

'Georgie helped me choose it,' I said. 'Georgie did the whole transformation thing. She's incredibly generous – and not just with my credit card.'

'Could we stop talking about Georgie?' He essayed another smile, but it went awry. 'I'm trying to come on to you.'

'Then don't,' I said. 'Aside from the fact that Georgie's my friend, you're treating me like – like one of those temps you used to get off with. Or the estate agent. You only want a quickie. D'you think that's all I'm worth?'

''Course not. But you'd never take me seriously; you're too smart. Oh, I know Georgie's smart, but you're smarter. I'm just a dumb guy who can draw.' I noted the contents of his glass were now mostly brandy, with a cursory bubble or two floating on the top. He took a large gulp. 'All you would want from me would be to – to use me for a night of lust, then toss me aside. That's okay. I could do with being used.'

'You love Georgie,' I reminded him, a little sharply.

'Leave it.'

'You love *Georgie*,' I persisted.

'Georgie's in my gut,' he said, through what sounded like gritted teeth. 'She's in my blood – in my bones – in whatever part of the body women get into, when you can't get them out.'

'Heart?' I suggested.

'Balls,' he said. 'She's in my *balls*. Damn her. I haven't had sex for weeks, and I need a shag. You look like . . . like a goddess in that dress. The Goddess of Lust. The Scarlet Woman. You should be surrounded by devil-cherubs with pointy horns and spiky tails.'

'Sounds very artistic,' I said. 'Positively Baroque.'

He grinned, gazing rather muzzily into my eyes, and then suddenly leaned forward and kissed me.

Somewhere, I could hear the Wyshing Well fairy, laughing and laughing, but this time it wasn't funny. It *really* wasn't funny . . .

'What the hell's going on here?' Georgie. One look at her face told me she too had had far too much champagne – even without the addition of brandy. Behind her, Lin was making anguished faces at me.

'I'm propositioning Cookie,' Cal said. Ouch. 'She's being nice to me, and I'm taking advantage of her. Pretty low, isn't it? But there you are. I always was an arsehole.'

'How nice is she being?' Georgie rounded on me. '*How nice?*'

'Don't be ridiculous,' I said. 'You know I wouldn't—'

But Georgie wasn't listening. Nor was Cal. 'Dog-in-the-manger,' he said to her. 'Just 'cos you don't want me, doesn't mean – doesn't mean – well, maybe Cookie does.'

'I *don't*!' I was yelling now, as if it would do any good. In our vicinity, people were staring. Nothing like a good row to liven things up. I *felt* like a scarlet woman – and it wasn't any fun at all. Georgie's face was ablaze with rage and pain.

'You bastard!' she screamed, I'm not sure who to. 'I thought you were my *friend*!' Me. Definitely me. 'I *trusted* you, I *cared* for you – I made you buy that dress – and all the time you were planning to – scheming to – You have him. Go on. You want him, you have him. I wish you luck. He thinks he's got a big dick, but you know what? He *is* a big dick. You have him. You're welcome.'

She headed for the stairs like a small tempest, leftover poets scattering from her path. 'I'd better go with her,' Lin said. 'Cookie—'

'It's all nonsense,' I said. 'You know that, don't you?'

'I hope so.' She threw me a last look, then followed Georgie.

'Right,' said Cal. 'Let's go and have sex.'

I removed the glass from his hand and set it down on a nearby table. Then I slapped him round the face. Hard.

For a moment he stood perfectly still. Then he took off his specs, straightened a bent ear-piece, and put them back on again. 'Shit,' he said. 'Sorry. Sorry . . .'

'If you've lost me one of my best friends,' I said in a shaking voice, 'I hope you burn in hell.'

'I'll talk to her,' he said. 'It wasn't your fault. It was me – all me. I'll fix it for you.'

'You'd better. I wanted to help you – I wanted you and Georgie to get back together. She's my friend, and I thought you were my friend too. I never imagined you would come on to me. Even when you've flirted a little, I just thought you were kidding.'

'I'm a man,' he said ruefully. 'That's the problem with all of us at the blunt end of a prick. You want us to be caring and sensitive and wonderful, and we ain't. We always let you down. I *am* your friend, Cookie – at least, I hope so – but put me near an attractive woman and the good old hormones kick into action. That's how blokes work. Women are the superior sex: you girls have always known that.'

'You do *want* to be with Georgie, don't you?' I said, suddenly scared.

'God, yes. I want to be with her so much it's tearing my heart out. All I wanted from you was comfort. And the tits, of course.'

'I encouraged you,' I said, smitten with a surge of remorse. 'You thought I was coming on to you, didn't you? I was being all cosy, and – this dress. I should never have bought it. I just wasn't cut out to be sexy.'

'Bollocks,' said Cal. 'All women are sexy – or they should be. I didn't need encouragement. I'm a bloke: remember? I keep my brains in my dick.'

'You said it.' But I was still feeling horribly guilty. I'd enjoyed his company, and his admiration. I'd been too pissed to think straight. How could I have been so *stupid*? And how on earth would I put things right with Georgie?

'Don't worry,' Cal said, reading my face. 'I'll speak to Georgie. It'll be okay – at least for you. She doesn't bear grudges.' And, after a pause: 'Shall I take you home now, or do you want to pick up a poet?'

I managed a smile. 'Just get me a cab.'

Outside, we stood on the pavement while Cal scanned the passing traffic for a 'For Hire' light.

'What will you do now?' I asked.

'Go home. Crash out on the sofa in front of the late-night movie, probably.'

'Do you still sleep with Christy?' I said.

'Yes. Me on one side of the bed, she on the other. Clear blue water in between. We don't even touch.'

'D'you mind?'

He shrugged. 'Not any more. It's been over for a long time now.' An available taxi approached, and he summoned it for me. When he opened the door I hesitated, turning to say goodnight. 'You should get yourself a decent guy,' he said, squeezing my hand.

'According to you, there aren't any.'

'Nah – the best ones are all like me. There are a few sensitive types, but they're all wimps. You'll just have to make do.'

'I'll bear it in mind.'

I got into the cab and it drove off, leaving him alone at the curbside. Looking back, I thought he appeared solitary and rather forlorn, standing there in the lamplight, with the bleak look settling over his face again. So much for my night of triumph. I'd been hailed a sex goddess – I'd been seductive and sought-after – my wish had come true. And what good had it done me? I'd hurt someone I cared for, I'd let people down, *I'd lost my friend*. I'd lost friends in the past through what might be termed natural wastage – growing apart, moving away, taking divergent paths – but never through anger. Never like this. I knew a horrible squirming feeling inside of mingled shame and regret and self-loathing, and worst of all, the sneaking urge to justify my actions, to tell myself: 'I didn't mean it. It wasn't my fault. Things just happen.' There I was, being beautiful and irresistible, and things just happened around me, the way they do around beautiful irresistible people. We don't mean to inflict pain on others, but we can't help it. Us *femmes fatales* . . .

Don't let me get like that! I prayed to whatever powers might be listening. Don't let me be someone who hurts people, and says it's not my fault, and is secretly smug about my fatal attraction. (If I had any. I felt like a fraud.) I don't want to be beautiful any more. I don't want to be a sex goddess. I just want my friend back.

I found I was crying, helpless tears oozing out of my eyes and trickling down my cheeks, probably making snail-tracks in my makeup. The cab driver was watching me in the mirror, but I didn't care. I fished in my bag for a tissue, but I hadn't brought any.

'Break up with your boyfriend?' asked the driver.

'No,' I said. 'My girlfriend. My best friend.'

'Oh. Like that, is it?'

At the time, I didn't catch the inference. It wasn't important. All that mattered was I'd hurt Georgie – I'd betrayed her – and I didn't know how to put it right.

Chapter 10

When the sky began to roar
'Twas like a lion at the door;
When the door began to crack
'Twas like a stick across my back;
When my back began to smart
'Twas like a penknife in my heart;
When my heart began to bleed
'Twas death and death and death indeed.

FOLK RHYME

When I set out to write this book, I meant it to be light-hearted and funny, a flippant account of three girls, and three wishes, and how we tried to help those wishes come true. I didn't know if they would or not, I just thought it would be entertaining to make a story of it, good practise for an aspiring writer. I meant to leave out the dull bits, the dark bits, the moments of gloom and despondency, the small failures and petty humiliations – but of course they crept in. As soon as you start to think about people, and life, you have to deal with the dark side. It's always there: the black underbelly of comedy, the shadow behind the light romance. Without it, my story would be only half-coloured, the characters only half-alive. I thought I could joke about it, make a mockery of the bad times – but it hasn't worked out that way. The problem is, I suppose, that nothing very dreadful has ever happened to me. (Yet.) Georgie lost a husband to alcoholism; Lin was betrayed by the man she adored and then ran off with someone else, who died after an excess of drink and drugs. I was just dumpy and dumped – and I dealt with one and got over the other. But writing this, I learnt to see through my friends' eyes. My experience has widened even as I took on theirs. I've grown up, and the story has grown up, and I don't know where it's going any more.

All of which brings me to this chapter. If you thought things were bad at the end of the last one, just wait. Up to now, I could be flip about the bad stuff: I made comments about worst fears being realised, and shit-fan situations, but there was no big tragedy, no major catastrophe, only everyday disasters. But this is the point where the jokes stop, where there's nothing to laugh at any more. And I'm scared to write it, because I don't do gloom and doom; it isn't my thing. I just have to tell it the way it happened, and keep hoping it'll work out in the end.

At Ransome on Friday, Georgie wasn't talking to me. I asked Lin to explain things to her – 'There was nothing between Cal and me. He was pissed and being provocative: that's all' – but Lin looked sad, and faintly unconvinced, and said she didn't think she could do anything. When Cal headed my way I begged him to sort it out, but he said Georgie wasn't talking to him either.

'She'll speak to you first,' he said. 'Bet you fifty quid.' He was leaning on my desk as he said it, and at that precise moment Georgie went past. She paused for a second, fixing us with a stare that would have split the atom, then walked on, ignoring my pleas to *Listen, please listen* . . .

'Bugger,' said Cal.

'Would you mind not coming near me,' I said, 'for the next year?'

He gave a resigned nod and returned to the Design Department, leaving me to sink quietly into a morass of misery and frustration.

Later, Lin admitted to me that she was going to the pub after work with Georgie. 'She needs someone with her,' she said. 'Ivor's been a star. He's babysitting again – though it's only Meredith tonight, so he might get some peace and quiet.' I thought it unlikely, but didn't say so. I suggested coming along with them to the pub and attempting to patch things up, but Lin was discouraging.

'Look,' I said, '*nothing happened*. You couldn't think – you *can't* think I would've . . .'

'You flirted with him, didn't you?' Lin sounded more unhappy than accusatory. 'He was coming on to you, and you didn't exactly repulse him.'

'He wasn't serious. It was just words. He kept saying how much he loved Georgie. But she's hurt him so deeply, I think he wanted to hurt her back, so he used me.'

'And you let him.' Lin turned to go. 'I think you should leave it for now. Maybe in a couple of weeks . . .'

But I didn't want to leave it. That was like an admission of guilt, and although I *felt* guilty, when I went over the events of the previous evening in my mind I didn't think I'd been leading Cal on. Instinct told me that the longer I left it, the harder it would be to put things right. But I didn't want to go to the pub alone, so I went to find Laurence, hoping this would be one of his going-out-with-the-gang nights. By then it was late-afternoon, and the undercurrents in the office had become overcurrents. Everyone knew there was something badly wrong, and most of Ransome was waiting with bated breath for the big explosion.

Except, as it turned out, for Laurence.

'Not tonight,' he said. 'Sorry, Cookie. Hector's giving a dinner party for some of his chums from work.' Hector, Laurence's partner, was in the social services. 'I have to get out my pinny and put the beef in my Wellingtons.'

'*You're* not the cook,' I said. 'I know that. What's more, I don't believe you have a pinny.'

'I do now,' he said. 'It's got Princess Di on it.'

I laughed, if half-heartedly, and went back to my desk. Cal was there. 'You going to the pub?'

'Yes, but—'

'Good. We'll go together. Georgie shouldn't be blaming you for what happened yesterday. It was my fault, not yours. You didn't even encourage me.'

'This isn't a good idea,' I said. 'Anyway, Georgie isn't talking to you.'

'Doesn't matter. *I'm* going to talk to *her*. I'm off on holiday for the next fortnight, and I want this business sorted before I go. I won't leave you to deal with the fallout; it isn't fair. I may be an arsehole, but at least I'm not afraid to say so.'

'I *really* don't think—'

'Yes you do. You think much too often: that's the trouble with women. Time for action.' He had obviously had an attack of grim resolve, and there was no point in arguing, though I tried.

Around half-past five I saw Lin and Georgie leaving. Cal and I followed after six – he was always the last out of Design – with me looking furtive, making sure there was at least a yard of clear space between us at all times. He paid no attention. When we reached the pub I hung back, feeling a coward, unwilling to be seen walking in with him – but Cal seized my wrist and pulled me through the door in his wake. It wasn't the entrance I would have chosen. Across the room, Georgie looked up at exactly the wrong moment. Lin told me later she was on her second double gin with very little tonic, and the glitter in her eyes would have daunted a black mamba. Cal took in the scene with a stiffened lip, bought drinks for both of us, and headed for Georgie's table. I lagged behind.

'Give us a moment,' he said to Lin.

'No,' said Georgie. 'Don't.'

Lin got to her feet, hesitated, then joined me. We didn't speak, just waited at a safe distance, trying to look as if we weren't watching the confrontation at the table.

'Fuck off,' Georgie said.

'If you wish. But first, we need to straighten something out. I made a pass at Cookie last night, yes, but she brushed me off. She's a good friend to you; she always has been. Stop blaming her for something *I* did. She wouldn't even flirt with me.'

'It's not important,' Georgie said, sick at heart. 'You wanted *her*, not me. I can't – I can't bear to look at her.'

'Don't be silly,' Cal snapped. 'Of course I want you. But we keep fighting, and Cookie was there – she looked great – she was kind to me—'

'*Kind* to you? How generous of her!'

'Yes, kind. It's an attractive quality. You should try it some time.'

'How dare you!' Her face blazed. 'You don't have the *right* to lecture me! You're a married man screwing around, and you think you can take the moral high ground—'

'I'm not screwing around. I wish I was.'

'You *bastard*!'

'I've had enough of this. All I get from you these days is tantrums. Yes, I'm married – you knew that all along. I thought we had a good thing going—'

'You made me fall in love with you!' Georgie all but screamed, abandoning any attempt at reason.

'I didn't mean to. I didn't want to fall in love either. I can't deal with it any more than you can. When you go with other men it destroys me, but I can't leave my wife, I can't leave my *family*. I don't think there's any way out of this—'

'There is,' Georgie said, going from stormy to stony in rather less than a second. 'The way out's over there.' She pointed at the door.

'If that's what you want.'

'It's what *you* want. You said so.'

It was another half hour before Cal finally walked out, looking furious, and wretched, and bitter. Georgie was left alone, looking – bitter, wretched, and furious. Same old scenario, but that didn't make it any less painful. Lin went over to her; I followed more slowly.

'I don't want to see you,' she said to me, I hoped with less acrimony than before. 'What I want to see is another gin. A triple.'

I got her the drink and went back to the bar, taking up a position beside a refugee from Ransome (Sales) who had evidently come to spectate. Georgie was going to feel like hell the next morning – if not sooner – but I knew it would be no use trying to stop her. As the evening progressed I saw Lin failing in the attempt, and Georgie getting through a couple more large gins, with only a packet of peanuts to soak up the alcohol. Booze doesn't solve your problems, I thought, but at least it makes you feel like shit. Tomorrow, Georgie would be too busy with her hangover to agonise over Cal, if only for a few hours.

Some time later, she called me over. 'You're still here,' she said accusingly.

'It's a pub,' I responded. 'I wanted a drink.'

'What really happened with Cal?' she asked, not looking me in the face.

'We talked about you. He said he loved you. He said you were in his bones, in his blood. He's desperate for you.'

'Then why did he go?' She looked up at me now, her eyes filling. 'Why does he always go?'

'You never ask him to stay.'

'I shouldn't *need* to ask him. He should . . . he should . . .' She groped for phrases that wouldn't come.

'He should stay even when you tell him to leave?' I suggested.

'Yup.' Sometimes, there is clarification at the bottom of the bottle.

'It's time you talked to him without rowing,' Lin said optimistically. 'On Monday—'

'He won't be there on Monday,' I said. 'He's off for two weeks. Holiday.'

'What?' Georgie's fury returned, first in a trickle, then in a flood. 'He left me – like that – and he's going away? Two weeks – *two weeks* – and he just walked out! He can't – he *can't*—' She banged her glass down on the table. They'd run out of tumblers: it was only a wine glass, and it smashed. She crushed the pieces in her hand; the blood ran over her fingers. Her face distorted.

Lin and I stared in horror. 'Georgie, your hand – !' Lin gasped, groping for tissues in her bag. She was the sort of person who always carried tissues.

'I won't let him!' Georgie was saying, fumbling with her mobile. 'I won't let him just *go*. I must talk to him. *Now*.' She pressed out the number, but evidently there was no answer.

'It'll be on recharge,' I said. 'Probably silent. He'll have gone to bed by now.'

It was the wrong thing to say.

'With her!' Georgie said. 'Bloody Christy. I can't stand it. If he loves me, why is he in bed with *her*? Why is he going on holiday with *her*? What kind of love is that?' She picked up her bag and made for the door with an alarmingly steady step. We ran after her.

Outside, she hailed a cruising taxi and got in, thrusting Lin away when she tried to follow.

'Where are you going?' Lin demanded.

'I must see him. I *have* to see him. He can't just walk out on me and bugger off on holiday with his wife . . .'

'What're you going to do?'

Georgie slammed the door, and the taxi leaped forward. 'Boil the rabbit!' she screamed.

Fortunately, we were on a main road and the closing-time rush hadn't yet started. Taxis streamed past, many of them for hire. I grabbed the next one and we jumped in. 'Follow that cab!' Lin cried, getting carried away.

'Which cab?' the driver asked, bored. Plainly he had heard it all before.

'That one,' said Lin, pointing. 'No – that one . . .'

'It's all right,' I said. 'I know Cal's address.' I'd had to send some stuff round to him once when he had a day off. I couldn't recall the house number, but I knew the street. Our driver took his time, getting bogged down in traffic, and we didn't see Georgie anywhere up ahead. When we eventually reached Lyndhall Road it was dark and quiet, with no sign of any other vehicle.

'What do we do now?' Lin said in an undervoice, while I paid the fare. 'Knock on all the doors?'

'Walk along till we come to the scene of the crime?' I offered.

We found Georgie leaning against a wall about halfway down the road. She, too, couldn't remember the number. 'I rang the doorbell,' she said, 'but it was the wrong house. There was an old woman in a dressing-gown who was cross. I asked if she knew the McGregors but she said no . . .'

We coaxed her to walk back with us, or at least to start walking. We each put an arm round her; the gin was taking effect and she needed support. At one point she stopped, insisting she wanted Cal – she had to go to him – and there was a struggle, and she lashed out at me, saying I'd tried to take him from her. Then she began to sob, dry racking sobs that tore at her gut, growing more and more violent, until her body shook with them. She doubled up, expelling a stream of thin vomit flecked with peanuts. Some of it splashed over my leg. There were no taxis any more, and even if there had been, I was sure the driver would have refused to take us. In the end, I called the minicab firm used by Ransome and booked one on the company account. (I could pay it back later.) We waited what seemed like ages, and Georgie was sick again, though she had very little left to be sick with, and then passed out on Lin's shoulder. I saw a curtain twitch in an upper window, and wondered which house Cal was in, and whether he was sleeping, and if he knew what was happening outside. But no; if he'd heard Georgie, he would have come out to help her, I was sure of that. Nearly sure, anyway.

When the minicab came we roused her enough to get her in, and gave the driver her address. Once there we asked him to wait, found her keys, took her indoors and arranged her on the sofa (the stairs were out of the question). 'Will she be all right?' Lin asked, doubtfully.

'I think so. She can't be sick any more: she's too empty. I expect she'll just sleep it off.'

We removed her shoes and covered her with a throw which was draped over one of the chairs. Lin scribbled a note which she hoped would be reassuring – 'Cookie and I brought you home. Call when you feel better' – and we left it on a nearby table with a bottle of Paracetamol from the bathroom and a glass of water. Then we went back to the cab. By the time he had taken us both home I calculated the fare would be astronomical. Perhaps I wouldn't pay it back after all.

When I crawled into bed at last I was exhausted and

desperate for sleep, but it didn't come. My brain was still in overdrive, fizzing away with unwelcome thoughts like a bottle of cheap champagne. I was shocked to the core that Georgie – Georgie who always seemed so on top of things, so in charge of her life (if not her credit-card bill) – could suddenly fall apart like that. She had invariably been poised, self-assured, sophisticated, funny, taking nothing too seriously, feeling nothing too deeply, a role model for those of us (i.e. me) who were gauche and unconfident and took everything to heart, falling over our own feet in the process. Whatever her troubles she'd dealt with them, laughed at them, made light of them, one of the natural winners at the great Monopoly-board of destiny. Georgie never came a cropper.

But tonight I'd seen her reduced, like other women, sobbing and frantic and helpless, battered by emotions she couldn't control. There was an element of shame in it, a kind of guilt because I'd seen her that way. That's what love does to you, I thought. Suddenly you don't own yourself any more. Someone else pushes the buttons that work your spirit, the ones marked 'Happiness' and 'Sorrow' and 'Pain', not to mention the red one marked 'Danger: Do Not Touch'. It can happen to anyone, at any time, any age. It terrified me. I tried to visualise what I'd felt for Nigel, multiplied by about a thousand. Wherever Georgie had gone was a place I hadn't been and didn't wish to go, however bittersweet the rewards. What was the poem?

> *I am the master of my fate;*
> *I am the captain of my soul.*

I didn't want to be beautiful, and I didn't want to be in love. I fished for pleasanter thoughts to divert my mind, and the image of Todd Jarman hovered, but I banished it. That way lay trouble – or it might, if it hadn't been for Helen

Aucham getting in the way. Thank God for Helen Aucham. At least, I thought, drowsing at last, nothing further could happen this weekend. I'd had two days of soul-searing emotion, upheaval and trauma. It couldn't possibly get worse.

I was wrong.

It must have been about eleven the following morning when the buzzer sounded on my entryphone. I was making tea, and I might not have heard it over the hiss of the kettle if the caller hadn't been so persistent. I picked up the handset. 'Who is it?'

A very small voice said: 'Is that Cookie, please?'

'Yes.'

'It's Meredith Grimes. Can you come down and pay my taxi?'

I've measured out my life in taxi fares, I thought, paraphrasing T. S. Eliot. I had no idea what Meredith was doing there, but I'd only just got up and my brain wasn't working well enough to think about it. I tied the sash more tightly round my tatty kimono and ran downstairs. I'd paid the cab and taken Meredith up to the flat before I got a good look at her, but I knew already something wasn't right. Not just because she'd turned up at my place alone, unannounced, unsupervised. When I put my arm around her I could feel the tension in her little body: the muscles in her shoulders were tight as wire. In the kitchen, I saw her face for the first time. She was never a pretty child, with her squashed-up features and lumpy brow, but now she looked uglier than ever, a small brown gnome knuckled inside herself as if her spirit was bunched into a fist.

'What are you doing here?' I asked her. 'Where's Mummy?'

'I've run away.'

'I see.' It might be important, it might not. I remembered my own childhood, and the huge miseries that seemed so

283

trivial now. 'I was just making some tea, but I expect you'd prefer juice.'

'I like tea,' Meredith said. 'Lots of sugar.'

'Magic word?'

'Please.'

'Why did you come to me?' I ventured, pouring water on tea-bags.

'I couldn't think of anyone else. Grandma Vee belongs to the twins, not me, and Grandma Grimes doesn't like me, and Nana and Grandpop Macleod are in Scotland. I thought maybe I could go to them, but I haven't enough money. Could you lend me some?'

'Of course,' I said. 'D'you want a biscuit with your tea?'

'Yes, please.'

We went into the living room and sat on the sofa. Meredith looked at her biscuit, then put it down. 'I thought I could live on the streets,' she went on, 'like a beggar or a gipsy. But I'm not old enough, and there are people who come and find you, and make you go to school. And there are bad men who steal little girls, like the Child Catcher.'

I remembered she had just seen *Chitty Chitty Bang Bang*. 'Were you scared of the Child Catcher?' I said. 'I know I was, when I was your age.'

'I'm not scared of anything!' Normally, she would have said it without the exclamation mark. 'It's just make-believe. It's silly to be scared of make-believe.'

'I'm scared of lots of things,' I said. 'Most people are. You can't be brave unless you're scared first. Actually, I was scared of you, to start off with.' I grinned at her, but she barely responded. The biscuit was still untouched, though she sipped her tea. (I'd cooled it down with tap water.) 'Why have you run away? Did you have a row with Mummy?'

'Sort of.' Pause. 'She doesn't love me any more. It's all Ivor.'

Ah. The textbook problem. New boyfriend taking up mum's attention and affection; result: jealousy. If only Lin had taken things more slowly, given the children time to get used to him . . .

'Of course she still loves you,' I said. 'It's just that she loves Ivor as well. That's natural. I thought you quite liked him. You said he was sensible.'

Meredith said nothing.

'Did you have a row with *him*?' I asked.

Eventually, she gave a tiny nod. 'He says I'm wicked.'

I was aware of a flicker of anger, but I didn't show it. 'He didn't mean it,' I said. 'Children aren't wicked; children are naughty. Only grownups are wicked.' She looked at me, her face unreadable as ever, but I sensed something hidden, a secret tumult of feeling. Rage, hatred, distress – I wasn't sure. 'What happened?' I inquired gently.

A further pause. 'It was about the porno stuff I got for the twins. I don't *like* it; I just did it for them. They pay me. I think sex is yukky and boring. But he said . . . he said . . .'

Suddenly, my skin crawled. A lot of things flashed through my head very fast: *'Ivor's been a star – babysitting again'* – *'he found them looking at porno pictures – he laughed'* – *Lin meeting a stranger in a chatroom, getting the bad news out there first – 'I'm a single parent, twin boys and a girl – no dads around—'*

There are some things so terrible that you don't even want to think them. You read them in the newspapers, you see them on the television, but that's at a distance, unreal; you don't expect them to invade your life. The big horrors belong in thriller fiction, in tabloid headlines – they don't happen to you, or to people you know. That's a cliché, of course, but when horror comes you think in cliché: your imagination freezes. You think: *No. Please no* . . .

'What did he say?' Somehow, I kept my voice gentle.

285

'He said . . . I *did* like it. He said I was wicked. It's not true. I *don't* . . .'

I put my arms around her, but she was still rigid, unyielding. I stroked the knotted braids of her hair. 'Did this happen last night?' I had to repeat the question before she managed another nod. 'Listen . . . I want you to tell me everything. I know it's difficult – you'll have to be very brave. Sometimes, bravery isn't what you expect. It can mean having to tell things, bad things, that you don't want to tell. But I promise you, I don't think you're wicked. Whatever you tell me. Understand?' Hesitant nod. 'Believe me?'

'Mm.'

'D'you know what a paedophile is?'

'Someone like the Child Catcher,' Meredith said promptly. 'Only they offer you sweets and presents, and you mustn't go with them, or you could end up dead, like those children on the news.'

'Okay. Now back to Ivor. He said you liked the porno stuff. What did he do next?'

'He said – he would show me some I would like better. Just for me.' The words came out brokenly, in a shrinking whisper. I had to lean closer to hear it. 'He went on to a website with pictures of children. They were undressed . . . doing things. Porno things. He said he could get the pix because I'd bypassed the security. He said, if I told Mummy, she'd think it was me. She'd think I wanted to look at those pictures – do those things. She'd know how wicked I am . . . He said he wouldn't tell her if I didn't, it would be a secret, our secret . . .'

'He lied,' I said. 'He lied and lied. He's the wicked one.' I coaxed her to drink more tea, gave her the biscuit. She still didn't eat, just sat clutching it, tight, tight, like a comforter. 'Did he do anything else?'

Silence.

286

I fished for the right words, the necessary words – words to encourage and reassure. It was like groping in a pitch-black room for something that is lost, when you're not even sure what shape it is.

'There will have been other girls, did you know that? He'll have told them they were wicked, just like you, and made them do things. There'll be more after you. You're not alone. If you're brave – if you tell – we can stop him. D'you want to stop him?'

'How do you know,' she said, 'about the other girls?'

'I just know. There always are.'

Mandelson jumped up on the sofa beside her, sniffing the biscuit. 'Can I give it him?'

'Yes.'

He took it in his mouth, played with it and discarded it, in the way of cats. I lifted him on to Meredith's knees, where he dug his claws in and settled down, allowing her to stroke him. His warmth and softness and the rhythmic motion of her hand seemed to help her. Or so I hoped.

'Did he do anything else?'

'Rude things,' she said at last. 'Like . . . in the pictures.'

My heart clenched – that's how it felt, like a cold hand clenching inside me. I thought of Lin, all shiny with love and happiness. Oh Lin . . . Lin . . .

I said, very softly: 'What things? You have to tell, Meredith. If we're going to stop him, you have to tell.'

'He touched my . . . my rude bits. He took my knickers off, and put his finger . . .' The stroking stopped. Her grip tightened on Mandy, who whined in protest, and wriggled free. 'He said . . . I was pretty there. Those bits. How can they be pretty?' For the first time, there were tears. Her voice rose. 'I'm ugly – I know I'm ugly – but he said he'd make me pretty . . . buy me pretty clothes. He said we'd do pretty things together . . . I said how could it be pretty, if it was

287

wicked? He said he'd show me. He'd show me lots of things
. . . I want Mandy back. Give me Mandy!'

I retrieved the cat, and put him back in her lap, and daubed
her eyes with the tissue. I was a bit surprised to find my
hand didn't shake. When she started stroking again, she grew
calmer.

'What happened next?' I said.

She went on stroking. Then she looked up at me, her
expression oddly flat. When she spoke, her voice was
different. Sharper. 'I said . . . I'd like some ice cream.'

A faint warmth flowed through me. 'And?'

'He got some. Two spoons. He said we'd share it. He said
he didn't know why Mummy didn't like me to eat ice cream.
If I did what I was told, he'd see I got lots. He – he got his
thingy out. While I was eating the ice cream. He said . . .
he'd show me something, and he got his thingy out. It was
disgusting. It looked – wrong . . .'

'How – wrong?' I asked involuntarily.

'Not floppy like it's supposed to be. Sticking up. Anyway,'
she added, 'you're not meant to touch your rude bits when
you have food. It's unhygienic.'

'Very,' I said. 'So did you—?'

'I did a sicky.' There was a note of defiance in her voice.
'I did a really good one. All over him – all over his thingy.'

'Well done,' I said. I was crying. 'Bloody well done.' I
hugged her, taking care not to dislodge Mandy, feeling a little
of the tension ooze out of her. 'Was he very angry?'

'He was scary – he said he'd punish me, make me sorry,
really sorry. I thought he was going to hit me, but he had
to go and wash first, and change his trousers, and I locked
the bedroom door so he couldn't come in. Then he stood
outside and said how wicked I was, and he would tell
Mummy, and she would be very angry. When she came back
he told her he'd been nice to me . . . I'd done a sicky when

he'd been nice to me . . . and she believed him . . . she *believed* him . . .'

'Did you try to tell her what he'd done?'

'No. I thought she'd be angry – about my helping the twins to watch porno stuff. Ivor said she would – he said she'd believe him – and she did. She kept on believing him—'

Meredith was tearful again – I could imagine her sense of betrayal – and I reassured her, telling her it would be all right now, I'd talk to Lin, and she'd be believed, not Ivor. I don't know if she was completely convinced, though I told her '*I promise*', which is always sacred to children. I didn't want to think of Lin's reaction when I pulled the rug out from under her world . . .

'How did you manage to run away?' I asked Meredith.

'I had to open the bedroom door, when Mummy came home, and Ivor took the key, and this morning he locked me in, and Mummy didn't stop him, and he said in a horrid quiet voice that he would deal with me later. So I climbed out of the window and down into the garden. There's a drainpipe – it's a bit slippy, so I fell some of the way, but I made it, and then I could get out the back. I remembered where you lived, so when I found a taxi I told him to come here. I didn't know where else to go.'

'You did quite right,' I said. 'You've been really brave and clever, and I'm so proud of you . . . so proud . . .' I hugged her again. 'Your mummy will be too, when she knows everything.'

'You won't tell her about the porn pictures?'

'Don't worry: it'll all be fine now. I'm going to call Georgie, and tell her about it. That's okay, isn't it? She never liked Ivor very much.'

'I thought she didn't,' Meredith said, with a trace of satisfaction.

I gave her another biscuit which I suspected would go the

way of the first, and put on a video. Then I phoned Georgie.

Horror and fury at Meredith's story possessed me so utterly I'd completely forgotten the drama of the previous night – or that Georgie and I were still on questionable terms – or the fact that she must be suffering from the mother of all hangovers. She answered the phone in a voice that seemed to have sawdust in it: I could hear the fur on her tongue. I paid no attention.

'Something's happened,' I said. 'Get round here. It's urgent.'

'I feel like shit,' she said stonily. 'And I don't know if I want to see you.'

Memory clocked on, but I ignored it. 'Meredith's here. She ran away. Thank God, she remembered my address. She turned up in a cab about an hour ago.'

'Have you called Lin?' Georgie sounded baffled.

'No.'

'She'll be frantic. Why did Meredith—?'

'Ivor.'

There was a silence which lasted some time. I could hear Georgie thinking, kicking her numbed brain into gear. 'What did he do?'

'You were right about him,' I murmured, obliquely. In front of Meredith, I wanted to keep the conversation innocuous. 'You were right all along.'

This time, the silence was much shorter, punctuated by an intake of breath. 'Is she okay?'

'I think so. She will be. She's a bloody star,' I added, getting weepy again.

'I'm coming.' The sawdust had trickled away; her tone was brisk. 'Just give me time to wash and dress: I'll be as quick as I can. Wait for me?'

'Yeah.'

I sat down with Meredith in front of *Shrek*, but very little of the film registered on me. Lin must be worrying, I knew, but that was tough. I had no intention of calling her; Georgie and I would go round there. (I couldn't possibly confront Lin alone.) It occurred to me that we couldn't take Meredith with us so we'd need a babysitter. I called a neighbour, giving her few details but stressing the urgency of the situation. Meredith wasn't too happy at the prospect of being left with a stranger, but as it was a woman, and they were to remain in my flat, she accepted it. 'We have to deal with Ivor,' I told her. 'We'll fix it so you never have to see him again.' I wasn't sure how – I had no plan of action – but it didn't matter. We'd fix it. I knew I ought to call the police, but not yet, not till we'd spoken to Lin. They would have to be involved, sooner rather than later – presumably Meredith would need to make a statement to some specially trained, sympathetic officer (didn't they video children nowadays, so they wouldn't have to appear in court?) – but all that was for the future. The first thing was to tell Lin, and get Ivor out of her house, out of her life.

We'd finished *Shrek* and moved on to Indiana Jones before Georgie arrived. Meredith had begun to be hungry at last; I gave her some tabouleh from M&S which I had in the fridge and some chocolate which I found at the back of the vegetable drawer, left over from pre-diet days. She greeted Georgie with something that was almost a smile and turned her attention back to the film.

I took Georgie into the kitchen to fill her in. She didn't look good: the fading tan gave her a sallow pallor and the disorder of her hair seemed less artistic than usual. But the tag-end of her hangover had evidently been consigned to history: her manner was sharp and alert, like a flick-knife with the blade ready to spring. She didn't say anything about last night; nor did I. She just listened.

'We have to go see Lin,' she said when I'd finished.

'Yes.'

'Oh God . . .'

I knew she'd started thinking, as I had, not of what Ivor had done (or tried to do) to Meredith, but of what he'd done to Lin. Lin with her romantic ideals and loving heart – Lin standing there in Waitrose with fairy dust in her eyes – Lin saying she'd found her Mr Right, her soulmate, her one and only love. Lin who thought wishes really did come true.

If he fried in hell for all eternity, it wouldn't be too long. (Not that I believe in hell, or capital punishment, or any of those things, but there are times when primitive emotion takes over.)

'What do we do?' I asked.

'Go round there.' Restlessly, Georgie opened and closed the kitchen drawers, a purely nervous action, like biting your nails. Or not. I saw her take out a fruit knife with a four-inch serrated blade and thrust it into her waistband, where it was in imminent danger of puncturing her stomach.

'What's that for?'

'I thought it was for cutting up fruit,' she murmured, with an echo of her old self. 'It's just a precaution.'

I didn't like it, but I didn't say any more. We left Meredith with my neighbour, and went out.

I hadn't thought about it, but I should have realised that Georgie was on the edge. The disintegration of her relationship with Cal, the paralysing discovery of her own depth of feeling, the realisation that she too could plumb the abyss of drunken humiliation – these things had pushed her beyond the limits of normal human reactions. Most of us have a sense of proportion, an internal equilibrium that keeps us rooted in the real world; but Georgie's equilibrium had gone with the raggle-taggle-gipsies-oh, leaving her off-balance, off-message, no longer safe to be around. But I was too absorbed with the problem of Lin and Ivor to notice. I remember very vividly the terrible shrinking sensation in my stomach when we arrived outside her house. They say the seat of emotion is in the heart, but it isn't. The heart may quail or leap occasionally, in response to powerful stimuli, but it's the stomach that bears the brunt of the punches. Fear, panic, revolt, anticipation – that's where it gets you. Right in the gut. We stood on Lin's doorstep and rang the bell, and my stomach ran the gamut of every emotion in the book. Lin opened the door. She looked too anxious to be surprised to see us.

She said: 'What?' and 'Come in', in an abstracted way, glancing over her shoulder to where Ivor appeared from the living room.

'Meredith's run away,' he said, looking grave. The hypocrite. 'Lin wants to call the police, but I don't think. . .'

'I'll bet you don't,' said Georgie.

Lin didn't seem to register her tone, but Ivor did; I saw it in his eyes. For an instant, it was like looking into the eyes of a calculating machine – or it would be, if machines *had* eyes. I could see his brain doing sums.

'I feel awful,' Lin was saying, on the edge of tears. 'We told her off – we locked her in her room – what else could we do? She'd behaved so badly . . . You have to have discipline. Ivor's right about that: he *knows* kids. I suppose I've been lax; I've let her get away with things for so long. She must've climbed out the window . . . I can't think where she could've gone. I've called some of her friends, but she isn't there . . .'

I said: 'It's all right, Lin. She came to me. It's all right.'

'Oh God. Oh Cookie – !' She hurled herself on my chest, hugging me, passionate with relief.

Lax, mouthed Georgie. She was looking at Ivor the way a snake looks at a bird – but Ivor wasn't a bird.

He joined Lin in expressing his gratitude and thanks, though we hadn't done anything. 'Where is she?' Lin demanded. 'Why haven't you brought her back? Is she okay?'

'I left her with a neighbour,' I said. 'She's fine. We wanted a word with you first.' Like Georgie, I was looking at Ivor.

His expression was a masterpiece: rueful, regretful, compassionate, a little sad. If there was an award for Most Appropriate Expression Under Very Awkward Circumstances, he'd have won hands down. But I knew him now; I could *feel* the well-oiled confidence underneath, the vein of smugness. 'She threatened to tell people I'd been abusing her,' he said on a sigh. 'You must realise it's nonsense, but . . . well, you know what she is. I'm afraid she's a lot too clever with that computer of hers. I didn't want to tell you, darling –' this to Lin '– but she's been accessing porn sites. She *says* it's for the twins. But . . . I caught her looking at child porn last night.'

Lin stared at him, her colour draining. He took her hand, looking kind, so kind, sorrow and sympathy coming out all over his face like a rash. In that moment, I could have killed him.

But I wasn't the one with the knife.

'Yes,' I said, 'she did mention what you tried to do. Funny how convincing she was. I think Lin should get her film career off the ground right now. With that sort of talent, she'd be an Oscar winner from scratch.'

'Meredith's a very good liar,' he said gravely. He was good at gravitas. 'The trouble is, she's always got away with it. You wouldn't believe how savvy kids are nowadays. They know it all, poor things. Colleagues of mine have to deal with this sort of accusation all the time.'

A little of Lin's colour returned. She said: 'Ivor would never . . .'

'She wasn't lying.' My voice was one I'd never heard myself use before. 'She *did* get pornography for the twins: they've hit puberty with all its urges, and it was a way of augmenting her pocket money. But it was Ivor who accessed the child porn. That wouldn't interest Sandy and Demmy: they like tits. And it certainly wouldn't interest Meredith: she's still young enough to think sex is yukky. She may think it for a long time now.'

'It's not true,' Lin whispered.

'What was the first thing you told him, when you met in the chatroom?' I must've sounded hard – implacable. I had to. 'You wanted to get the worst over with, didn't you? So you explained you were a single parent with twin boys and a girl. A *difficult* girl. He must have thought Christmas had come early.'

'No . . .' Lin's whisper had shrunk till it was almost inaudible.

Ivor had begun to protest, with just enough weariness in his tone to give it conviction. Georgie, untypically, wasn't saying anything. She'd moved round, so she was standing beside and a little behind him. Her left hand went under her D&G T-shirt and reappeared with the knife. Then her right grabbed his arm, and the blade whipped round – and stopped.

Everything stopped. Ivor's weary protest, Lin's awful whisper. I can't remember if I was talking, but if I had been, I shut up.

The tip of the knife was embedded in his trousers, low down next to the fly. From the look on Ivor's face, metal was touching skin.

'The truth,' Georgie said. 'Now.'

'I've told the truth. You've been watching too many documentaries . . .'

'*Now.*'

The knife-hand moved. Lin screamed. At the same moment Ivor's body jerked backwards – twisted – he seized Georgie's left arm, deflecting the knife, flinging her aside. Lin tried to clutch him in relief but he threw her off too, shoving past me, bolting through the front door like a bat out of hell. Evidently he'd had enough. Lin ran after him, calling his name. 'Fucking psychos!' he cried, half turning. One hand held his groin: there was a hint of red showing between the fingers. 'Fucking psycho bitches! I'm getting out while I still can. I'll send for my gear.'

'But what about me?' Lin wailed.

'Sorry, but . . . with friends like those, there'll never be a man in your life.' He went off down the street, his walk breaking into a wobbling run – not easy when you are trying to keep hold of your genitals and are clearly in pain. I might have laughed, if there had been any humour left in the world. But Lin's face left no room for laughter. We got her into the living room, attempted to relate Meredith's story as calmly as possible, but she didn't want to listen, or listening, didn't want to believe. I stayed with her while Georgie went to fetch Meredith. She kept accusing me of destroying her life, and then collapsing into a sobbing so violent I was afraid she would choke herself.

'If it wasn't true,' I said, 'he wouldn't have run off like that.'

Then Georgie arrived, with Meredith, and when Lin saw her daughter's face she knew it was true.

The next few days were an ongoing nightmare. The police were called and statements taken; there was endless praise for Meredith's courage and resource – not to mention the fact that she was extremely articulate for her age – which, while it didn't heal her, did help her to cope with the trauma of what she had been through. Mummy's betrayal seemed to cut as deep as the abuse; only time would close that particular wound.

Lin was torn between intolerable guilt and the pain of

Ivor's perfidy, one moment hysterical with grief, the next struggling to scrape herself together for the sake of the children. She didn't want people to know what had happened, so we couldn't summon relatives from Scotland to support her, but we told Alistair in confidence so she could take time off, her doctor gave her a sick certificate, and Vee Corrigan looked after the twins as much as possible. Georgie and I came round every evening after work, stayed the night regularly, and did what we could for her – which wasn't much, because all you can do in such a scenario is to be there. There was no remedy but time, no panacea but to listen as Lin went through it all, over and over again. She showed little anger against Ivor: it was all turned inward on herself.

Georgie, with real nobility, never said *I told you so*.

Investigations revealed that, while Ivor had no record, there had been complaints against him in the past. But the children concerned were all very young, and none of the allegations had been substantiated. He had left one school rather abruptly, no reason given; the headmaster, now retired, admitted in an interview that there had been 'issues' with some of the girls, but insisted he'd had no suspicion of 'anything really wrong'. He had just thought it best for Ivor to leave, and had passed the problem – and the responsibility – on to someone else. One girl, then eleven, now eighteen, made a statement.

Ivor was traced, arrested, bailed. He *did* come back for his things, fleeing down the steps when Georgie opened the door. We don't know when the case will come to court, but he's got an expensive lawyer (so there's money somewhere) and he's going to plead Not Guilty. Lin's horrified at the prospect of Meredith being a witness, even though, as I thought, she'll be questioned elsewhere, on video. Meredith is nervous of it, but hugely proud of the most famous sicky of her career. Because of that, she doesn't have to see herself

297

as a victim, and even at nine years old, that matters. Whether you win or lose, it's the fightback that restores your self-respect.

She now says she wants to be a detective when she grows up.

Georgie and I never really made it up – we didn't need to – our falling out just wasn't important any more.

There was an occasion in Lin's kitchen when we talked about it, just a little. (Lin was upstairs with Meredith.)

'Cal's back next week,' I said. 'Are you going to patch things up with him?'

'I don't know. I don't know if I can.'

'But you love him,' I said, for the umpteenth time. 'He loves you. Real love, not lies and fairy dust. Isn't it worth putting up with anything for that?'

And, when she didn't answer: 'There was nothing between us. Nothing that mattered. Just . . . Cal being a bit flirty, because you'd hurt him, and perhaps a little because he felt safe with me. He knew I wouldn't take it seriously.'

'It's okay.' She squeezed my hand. 'It isn't that. I lost it the other night – I mean, completely lost it. I've never done that before, over anyone. Supposing it happens again. What if, next time, I ring the right doorbell?'

'There won't be a next time,' I said, being positive, but it didn't reassure her.

We had to field all Lin's telephone calls: she couldn't cope with casual conversation and dreaded inquiries about Ivor. She flinched every time the phone rang. Inevitably, Andy Pearmain was one of those on the line. Andy? I said soundlessly, making a beard-stroking gesture in the vicinity of my chin. No! Lin responded, shaking her head violently. Don't tell him anything! I duly explained to Andy that Lin was ill – no, nothing serious, just some bug the kids had brought home from school – and I was there to help out. Could I take a message? Andy provided a fount of information about Dryden and Acme City, the gist of which I scribbled down on a piece of paper. I threw in a question about Sir Harold Chorley, and noted down more details. Jerry Beauman's activities didn't seem quite so absorbing right now, but they did offer a diversion. Andy went on to ask about Ivor, and why wasn't he taking care of Lin instead of me. Lin and I swapped a succession of agonised grimaces, after which I said hesitantly that he had to go to the school, a parents' evening or similar, but should be back later. Lin gave a vague nod of approval and then began to cry, silent tears snaking down her cheeks. Andy said: 'I see,' sounding unconvinced, and added that he would call back soon to arrange when he was coming to London. I didn't think I was imagining his proprietorial attitude towards Lin, but there was no point in commenting on it.

'He *can't!*' she said tragically when I repeated his last remarks. 'What am I to do? I can't face him. You'll have to put him off.'

'Me?'

The next problem caller came to the door late on Saturday afternoon. Georgie and I were both there, losing to Meredith at Monopoly. I escaped bankruptcy to answer the bell, and found myself confronting a man of forty-odd who looked faintly familiar. He must have been good-looking once but he wasn't wearing well: his jaw-line was blurred and beginning to be jowly, his thinning hair was a little too long on the collar, and his waistline bulged over the top of his jeans. To complete the picture, his eyes were pouchy and he had the sort of incipient beard that only works if the man is ruggedly beautiful, like Viggo Mortensen's Aragorn. Otherwise he just looks the way this one did: badly in need of a shave. I was trying to recall if I had met him at a party or a launch recently when light dawned.

'Lin here?' he asked.

Sean Corrigan.

I'd seen him as one of the guest stars in a who-dunnit series a few weeks earlier, *Midsomer Murders* or something like that. He'd changed a lot from the youthful Irish charmer Lin had fallen so desperately in love with; even the brogue had faded, at least in everyday speech, revived only in appropriate roles. His drinking binges still happened from time to time, to judge from his appearance, but the tabloids weren't very interested any more, and, at a guess, his high living had shrunk to low living, which is much the same but without the celebs and attendant paparazzi.

I said: 'Yes, but she hasn't been too well lately . . .'

'Mum told me. I'm going to find the bastard and kick the crap out of him. Can I come in?'

'I'll ask.'

He came in anyway, pushing past me, breaking in on the Monopoly game. I saw Lin's face look startled but not too horrified. Sean said: 'Mavourneen,' holding his arms out to her. Evidently he still used that one.

Lin said: 'What on earth—?'

'You should've called me,' Sean said. 'I've always been here for you, haven't I?' No comment. And then: 'What were you after, letting a man you hardly knew come and live with you? And you with the children and all.'

'Why not?' Lin retorted, uncharacteristically tart. 'I *married* you, and we barely knew each other.'

'D'you want him out?' Georgie said, giving Sean the steel-hard look of a woman who had recently knifed a man in the balls (if not too far in).

'No, it's okay.'

'We want a word in private,' Sean said. 'If you don't mind . . .'

Georgie ignored him, glancing at Lin, who nodded

reluctantly. We retreated to the kitchen, where Meredith said: 'Bugger. I was winning that game. I know what you'll say when we go back. You'll say we've forgotten where we were, so we can't go on playing.'

'Probably,' Georgie replied. 'And don't say bugger.'

'Why not? You say it.'

'I'm grown up. I'm allowed.'

'How old do I have to be to say bugger?'

'Eighteen. On your eighteenth birthday you can say it all you like. Bugger bugger bugger bugger. Until then, you have to say bother instead.'

'Bother!' Meredith echoed scornfully.

'How do you get on with Sean?' I asked. I noticed he hadn't even greeted her.

Meredith shrugged bony shoulders. 'He doesn't like me. Mummy says it isn't because I'm me, it's because of Daddy. She left Sean to live with him, so he doesn't like me. I think that's stupid. I wasn't even born then.'

'Some people react that way,' I said.

'Maybe I could start eating some ice cream?'

'*No*.'

Sean went about half an hour later, leaving Lin strained and anxious. 'He said Ivor could've abused the twins,' she complained. 'I told him, Ivor's thing was little girls. There's nothing in his record about boys. Sean said a paedophile is into any kind of child, which is totally wrong but I couldn't make him listen. He came over all paternal and protective – all very well, only he doesn't contribute very much as a father under normal circumstances. It's like . . . he's using this as an excuse to be macho.'

Lin wasn't usually so critical – or so perceptive.

'Could well be,' Georgie said. 'Still, what harm does it do? You're not worried about him beating up Ivor, are you? I mean . . . would it matter if he did?'

'No. I'm just . . . worried. Generally.' She tried for a smile that didn't come off.

'That's a natural reaction,' I said. 'But I'm sure the worst is over now.'

'I hope so,' said Lin.

Chapter 11

If I or she should chance to be
Involved in this affair,
He trusts to you to set them free
Exactly as we were.

It seemed to me that you had been
(Before she had this fit)
An obstacle, that came between
Him, and ourselves, and it.

Don't let him know she liked them best,
For this must ever be
A secret, kept from all the rest,
Between yourself and me.

LEWIS CARROLL: *She's All My Fancy Painted Him*

The next week started badly. Cal was back from holiday, not looking particularly rested but rather grimly resolved. Holidays are difficult with a disabled child: they'd gone to a hotel in the West Country which they'd visited before, where the staff understood Jamie's needs. There were wheelchair ramps everywhere, a shallow pool where he could splash around supported by his parents, and an adjacent farm with a children's area where he liked to stroke the animals. And for Allan there was a much deeper pool, a beach a short drive away, tennis and golf. Cal said with some pride that he was the new Tiger Woods and could even beat his dad. But it was clear Georgie had been on his mind. He'd obviously missed the scene in Lyndhall Road that night, since he didn't mention it, and Cal wasn't the sort to conceal what he knew, but he went into Georgie's office early on, asking her if they could go for a drink later and talk.

'Preferably without having a row.'

Georgie said: 'Okay,' but she didn't feel optimistic.

'This isn't working,' he said when they met after six. 'We have to sort it out – stop arguing – stop hurting each other. After all, we're in the same office.'

'Sort it out how?' said Georgie.

He avoided her eye, fiddled with a pen, spinning it between restless fingers. When he spoke, the sentences came out in short bursts, with silences in between. 'I think we need to accept that it's over. We're not going to be able to fix it. You want . . . more than I can give. The children need me, Christy needs me. I can't walk away from that. Things may never change. Allan will grow up, but Jamie – Jamie will always have to have care. I can't be there for you, not the way you want. You deserve so much more.'

'You said you loved me,' Georgie said numbly. 'You said I was part of you, part of your life. You said you'd always be there for me.'

'I'll try. As much as I can. We'll be friends . . .'

'We've been lovers.' Georgie's voice was bleak. 'How can we be friends?'

'Of course we can. We *are* friends, best friends. That won't change. It may take a little time, but . . .'

'One day we'll go out for a drink – reminisce – compare notes on our new loves? Is that it? Everything we felt –

everything we were – will just be a comfortable memory?'

Cal looked far from comfortable. 'No. More than that.'

'More than comfortable – less than passionate?' She stopped. 'Sorry. There's no point in talking, is there? You've made up your mind.'

He didn't answer. The pauses between them stretched out, becoming yawning gulfs of non-communication which even Georgie could not bridge. Georgie the articulate, the professional communicator.

Eventually they said goodnight, and she walked away, feeling that awful emptiness inside when your heart has gone out of you, and your soul has gone out of you, and there's nothing left, and nothing weighs as heavy as lead. Cal had offered to get her a cab, but she said no. The nights were getting cooler now, and she shivered in her light jacket, but the discomfort didn't matter. She thought: I had love in my life, the deep thing, the true thing, and now it's gone, and it will never come again. Never again. She'd always believed that somehow they would make it work, their love would make it work, but he'd given up trying. Maybe if she'd been a better person, more patient, more unselfish, less demanding . . . But I'm me, she told herself, in realisation, in revelation. I can't change that. And it was me he loved – wasn't it?

She crossed a road, nearly walking under a bus, not deliberately, but because she wasn't paying attention. The bus creaked to a halt while the driver honked his horn. Georgie glanced round vaguely and waved, knowing how maddening that is, but she didn't enjoy it the way she used to. For the first time she understood how people could want to kill themselves, because the vacuum inside drained all colour and joy out of the world, and life was no longer worth the struggle. She had dealt with Franco's alcoholism, the disintegration of her marriage, all the failure and futility of human existence – she'd never looked back, never looked down, lived for the present, kept her eyes on the future. She'd been brave and hopeful and naturally buoyant, with the bounce-back quotient of a large rubber ball. But someone had let the air out, and the bounce was gone, and there was nothing left to hope for any more.

Back at home she thought about crying, because crying was what you did at these times, it was supposed to heal you; but she was too empty for tears. She sat on the sofa all night, motionless and awkward, with the emptiness going round and round inside her head. Only when the dawn came did she stumble to her bed and sleep at last, and sleep and sleep, oblivious to the alarm that called her to go to work.

Cal got in on time, but I knew as soon as I saw him that things hadn't gone well. He didn't even smile at me, not out of rudeness, but because he seemed to have forgotten how. ''Lo, Cookie,' he said in passing, and that was that. No flirty remarks, no mischief-grin. This wasn't the Ice Age: he had the preoccupied look of a senior staff officer in a war movie, overseeing the downfall of Norway from a backroom, knowing there was nothing he could do. He went to immerse himself in work and was barely seen all day.

Georgie showed up at lunchtime, pleading an upset stomach.

'You don't look well,' Alistair said, giving her an automatic once-over. A more kindly, compassionate boss (if there are any) would've suggested she went home early, but he didn't. 'We've got the preliminary meeting at three about the PR for Jerry Beauman. Hope it hasn't slipped your mind.'

'No,' said Georgie. 'I've prepared some suggestions.'

'Good. At three then, my office. Cookie, you're coming too.'

I failed to radiate energy and enthusiasm, but he didn't notice. 'Why is it,' I asked the world at large, and Georgie in particular, 'that publishers spend a fortune promoting writers who are already hugely successful, and practically zilch on the ones who really need it?'

'You know the answer,' Georgie said wearily. 'Egotistical literary stars always demand a colossal publicity budget, regardless of whether or not it's really necessary. It's a question of vanity. And the sales justify it, even if they would've done anyway, so the Accounts Department can accept it. Lesser lights have to sell a certain number of books without backup before anyone thinks they're worth the outlay. So unless they're picked up by a magazine or newspaper, they haven't a chance.'

Cynicism without humour wasn't her style, and it worried me. To divert her, I filled her in on the info I'd received from Andy Pearmain about Beauman's nefarious financial dealings. She showed a little interest, but not much. Lin showed none at all.

'Dryden's the company which sold the land to the developers who are building Acme City,' I explained, hoping to elicit a brief spark of curiosity. 'Andy said they got about twenty million – I think I remember Jerry mentioning a similar figure. Apparently, all that was there originally was a group of derelict warehouses in the jewellery quarter. I didn't know Birmingham *had* a jewellery quarter – I thought jewellers hung out in places like Hatton Garden, all glamorous and expensive – but I was wrong. Anyway, the area was pretty run down. Andy said it used to belong to a family business, Bryan Fortescue, but *they* sold it at a knockdown price to a company based in Switzerland, who sold it to Dryden. Now, this is where it gets really interesting.' Georgie looked automatically attentive, Lin lacklustre. 'Jerry took this call from Sir Harold Chorley, right? And it sounded as though he was being put through the wringer. Well, Sir Harold is on the board at Bryan Fortescue – and so's Jerry. And the Swiss company who bought the warehouses is a one-man show: Pierre Wahid. *That* was the name of the caller Jerry was talking to the first time I overheard him. From the sound of things, they were partners in the deal. Which seems to mean that Jerry sold a clutch of tumbledown buildings to himself on the cheap, and then sold them on – to Dryden – at a profit of half a mil each for him and his chum Wahid. All very underhand and unethical.'

'So he's a crook,' Lin said. 'We knew that anyway.'

'Is it actually illegal,' Georgie wondered, 'or just sneaky?'

'According to Andy, it's fraud,' I said. 'Like insider trading. He abused his position on the board at Bryan Fortescue.'

'And he's got half a million quid tucked under the bath in Berkeley Square,' Georgie said, a note of wistfulness creeping into her voice. But it was faint. She really wasn't herself.

'Why can't he use it?' Lin asked. 'Launder it or something.'

'That's the catch. Acme City is a high-profile project – that's why attention's focused on Dryden and Jerry's deal – and people at Bryan Fortescue are starting to take notice. They could hardly fail to see that this bloody great shopping mall's going up on their land and they didn't make any money out of it. *Vid.* Sir Harold Chorley. Wahid is the dodgy link in the chain; Jerry must've engineered the sale to him, and they've begun to suspect a connection. So Jerry has to be very careful that his dirty money can't be traced. It's too large a sum for a quick spending spree or to slip in an account somewhere.'

'So he's stuck with it,' Georgie said. 'How awkward. To be stuck with half a million quid.' The wistful note had intensified; she was paying attention now.

'What are we supposed to do about it?' Lin said tepidly.

'What do you suggest?'

'Appropriate it,' said Georgie. 'Ill-gotten gains belong to anyone who can get their mitts on them.'

'Who made that rule?' I demanded.

'*Appropriate?*' Lin said. 'You mean steal.'

'You don't have to be so literal,' said Georgie. 'Anyhow, we could . . . we could give some of it to charity. *After* I've paid my credit-card bill.'

'It's wrong,' said Lin, but without her usual vehemence. 'You know it is.' Her moral fibre – like her nerves – was evidently worn to the consistency of a rubber band. One big twang and it could snap. 'Shouldn't we pass the information on to the police?'

There was an unreceptive silence.

'Would they listen?' said Georgie with a trace of contempt. She'd been a student in the seventies, and sometimes it showed. 'We don't know any of this for sure. It's all hearsay and surmise, as they say in court.'

'*Do* they?' I murmured.

'If we tell them the money's under the bath, and there's nothing there but plumbing, we're going to look prize idiots. Whatever we decide to do, we can't do it until we've located the loot.' I detected fiendish subtlety here. I was quite sure Georgie had no intention of calling in the cops. 'I think I need to work more closely with Jerry Beauman on the PR campaign. Meetings at his flat: that sort of thing.' She nodded to Lin. 'You're my assistant. You'll have to come with me.'

I opened my mouth to say something discouraging – and shut it again. With the end of her affair with Cal Georgie needed something to think about, something to plan, a fantasy to fill the space in her head, if not in her life. I'd hoped to intrigue her, hadn't I? And I'd succeeded. As for Lin, at least being drawn into Georgie's schemes would offer her a slight distraction from chronic guilt, pain and anxiety. Any distraction was better than none.

'I'm not crawling around in Jerry Beauman's bathroom sounding the Jacuzzi for secret passages,' she was saying with more animation than she had yet shown. 'What if someone came in?'

'Then you can be the lookout,' Georgie said.

'You've got to get there first,' I reminded them. 'The PR meeting's in half an hour.' I looked at Georgie. 'Have you got your spiel prepared?'

'Don't need to prepare,' said Georgie. 'I can spiel off the cuff. You should know that by now. All I have to do is ring Beauman myself, tell him what a big star he is, and say I want to discuss extensive publicity. He'll jump at it.'

'I got the impression Alistair wanted all discussions filtered through him,' I said. Presumably to stop things getting out of hand and over budget. 'He won't want you doing that.'

'He hasn't told me so, has he?' Georgie said. 'Which is why I'm going to do it now – before he does.'

Jerry was unavailable that week but was only too eager for a meeting the week after. As predicted, Alistair greeted this news with marked disapprobation. 'Georgie, what were you thinking of? The plan was to sort out our ideas this after- noon, sketch out the campaign, and present him with a *fait accompli*. The last thing we want is writers' input in their own PR – that's always been a house rule.'

'Yes, but . . . this is Jerry Beauman,' Georgie said inno- cently. 'He must be our biggest star. I thought he was a special case.'

'Our biggest star is that American chap what's-his-name who, thank God, never visits this country at all. Jerry just *thinks* he's our biggest star. All right, all right, he's bloody important, a sizeable bite of our annual sales. All the more reason to keep him out of our PR plans. He'll want us to go mad with stunts and tours and Lord knows what. These writers are all the same. Carry on like rock stars – and really, nobody gives a damn about them, least of all the people who buy their books.'

'They'll give a damn about Jerry, won't they?' I said

cautiously. 'What with his prison record and so on. You said we should be capitalising on that.'

'I said, I *said* . . . Yes, of course we should.' Alistair charged on, unfazed by his own inconsistencies. '*But* we don't want to drag him into it – not till we absolutely have to. He can pay for his own launch party – Bolly and toad-in-the-hole, it always is – sign when he's told to sign, smile for the cameras, though not too much, his readers' stomachs may not be *that* strong. Point is, to keep him under control. Invite him in on the ground floor and before you know where you are he'll have a beachhead in the attics.'

Quite a metaphor, I thought, mildly stunned.

Georgie was looking contrite. 'I'll do what I can,' she said.

'You'd better,' said Alistair.

The little fracas was the only incident to enliven a week that badly needed enlivening. We weren't spending every evening at Lin's any more, but I was round the night Andy called back, and once again, I answered the phone. (I suspected that when alone Lin had been leaving the machine on full-time to screen out most callers.) I couldn't tell him the truth, Lin still refused to talk to him, and he was sunnily planning a trip to London to give Ivor the once-over and send his fiancée on a designer shopping spree. 'I was thinking of Saturday week,' he said. 'Lin may've forgotten, but the wedding's next month and there's still a hell of a lot to do. She *is* well now, isn't she?'

'Fine,' I assured him, while Lin shook her head in frantic denial. 'Absolutely fine. She's . . . out tonight, that's all. I'm sure she's really looking forward to seeing you.'

'Time she got her mobile fixed. I can never get through.'

Lin's mobile had run out of credit nearly a fortnight earlier and she said she couldn't be bothered to do anything about it.

'She – she might be out of range,' I floundered. 'On the

Underground . . . or in some place really noisy where she can't hear it ring.'

'I'll keep trying. Thanks, Cookie. May see you.'

He hung up, and I was left facing Lin, whose panic was bordering on hysteria.

'I can't see him!' she repeated, over and over again. 'He thinks all my men are useless, and he's right – he's right – and I can't stand the *humiliation. I can't.*'

'What about Catriona?' I said. Wholesome, squeaky-clean Catriona, who probably suffered from the wind off the loch, at least after too much haggis. 'You're supposed to take her to Harrods.'

'Oh *no* . . .'

In the end, Lin put off thinking about it (she had over a week left for putting off, after all) and Georgie and I squabbled regularly over which of us would draw the short straw and have to tell Andy the true story, and which would draw the *other* short straw and have to spend the day trailing round after Catriona in the bridal departments of Knightsbridge. Normally, that would have been right up Georgie's street, but she said she could tell Catriona wasn't her type ('Or mine,' I interjected) and anyway, she had lost interest in shopping. She was struggling valiantly to remain herself, or the self she used to be, but when she forgot to struggle a weary listlessness took over, and the emptiness of her soul showed in her eyes. She and Cal had barely spoken since the break-up. He seemed much as usual, on the surface, only rather tight-lipped, and somehow older. The brash, flirtatious manner had gone; he didn't joke or laugh any more. On the one occasion I'd seen him in the pub he kept his distance, absorbed in conversation with a colleague, drinking steadily but without enthusiasm. He said hello, but that was all.

'They aren't happy,' Lin said. 'But then, they can't be, can they? There isn't any way to work it out. Why is life like this?'

I thought of saying: At least things can't get worse – but didn't. Experience had taught me that was asking for trouble.

Things got worse anyway.

They frequently do.

I don't care what the scientists say, there is definitely such a thing as Luck. After all, according to modern thinking, everything happens *somewhere*, so Luck must happen somewhere too, and as far as I can tell, somewhere is here. Forget all those probability laws and Uncertainty Principles: Luck is alive and well and living in Central London. You must have noticed how some people attract good luck (or bad), a trend that can last throughout their lives. My sister, for instance, has always been lucky: even her brief spells of bad luck worked out well in the end. And there's an old school-friend of mine who invariably had it easy, romping through love and marriage and job fulfilment like a puppy, with never a hiccup on the way. Conversely, another one tottered from catastrophe to disaster, with unwanted pregnancies, sexual harassment in the office, dud boyfriend after dud boyfriend.

Mostly, however, luck goes in waves. Some enterprising physicist could probably calculate a pattern, relating it to such factors as environment, genetics, the state of the economy and whether or not Jupiter is in the ascendant this month. Georgie, Lin and I were obviously going through a trough of the bad stuff, crossing our fingers that sooner or later we'd get our chance to surf the crest again. Well . . . when I say *again* . . . Georgie and Lin had had their moments of surfing, but my life had generally hovered somewhere in between, without too much of either good luck or bad. (Nigel's departure had been bad at the time, but I had few regrets now, so that didn't count.) But things were changing. I was no longer the dumpy, frumpy girl who played safe because I had no option. Now, I felt voluptuous and adventurous, and I dared to hope that life might offer me something more.

The problem with that is, more what?

So we come to the weekend. Leaving Georgie and Lin to their troubles, I went to a dinner party in Hampstead.

My hostess was one of those people riding the good luck curve. She was a friend of my sister's who'd always been kind to me because, I felt, 'it must be so difficult for poor fat Emma Jane, trying to compete with someone like Sophie'. She never actually said it, but I could see the thought processes behind her smile. Pre-Nigel, she used to invite me to dinner every six months or so, usually seating me beside a single man so undesirable that even the most desperate woman wouldn't touch him with the proverbial barge pole. She herself had a trust fund, a job in television, a barrister husband and two daughters, Lucia and Clemenza, named after operas (or possibly high-profile Mafiosi). Her name was Laura. She was slim and dark, not exactly pretty but so well groomed it came to the same thing. Nigel had met her once, and loathed her (he had his good points). I wanted to loathe her, but I couldn't. She had so many admirable qualities I wasn't comfortable with loathing, and had to settle for feeling vaguely guilty because I didn't like her very much.

I accepted her dinner party invitations for all the wrong reasons. The food was wonderful, her husband Roger was lavish with the drink, and, bar the undesirable singles, they knew lots of interesting people. I never really enjoyed myself, mind you – I felt too fat and boring – but I kept going back, hoping that *this* time it would be more fun. Sophie had clearly told Laura about my split from Nigel – had probably asked her to invite me over – and yet again I went, trusting to my new image to make it worthwhile.

(In my secret heart, I couldn't help wondering . . . it was

a Hampstead party . . . Roger was in the Law, like Helen
Aucham . . . perhaps . . . perhaps . . .)

And yes, Todd Jarman was there. With Helen. I saw him
the moment I came in, his face averted in profile, with its
hook nose and light-fitting jaw. Even though I had been half
hoping for, half fearing, the possibility of this meeting, a rush
of confused thoughts flooded through me. He was terribly
attractive – why hadn't I noticed that from the start? – and
I'd been fantasising about him, like a schoolgirl with a crush,
not just about sex but about a *relationship*, and here he was
with his long-term girlfriend (she was chatting to the host),
and of course he had never given me a thought outside the
sphere of work. I felt a blush of shame creeping over me,
and suddenly I wasn't voluptuous any more, just a bit less
fat, and the flame-coloured dress which I'd given another
outing made me look tarty and vulgar. Laura obviously
thought so – she greeted my décolletage with faintly raised
eyebrows – and presented me to Todd with the hesitant
manner of someone who has had a bright idea and is now
regretting it.

'As you're both in the same field, I thought . . .'

'We know each other,' I said, emboldened by Todd's smile.

Laura looked relieved, and said she would see about drinks.
As she moved away Todd said: 'That's quite a dress you're
almost wearing.'

Damn. The blush returned with a vengeance; I could feel
my face burn. 'I don't usually . . . It was Georgie. She came
with me – she chose it.' Cravenly, I passed the buck.

'Georgie?'

'Georgina Cavari – publicity.'

'Oh, yes, I know. Goes in for cleavage herself, doesn't she?
But yours is much more impressive.'

Damn, damn. Now even my tits were blushing. 'It's not
my sort of thing,' I said. 'I shouldn't have let her talk me

315

into it. But Georgie always says you should make the most
of your assets.'

'Your main asset is your personality,' he said. (I wasn't
sure if that was a compliment or not: he might mean I was
so physically unattractive personality was all I could depend
on.) 'But don't apologise for the dress. It looks terrific, if a
little extreme for a Hampstead dinner party.'

Worse and worse. I didn't simply look tarty, I looked out
of place. Like an Essex girl who insists on wearing her skimp-
iest garments to a christening in November. I determined to
be self-effacing, but it was a virtual impossibility when there
was so much exposed flesh to efface.

Helen drifted over, glanced at me with vague non-
recognition, and began to talk to Todd in what I thought was
a proprietorial way. It might have been my increasing paranoia, but I was sure she too eyed my bosom with disapproval.

'This is Emma Cook,' Todd said. 'You remember? My
editor.'

Helen did a double-take, and looked me over rather more
thoroughly. She didn't raise her eyebrows as Laura had done
– too much Botox – but her expression, such as it was,
conveyed surprise, disdain, and, most unbearable of all,
amusement. Dear me, it said, what have we here?

What she said out loud was: 'Hello . . . Didn't you come
to the house once?'

'Mm.'

'She's been incredibly helpful,' Todd said, perjuring his
immortal soul and resuscitating my confidence in one short
phrase.

'Really?' What Helen lacked in facial expression, she made
up for in tone of voice. It unnerved me how much polite
contempt could be infused into a single word. 'I seem to
recall your telling me something rather different at the time.'
And to me: 'Of course, you looked a bit more . . . *casual*

316

then. Still, you could hardly go to work in a dress like that.'

'Work clothes are always a bit of a bore, aren't they?' I said, summoning up a false smile. 'I've always thought it must be pretty difficult for lawyers, having to stand up in court in a Batman cloak with a knitted sheep on your head.'

Helen looked startled – as if she had just been savaged by a hamster. She was wearing spaghetti straps and showing a lot of clavicle and sternum, with very little flesh on the top. My assurance had see-sawed back up again, and I felt a rare flicker of superiority. Maybe I wouldn't need the T-Rex after all. Then Todd grabbed her elbow, propelling her away with one of those 'I want you to meet So-and-so' lines, and I was left alone, slowly deflating again. Right on cue, Laura returned with the latest undesirable singleton. He had long, droopy hair, prematurely receding, and the sort of face that started broad at the brow and shrank out of existence towards the chin. Given five hundred years and a magic ring, you felt he would look exactly like Gollum. (Possibly even sooner.) My God, I thought, thirty looming, and already the only available men are going bald.

'This is Enoch,' said Laura. 'Enoch – Emma Jane.'

Enoch? What were his parents thinking of?

'Emma Jane's in publishing. Enoch's a microbiologist.'

I said nothing. I felt like a major example of macrobiology.

When Laura had moved on, Enoch struggled to make conversation and I struggled back. It was one of those guilt-trip sessions where you stay talking to the weediest man in the room because you're sorry for him and he's probably a nice chap underneath, and no man (or woman) is an island, and there but for the grace of God, and so on. It wasn't his fault his hair was receding (though he could have cut it shorter) and he had the face of a renegade hobbit. He was obviously very clever: I could tell by the way he kept stammering. I nudged him towards his specialist subject and he became far more relaxed, happily spouting microbes. Glancing round furtively for Todd, I saw he wasn't watching me.

At dinner, Enoch was seated next to me; Todd was down the other end with Laura. Her husband was on my left, at the head – or foot – of the table. I'm never sure which is which, or how you tell the difference – or if it matters. Perhaps there's some sort of mystic Feng Shui going on here. Apparently, in a bedroom you shouldn't have the foot of the bed turned towards the door, because that's how you'd be carried out if you were dead. So if you're seated at dinner facing the door, does that mean you're going to be the first to sprint to the loo because the prawns are off?

Enough of this waffle. If anyone can tell me which end of the table is which, and why – or whether – it's significant, please write care of Ransome Harber.

Back to Laura's seating plan. The worst feature of it was Helen Aucham. She was opposite me.

I thought of my fantasy dinner party, when Helen hadn't been there (a last-minute brief?), and Todd and I had been sitting side by side, and had talked privately all through the meal like something out of an old coffee ad. Fate had played me a cruel trick, bringing us together only to thrust us apart. But then, she always was a sadistic bitch. Fate, I mean.

Helen endeavoured to monopolise Roger (our host), talking about mutual friends in the legal profession and similar matters. My one satisfaction was how often he turned to me with a murmured apology for the lawyerly small talk, even snatching the odd moment to tell me how good I looked. I still couldn't get used to the compliments – I found them embarrassing and somehow false, perhaps because I didn't feel like a sex bomb inside – but I didn't show it. When Helen took a break to eat (she didn't do much of that) he asked me how things were going in the literary world.

'Words, words, words,' I quoted. It was my stock answer,

and I swear I'd used it before with Roger, but this time he laughed. Helen looked piqued. So I'm a lump, am I? I thought viciously. Ha! The lumps have it. And they did, holding Roger's attention more and more as the wine sank in several bottles.

Occasionally, I looked Todd's way, hoping our eyes would meet, or at least catch, but it was a large dinner party, twelve people, and he was too far away. Opportunity was slipping between my fingers, and there was nothing I could do about it. But the opportunity had only existed in my imagination, I reminded myself. The Scarlet Woman dress might get me attention, some of it unwanted, but it had never got me anything more. No one falls in love with a sex goddess: just lust. Roger was now so drunk he showed a tendency to lean over me and breathe down my neck. Enoch had started, rather unexpectedly, to hold forth on his first love, though this turned out to be tropical diseases. Helen looked dauntingly sober.

We migrated into the sitting room for digestifs. I made up my mind to try and talk to Todd – I was his editor, so it would be perfectly natural, indeed rude not to do so – but Helen went to his side and latched on to his arm like a parasitic fungus, and I was left with bilharzia. They formed part of the bright centre of the room, and as usual, I was on the outer rim, feeling it would be mean to abandon Enoch, and knowing I wouldn't be able to relax with Todd in front of Helen.

Then, as the evening dragged to a close, she went to the loo, and he came over to me.

'Am I interrupting?' he said, glancing at my companion.

'Not at all,' I gasped. 'Enoch here was just – was just—'

'Sleeping sickness,' he declaimed. 'Swamp fever. Beriberi.' Standard phrases flowed over us: '. . . has been partially eradicated . . . mutations . . . new strains . . . resistant to antibiotics . . . poor medical facilities . . . eradicated . . . strain . . . antibiotics . . .'

319

Todd listened with the respect we always accord to scientific knowledge, even when it's pissed. Presently, he murmured to me: 'Have you had this all through dinner?' I nodded. 'I'm surprised you managed to eat anything. I thought what Laura calls her timbales were a little peculiar anyway.'

'*I* thought a timbale was a kind of drum.'

He raised one eyebrow and one corner of his mouth.

'I know it's a bad joke,' I said, 'but it's late, and I've had far too much to drink.'

Enoch was winding down and hadn't seemed to register that he no longer held his audience. We saw him lurch slightly, and assisted him into a chair. 'I'm sorry we didn't get more time to talk,' Todd said.

'Me too.'

And then, just as things were looking up, Helen came back, sweeping him away – 'Darling, we must go. Lovely party, Laura. Adored the timbales . . .' – and he was gone. I wondered how many dinner parties I would have to attend before I ran into him again.

The PR meeting in Jerry Beauman's flat was something of a disappointment. We colonised an area of the living room where I hadn't been before, sitting on a nest of sofas with coffee on a table in the middle while Georgie did her stuff. She'd brought her briefcase (the kind on a shoulder-strap) which she said, for all practical purposes, was quite unnecessary, but she carried it to meetings like this because it always made a good impression. She produced busy-looking files and expounded on the essential ingredients in a large-scale marketing and publicity push: poster campaigns on the Underground and mainline train stations, advertising in magazines and colour supplements, display space in book-shops and point-of-sales promotion. 'We've got a big budget,' she said, 'but we need to make sure it's targeted on the important things.' Targeting is a favourite term in publishing PR, generally used to convince lesser writers that money is being spent on them when it isn't. We don't have the cash for a full-page spread in *The Times*, because we're *targeting* other areas. Georgie was so used to flourishing the word it slipped in even when she didn't really need it. The budget for Jerry Beauman was substantial – but of course, she was trying to avoid paying for the party.

Launch parties, though fun, contribute little to writers' sales. (And if nobody turns up, it's embarrassing.) There are only two reasons for having one: a) if the writer is so well known or well connected you can guarantee wall-to-wall celebs, and diary and literary hacks who will all do puff pieces the next day, or b) if you are pushing the writer more than the book, usually a first timer, like Vijay Ramsingh. Jerry Beauman, of course, came into category a), but fraud and prison had rather damaged his party cred, and former celebrity mates might be unwilling to risk their reputation being seen drinking his champagne. However, Alistair's main reason for not wanting to finance the launch was much simpler. He was as tight as a duck's backside.

'We're up for one of those book-of-the-month things in Smith's,' Georgie was saying. 'Recommended Thriller for Christmas, something like that. It'll give us plenty of poster and shelf space instore.' Most people don't realise this, but although booksellers 'choose' titles for those promotions, publishers then have to pay them, so the chances of someone getting picked out of the pile on literary merit alone are zilch. 'Then we're going to have signing sessions in—'

'What about the party?' Jerry interrupted. 'I'm famous for my launch parties. Bollinger and toad-in-the-hole: it's my trademark.'

'We don't do parties much nowadays,' Georgie said. 'The climate has changed in recent years.' (i.e. while Jerry was inside). 'They don't generate sales and the press can be hostile to anything they see as pretentious.' She was improvising furiously here: the press are never hostile to free drink.

'Nonsense,' Jerry said. 'The press have always hung on my every word—' though *what* they hung on his every word was another matter '– I'll be in every diary, every gossip column, I always am. Good God, do I have to spell it out for you? I'm high-profile, I'm *glamorous*. My dear girl—'

'We *can* see that,' Georgie assured him sycophantically, bringing a sexy smile into play. 'But this is a sensitive issue. You're an ex-con – the ultimate comeback kid – and some people will be itching to put a spoke in your wheel. There'll be jealousy – you've met it before. The British press hate success: they're famous for it. They're *really* going to hate the idea that after all you've been through you can come back fighting and top the bestseller lists again. A party gives them a focus, somewhere to put the boot in. I knew you'd be up for it, but Alistair's nervous. He wants to protect you from the envy of small-minded hacks who won't miss the chance to stab a genuine star in the back.'

Georgie really earned her keep, I reflected. I'd never heard so much bullshit condensed into such a short speech.

'I'll pay for it myself,' Jerry declared. 'Nice of Garnett to worry, but if his nerve's failed, mine hasn't. I've *always* had a party; I'm not going to stop now.' He might have been setting up a beachhead in a war. 'I hope I'll have your support?'

'Of course,' Georgie said instantly.

Lin and I found we too were being fixed with a demanding stare.

'Absolutely,' I said.

'Um – yes,' said Lin.

'All for one and one for all!' Georgie said, getting carried away.

'That's the spirit!' Jerry said. 'We'll drink to that. I'll open a bottle now.' He went off to the kitchen, where he had once told me there was always champagne in the fridge.

'All for one and one for all?' I repeated. 'I thought that was *our* motto?'

'Sorry,' said Georgie. 'He's so ham, it brings out the worst in me.'

'Will anyone come to the party?' I asked.

'Put it like this,' Georgie said. 'If we ask half London, the other half will be pissed off they've been overlooked. Big stars will give it a miss – they'll be too anxious about their public image – but the rent-a-celebs will show up for anything, and the press'll fight to be there. The important thing is, we're not picking up the tab.' With Jerry's return, she switched the smile back on. 'Champers! How lovely.'

We talked more business, drank the champagne, and waited in vain for an opportunity to check out the bathroom. At one point Jerry went into his study to answer a telephone call, but we couldn't rely on his being gone long enough for us to take a look around. 'You'll have to distract him,' Georgie said, 'while I make some excuse to go to his room.'

'Why me?'

'You're his editor. He's got a fancy for you. Didn't he encourage you to sunbathe nude on the roof?'

'Not *nude*. You distract him. He's much keener on you, especially after all that buttering up. I've seen the glint in his eye.'

'You're the new sex goddess.'

(God, I was getting to hate that phrase.) 'Well . . . you're the *old* sex goddess. You've got far more experience. I can't do that vamp stuff.'

'Who are you calling old?'

When Jerry re-emerged Georgie, choosing her moment, asked for the loo. 'I hope you won't think it awfully cheeky,' she said, 'but could I use *your* bathroom? Cookie – Emma

– tells me it's amazing. Jacuzzi bath and everything. I'd adore to have a look.'

'Of course,' Jerry said, expansively. 'Another time, I must show you around. I've got this flat the way I want it now: simple, but not minimalist. I believe in the optimum amount of comfort. Comfort *and* quality – those are my watchwords. This rug's a Bokhara, naturally, and that sideboard was originally made for Brighton Pavilion . . .'

While Georgie allowed herself to be pointed in the direction of the master bedroom and ensuite, I encouraged Jerry to talk more about furniture. He held forth on occasional tables, gilded mirrors, Chippendale chairs and his collection of paintings, while Lin, nudged urgently by me, expressed appreciation at random. I couldn't help wondering how many of his claims about the provenance of his pieces were exaggerated. I resisted the temptation to inquire the pedigree of the sofas, which looked as if they had been made originally by the furniture department in Liberty's, or somewhere similar. When Georgie failed to reappear promptly Jerry became slightly twitchy; his Antiques-Roadshow exposition ran down. I was cudgelling my brains to come up with more diversionary tactics when he said abruptly: 'Do you think Georgie's all right?'

'I'll go and see,' I said, clutching at the straw of opportunity.

I found her in the master bathroom (if that's the term) with the door unlocked, on her knees beside the Jacuzzi examining the surround. She didn't even hear me come in.

'Hi,' I said.

Georgie jumped so violently she dropped the nail file which she had been inserting into the crack in the faux-marble. It was metal, and clinked loudly on the ceramic floor. 'Cookie!' she gasped, pressing a hand to her bosom. 'God, you scared me! I thought—'

'I know. I could've been Jerry Beauman, too. He's getting restless. We have to go back. Any luck?'

'No,' she sighed. 'But there's got to be something here. There's no other reason for this section to be in two pieces. Just give me another minute . . .' She retrieved the file and reapplied it to the crack.

'We haven't *got* another minute. If we all disappear into the bathroom and don't come back he's really going to smell a rat. Remember, he'll be thinking about the money he's hidden here – if it *is* here – and that'll make him seriously paranoid. I'm surprised he ever agreed to your seeing the room alone.'

'He could hardly keep me company in the loo,' Georgie said as I dragged her to her feet. 'The money's here: I can smell it.' There was a familiar glint in her eye. 'All we have to do is get it out.'

'Look, I don't know what you're planning but we're not crooks, right? Don't go all *Shallow Grave* on me.'

'It isn't drug money. There are no gangsters on its trail. It's just fraud money, greed money.'

'And you're greedy!'

'I'm *desperate*.'

Back in the living room, she erased the frown from Jerry's face with a gush of enthusiasm. Sorry she'd been so long, but she was admiring the gorgeous bedroom (she managed without too much difficulty to charge the phrase with sexual undertones), and then there was that amazing bath! She'd been speculating on what all the different buttons were for, and which jet targeted which part of your anatomy (more undertones). She simply adored Jacuzzis, but she'd never seen one as good as that. Perhaps – one day – would it be an awful nerve . . . ?

'We'll see,' Jerry said, flicking on a smile.

Faintly stunned by Georgie's audacity – and the fact that

she seemed to be getting away with it – I heard her return to the subject of the party. One of the dangers of spending too much time with Jerry Beauman was that, if you lost concentration, you would start to pick up his world view. He had been wrongly maligned, and we had to fight the good fight to expunge the stain from his honour. There were nameless powers out there, trying to do him down. The tabloids were obsessed with scandal and would print any insinuations to pander to the blood lust of the uneducated masses. And so on. Throwing the party (if only to see what it hit) would be a gesture of defiance, a gauntlet in the face of canting hypocrisy, the gutter press, and the aforementioned nameless powers. It would be his way of saying: 'I'm still the same Jerry Beauman – gallant, unrepentant, triumphant. I'm still king of the heap!' And inevitably we found ourselves compelled to jump on the tail of his wagon and hang on like grim death for the ride.

'All for one and one for all!' Georgie said yet again, raising her glass in a toast.

But she directed the ghost of a wink at me, and I suspected darkly that it wasn't Jerry's success she was toasting.

Friday brought no respite from our troubles. The weekend brought Andy Pearmain and Catriona to town.

Chapter 12

Are you going to Scarborough Fair?
(Parsley, sage, rosemary and thyme.)
Remember me to one who lives there.
He once was a true love of mine.

ANON

The farmer's daughter hath ripe red lips;
(Butter and eggs and a pound of cheese.)
If you try to approach her away she skips
Over tables and chairs with apparent ease.

The farmer's daughter hath soft brown hair
(Butter and eggs and a pound of cheese.)
And I met with a ballad, I can't say where,
Which wholly consisted of lines like these.

CHARLES STUART CALVERLEY: Ballad

Summer was fading into autumn (it always does, of course, but that doesn't make it any better), the Big Heat was over, and the trees were changing into their seasonal tints of orange and gold. Not that you see many trees on your average London street, but those we did see looked good. I was told there were spectacular sunsets, if you could only get the buildings out of the way. And with the autumn came Andy Pearmain.

Lin had screwed her courage to the sticking point – after constant urging by Georgie and me – and had declared, with wan resolution: 'I'll tell him myself. I'll tell him everything. But *not* with her there.' So we had to deal with Catriona, sweeping her off for an orgy of shopping in Knightsbridge and Bond Street. Never had two fully paid up members of the shopping sex felt less inclined for retail therapy. To further complicate matters, Vee Corrigan was ill, and as we couldn't babysit both Andy's fiancée and Lin's children, she had to do a last-minute search for a child minder, and was forced to settle for Sean, who was staying at his mother's after a job abroad and had been trying to rediscover fatherhood. 'I made him *swear* to be nice to Meredith,' Lin said later.

We were all due to meet at the Groucho around eleven, but I was the only one who was on time. Georgie tends to chronic lateness, except for business appointments, and Lin is often delayed by parental matters, but after I'd been waiting twenty minutes in the lobby I was getting restless. Andy Pearmain got there first, greeting me with faint surprise. He and Lin had spoken to fix the rendezvous, but obviously she hadn't told him any more about the plan of action. I smiled nervously and wondered what the hell to say. With him was a girl with soft uncoloured hair, springy like heather, and the fresh complexion of someone who spends lots of time outdoors. (In a decade or two she'd be weatherbeaten, but that wasn't relevant now.) We were introduced over cappuccino, swapped a few polite nothings, and then the three of us sat around, feeling awkward, glancing unobtrusively at our watches every so often.

'Is Lin all right?' Andy asked me at one point.

With an eye on Catriona, I said: 'Fine. She's fine.'

'Only I thought she sounded rather . . . Anyway, what do

you think of this chap Ivor? She seems to have rushed into it just a bit.'

'Just a bit,' I said.

'Trouble is, she's always been impulsive in her relationships. When she falls in love, she has to do it at first sight. Most of us start off as friends and then work up to it, but not Lin.'

'We started as friends,' Catriona volunteered. 'When I was a little girl, Andy would come over to see my parents, and bring me boxes of chocolates.'

'Our families go way back,' Andy explained. I might have been imagining it, but I thought he looked uncomfortable with her reminiscence, since it emphasised the fact that he was nearly twenty years her senior.

Another silence fell, which lasted until Georgie arrived. She apologised fluently for her lateness, blaming it on tube delays, I glared at her, and Andy ordered more cappuccino all round. I don't normally drink a lot of coffee, and as I sipped my way through my second cup I could feel the lining of my stomach wrinkling up. Georgie was doing her best to kick-start the conversation, but with only limited success. Catriona perked up in response to her questions, telling us how they had flown down from Edinburgh the previous day and spent the evening at the theatre, Andy had suggested Shakespeare but she'd chosen a musical, then they'd had dinner some-where very smart ('Le Caprice,' Andy supplied), and it was so much fun, she always felt like a princess when she was with him. Would we like to see her ring?

We duly admired a large emerald surrounded by diamond chips. Although her chatter was sprightly enough I felt she wasn't completely at ease: she stole sidelong looks at Andy every so often, as though seeking his approval, and there was a false note in her vivacity as if she were talking out of tune. In between spurts of conversation, the pauses stretched out, prickly with silent thoughts. Andy appeared to be smiling on automatic, giving the small talk very little of his attention. When Lin got there at last his whole demeanour changed; it occurred to me he had been afraid she wouldn't come.

He kissed her on both cheeks and asked: 'Where's Ivor? I thought I was going to meet him.'

'He – he couldn't make it,' Lin stammered.

'I've got a suggestion,' Georgie said, rising nobly to the occasion. 'Why don't Cookie and I take Cat for a wander round Harrods – I gather that was half the reason she came to London – and leave you two to chat for a while? That way Andy misses out on being dragged round the shops and you both get a chance to catch up.'

Catriona looked pleased, Andy grateful. Lin was pale and almost haggard; I only hoped, once they were alone, she'd manage to get her story out. Meanwhile, the three shoppers left the club, piled into a convenient taxi, and set off for Brompton Road.

In Harrods, Georgie scanned the store guide for the bridal department: it was the only one with which she wasn't familiar. But Catriona had other ideas.

'I've got all I need for the wedding,' she said. 'Mummy had my dress made, and I'm borrowing a tiara that belonged to Andy's grandmother. What I want is some *real* clothes, the kind I've never had. Clothes like Victoria Beckham wears, or Liz Hurley.' She added with pride: 'Andy's given me a credit card on his account. He says I can spend what I like.'

For an instant, a spasm crossed Georgie's features and I could see she was unable to speak. I rushed into the breach. 'You mean, you're after designer labels?'

'Yes, but . . . I want clothes I can choose myself.' I must have looked surprised, since she hastened to explain. 'You see, I live at home most of the time. I don't earn enough to pay rent on a place of my own, and Daddy's a farmer, so he's not too well off these days, what with foot-and-mouth and everything. Mummy makes such a fuss if I buy things she doesn't like. But Andy said I could choose whatever I wanted.'

'He told us you worked in publishing,' I said, still baffled.

'It's a very small company, doing books in Gaelic. Mostly, I work from home, copy-editing and stuff. I did Gaelic at college.'

'Didn't you live away from home then?' Georgie asked.

'No. It was only just up the road, in Larnock, so I drove in every day. I've got my brother's old car.'

We said no more, but made our way to the escalators and up to Ladies' Fashions. 'She isn't in love with him,' Georgie said to me once Catriona was safely installed in a changing room. 'She's only marrying him as a way of escape. That, and the unlimited spending spree.'

'Who are you to criticise?' I said. 'You were all set to marry money, not so long ago.'

'Yes, but I didn't, did I? I didn't even get engaged to money. I wouldn't even *sleep* with money.'

'Maybe you just never met the right millionaire.'

At that point Catriona called out, demanding our opinion, and proceeded to parade for our benefit in an assortment of very revealing garments. Her rather boyish, small-breasted figure could carry off the wispy tops and bare midriff, but I couldn't help thinking it would be something of a shock to Andy, who liked his women wholesome and *au naturel*, with no dress sense. Clearly, the same thought occurred to Georgie. 'You look great,' she said, 'but you need a tan.'

'I never tan,' Catriona said sadly, gazing down at her pallid stomach.

'Never say never,' said Georgie. 'Haven't you heard of faking it?'

'Doesn't it turn orange and go all streaky?'

'Not if you have it done professionally.'

'I'd love to,' Catriona sighed. 'I've always wanted to be really brown. Not that it would be much good against my hair. I wish I was blonde. Sometimes I go a bit fairer in the sun, but . . .'

I detected a diabolical gleam in Georgie's gaze. 'We can fix that,' she said. 'What do you think that credit card is for?'

At the Groucho, Lin was sitting in front of a cup of congealing cappuccino failing to meet Andy's eye. 'Are you going to tell me about it?' he said gently. 'Don't say everything's all right, because I can see it isn't. I'm not a fool, Lin. Your friend Cookie has been fobbing me off for weeks.' And, after a pause: 'I don't understand why you won't tell me. We've known each other so long. I've never let you down, have I? I've always been here for you.'

'You're getting married,' Lin said.

'That won't change anything,' he responded. 'When you get to know Cat you'll be bound to love her. The two of you have so much in common. She reminds me—'

'Yes, you said.'

There was another, longer pause.

Then: 'So what about Ivor? Where is he?' And, with the edge of a smile: 'Is Ivor over?'

Lin ignored the humour. 'Yes,' she said. 'I messed up again. I always do, don't I?'

'Oh my dear . . . I'm so sorry.'

'Don't be. Please don't be. You're always sorry for me. All the time we've been friends you've been sorry for me. It makes me feel so . . . *pathetic.*'

'Don't say that. Look, I didn't like Sean: he was spoiled and superficial and thoroughly selfish. And Garry – he was just a poor mixed up kid with a lot of talent and not enough

332

heart. Neither of them loved you or appreciated you the way they should have done. You did all the giving and they did all the taking, and I think you deserve better than that. You're not pathetic – never that. It's just . . .'

'I'm a bad picker?'

'I didn't say that. Maybe . . . unlucky.'

'Thanks,' said Lin. 'You're saying I wasted my time with Sean and Garry – and you're right. You're right. Except for the children: they weren't a waste of time.'

'No, indeed. Your kids are great.'

Pause. Again. The conversation was laden with them, like a play by Harold Pinter.

'How about a drink?' Andy suggested.

'Just mineral water. Thanks.'

He ordered mineral water and two martinis, with olives.

'I've never drunk a martini,' Lin said. 'Except the pre-mixed kind.'

'This is different.'

When the drinks came she sipped cautiously, ate the olive, and progressed to sipping incautiously. There was a loosening effect, both physically and mentally. She sat more easily in her chair, and began to talk through the pauses. The drawn lines he had noticed in her face softened a little.

'I never drink this early in the day,' she remarked.

'Maybe you need a few bad habits,' he said. 'For special occasions.'

'Men are my bad habit,' Lin said. 'The wrong men.'

'Ivor was another Mr Wrong?'

'Yes. Oh, yes.' He saw her wince, as if in pain.

'How did you meet him? Am I allowed to ask that?'

'It was in a chatroom,' Lin said. 'I was stupid. I know you have to be careful with all that Internet dating stuff – I mean, I never tried it myself, of course, but Georgie did a bit, for fun, and I used to worry about her – *I* worried about *her*!

– and then she seemed to be having a good time, and I couldn't get out much, because of the kids, so I thought it was okay to use a chatroom. It felt so *safe*, sort of anonymous – I said my name was Lin but lots of people are called Lin – and it meant that every evening, with my computer, I could have a social life. I love my children but their conversation is a bit limited. When I started talking to Ivor it was – magic. We got on so well – I mean, I thought we did. We had – we seemed to have – so much in common. We'd been e-mailing each other for a few weeks when we arranged to meet. I panicked a bit at the last minute – instinct, I suppose. You should always listen to your instincts, shouldn't you?' Andy didn't answer, not wanting to interrupt the flow. 'And then we met, and he was so attractive, and he looked at me as if I was – You know. I'd always dreamed of it happening like that. I was stupid, *stupid* . . .' She put down the martini with a shaking hand, tears starting.

Andy took her other hand between both of his. 'What happened?' he said, his face sharp with concern, soft with tenderness. Lin could only see the expression dimly through her tears but somehow it made her descent into weakness bearable. 'I've never seen you like this. Don't blame yourself, whatever it was. If he deceived you – if he let you down – that's not your fault. Lin . . .'

'I let him,' she said. 'I wanted to believe – all the fairytale stuff. That was my fault.' She took too large a mouthful of the martini, and gasped as the raw spirit scorched her throat.

Andy handed her the water.

'Thanks. Sorry – it's so hard to tell you. I'm so ashamed.'

'*Ashamed?*'

'Ivor wanted to move in. He was living in this awful bedsit, and he came to stay the night, and it seemed silly to wait, so I said yes. I'd always fallen for people quickly, like Sean, and then Garry – that took a bit longer, but not much – and

334

I was so sure this time, or maybe I just wanted to be sure. I wanted my life to come right, fast – and it was like everything fell into place, and we were going to live happily ever after.'

'Things don't usually work out fast,' Andy said. 'It takes time.' And, probing carefully: 'How did he get on with the children?'

The trickle of tears resumed. 'He seemed all right,' she said. 'All . . . perfectly . . . all right. He was a teacher – he got on with kids. He was always offering to babysit so I could go out with the girls. Georgie split up with Cal – her married boyfriend – and she needed a lot of support. There was one night when it was just Meredith – a Friday, the twins were with Vee – and he said she'd been naughty, and I believed him, because she's always been difficult. I *believed* him. We locked her in her room the next morning, and she climbed out of the window and ran away, and I didn't know where she'd gone, and I was going frantic. Then Cookie came, with Georgie, and they said she was at Cookie's flat, and she'd told her – told Cookie – about Ivor . . .'

Andy was out of his chair, crouching down beside Lin with his arms around her. 'Lin . . . oh Lin . . . my dearest dear. . .'

'It was my fault,' she said, between sobs. 'I let him into our lives – I trusted him – I wanted to be in love – I wanted a date for your wedding—'

'What?'

'I didn't want to be a pathetic failure any more, always messing up. I didn't want you to be *sorry* for me . . .'

'I'm not sorry for you! That is, I am, but – damn, I'm saying this all wrong. You're so special, so wonderful – so trusting and loving. You get hurt so easily, just because of that, but I couldn't bear you to change. I don't want you to be hard and cynical and worldly-wise. You need someone to protect you, someone to— Oh *bugger*.' A bar, even in a private club, is not an ideal location for heart's outpouring. Pre-lunch drinkers were gathering in the vicinity, trying not to look interested. Lin pulled herself together, a little reluctantly, blotting up the tears with her napkin. There had been a moment when it was bliss to let go, to feel a strong arm around her, an available shoulder to cry on. She had forgotten about Catriona and she thought, for a minute or two, so had Andy.

'Can you face lunch?' he asked.

'I don't think so. I haven't been eating much lately.'

'I can see that. You're far too thin. Food will do you good. Finish your drink and we'll go eat in Zilli's, in a nice quiet corner.' He went next door to reserve the table and specify the corner in question, and Lin returned to her martini. She felt warmed by his concern, and afraid it was nothing more, and she knew now that what she really wanted – what she ached for and yearned for – was just to melt into his arms, if only they hadn't been pre-booked by someone else.

It was six-thirty before we got back to the Groucho where Lin was waiting with Andy. Encouraged by us, and sustained by her fiancé's credit card, Catriona looked . . . different. As I knew, Georgie loved playing the fairy godmother in the transformation scene, and with an unlimited budget and such very *raw* raw material any underhand schemes she might have had were forgotten in the flood-tide of her enthusiasm. Catriona had a hazy idea of how she wanted to look; Georgie could turn fantasy into reality. When we got back to Dean Street Catriona had a flawless crème caramel tan, a mass of streaked-blonde hair, full metal jacket, low-slung hipster trousers, scanty halter-neck top. Her face was no longer as Nature intended, with a subtle hint of blusher under the cheekbone and unsubtle gold spangles above it. Heavy black mascara and a blurring of shadow enlarged her eyes; her lips had been painted into a full cherry-red pout. The rock-chick effect was completed with an assortment of designer costume jewellery and strappy sandals with twists of steel chain and four-inch heels.

'Now,' Georgie had said to her, 'you really look as if your name is Cat. As in Cool For.'

Catriona was so pleased with her appearance she clearly hadn't stopped to think how Andy would react. She was more like a teenager putting on sexy clothes for the first time than a twenty-four-year-old, which only goes to demonstrate the hazards of living a sheltered life. But in the taxi to Soho, she had become rather quiet.

'He will like the way I look, won't he?' she said.

'It's the way you *want* to look,' Georgie replied. 'If he isn't happy with it, that's his fault. He shouldn't try to super-impose his own idealised image on the person you are. But I'm sure he'll think you look great. We do.'

I was too busy feeling guilty to say anything. Of course, what Georgie said was true (most of it, anyway), but that didn't make it any better. Catriona, who came across as a nice quiet girl even if she did support fox-hunting, had walked straight into our trap, and it was mere quibbling for me to tell myself that at the beginning it had been her own idea. We had nudged, tempted and lured her all the way. By the time we got to the club, I felt as evil and manipulative as Cruella de Ville, and it wasn't fun.

When we walked into the bar, Andy totally failed to recognise his bride-to-be. 'Where's Cat?' he asked.

'It's me,' said the *nouvelle* blonde. 'What d'you think? Isn't it wonderful?' She fluffed her hair, twirled – and stopped, waiting for approval, looking like a puppy that has brought something particularly unpleasant in from the garden and deposited it at his master's feet.

Andy's face was a picture, though not the kind they would

hang in the Tate. The beard partially concealed the dropped jaw and shocked pallor, but nothing could hide the amazement in his eyes. 'What – what have you done?' And to Georgie and me: 'What have you done to her?'

'We fulfilled her dreams,' Georgie said. 'This is who she wanted to be.'

'I liked who she was,' he retorted grimly.

'But – I hated my boring brown hair, and my boring country clothes,' Catriona said. 'I always wanted to be blonde, and sexy, and have a sun-tan and a navel stud.' She glanced down fondly at the glitter in her belly-button. 'This is fake, but I'm going to get a real one. I think I look *wicked*. I've never looked wicked before. I've never felt this good about myself. I thought – I hoped – you'd . . . like . . . it . . .'

'Well, *I* think you look absolutely terrific,' Lin said, rushing into the breach with a generosity that was magical because it was so genuine. 'I used to dream of wearing clothes like that, sometimes, but I knew they wouldn't work on me, I haven't the right personality. But you look *fantastic. Doesn't she, Andy?'*

'Yes,' he said grudgingly, picking up his cue. 'It's just . . . a bit of a shock. Rather a dramatic change . . .'

'Are you sure it's okay?' Catriona said. And, belatedly: 'I won't be happy if you don't like it.'

'It's fine . . .' Funny how people always use the word *fine* to mean exactly the opposite.

'I bought a Liz Hurley dress too, all backless and slinky, and some more shoes, but they're quite low, only three inches, and this white thing that crosses over at the front and ties, and a bra-top with sequins round the nipples, and . . .'

Lin threw a tragic look at Georgie. 'How could you let her do this?' she whispered.

We didn't *let* her, we encouraged her, I thought, but didn't say so.

'It's all come from her,' Georgie whispered back. 'Andy doesn't have the right to keep her looking like a sprig of heather in tartan drawers if she doesn't want to.'

'She wasn't wearing tartan drawers!'

'In spirit.'

Andy, meanwhile, had plainly decided to put a brave face on things. It didn't suit him. 'How about us all going out to dinner?' he said.

'I had lunch: remember?' Lin said. 'I don't usually eat a proper meal twice a day.'

'You need fattening up.'

'Georgie and I ought to be going,' I threw in, hastily.

'No you don't,' Andy said. It was clear that the prospect of being alone with his fiancée wasn't something he could handle right now. 'We'll all go.' He added, rather nastily: 'You two deserve a treat, after all the help you've given Cat.'

We went to the Red Fort for superior Indian, but none of us ate much. It is a little-known fact, but embarrassment is a big appetite-killer, and Georgie and I, if not actually cringing, were definitely ill-at-ease. Andy didn't brood because he wasn't the type, but he spoke rarely, and what conversation he did make sounded forced. He spent most of the time watching Catriona, who alternated between expressions of self-doubt and head-tossing defiance.

'If you really don't like these clothes,' I heard her say, 'you shouldn't pay for them. I'll get the money, somehow. Or take them back . . .'

'Don't be silly.'

As often happens when the man is much older, he came across more like a teacher or guardian than a lover. Cat was clearly aiming for the penitent schoolgirl effect, but it was difficult in that get-up, and I sensed she was losing her taste for the role.

'How did it go?' I asked Lin in a low voice, when the

339

others were sufficiently distracted. 'Did you tell Andy all about it?'

'Yes.'

'And?'

'He was lovely.' For a second, there was a flicker of wry pain in her face. 'So understanding and *kind* . . .'

I seemed to recall she had been dreading his kindness for the last few weeks, but all that was clearly forgotten. I suppose there is kindness and *kindness*, under these conditions. The disinterested, slightly patronising sort (*vid*. Laura in Hampstead), and the sort that comes from the heart and is given with love. (And then there's the everyday sort, the effortless gift of a generous spirit, which costs nothing and warms the recipient and is a lot rarer than it should be.) Anyway, Andy's kindness obviously came into the right category, but I detected without much surprise a touch of the might-have-beens in that passing flicker.

Across the table I studied Catriona, who, prompted by Georgie, was now talking about hunting. It wasn't cruel, it was natural; city people just didn't understand. Foxes could be really savage: they would break into a hen-house and kill every bird, not to feed but for the sake of killing. Is that any reason for humans to do the same? Georgie wanted to know. Cat argued her point with pretty eagerness, not the thrusting anger of one who is deaf to all other opinions. It was easy to see why Andy had been attracted: she seemed young for her age, with that wind-off-the-loch freshness and slight naïveté which evidently appealed to him. But both would go with time, I thought, and the opinions would harden, and one day he would feel nostalgic for the rock-chick clothes.

If he was really in love with her, of course.

The weather might be cooling down a little outside but in parts of the office the temperature seemed to plummet. When

340

Georgie and Cal encountered one another, they would exchange polite greetings and walk on, leaving behind the sudden chill that you get when two people are determined to place their hearts in cold storage. Laurence Buckle, too, seemed to be nursing his resentment, both against Jerry Beauman's homophobia and Alistair's acceptance of it. This was unlike Laurence, who had always been fairly easy-going, at least on the surface – though I wondered if his past tolerance had required an effort. Now, he showed glimpses of bitterness, and was often aloof. Lin was deeply unhappy, for more reasons than one, and I – well, let's just say that when I went to bed it took a struggle to keep my mind on Hugh Jackman. I tried transferring my affections to Johnny Depp in *Pirates of the Caribbean*, James Marsters in the final season of *Buffy* (Laurence lent me the tapes), and even Orlando Bloom as a cool but subtly seductive Legolas, but it didn't really work, though there was a certain amount of originality in having sex with an elf. (Elves have highly sensitive ears: I could drive him mad by just licking the tips.) We all tried to maintain a façade of optimism for the benefit of other colleagues, but an autumnal fog had settled over Ransome Harber which none of the seasonal parties could disperse. Work provided a few highs, but the lows were always there underneath.

'I told Hector about that business with Jerry Beauman,' Laurence said one evening in the Grinning Gibbon, a new local we had taken to patronising. 'D'you know what he said? He said – he *said* – I'd never really come out. He said *that* was my problem. I didn't think I had a problem! Apparently, I don't really like football and beer and being one of the lads; I'd rather be mincing round home furnishings in Peter Jones choosing kitchen curtains. He says I don't ask you all to dinner because I'm ashamed of him.'

'Well, you *don't* ask us to dinner,' Georgie pointed out.

'Yes, but I'm not a dinner party person. Hector's the

socialite: he asks people to dinner every bloody week. If I did it too we'd never have an evening alone. Anyway, I prefer going to the pub.'

'We could come to dinner one night if it would help,' I offered.

'That's not the point,' Laurence said with what was, I realised, unintentional rudeness. 'The point is that we've been together eight – nine years, and suddenly he's saying I'm not committed, I'm not *gay* enough for his taste. Like he's been thinking it, all this time, and keeping quiet, bottling it up . . .'

'He'll get over it,' Georgie said. 'At least you're still together.'

'Any word from Andy?' I asked Lin hurriedly, to break the ensuing pause.

'He called and left a message,' said Lin, 'and I called and got his voice-mail, and so on for the past week.'

'If he marries Catriona,' Georgie said, 'they'll be in the divorce court in a year.'

'She seemed very sweet,' said Lin, 'except for supporting hunting, and I don't suppose she can help that. It's how she was brought up.'

'Rubbish,' Georgie declared. 'She goes in for sadistic blood sports and she's a gold-digger to boot.'

'A successful one,' I said. 'Sour grapes. Anyway, I think you're wrong. She may be a gold-digger but she's fooling herself it's love, playing beggar-maid to Andy's King Cophetua. He sweeps her off for glamorous weekends in London and gives her a credit card to spend. It would be awfully easy to get carried away by all that.'

'Don't rub it in,' Georgie said, wincing at the credit-card reference. But such was her despondency she hadn't bought so much as a pair of holdups lately, and I dared to hope the bill might be inching down a fraction.

'Have you seen the new temp?' Laurence asked when she went to the loo.

'No.' Lin and I looked round simultaneously, fixing him with a steely double stare. 'What new temp?'

'Working for Larry in Phoenix. Started this morning. His PA was rushed to hospital with an appendectomy: they say she'll be off for a month at least.'

'Poor Clare.' I was a little perfunctory. 'What's this temp like?'

'Looks about twenty, blonde ponytail, short skirt.'

'Shit.'

'Saw Cal chatting her up at lunchtime. Back to his old ways. She was giggling a lot.'

'*Shit.*'

'I didn't want to say anything in front of Georgie,' Laurence said. 'Too chicken. But I thought perhaps one of you should tell her. Don't want someone catching her off guard with it. Trudi Horn's never forgiven her for hooking Cal long-term when he slipped through her fingers in less than a month. She'd love the chance to stick a dagger in and twist it.'

Lin and I gazed at each other in mutual despair.

'Thanks, Laurie,' I said. 'You've cast a gloom over the evening – and it was pretty gloomy already.'

'Cal can't mean it,' Lin protested. 'Until a few weeks ago they were so much in love. Even when they were fighting, I thought . . .'

'He doesn't have to mean it,' I said. 'He's a man. He's just doing what men do – trying to get laid. That has nothing to do with love.'

Georgie rejoined us before the conversation could continue. 'You look like a convention of depressives,' she remarked. 'I hate winter. Is it my round?'

'Mine,' said Laurence, heading for the bar.

This time, Lin and I avoided each other's gaze. Neither of us wanted to break the bad news yet.

'Why is life so bloody?' Georgie demanded rhetorically.

'Cookie's all right,' Lin said, fishing for a cheerful thought. 'Your wish worked out – didn't it?'

'In a way.' I hadn't told them anything about Todd. There was so little to tell.

'You *are* all right, aren't you?' Lin persisted, looking vaguely anxious.

'Of course.'

'No, she's not,' said Georgie, with alarming perspicacity. 'It's not Nigel any more, but there's someone. And it isn't going well.'

'Is that true?' Lin asked.

I said nothing.

'This sort of stuff never happened to Charlie's Angels,' Georgie commented. 'Maybe we should re-name ourselves. The Three Stooges.'

'Who're they?' Lin inquired.

'Some old comedy act.'

'The three witches,' I said. 'As in *Macbeth*. "Double double toil and trouble . . ."'

'I like that,' said Georgie. 'I feel evil. (And she hadn't even heard about the temp yet.) Bags I be the hag.'

'I thought they were all hags,' Lin said.

'No. The hag is the boss, the one who controls the trio. Then there's a vague one with Sight – you – and one who raises the dead – that's Cookie. The happy medium.' I groaned. 'The hag is the oldest and the ugliest and the nastiest – and that's how I feel. The hag is astride, This night for to ride . . . We've spent too much time suffering in silence – or just suffering. Time to get positive again. Let's make some magic – *black* magic. Let's make trouble for someone.'

'Jerry Beauman,' said Laurence, returning with drinks.

Georgie brightened.

Jerry Beauman . . .

There's nothing like having a hate figure in your work environment, somebody you can rely on to be irredeemably nasty and on whom you can turn whenever the bile is overflowing. A legitimate target. Jerry Beauman had his uses. Georgie wangled a further meeting at his flat to discuss party strategy, though we had no opportunity to go near the bathroom. I suggested Andy should put his banker's ear to the ground, but Lin still hadn't spoken to him since he left London with the new-look Catriona and was unwilling to keep calling. 'Something's up,' I said, or rather hissed, as Jerry quit the meeting for the second time to take a private call in his study.

'You could pick up the extension,' Lin postulated, looking round for one.

'People don't have them much any more,' Georgie pointed out. 'There's a phone in the hall and one in there—' she indicated the study door '– and that's it. Who needs extensions when you've got cordless? Besides, there's a kind of click on the line when you pick up, so he'd be bound to realise there was someone there.'

I wondered how *she* knew about the click, but let it go.

We hadn't told her about the temp: we didn't need to. Back at the office, Georgie saw for herself.

'Just Cal's type,' she said, and something in her face – something very firmly closed – meant we didn't venture further comment.

Todd Jarman left a message on my voice-mail, and for a dizzy hour I let myself believe all kinds of things, but when I called back it was just a query about promotion for *The Last Harlot*.

'When's the exact publication date?' he asked me. 'I know

345

it's January, but I'm booking a skiing trip around that time and I want to be sure not to overlap.'

'Beginning of Feb,' I said, consulting my computer. 'The . . . third. We should have lunch very soon – to discuss PR.' At least Todd wouldn't demand a champagne launch – or would he?

'Yes, we should,' he said.

'With Georgie Cavari,' I added, trying not to sound reluctant. I must stop hallucinating that he fancied me. This was just normal author/editor conversation.

'Give me a date,' he said after a pause.

'I'll have to check with Georgie.'

'You do that.' His voice, while not actually saturnine (*can* a voice be saturnine?), had dark undertones. I worried suddenly that I'd given myself away at that awful dinner party – that even now I sounded fluttered, flattered, all a-gush. I terminated the call as quickly as I possibly could, and then worried all over again that he would think me brusque and unfriendly.

Being attracted to someone when you aren't sure if they're attracted back (and, since it's me, they probably aren't) is a situation fraught with potential embarrassment. I'd been there before, of course, but not in a work situation, and it had never been this strong. Every time I remembered how we'd made love on my sofa I blushed inside (and sometimes outside). And whenever I talked to Todd now there was a small treacherous corner of my mind which couldn't help thinking of that.

On the whole, I was glad to be distracted by a call from my sister – at least until she spoke.

It was my birthday next week, my thirtieth, a big deal. (Ugh. What was there to celebrate? Incipient spinsterhood?) Was I having a party?

No.

'And don't tell me I ought to get hitched,' I said.

'I wasn't going to,' Sophie responded indignantly. She obviously thought I was a hopeless case.

She was probably right.

'What d'you want for a present?'

'A hot-water bottle,' I said. At the rate I was going, that was all I'd ever cuddle up to.

Then came the evening when Georgie and I went to the pub, and Cal was there with the temp. Georgie didn't say anything. She drank quickly, soberly, without effect. She left early. (Georgie was the sort of person who never left anything early.) I went with her, wanting to offer support and comfort, knowing there was nothing I could do.

'He isn't serious,' I said awkwardly. 'It's just . . .'

'Just lust?' She made an odd, dismissive gesture, something between a nod and a shrug.

'D'you want me to come back with you? I'm always here – if you need me. I mean—'

'I'm all right.' She got into a taxi, and went home.

I took the tube.

I'd been in about an hour when the phone rang.

'Cookie?' Her voice was almost unrecognisable. 'I'm very sorry to disturb you, but – can you come over? Now? I – I need someone . . .'

I dressed hastily, and went out.

At the house she let me in, offered me tea, forgot about it. She sat down on the sofa in the living room – a big room, two knocked into one, with a high ceiling and shabby old furniture she couldn't afford to replace – and hugged herself like a lost child. The house was warm, but she looked cold. Cold and small in that big space. She'd switched on one of the lamps but left the overhead light, and in its uncompromising glare I could see the lines on her face, all fifteen of them, and the sad droop of her mouth now the laughter had gone out of her. For once she looked all of her forty-three years, but in some way she also looked like a girl, young and vulnerable and horribly bruised by her first encounter with the cruelty of love. Because it was the first for Georgie, I knew. This was somewhere she'd never been before.

I said: 'Shall I make the tea?'

It was trivial, but I didn't know what else to say.

'I – sorry. I should've . . .'

'I'll make it.'

When I gave her the mug, she cradled it like a heat-source on a winter's day. I tried to find the right words – words of sympathy, consolation, comfort – but there weren't any. There never are.

'I was such a fool,' she said at last.

'Lots of people go out with married men,' I said. 'Sometimes they leave their wives. You weren't a fool, just. . . reckless.'

'I didn't mean that. I knew he wouldn't leave, though I used to fantasise about it occasionally. But he loves the children so, and he's got such a strong sense of responsibility. I meant . . . I was a fool to make it difficult for him, when things were so difficult anyway. I was a fool to waste time picking fights, and going off with other men. Christy could've had all the couply stuff, the family stuff, the marriage – she was welcome to it. All I wanted was the loving, the being loved.'

I murmured something inadequate, stroked her shoulder. I thought it would be better if she cried, but she looked too desolate for tears.

'I miss him so,' she said. 'I didn't think it would be like this. I didn't know it would *hurt* so much, seeing him with someone else. Before that, I kept thinking we might get back together. If it was just my pride – but I don't care about that any more. I'd probably crawl to him on my knees, if I thought it would do any good. Isn't that shaming?'

'No,' I said. 'It's love. Love isn't anything to be ashamed of. The people who hang on to pride are the people who love by halves. There was that stupid book *The Rules*: remember?' (I'd read it, of course.) 'All about getting yourself a man you don't really love so you can stay in control. How to be comfortable – and a coward. You don't want to be like that.'

She tried to smile. 'No I don't. *Sensible* Cookie. He always said you were sensible . . . It was so wonderful, being loved. Like . . . thermal underwear. This layer of warmth that wrapped me round, wherever I was, whatever I did . . . even if we didn't see each other very much. He didn't say romantic things, but it didn't matter. He isn't a smoothie. I liked the things he said because he *meant* them. Mind you, he said we'd always be friends, but . . .'

'You will,' I assured her.

'I don't think so. Not *just* friends. I couldn't bear it, if he looked at me in that cosy, ex-boyfriend way: Hey, didn't we have a blast? I couldn't *bear* it . . .'

Some time later, she said: 'I don't regret a thing, do you know that? It hurts so bad I wish I was dead, but I don't regret it. How could I regret the best thing in my life? One day I'll turn into a boring old woman, going on about all my lovers, but Cal is the one who'll make me cry. Oh Cal . . . Cal . . .'

The tears came, but only briefly. Then she sat up and blew her nose. 'Oh well, I suppose there's nothing left for me but to be utterly ruined and imprisoned for debt. It doesn't matter now, after all. I'll have to wear convict-gear and they'll cut my hair off . . .'

'You have your hair short anyway,' I pointed out. 'And they don't send people to prison for debt any more. I don't think you have to wear convict-clothes, either.'

'Damn. Some people have no concept of sticking to the story. I'll just have to turn to real crime.'

'Don't start that again.'

'Thanks for coming,' she said suddenly. 'Thanks for not saying *I told you so.*'

'I don't think I *did* tell you so – did I?'

'Probably not. You're too tactful. Could you – would you stay?'

'Only if there's alcohol,' I said. 'Or more tea.'

We had both, and watched the late-night thriller, which was strange, and strangely depressing, and then a vintage horror film on Channel 4, all human sacrifice and heaving bosoms (much more fun). I crashed out in the spare room but Georgie stayed on the sofa, and in the morning she was still there, hollow-eyed and unsleeping, watching children's TV and letting her tea go cold.

The months rolled on towards Christmas, and the year darkened. On my birthday I got mildly drunk and a male friend who I'm sure had never fancied me before made a pass, but I turned him down. Good for my ego, but nothing else. Everyone in the office decided they were suffering from Seasonal Adjusted Disorder, or whatever it's called. I arranged lunch with Todd Jarman in order to discuss publicity, only to be summoned at the last minute by Alistair and delegated to entertain an important American writer who was in town. Was Fate trying to tell me something? I wondered. He's not for you. Keep Off the Grass. Bloody Fate.

'He seemed awfully disappointed you weren't there,' Georgie said afterwards. 'He kept asking about you, unobtrusively, trying to make it look like casual interest rather than real curiosity, but I wasn't deceived. Cookie . . .'

'If it was curiosity,' I said, 'it was the idle kind. He's got a very glamorous girlfriend. Helen Aucham.'

'Oh, I know. Seen her with him. Isn't she a lawyer?'

'Human rights.'

'A lawyer is a lawyer,' Georgie said obstinately, 'no matter what angle they use. They'll fight anyone's corner if the money's right. Besides, she looks like a bitch.'

I didn't comment.

Lin had decided not to go to Andy's wedding, it would be too painful, and apparently he hadn't called again, which, under the circumstances, was rather surprising, though she had had a couple of e-mails from him. When the grim day arrived Georgie and I joined her in taking the children out – the Planetarium, lunch, an afternoon film – an act of solidarity which, she said emotionally, she would never forget. Apart from saying things like: 'It's eleven o'clock. They must be going up the aisle now,' and 'He told me they're going to honeymoon on safari,' she bore up nobly.

'Safari?' said Georgie. 'Oh-ho. Presumably so Catriona can shoot herself a lion, on the grounds that they're vicious and deadly predators who will kill the cubs of rival males if they get the chance.'

'*Will* they?' Lin was horrified.

'She was a nice girl, though,' I said unwisely. 'In her way.'

'So was Eva Braun,' Georgie retorted.

Clare of the appendectomy returned, the blonde temp departed, and Cal started talking to me again, once in a while, and even to Lin, though he didn't venture more than common greetings with Georgie. But I thought I detected a note of yearning behind his backchat, and the sad look in his eyes seemed a little sadder, though it was hard to be sure because of the glasses. But he didn't make any moves and maybe he never would, choosing a safer, duller life. Love is always a high-risk option, especially for someone in his position.

And then, in November, two things happened. Firstly, I got a call from Catriona. I'd given her my number in the way you do, without ever expecting her to use it, so I was taken aback when she said her name and had to ask her to repeat it. She was in town for a few days – no, not with Andy, though she was staying in his flat – and could we meet? Just her and me and Georgie, like when we went shopping. She was so grateful to us, we had no idea, she'd never *enjoyed* shopping before . . .

We met in the coffee shop in Dickens and Jones. (We didn't tell Lin.) Catriona had retained much of her rock-chick style, though suitably toned down, a polo-neck sweater instead of a skimpy top, faux-sheepskin jacket, boot-cut trousers. It was a minute or two before I noticed her left hand resting on the table. The emerald had gone and there was no wedding ring.

'We called it off,' Catriona explained. 'It was . . . sort of mutual, really. The thing is, he wanted me to still be the little girl he used to buy chocolates for. A bigger little girl, of course, but not changed, not sophisticated. And I wanted . . .' She stopped, fiddling with her napkin.

'To leave home?' Georgie said, not without sympathy. 'To be spoiled, and fussed over, and swept off your feet?'

'I suppose so. It sounds rather cheap, doesn't it? But I honestly thought I was in love. Andy's so *kind*.' People were clearly unanimous on that. 'He helped me get a job in Edinburgh, on a magazine, and he's paying my rent until I can get a bit more money. I didn't want him to, but he insisted. He even talked to Mummy and Daddy, tried to make them understand. They were frightfully keen on my marrying him.'

I'll bet, I thought.

'Anyway, I'm down here with Morag, my new friend from work, shopping again.'

'Andy's credit card?' I said with burgeoning suspicion.

'Yes – isn't it sweet of him? He says it's to make up for my being jilted – but I said *I* jilted *him*. Anyway, I wanted to thank you both. If you hadn't helped me that day, I'd never have this great new image, and I might have married Andy and been really unhappy, trying to be someone I wasn't.'

'Good luck,' Georgie said, evading my gaze. I seconded her.

When Catriona had gone she remarked bitterly: 'He gives her his credit card when they're not even together any more! Why don't I meet men like that? A couple of the credit-card companies are getting really nasty, threatening legal action. I saw a lawyer last week. I could lose the house.'

'Bugger.'

'And it isn't as if I've been running up the debt any more lately. I don't seem to care about clothes the way I used to. It's just that the minimum payment's got so big, I can't always manage it.'

'How *have* you been managing?'

'I took out a bank loan. Against the house, you know? The Loans guy fancies me a bit, so . . .'

We lapsed into a silence heavy with financial gloom.

'At least we've got some good news for Lin,' I said.

But when we called round for coffee on Sunday, she had other matters to think of.

(That was the second thing that happened.)

'Is there anyone outside?' she demanded when she admitted us, peering into the street with unaccustomed paranoia.

'No,' I said blankly.

And Georgie: 'What's the problem?'

'It's Sean.' Her voice had an unusual edge. 'Bloody Sean. He paid a private detective to trace Ivor, and last night he got drunk and went round there and beat him up. He was arrested but they've released him, and now he's making statements to the press. I've had the *Express* and the *Sun* on the phone already.' I saw the receiver was off the hook in the living room. 'He has to go and prove his stupid machismo! It wasn't as if anything happened to the twins. And now it'll be in the papers, the whole story, and they'll be pestering me and the children – it'll be worse than when Garry died.'

'Good for Sean's image, though,' Georgie said pensively. 'Beating up a paedophile will always be popular with the crowd. Revives his bad-boy aura while making him look like a hero at the same time.'

'Don't I know it,' Lin said with rare cynicism. 'This wasn't about punishment, or revenge, or anything like that. That was just the excuse. This was about *Sean*. He's always been selfish and thoughtless and – and *thick*. He didn't care about me and the children. He just wanted to act tough and look good. I could kill him.'

'That really *would* get you in the papers,' Georgie said wryly.

'We've just seen Catriona,' I interjected with an abrupt change of subject. 'Andy called off the wedding.'

Lin stopped in mid-fume. Her expression jolted – and froze. 'What?' she whispered.

'Mutual incompatibility,' Georgie said. 'He didn't like her new image. At least one of our best-laid schemes didn't gang aft agley.'

'He didn't tell me,' Lin said. 'He hasn't even called. I expect . . . he thinks it's none of my business.' But her expression didn't think so. Her expression said it was very much her business.

'He must have had a lot to sort out,' I suggested, by way of palliative. 'I'm sure he'll be in touch soon.'

'What did she say? Did she tell you—'

But what Catriona might have told us was never established. The doorbell rang, and Lin reverted to panic mode. 'It'll be Them,' she said with a distinct capital letter. 'Don't answer!'

'I'll deal with it,' Georgie said. While Lin fled into the kitchen, she went to the door, and I heard her sliding effortlessly into PR mode. '. . . a nightmare experience . . .

profoundly traumatic . . . need for privacy . . . your considera-
tion much appreciated . . . no further distress for children . . .
case *sub judice* . . .' From the tenor of the response, it seemed
to be working. But even though she closed the door without
a fight, we knew the problem wouldn't go away. If the columnists found out how easily Ivor had invaded Lin's life, they'd
be staking out the moral high ground within a week. She'd be
pilloried . . .

As long as no one told them. But we'd reckoned without
Sean. After years of being ignored, he was riding high on a
wave of fresh publicity, gushing like an oil well in a succession
of interviews. I doubt if he thought about the implications
of what he was saying, when he explained how Lin had
invited a man she barely knew to live in her home. He was
just anxious to present himself as a conscientious father and
supportive ex-husband – not an easy task in view of his
record. But it was Lin who got the fallout. The pundits saw
an issue, a chance to pontificate and condemn – and they
pounced.

Chapter 13

There is no Chapter 13. It's like the thirteenth floor in skyscrapers, which gets left out. We were in enough trouble, without throwing in a Chapter 13.

Chapter 14

And Crispin Crispian shall ne'er go by
From this day to the ending of the world
But we in it shall be remembered –
We few, we happy few, we band of brothers;
For he today that sheds his blood with me
Shall be my brother; be he ne'er so vile,
This day shall gentle his condition:
And gentlemen in England now abed
Shall think themselves accursed they were not here,
And hold their manhoods cheap while any speaks
That fought with us upon St. Crispin's Day.

SHAKESPEARE: *Henry V*

Now is the time for all good men to come to the aid
of the party.

TYPING EXERCISE

Lin had never liked the publicity attendant on her marriage
to Sean and subsequent relationship with Garry, but at least
it had rarely been critical of her personally. What followed
Sean's statement to the press was something else. The imminent court case offered some protection, more theoretical than
actual, and the tabloids had the decency to leave Meredith

357

alone, but once they learned that, on the strength of a few weeks' romance by e-mail, Lin had invited a paedophile into her home, there were plenty of voices ready to swell the chorus of condemnation. At best they called her a fool; at worst, criminally irresponsible, a bad mother who shouldn't be allowed to keep custody of her children. One or two suggested Sean should be their guardian, but when questioned on the subject he backtracked hastily, having no wish to be saddled full-time with a brace of pre-teenage boys. He rang Lin to make a grudging apology for the mud he'd stirred up, while Garry Grimes' mother emerged from seclusion to rake up old grievances against her late son's girlfriend, thus keeping the story going with fresh 'revelations'. Lin took to disconnecting the phone whenever she was at home, and once again Georgie and I were there as much as possible, fighting off any hacks who tried to doorstep the place.

At Ransome, the entire company did everything possible to protect her. A Blitz mentality developed, and inevitably barriers came down. One evening in the pub Georgie was waylaid by a persistent journo who had heard she was close to Lin. With a brief apology to her neighbour, she helped herself to his pint – G&T being too small for her needs – and emptied it over her would-be interrogator. The journalist retired, his enthusiasm somewhat damped, those in the vicinity applauded, and Cal, who had been watching, stepped in when she offered to replace the beer.

I noticed he had forgotten to be aloof and was chatting to her with animation and the old familiar glow in his eyes. We left early to return to Lin, and Cal kissed her on the cheek by way of goodbye. I felt hopeful, but Georgie was curiously down.

'He doesn't want to love me,' she said. 'He thinks there's no future in it. But there's no such place as the future. It's always in front of you, always receding, and you never get there, and then one day you're dead. There's only the present. That's where we live. You can't live in the future. You can't plan for anything. You can only take what comes.'

'Don't you think he might see it that way too?' I said.

'How can he? I was the one who complained, because I wanted a future for us. It's my fault.'

I wasn't sure what to say to this, and did my best to make the right kind of noises, but Georgie wasn't listening.

'Everything's my fault,' she continued sombrely. 'It all started with those three wishes. We were doing fine till then. But I had to go around trying to make wishes come true, and now we're up to our ears in shit. If I hadn't gone looking for a cardiac millionaire I'd probably still be with Cal. If I hadn't told Lin she could find her One True Love on the Internet she'd never have met Ivor. At least you came out of it okay, but—'

'As long as I don't try to be a sex goddess,' I said firmly. I'd consigned the flame-red dress to the back of my wardrobe and resolved never to wear it again. (Well, not for ages, anyway.) 'I'm glad I've lost weight and I dress better, but that's all. Looking sexy doesn't suit me.'

'Nonsense,' said Georgie, diverted from her private abyss of self-blame. 'You can look sexy without having to go the whole hog. There are degrees of sexiness. Mostly, it's down to how you feel. If you *feel* sexy, even though you're covered from neck to ankle you can exude a sort of aura.'

'I don't want to exude anything. It makes me sound like a bad case of environmental pollution.'

'I think you should have a new dress for Jerry Beauman's party . . .'

'No.'

'Something more restrained.'

The launch loomed ahead of us, an event of huge significance though we weren't at all sure what it signified. We anticipated it with dread and also with . . . well, anticipation.

As Georgie said, if the party was a catastrophe, it wouldn't be *our* catastrophe. Apart from specifying certain people he wanted to invite, Jerry had left the guest list up to her, and Georgie, after an open meeting with practically everyone at Ransome, had decided to ask the whole of London – media, celebs, the lot – in the hope that some of them would come out of sheer curiosity, some for the free booze, and a few because they didn't realise whom the invitation was actually from. (It was headed: 'The Staff and Management of Ransome Harber invite you to . . .' after a brief debate with Jerry, who was tactfully brought to realise the imprudence of putting his own name at the top.) I had contemplated adding Todd Jarman's name to the list – I was still running on forlorn hopes – but Alistair stepped in first, insisting we include all our high-profile authors living in the area. 'Time to show solidarity with their publisher,' he said. 'We've backed them for years; now they need to back us.' He had clearly slipped into an alternative universe where writer and publisher shared a warm, huggy-huggy relationship based on mutual respect and appreciation. In this world, writers hate their publishers on the grounds that their advances are too small and their efforts at promotion derisory – and, as I've mentioned before, publishers despise writers, since they know nothing about books and do everything they can to mess up the smooth running of business. But some might attend the party, if we were lucky. Writers cannibalise pain, preferably other people's. There were bound to be a few out there who would come, like Romans to the amphitheatre, in the hope of seeing Jerry eaten by lions.

As far as Jerry's private list was concerned, the refusals were mounting up. In general, people don't bother to accept (or refuse) an invitation to a launch party: it's the kind of sprawly, casual occasion when they think courtesy doesn't matter. But in this case the great and the good clearly wanted it set on record that they *weren't coming* – refusal was a gesture, not a mere social decision. Of course, arguably, so was acceptance, but we didn't have so many of those. All we could do, as Georgie put it, was to trust that, in theatrical parlance, it would be all right on the night. 'And if it isn't,' she concluded, 'it doesn't matter, because it's not our fault. Jerry was the one who wanted the bloody party, after all. If no one shows up, there'll be more Bolly for the rest of us.'

Bearing this in mind, anyone at Ransome who had anything to do with the project was preparing to turn out – 'It'll flesh out the crowd,' Georgie said, 'if there is a crowd' – plus a good few extras. I slipped an invitation to Cal, in case Georgie hadn't, and later that day he arrived at my desk, plainly in a state of indecision.

'I've had a couple of these,' he said. Aha. 'No one's ever bothered to *invite* me to a launch before.' He had a point. You don't usually invite staff: they just go. Or not. But this was – unfortunately – a special occasion.

'Everyone's getting them,' I explained. 'We're trying to rally people round. Let's face it, we could well be the only guests.'

'I thought perhaps Georgie . . .'

'This isn't *personal*,' I lied. 'This is for the company.'

'Balls to the company,' Cal said, looking startled. Corporate morale wasn't a big deal at Ransome. Publishers tend to take it for granted that it's a privilege to work for them; they don't think their employees need regular encouragement.

'Okay, then it's for your colleagues. For everybody who worked on the damn book. You did the dust jacket, didn't you?'

''Course, but . . .'

'Show – solidarity.' I borrowed from Alistair's vocabulary. 'It's just a party. You used to be a party guy.' I decided to take the bull by the horns. 'Is it us – is that the problem? Georgie – and friends? Don't you even *like* us any more?'

'Don't be stupid. I've always liked you, and as for Georgie . . .'

'Did that blonde really fill the gap,' I said, 'or did she just – temp?'

He made a half-grimace, gave part of a head-shake, a fraction of a shrug. 'You know it's hopeless.'

'No, I don't,' I said with sudden energy. 'It's only hopeless if you think it is. Love is special. Love is worth the effort. You could make it work if you both really *wanted* to. You've had plenty of time to dwell on the difficulties: all you have to do is come to terms with them.'

'Georgie doesn't want to,' he said, 'does she?'

'Ask her.'

Meanwhile, the columnists backed off Lin to stick their dagger-nibs into another scandal, but the damage was done. The photos which had appeared in the press were all either old ones from the files or the blurred sneak-shots of prowling paparazzi, but they were enough to make her so apprehensive she hardly dared go out. One day in her local supermarket she was harangued by a woman she knew only by sight, who called her a disgrace to motherhood, more interested in men than the welfare of her children. A manager rushed to her aid, and she was taken home in tears, but after that she declared she would never go shopping again. The Internet had its uses: she could buy everything online. She couldn't even face going to work any more . . .

'Are you going to let the bastards defeat you?' Georgie demanded. 'Where's your fighting spirit?'

'I haven't any,' Lin said flatly. 'I can't stand people yelling at me, *hating* me. It makes me shrivel inside. Not just strangers – people I know well, people I thought knew *me*. Vee won't take Meredith any more. She says I should spend more time with the kids, stop g-gadding about. I know I was stupid – I *know* that – but I don't gad about, I've always, always put the children first. It's like *I'm* on trial, not Ivor – like *I* abused them . . .'

'Vee's wrong,' I said furiously. 'She's just being smug and self-righteous and superior – she and all the ones like her. The broadsheet moralists and the tabloids who batten on people's suffering – and the morons who soak it up to feel good about themselves. People hurt other people – they let each other down – they let *themselves* down – and then they band together to victimise some poor sod whose little failings are out in the open. It makes them *feel good* – it's the real feelgood factor – and it's horrible. It's humanity at its most obscene. Like stoning adulteresses in Biblical times. People like to gang up, particularly against someone who won't fight back. There's the bully in all of us, but at least we can try to suppress it, instead of – instead of justifying it, instead of saying to ourselves: I'm right – I'm righteous – she's screwed up – she *deserves* to suffer . . .'

Lin was clasping my hand, evidently moved by any gesture of affection or support these days.

'Good speech,' Georgie said. 'Wish I'd made it. And *don't* say—'

'You will, Oscar. You will.'

The atmosphere lightened. 'Right,' Georgie said. 'First of all, you *can* go out. You must. You can wear a woolly hat pulled down over your ears and look a nerd; lots of celebrities do that. Or a wig – that might be fun. But you mustn't become a recluse. For the kids' sake—' she found the right button, and pressed it '– you've got to go on as normal. They won't like it if you fuss over them all the time. And you can't give up working: you need the money.'

'Demmy said I was a bad mum,' Lin whispered. 'His classmates told him . . . And Sandy doesn't say anything, but his teacher told me he keeps getting into fights, and he comes home with bruises, and sulks when I ask how he got them.'

'Has – has Andy phoned?' I asked hesitantly.

'No. I mean, I don't know. Mostly, I keep it unplugged, and my mobile's not working, and I don't check my e-mail any more 'cos people have found out my address, and I get so much hate stuff . . .'

'Maybe you should call him.'

'How could I?'

I didn't push it.

'At any rate,' Georgie said, 'you'll come to Jerry's party.'

'I couldn't possibly—'

'You'll come,' Georgie persisted, at her most inexorable, 'because we need you. *I* need you. We'll fix you up with a babysitter, someone from a reliable agency if we have to. I'll find a way to put it on the PR account. But you have to come. You can't let us down.'

'I've already let my children down—'

'Oh *bollocks* . . .'

The launch was at the end of November, carefully timed to start the Christmas season. At Jerry's insistence, we went to the flat the day before to discuss it in detail. He believed in planning a party like a military operation, something we thought of as overkill although, under the circumstances, perhaps it was necessary. But I suspected the circumstances had nothing to do with it; Jerry was just one of Nature's superplanners, a control freak who, having temporarily lost his grip on life, was determined to get every aspect of it back on track. The champagne corks would be fired *here* – the toad would be holed up *there* – a squad of catering staff would attack the west lounge – guests would be ambushed and stripped of their coats in the lobby – a welcoming line would be stationed near the door – hold until relieved . . .

'I don't think we need that,' Georgie said hurriedly. 'It looks as though we're trying too hard.'

'When I went to a reception in Downing Street—'

'They *have* to be formal,' Georgie said coaxingly. 'We don't. Much better to appear casual. We *know* this is the best party of the season; we don't have to ram it down anyone's throat.'

'Maybe you're right,' Jerry conceded, with a flicker of the mouth which might have passed for a smile.

'If the old religions are right,' I remarked in an aside to Georgie, while Jerry was diverted by the telephone, 'and people go to Purgatory for a single lie, you're going to be there for one hell of a long time.'

'Purgatory,' Georgie shuddered, 'is part of my job.'

Surprisingly – once he had realised she was undergoing trial by tabloid – Jerry was extremely, even embarrassingly, nice to Lin. In his view, they were kindred spirits, wrongfully targeted by the gutter press, and as such ranged on the same side. (At other times, he also felt he was a kindred spirit with Frank Bruno, Russell Crowe, Tony Blair and the late Princess Diana.) He kept making jollying remarks to her – 'Don't let the swine get to you' – 'Right is always right, even if a howling mob calls it wrong' – patting her on the shoulder, oozing sympathy. When she said she might not manage to come to the party, he became bracing and military again: 'We have to stand together. I know you won't let the team down.'

'I'm not *on* his team,' Lin objected pitifully, once he was out of the room. 'I don't think I can take much more of this.'

'I know,' Georgie said. 'There's a downside to being hounded by the press that you just don't expect. It puts you in such very bad company.'

'*Publishing* puts you in bad company,' I said. 'And they told me it was a respectable job.'

'When you consider what books are *about*,' Georgie retorted, 'you can't really expect publishing them to be respectable.'

With Jerry metaphorically laying out a party map and moving flags around we hadn't had another chance to search the bathroom. Lin, driven to breaking point by his sympathetic manner, declared he was capable of any crime and she would be only too happy to prove it – thus uniting with Georgie and me on our quest for his hidden loot. Against my better judgement, I was still eager to vindicate my theory about the cache under the bath. Call it sheer female curiosity, if you like. Yes, I know that's a sexist statement, but actually curiosity is one of the (many) qualities that make women superior. Listen to any conversation between a man and a woman: the woman will be asking questions, the man talking, usually about himself. (Most heterosexual relationships are based on this simple fact.) Men affect to despise us for being 'nosy', 'minding other people's business', but in fact they thrive on our spirit of inquiry. And curiosity leads to progress – you can bet it was a Stone Age woman who stuck a haunch of mammoth in the fire to see what would happen, and thereby invented cooking. I wouldn't be surprised if many of the great discoveries of history were made, not by the accredited males, but by their wives, overlooked because of their gender. Mrs Newton probably had to drop the apple on Isaac's head a good few times before he cottoned on. And one of the main things that's wrong with our police force is that the CID still consists predominantly of men. Yet women are natural detectives (Agatha Christie knew all about that) and much better at it than Sherlock Holmes.

Which brings me back to Jerry's bathroom. I wanted to see what was behind the faux-marble panel, Georgie had her back to the wall with financial hassle, and Lin, driven to the edge of a precipice, was horrified to find Jerry Beauman dangling from the same rope. We weren't really planning to steal the money – I don't think so, anyway – we just wanted to know if it was there. We weren't planning to inform the

Serious Fraud Office. We weren't planning *anything*. It just gave us something to be curious *about* – a distraction from broken hearts and hopeless love, from private rejection and public humiliation and guilty fantasy. It made us feel like Charlie's Angels again, swashbuckling adventuresses on the trail of a supervillain. Of course, Jerry wasn't plotting world domination, but from the way he organised the party it was clear he was exactly the kind of obsessive control freak who *might be*. Besides, he was the nearest we could get.

'We'll have to search under cover of the launch,' Georgie said. 'Guests are supposed to use the other bathrooms; that one's off limits, so we should be okay. When Jerry's preoccupied with critics and journos we can sneak off quietly.'

Unexpectedly, Lin agreed. 'That's what Farrah Fawcett would do.'

Georgie nodded at me. 'You'll need a new dress,' she reiterated. 'That red one's too noticeable. You can't sneak anywhere in that.'

'I wasn't going to wear the red one! As it happens, I'm never—'

'You want something dark. Black is good.'

So it was decided.

In the end, it was Laurence who was delegated to babysit Lin's children. As Jerry's rejected editor, he was the one person at Ransome who had no intention of going to the party. 'As long as Sean doesn't find out,' Lin confided. 'He thinks being gay is practically the same as being a paedophile. I only hope the twins haven't picked up any ideas from him.'

'Kids learn their prejudices at school, not from absentee dads,' Georgie said wisely. 'Which is probably worse. Still, it doesn't matter. How would they know Laurence is gay?'

'Hector's coming with me,' Laurence announced later. 'That's all right, isn't it?'

'Um . . . yes . . .'

'He feels we need to bond at every opportunity these days . . . after the problems we've been having.'

'Fine . . .'

Lin wasn't happy – she was on a permanent maternal guilt trip since the revelations about Ivor – but Georgie and I quashed her objections ruthlessly. We arranged to tart up in Publicity (as usual) and get a taxi round to Berkeley Square for half-past five. Jerry had specifically commanded our early arrival; Georgie said he probably wanted to make a speech. 'Something stirring and bellicose,' she said. 'For Queen and country and all that. I'll bet you a tenner.'

'No takers,' I said.

As far as possible, I cleared my desk (An editor's desk is never cleared: Ancient Literary Proverb), mostly by sweeping things into piles and putting them on top of other piles, thus creating an illusion of space in the middle. I was enjoying the unaccustomed feeling of achievement when the phone rang.

'Hello? Is that Cookie?'

'Yes?' I recognised the voice without being able to identify it.

'Andy Pearmain. Look, I hope you don't mind my calling like this—'

'Not at all.'

'– but I can't get hold of Lin. Her home phone doesn't seem to be working, her mobile's always off, and the switchboard has refused to put me through to her, so I asked for you.' Reception were faithfully filtering out all calls for Lin, since most of them were from journalists. 'I've been abroad for a couple of weeks. I don't know if you heard, but we called off the wedding—'

'I heard,' I said, but Andy wasn't paying attention to my side of the conversation.

'– three days before the event. It was a bit chaotic. I did what I could to protect poor Cat from the flak – her parents were pretty devastated, I think I was their dream son-in-law, presumably because our families are such old friends—'

Of course, the money wasn't a factor.

'It was a brave decision of hers, but I think she was right. Maybe I'm just not cut out for marriage. Every time I get within a mile of it, something goes wrong.'

'D'you think that Cat was really your type?' I asked tentatively.

'She was until you and Georgie got your hands on her,' Andy said ruefully. 'Then suddenly she was telling me that *this* was the real her – complete with navel stud and leather mini-skirt.' I couldn't recall a leather mini, but I let it pass. 'Anyway, I decided to go away for a while – clear my head.'

'Did it work?'

'I've been trying to contact Lin since I got back – I just want to know she's all right. I won't intrude on her if she doesn't want me – I realise she wasn't keen on telling me about Ivor – but I must know—'

'She's not all right,' I said bluntly. 'Order back copies of all the newspapers you've missed.' As succinctly as I could, I told him what had happened.

There was a long silence, punctuated by assorted oaths. Fairly moderate ones: Andy wasn't much given to obscenity, even under pressure. 'Some of these newspaper proprietors are going to be sorry,' he said finally. 'I've lent money to them.'

'Do they still owe you?' I asked, hopefully.

'You bet they do.'

There are pluses to knowing an influential banker which hadn't occurred to me before.

'Give 'em hell,' I said.

In Georgie's office, I didn't get around to mentioning the

call. We were too busy barricading the door against intruders so we could wriggle into posh dresses and apply our makeup in Georgie's illuminated mirror. Lin was wearing the inevitable ethnic embroidery effect, this time on panne velvet, with a little mascara, a pale lipstick, and some daring blue pencil eyeliner which was fortunately too faint to be noticeable. Georgie had gone for the Little Black Dress – one I'd seen before, showing she was still at too low an ebb for shopping – ruched around the hips and displaying what seemed to be less cleavage than in the past. 'I've lost weight,' she explained, tersely. Georgie's weight was normally fairly stable: unhappiness had evidently eroded her appetite.

As the only one in something new, I felt blatantly extravagant. But I *really* hadn't wanted to wear the red dress again, and my other party clothes pre-dated my diet, so I'd been able to justify the expenditure to myself in the way women do when we've decided to spend the money anyway. My dress was also velvet – velvet is one of the good things about winter – but soft and slightly stretchy instead of panne, clinging in the right places but not plunging, its colour a sort of dark purplish-brown which suited me better than black. (I don't know the technical name: possibly aubergine.) With Georgie's assistance I put my hair up, twizzling the leftover dangly bits into ringlets, which, with the aid of high heels, made me *feel* tall even if I didn't look it. We left the office on a heartening wave of appreciation from fellow workers and piled into the taxi.

'Well,' Georgie said, 'here we go. The Three Musketeers. All for one and one for all.'

'Charlie's Angels,' said Lin.

'The Weird Sisters,' I concluded. 'Clotho, Lachesis, and Atropos. The Fates who spun the threads of men's lives – and snipped them off at the end.' There's nothing like pretending you're in control, especially when you're not.

'Just because you went to Oxford that doesn't mean you can go all intellectual on us . . .'

At the flat, as predicted, Jerry made a speech. It wasn't quite Henry V but the intention was much the same, if you substituted the tabloids for the French and bore in mind that the enemy had numbers on his side. 'At Agincourt,' Georgie muttered, 'as far as I can remember, the British longbows decided the issue. Do we have longbows?'

'Nope.'

'Any equivalent?'

'Uh-huh.'

'We're doomed. We're all doomed . . .'

Jerry opened a bottle of champagne so we could toast his success, and Georgie was just persuading him to let us leave our coats and bags in the master bedroom, out of the way of the guests' things, when his girlfriend arrived. She was smothered in some endangered species and had a name which sounded like Ly Chee, though I'm sure it wasn't. We all availed ourselves of Jerry's bedroom to shed our outer layers. Meanwhile, the apartment started filling up, mainly with waiters and waitresses, coat-carrying maids, the staff of Ransome, and Jerry's chauffeur and minder MacMurdo, standing around surveying the room like a CIA agent at a presidential reception.

Around six-thirty, the after-work crowd began to arrive, first in a trickle, then a flood. Georgie's policy of inviting everyone in London had clearly paid off. There were no A-list celebs but a good few C-list ones – the kind who were eager for any exposure, no matter how dubious – and a score of low-profile glitterati who knew they weren't famous enough to attract attention and could therefore come out of curiosity and the natural human desire to witness what might be a débâcle. And then there were the hacks, pretending to be literary journalists, and the literary journalists, doubling as hacks. There were diarists, columnists, pundits, an investigative team specialising in City scandals, even a wine writer. There was a fading rock star too far gone to know what party he was attending, and a minor It girl who said large-mindedly that she didn't care about a person's past, some of her best friends had been to prison, and any man who was rich enough was entitled to a second chance (or words to that effect). Cal turned up late, at a guess after a visit to the pub, and fell into her manicured clutches. God knows what he told her, since he wouldn't be her line of country at all, but I saw him appropriating a bottle of Bolly while she gushed and sparkled at him like a fountain in overdrive. Georgie, catching sight of them, promptly began to flirt with someone who turned out to be the ex-TV presenter from her misspent youth. Lin was clinging to a colleague from Ransome by way of a shield, but none of the hacks had noticed her yet. They were intent on other prey. An official photographer roamed the throng; unofficial ones were being firmly discouraged by MacMurdo. Jerry, who had a notoriously short fuse with journalists, remained – for the moment – scrupulously polite, sweeping the crowd with a lighthouse beam of improbable charm.

'If numbers count,' I thought without satisfaction, 'it's a success. So far.'

Jerry didn't think so. 'Where are the Hamiltons?' he muttered in a tight-lipped aside to Georgie. 'I always gave him my wholehearted support, and this is how he repays me. And Rod – we used to go drinking together . . . Peter – the money I've spent in his club . . . The Viscount – God, I once paid his bail . . .'

'The press are all here,' Georgie pointed out. 'They're the ones who'll give us the coverage. And two actors from *EastEnders* and one from *Emmerdale*, and a blonde from one of those property shows, and the latest guy to be fired from children's TV for a sex-and-drugs scandal. And there's – good God – Todd Jarman . . .'

'I don't recall inviting him. I hardly . . . Of course, he's a terrific writer. Top-notch thrillers. In some ways, we're two of a kind, though he hasn't quite achieved my status yet. I must go and have a word with him.'

I'd seen Todd almost the moment he arrived, and to my horror my heart leaped, or at least jolted. I was in mid-conversational flow with a reviewer who was telling me he'd been agreeably surprised by Jerry's new book ('Really quite well-written . . . derivative, of course, but a page-turner . . . I must say, Jerry's books always are . . .') and suddenly I found I'd lost the thread. My mind was jerked off course – I floundered in a sea of meaningless chatter.

Todd, approached by Jerry, was looking particularly sardonic and, I thought, vaguely uncomfortable; Helen Aucham, on his arm, had the air of someone with a bad smell under her nose who's trying very hard not to inhale. I found myself wondering how on earth Alistair had been able to persuade them to come. Of the other writers asked, only one had put in an appearance, a plump, pretty authoress of darkly convoluted mysteries who was, I suspected, only here for the murder. I forgot to feel gratified by the reviewer's unwitting praise for my efforts, and began to sidle casually through the crowd towards Todd. The party currents tugged me this way and that but I persisted, striking out against the tide. When I was within a couple of yards, I saw Helen had become unlatched from Todd's arm and had allowed herself to be drawn into an adjacent group which included a well-known face of some sort, though I couldn't recall whose it was. Over three or four intervening people, Todd smiled at me. Bugger – I was remembering the way he'd looked that night on the sofa when we . . . I started to blush, and had to pause for a quick chat with whoever came to hand to give the blush time to burn itself out. The exchange might have been in Latvian for all I knew. And then somehow – I don't know if he moved or I did – I was talking to Todd.

'What are you doing here?' I demanded, in a tone that came out more accusatory than I'd intended.

'I was invited.'

'I know *that*. I'm sorry, I didn't mean – I just didn't expect you to come. This isn't exactly a cool place to be seen, is it? And Helen didn't look too thrilled . . .'

'She wasn't. Still, for an uncool party it seems to be fairly popular. Plenty of people here.' He hadn't answered the question.

'It's mostly press and C-list padding,' I said. 'Oh – and anyone too nosy to stay away.'

'Which category do you think I belong in?'

I began to blush again, this time from embarrassment. 'I don't,' I said. 'That's just it. Did – did Alistair twist your arm somehow?'

'My arm isn't easily twisted. Call me nosy, if you like. I was so staggered to get the invitation I couldn't bring myself to turn it down. Besides, I had nothing else to do.' I didn't believe him, but I let it rest. For now. 'You're Jerry's editor, aren't you?'

'They give me all the dirty jobs.' I spoke without thinking. Todd laughed.

'Oh *shit*. Sorry . . . sorry . . .' I gave up trying to apologise. After all, it wasn't the first time I'd been rude to him. 'It's a tough life being an editor.'

'You meet such a low class of people, don't you?' He accepted a top-up from a passing champagne bottle and went on: 'Where's the toad-in-the-hole? I understood that was a staple of Jerry's parties. Actually, I was quite looking forward to it – though it'll have to be good to match my mother's.'

'After the speeches.'

'*Speeches*?' He did the eyebrow trick.

'Haven't you ever made a speech at any of your launches?'

'Well, last time I think Alistair said a few suitable words

– great book, straight up the bestseller list, going to make us all lots of money – and I said something in acknow-ledgement – thank you, probably – and that was it. Nice and short. Not what you'd call *speeches*.'

'These won't be short,' I said sweetly. 'Alistair will say what a great writer Jerry is and how lucky we are to publish him. Then Jerry—'

'Will say what great publishers you are?'

'Fat chance. But I should warn you, it's a lot more than thank you. He's written it up in advance. Several pages. I've seen them.'

'My God. Why *did* I come?'

'That,' I said, 'is what I'm still wondering.'

'Are you?' He was looking at me with something in his eyes which I didn't recognise, not quite mockery, almost a chal-lenge. I found myself noticing their colour – grey with a hint of green – and the crinkling of his eyelids, and the downward sweep of his werewolf brows over the bridge of his nose, all in great detail. The intimacy of my perception disturbed me; I felt myself going hot inside. He said something else but for a few seconds I was so absorbed in his face I didn't hear.

'Sorry?'

'I said, "Take a guess". Never mind. Your face glazed over. You're obviously saturated with small talk.'

'No, I . . .' But he had turned away to include his neigh-bour in the conversation, and whatever had nearly been said was lost.

Jerry had scheduled the speeches for half-past eight. The vast living room was crowded and the party buzzed, but it still lacked the top-rank stars, aristocracy and – probably – royalty that Jerry considered his due. Nonetheless, he continued to give his Klingon impression of a good host. The ominous moment arrived when Alistair stood on a chair, and a hush ran through the room. A hand fell on my arm. Georgie.

'Come on,' she said. 'Lin's done a bunk somewhere. I think she's in trouble.'

I whispered: 'Excuse me,' to Todd and we slipped out.

We found Lin in the master bedroom, hunched up on Jerry's fourposter looking like an abandoned orphan in a period novel. Her face was pale and pinched under the long fall of her hair. 'One of the journalists recognised me,' she said. 'She started on at me – why was I out, leaving my children? Who was looking after them? How did I feel about having my name linked with paedophiles and ex-cons? I said it was work, that was why I was here, but she wouldn't listen. She just kept going on and on. How friendly was I with Jerry? I claimed the press had treated me unfairly – did I think they'd treated him unfairly too? I didn't know what to say. I ran off – she tried to follow, but that minder of Jerry's got in the way.'

'MacMurdo,' I supplied.

'I can't go back out there. I'm sorry, Georgie, I just can't. I'll wait in here till everyone's gone . . .'

'It's the speeches,' Georgie said. 'We're not going back out there either. Let's have another go at taking the bath to bits.'

'Shouldn't someone keep watch?' I said.

'No need. We'll just lock the door.'

In the bathroom, we all crouched down by the faux-marble panel. 'It's got to be here,' Georgie told Lin. 'Why else would this section be in two pieces? I've tried levering it open *here*, but—'

'Did you try the other end?' Lin asked. 'Maybe it opens that side instead.'

'That's too obvious.' Georgie gave her a severe look and got out her all-purpose nail file. She slid the tip into the crack at the corner of the panel, working it to and fro. 'I can feel something,' she said abruptly. 'Like . . . a latch . . .' She wriggled the file more vigorously. There was a tiny snick, and the panel swung open a fraction.

'See?' Lin's face had lightened. 'It worked.'

'I hate it when people do that,' Georgie remarked. 'You wrestle with something for ages and then somebody comes along and says brightly: "Why don't you do it *that* way?" and they're right. That's *so* infuriating.'

'Open it wider,' I said, disregarding her. 'Let's see what's in there.'

The cavity was dark and the overhead lighting did little to illuminate it, but there was a bulky object inside, squashed against the curve of the Jacuzzi. A bag. Quite a big bag. Georgie seized it and tried to pull it out, but it was wedged. It came free with a wrench that sent her rocking backwards, and there it was. An ordinary sports bag, rather dirty from prolonged incarceration, bulging at the seams and zipped tight.

'My God,' I said – or something like that. 'We were right. We were *right* . . .'

Georgie undid the zip.

The bag was full of money. Lots and lots and *lots* of money. Great wodges of scarlet and mauve notes, sealed in plastic, presumably in case the bath leaked. We couldn't begin to count it, but it didn't matter. It *looked* like half a million quid, and that was good enough for us. I'd rarely seen a fifty-pound note, and here there were fat bundles of them. Money is – money. The purchasing power of life. It's food and drink and shelter, new-reg cars and first-class travel and designer clothes. It's security and status and influence and bank managers who kiss your arse. It may not have the glitter of jewels or the lustre of gold but in this day and age – in such large quantities – it has magic. We stared and stared. At the bag and the money and each other.

Lin said faintly: 'Wow.' Her troubles were (briefly) dimmed by the glow of our discovery.

Georgie began to scrabble at the plastic, trying to tear it open.

'Why wasn't the panel locked?' Lin said. 'I *mean* . . .'

'I suppose Jerry didn't think anyone would look there,' I said. 'We'd never have thought of it if I hadn't hidden stuff under the bath when I was a student.' And, glancing at Georgie: 'We have to decide what to do.' I only hoped I sounded forceful enough to get through to her.

'Call the police?' Lin.

'Pay my credit-card debts.' Georgie.

'We can't just *take* it. Leave it alone.' I pushed her hands away from the bag. 'We've got to talk.'

'What about ethics?' Lin demanded with less conviction than I would've expected.

'What about them?'

'Perhaps . . . if we gave some of it to a good cause . . .'

And then – with the sort of timing that normally only occurs in books – there was a knock on the door. 'Hello? Mrs Corrigan?' A Scots accent. MacMurdo. 'Are ye all right in there?' There was a note of rough concern in the voice, and I realised he must have noticed Lin's flight and come after her. Even musclemen have a small dose of the milk of human kindness in their system. I nudged her violently.

'Yes,' she said in a sort of gasp. 'I – I won't be long.'

'I'll see to it ye're not troubled nae more,' he assured her.

'Thanks.'

Now what? I mouthed.

'Supposing he's still out there?' Lin whispered. 'Waiting for me.'

'We can't stay in here forever,' I said.

'You go,' Georgie said to Lin. 'We'll wait in here, then we can follow when the coast's clear.'

'What'll you do with *that*?'

'Take it with us.'

'How?' I hissed. 'Under your coat?'

'I'll . . . improvise . . .'

She'd managed to tear the plastic by now and there was a breathless moment when she pulled the rip wider and we each snatched a wad, feeling the thickness of it, the crisp smoothness of new notes. Money really does feel crisp: did you know? Not crisp like crisps but crisp like the best bed linen, and every bit as sexy. Then came the voice again: 'Are ye sure ye're all right?' and the spell was broken.

'What kind of a world is it,' Georgie muttered as we shoved the money back, 'where a girl can't have a pee in peace?'

'I'm not having a pee,' Lin said.

'No, but you might be. Now, get out there – distract him – get him out of the bedroom.'

Georgie and I flattened ourselves on either side of the door, Georgie clutching the bag to her bosom. Lin went out, omitting to switch off the light behind her – I trusted MacMurdo wouldn't notice that someone else had done it. Their voices retreated and I peered round the door-frame.

'Okay.'

In the bedroom, Georgie said: 'Our best chance is to sneak out with it now, under cover of the party.'

'Don't be an idiot. Jerry would be bound to spot you – he watches the entrance lobby like a hawk in case anyone important shows up. And you can hardly pass that off as your handbag.'

'I should've brought an overnight bag with my work clothes instead of leaving them at the office. Why didn't we plan this better?'

'Because we never *really* expected to find anything.'

'I could throw the bag out of the window for you to collect down in the street.'

The window was locked.

'We shouldn't be removing it at all. It's evidence. You have to leave it *in situ*.'

'Are *you* going to tell the SFO?'

We were glaring at each other, locked in conflict – how fast money can undermine the deepest friendship! – when we heard the door opening. Georgie threw my koala fur over the bag, just as a woman walked in, raking the room with a ferret-like gaze. She had a short skirt, very thin legs, and a hairdo that combined back-combing and sticking-out ends in a tangle of such complexity it had to be deliberate. I didn't recognise her but Georgie did. 'Jocasta Tate,' she said, *sotto voce*. The name was familiar. A Glenda Slagg working for the *Mail* or the *Express* or the *Mirror*, I couldn't recall which.

'I'm looking for Lindsay Corrigan,' she said. 'I know she came in here. Skinny little thing, sandy hair.'

I opened my mouth to say she'd left – and shut it again. Loot or no loot, we had to divert the enemy from Lin.

'She went into the bathroom,' Georgie said glibly. I detected a note of inspiration in her voice, and my heart sank. 'I think you can get out that way. There's a balcony or something.'

A balcony? Outside the *bathroom*?

But Jocasta was too hot on the trail to smell a red herring. She pounced on the door, knocked, pushed it open. 'Keep her there!' Georgie adjured, and bolted back to the party. It took her a few seconds to locate Jerry.

'Jerry, have you got a moment? There's some woman in your bathroom – I think she's a journalist. She says she's found a secret panel in the side of the Jacuzzi. She took something out of there—'

Jerry snarled a summons to MacMurdo and they all burst into the bedroom at a run, with Lin – who had been clinging to the minder for protection – tagging along behind. Jocasta had found the panel ajar – the way we left it – and paused in her pursuit of Lin to peer inside. Seeing the cavity was empty, and there was no sign of any alternative exit to the room, she re-emerged just in time to collide with Jerry. He grabbed her, tossed her into MacMurdo's grasp – 'Don't let the bitch get away!' – and dived through the door. An instant later he appeared again, his face white and lipless with rage. He plucked Jocasta by the shoulders and shook her so savagely I was afraid she'd be really hurt. 'What've you done with it? You thieving whore! What – have – you – done – with – it?' Jocasta, her head jerking like a rag doll, couldn't have answered him even if she'd known what to say.

Georgie, meanwhile, had picked up the bag – still covered by my coat – and strode purposefully to the door (she knew better than to sidle). Everyone's attention was fixed on Jocasta. Once Georgie was out of the bedroom, the party crowd would engulf her . . .

It was a bold plan and it might have worked. It very nearly did.

But Jerry's departure from the party had been rapid and noticeable. Several of the guests, scenting drama, had trailed in his wake. In the lead was Cal, who had been keeping an eye out for Georgie; behind him came Todd, who – well, I still hadn't worked out what his agenda was. With them, the It girl, a spare EastEnder, assorted representatives of the press, and the official photographer, who was employed by Ransome and blithely continued taking pictures when Jerry had long passed his save-by date. Even as Georgie reached the door, it was blocked by people.

'Let me through!' she commanded Cal, but the crowd was building up behind him and escape was becoming impossible.

'What have you got there?' he asked, catching a glimpse of the bag.

'Shush!'

But it was too late. A couple of hacks were shouting at Jerry – one went to Jocasta's assistance – and he spun round, saw Georgie struggling to get out, guessed what she was carrying. He leaped towards her – made a grab for the bag

– my dead teddy slid to the ground – and then the two of them had hold of it and were tugging in opposite directions. Lin and I ran to support Georgie, hooking our fingers into the gaping zip, but Jerry, inspired by greed, must have had the strength of ten – or at least of four. In an ideal world the bag would have split apart, showering money into the air which would have come fluttering down like oversized confetti. In fact, Jerry called MacMurdo to his side and, letting go with one hand, punched his principal opponent in the face. Georgie reeled backwards, letting out a screech of fury. 'You *bastard*! My blusher—' Cal, operating on instinct, sprang into the breach and hit back.

Not for nothing did he go running and play squash regularly. The blow was a good deal harder than Jerry's, and sent the recipient crashing to the floor. Meanwhile, the guests were pushing forward into the room, anxious not to miss any of the action. MacMurdo, who knew his job, swung in retaliation – Cal dodged sideways – and somehow the Scotsman's huge fist encountered Todd's lantern jaw. Todd would have fallen, if there hadn't been too many people getting in the way. I let go the bag and went to his side, and there was a moment when he collapsed against me, his arm clamping my shoulders. (It should have been a moment of bliss, but I had no time to feel blissful.) Somewhere in the background, Helen Aucham shrieked: 'We'll sue you for millions, Beauman, you arsehole!'

Todd sat down on the bed, evidently dizzy. His lip was bleeding. There was a box of tissues on one of the tables and I snatched a handful and began to staunch the flow. Lin dropped the bag to harangue MacMurdo – Jerry was trying to sit up – Cal was kissing Georgie's swollen cheek. The photographer went on snapping industriously at what was clearly the most photogenic launch party in history.

There was a minute when the bag was unattended. Jocasta

Tate and the It girl almost smashed head-on in their haste to look inside, yanking it open between them and gazing fixedly at the contents. Then Jocasta up-ended it and the money came pouring out, thick wads of banknotes pounding into a heap on the floor, skidding across the carpet. For a second, there was almost silence. Jerry, tottering to his feet, cried: 'Leave it! It's mine!' but no one paid any attention. They all knew ill-gotten gains when they saw them. That crowd of literati and glitterati – society girls and celebs – journalists both famous and infamous – burst through the confines of the door and rolled forward like a wave. Half a million disappeared under the rush. Georgie, I am sure, grabbed a bundle or two before Cal pulled her away; Lin was in danger of being trampled but MacMurdo lifted her clear. Jerry plunged into the free-for-all and temporarily vanished, though his voice could be heard from time to time.

'Thieves – you're all thieves! *Get out of my house!*'

'I told you I was no good at the fights,' Todd remarked. I was still daubing his mouth, though it wasn't bleeding much any more. 'Are you going to tell me what the hell's going on?'

'It's a long story,' I said, unable to resist a grin. Helen, too, was swamped in the mob.

'That's all right,' Todd said. 'I've got time. After all, I only came tonight to talk to you.'

Chapter 15

Let other pens dwell on guilt and misery. I quit such odious subjects as soon as I can.

JANE AUSTEN: *Mansfield Park*

All tragedies are finished by a death,
All comedies are ended by a marriage;
The future states of both are left to faith.

BYRON: *Don Juan*

Afterwards, Georgie said she couldn't decide if the party was her most spectacular failure – or her greatest success.

'You always said it was Jerry's responsibility,' I reminded her.

'Only if it was a failure. If it was a success, it's down to me.'

'It all depends what you mean by success . . .'

The wave of marauding guests had retreated at last, leaving a dishevelled Jerry, one eye puffed up and slowly turning black, clutching the remnants of his half a million. There wasn't much of it. He was shaking visibly, his face shrunken into taut lines, the gleam of his good eye almost demonic. He strode towards Georgie, his left arm still pressing the crumpled bank notes against his chest, his right

384

jabbing at the air with a malevolent finger. 'You did this! – you – *you*—'

'Leave her alone,' Cal said tersely, stepping in front of her, 'or I'll black the other one.'

'MacMurdo!'

'You can't make him beat people up!' Lin declared unexpectedly. 'He's supposed to be your chauffeur – your minder – but not your – your private thug! Anyway, he's not like that.' She was holding him back with an outthrust hand. It was a small hand, and it looked child-sized against the looming mass of MacMurdo. I stared at Lin with new respect. The bodyguard appeared decidedly uncomfortable.

('He comes from the same village as my mother,' Lin explained later. '*His* mum knows *my* aunt. Once I learned that, I knew I could deal with him.')

Jerry's lower jaw was thrust so far forward it seemed only loosely connected to the upper. 'Get him,' he said, 'or you're fired.'

'Erm . . . sorry, sir.'

Jerry started yelling for other minions, giving orders right and left – Re-cork the champagne! – Stuff the toad back in its hole! – Get rid of the remaining guests! In the middle Helen Aucham walked in, adopted a protective stance close to Todd, and threatened to issue a writ, or whatever it is lawyers issue under these circumstances. To give her her due, before very long she was also offering to represent MacMurdo in a suit for unfair dismissal. 'I'd better take her home,' Todd said. 'I'm damned if I want to star in a court case over a split lip, but I'll need to talk her out of it quietly. Will you be all right? I'm going to call you tomorrow, and we'll get together, preferably over dinner, and then you'll tell me everything. Okay?'

I nodded.

He turned to Cal. 'Would you look after her?'

''Course. Sorry about that—' he indicated the lip '– I think it was meant for me.'

Todd grinned crookedly. 'My pleasure.'

In the living room, half the party hadn't quite realised what had happened to the other half. Embarrassed waiters stood around, not too sure about hurling the leftover guests into the street: it wasn't a task which had previously come their way. Rumours of the scrum in the bedroom were spreading, wildly distorted (or so everyone assumed), and there was a wailing and a gnashing of teeth among those who had missed the fun. The one person who remained completely oblivious to disaster was Alistair Garnett. In the aftermath of the speeches he was talking to John Walsh of the *Independent* – they'd been at Oxford together – and he continued in lofty ignorance until the moment when Jerry lighted on him as an adequate target for his rage. 'He demanded I fire you,' Alistair told Georgie the next morning. 'And Cookie – and Lin – and Cal McGregor. In fact, he demanded I fire practically the entire staff of Ransome, as far as I could tell. I don't know what you did – the poor chap was babbling, virtually incoherent. I swear he was actually frothing at the mouth. *Writers.*'

'*Are* you going to fire us?' Georgie inquired.

'Lord, no. He's the one who wanted the bloody party. I always said it was a mistake.' Alistair looked gratified at his own foresight. 'Of course, he can't tear up the contract – too late now – but he'll go elsewhere next time. Doesn't matter, though. We've got him at his peak. His sales have nowhere to go but down.'

As the evening disintegrated, Cal had put Lin and me into a taxi, obviously intending to see Georgie home personally. On an impulse I gripped her lapel and said for her private ear: 'Sort yourself out this time. Tell him why you needed a millionaire. Tell him about your credit-card debts. Tell him there's no such thing as the future. Tell him—'

'All *right*.' She detached herself, and we drove away.

Cal found another cab.

'Are you taking me home?' Georgie asked.

'I'd better, hadn't I? Before you get into any more trouble. Where did that money come from?'

'Under the bath,' Georgie said, and proceeded to explain.

'He should have hidden it in the washing machine,' Cal commented. 'Then he could have laundered it.'

'Jokes really aren't your forte, are they? I can't believe I had a serious affair with a man who has no sense of humour.'

'I've got a big dick, though.'

'Sometimes,' Georgie said darkly, 'you *are* a big—'

'All right,' Cal said, 'I'm sorry. I'm sorry I've been a dick. I've always asked too much from you, and I'm married to another woman, and you could do so much better – but I do love you. Anyone else would cry if some guy thumped her, but you just worry about your blusher. You're the best, d'you know that?' He stroked her swollen cheek with one finger.

Presently, they kissed.

'Are we back together?' Georgie asked.

'Suppose so. It's up to you.'

'No, it's up to you. You were the one who finished it.'

'You wanted to see other men. You have every right, but—'

'Look—' she gave a deep sigh '– there are some things I ought to tell you. Important things.'

'Go on.'

'The problem is, our relationship has never been about – well, business stuff. It's just been about sex and love and things. The nice things. We don't have to share the everyday nitty-gritty of life. I didn't feel it was fair to burden you . . .'

Cal was looking bewildered. 'Burden me.'

'I'm broke. I owe so much money on my credit cards

they're threatening to bankrupt me. I could lose the house. I thought if I married a millionaire it would solve my problems, but I couldn't even bring myself to sleep with one. I only wanted you.' She sat staring in front of her in the darkness, her gaze fixed on the back of the cabby's neck. Fortunately, Cal had closed the intervening window early in the conversation. 'I've made such a mess of it – such a mess of everything. I never stopped loving you, though God knows I tried. Even if being with you is complicated and – and stressful and sometimes painful, I can't bear being without you. It doesn't matter if we haven't any future, as long as we always keep the present . . .'

Cal wiped away a tear, further smudging her makeup. 'You're *broke*? That's *all*? Why didn't you tell me?'

'I was ashamed. I thought you'd say I was hopelessly extravagant . . .'

'You're hopelessly extravagant.'

'Only when we split up, I was so unhappy I didn't even want to buy clothes any more.'

In the dark, she saw the ghost of his mischievous smile flicker across his face. 'My God, you *do* love me after all . . .'

'He was wonderful,' Georgie said the following morning. 'He was utterly wonderful. That's what love is: you meet some ordinary guy who isn't rich or famous and makes very bad jokes, and suddenly you know he's wonderful. He's going to arrange a bank loan to cover my debts – in his name – and help me pay them off. This friend of his who's opening a restaurant has offered him a commission to do some pictures for it. It's lots of money, and he says he'll give it to me. There's a trust fund for Jamie and Christy has a good income so they're not short at home. And he's going to tell her he's seeing someone, so he doesn't have to make up lies for her, and then it'll be easier for us. And he says when we're very old he'll still be coming round to make love to me, dosed up to the eyebrows with Viagra.'

'How romantic,' sighed Lin, with such obvious sincerity I concluded she'd missed the last bit.

We were meant to be checking the newspapers for coverage of the party (or even the book), but so far we hadn't found a single line. The diarists burbled on about other matters; the columnists were strangely mute. Two days later, Jocasta Tate came out with a lengthy piece on the glamorous life of the It girl, but there wasn't a word about Jerry Beauman. Georgie, buoyed up by the renewal of her relationship with Cal, had decided the party must have been a success after all, and was inclined to view the lack of publicity in a positive spirit. 'Anyhow,' she pointed out, 'what could they have said? That Jerry had a stash of money which he'd obviously acquired illegally and which had mysteriously disappeared along with most of the guests? They're not going to print that, are they? They were the guests who were busy disappearing.'

'Not all of them.'

'Yes, but the ones who actually saw what happened were involved in it. The more I think about it, the more I feel no one's going to run the risk of going public. Otherwise they'll all end up with egg on their faces – not to mention dirt on their hands.'

'Could you sound out some of your contacts?'

'I'll try.'

In fact, Georgie's hypothesis was proved right. There had been no secret confabulations, no formal conspiracy of silence. The journalists present at the final mêlée had gone away with a hot story and hot money in their pockets – and each had waited for one of the others to rush into print. The herd instinct is very strong in the press, and with nobody ready to stampede the herd made no move. A state of *omertà* kept the whole incident off the record. Those guests who had avoided the scrimmage knew what had happened, but hearsay wasn't good enough for publication on such a sensitive issue, and anyway, too many of their friends and colleagues were compromised. The story passed into journalistic myth and was revived with the brandy at the tag end of drunken dinner parties, and whispered in intimate circles, as proof of a mystic truth – the biggest scandals never see the light of day. The investigative team deduced where the money had come from and printed a few hints, but dared not venture further. Only the *Independent* gave the matter a mention, concluding: 'There was a minor fracas in one of the bedrooms – a falling out between the host and some of his guests – which resulted in a disgruntled Beauman calling off the party early and sending revellers home without any toad-in-the-hole, a sad come-down from Beauman's former standards of hospitality. Prison has clearly had a detrimental effect on him. A rumour that he had terminated his contract with Ransome Harber has not been confirmed.'

Alistair admitted later that Jerry had tried to block distribution of the book at the last minute with a view to selling it elsewhere – he wasn't the sort to worry about breach of contract, and told Alistair that after Georgie's behaviour we were in no position to sue. But thanks to the persistence of the official photographer, Alistair was able to change his mind without having to shell out for legal fees. The book was selling well, though the *omertà* seemed to have spread to the reviewers: even the one who'd spoken to me never actually gave it a write-up. A sort of collective media embarrassment settled over Jerry, blotting him out of the public eye. Even his girlfriend was reputed to have dumped him.

'Oscar Wilde got it right,' Georgie remarked the following week, as we looked in vain through the book pages. 'The only thing worse than being talked about ... There's got to be a moral here.'

'Don't get found out,' I said. 'The wages of spin is professional death.'

'Particularly if you hide them under the bath,' Georgie added.

'I've just realised,' I said, my editorial instincts clicking in, 'that's all wrong. It should be "the wages *are* death". Am I misquoting, or does the bad grammar come from the Bible?'

'The moral should be for us,' Lin said thoughtfully. 'After all, everything was our fault.'

'Phew!' said Georgie. '*Everything*? That gives me a *real* sense of achievement.'

With all the excitement, I'd forgotten to tell Lin about Andy's telephone call. Now that the press had cooled off a bit, she started plugging her landline in again, and eventually he got through. 'I don't want to push you,' he said. 'I know you've been through hell. Sean's a selfish, thick-headed—'

'He just didn't think,' Lin said, annoyed to find herself automatically apologising for the men in her life. 'He's desperately sorry now.'

'He'd better be. He's a lousy father and you're a wonderful mum, and he landed you right in it. But that isn't what I wanted to say. When the case comes to court it could all blow up again. I'll do what I can – I've got influence with some of the papers – but it would be easier if I was there. I hoped . . . you would let me help, support you . . .'

'*Let* you?' Lin said. 'Of course . . . I mean . . . that would be . . .'

'The thing is,' Andy persisted, 'we've been friends a long time, but I've never really been able to . . . When we first met I gave you a bed for the night, and I've bought you dinner fairly often, and you've talked to me – confided in me – but it's always been . . . Look, I've never been able to *do* anything. Sometimes, I feel a bit like Buttons in *Cinderella*. I never get to punch the villain or escort you to the ball in a pumpkin.

I want it to be different now. I don't just want to be your friend and confidant: I want to *help*. You're going to need someone to lean on in the next few months. I'll be your – your rock . . . Lin? Are you still there?'

'Yes.'

'You've gone very quiet. I'm not trying to take over your life or anything – just get you through a bad patch. Tell me it's okay. I know how independent you are at heart.'

Lin, who wasn't in the least independent, murmured: 'Yes, of course,' and 'It's okay – it's more than okay.'

'Good. You should have the best legal help. I'll fix you up with a friend of mine.'

'Aren't posh lawyers very expensive?'

'Don't worry about that. The important thing is to have someone who knows every trick of the trade. This Ivor sounds like a smooth operator. People like that know how to work the system. Sorry – I'm being tactless.'

'No. No, you're right. He was – smooth.' Her expression went awry. 'He fooled me easily enough.'

'Don't say that. You're very trusting – optimistic – you always believe the best about people. I don't want you to change. I don't want you to be hard and bitter and disillusioned. Somehow, you're going to come through this with your faith in humanity intact.'

'I'll try,' Lin said. 'People like you – do a lot to restore it.'

Emboldened, Andy went on: 'Actually, that wasn't quite everything. I was wondering . . . what you're doing for Christmas? Perhaps you'd like to come up here? With the kids, of course. The castle's a bit bleak, but we've had central heating installed and most of the plumbing works now. It usually snows, but I expect the boys'll like that.'

'Girls like snow too,' Lin said. Her eyes were misting over. 'We were going to get together with Sean and Vee, but she's still barely speaking to me, so . . .'

'Great!' Andy seemed almost unnerved by his own enthusiasm. 'Great. You don't need to do a thing. I'll fix up the flights – meet you at the airport . . . What date d'you want to come? How about Tuesday the 23rd? Better still, Monday. Tuesday's bound to be booked out. Or the weekend . . .'

In the office the next day, Lin wasn't as happy as I would have expected. A vague apprehension still hovered over her.

'What's the matter?' I said. 'You can't think he's acting out of pity now.'

'No, but . . . I'm afraid.'

'Afraid of what?'

'I'm not sure. I've known him so long. Afraid of – hoping. I've been hopeful so many times, and it's always gone wrong for me. Afraid of being happy, of thinking we could – things could – really work out for me . . .'

'That's because it's real,' Georgie said. 'All that love-at-first-sight stuff, that's just fantasy and fairydust. When you really know someone, then it's scary, because it has to go all the way. You can rush into love with a stranger, but not with a friend, because then it's too deep – too dangerous – and you'll never get out.'

'I didn't say anything about *love*,' Lin said. 'I just *like* him, care for him – too much to—'

'Too much to get it wrong?' Georgie finished for her.

'I don't know . . .'

'Have a great Christmas,' I said.

Later, Georgie took me on one side. 'We ought to do something about this. Lin's got a jinx. It's *got* to come right for her this time. Andy's not some flash-in-the-pan, flash-in-the-*pants*, this-is-it-forever-until-next-month deal. He's the guy who's loved her faithfully for over a decade. The Captain Dobbin type. That's the kind of security she needs.'

'Faithfully?' I queried, remembering Andy's numerous engagements.

'You know what I mean. He's been faithful *underneath*.'

'"I have been faithful to thee, Cynara, in my fashion",' I quoted.

'Exactly. Well, no, not exactly. I expect he's always loved her but without knowing it, or without letting himself know it, and now we need to make damn sure he knows it.'

'We do?'

'You've got his number, haven't you?'

'Yes.'

'Give it me.'

I complied, but reluctantly. 'I don't think we should interfere. Despite evidence to the contrary, Andy's no fool. He'll sort her out . . .'

Georgie was already dialling. 'Hello? Andy Pearmain? It's Georgie Cavari – Yes, Lin told me. I think that's terrific. She's had such a rotten time, she needs lots of pampering and tlc – I'm sure you will. I hope you don't mind my phoning – it's just that we've been so worried about her, and we wanted to be sure – That's just it. She's been let down so often. She's very fragile right now – No, not *that* fragile. What she really needs is a strong man who'll adore her and look after her and shield her from – from – '

The wind off the loch? I hazarded.

'– shield her from the wind off the – from the storms of life. You've been such a great friend to her – Yes, I know. You must be very bruised from what happened with Cat – Oh. Oh, good.' Not bruised, she mouthed. Merely *punctured*. 'Of course Lin's been damaged too, but - No, I don't think it's gone deep. I really don't. They were only together a little while, remember – I think it was more infatuation than love – It doesn't take any time to get over that – I want you to know – Don't be afraid to say what you – Yes, that's it. Honesty is the key – Great – Oh, and – Andy? Why don't you shave off the beard? Give yourself a new look? – No, of course I'm not trying to revamp your image, it's just – Most girls don't like beards. Trust me on this – They were probably lying. You'd look years younger – No, I don't mean you look old, but – Okay. 'Bye.'

I stared at her in horrified fascination. 'Georgie! Did you really have to go on about his beard? It's not that important, is it?'

'Of course it is. Once he gets rid of the beard Lin will be all set to see him in a new light. Probably a halo, knowing her. They've known each other for years and nothing's happened. There has to be a reason for that. Anyway, *no* women like beards. It's one of those gender secrets that men never twig. When did you ever see a Mills & Boon with a beard on the cover?'

'I don't read Mills & Boon.'

'Nor do I, but you *see* them. Anyway, I was just helping Andy out. Even if he's in a huff, it's in a good cause.'

'Should I ever fall in love with someone,' I said, laying some stress on the subjunctive, 'remind me not to tell you – in case you try to be helpful again.'

'Don't be silly,' Georgie said. 'I'm not blind. You've definitely got a thing for Todd Jarman.'

'What – utter – nonsense!' I managed, hoping I looked taken aback for the right reasons. 'Anyway, he's with that lawyer, Helen Aucham . . .'

'He seemed pretty fed up with her at Jerry's party,' Georgie said. 'And when we took him to lunch he was *really* disappointed you couldn't come. And I saw you doing the ministering angel after he got hit. Besides, you've been showing symptoms for some time.'

'W-what symptoms?'

'Bottling things up. Not mooning over Nigel any more. Blushing when anyone mentions Todd's name.'

'You're imagining things.'

'When are you seeing him?'

I gave in. 'He said he'd phone, but he just wants to find out what was really going on at Jerry's party. You can't blame him for that: he got a blow in the face, after all. I don't think he has any *romantic* intentions.'

'Then give him some,' Georgie said. And, inevitably: 'You'd better have a new dress.'

I had of course been on tenterhooks ever since the party waiting for Todd's call, but when it came, he caught me off guard. It's always the way. If I hadn't been off guard, he probably wouldn't have called. It was a Wednesday afternoon at work, and I was between meetings, snatching a sandwich by way of lunch. Needless to say, I answered the phone with my mouth full.

''Lo?'

'Can I speak to Emma Cook, please?'

I swallowed prawn and low-fat mayonnaise in haste, nearly choking on one of those seeds that litter granary bread like lead shot in game. 'Sorry. It's me. Just . . . eating something.'

'Didn't mean to interrupt your lunch. Isn't it a bit late though?' It was almost three.

'Busy day.'

'Let me make it up to you. How about dinner on Friday? You promised me the whole saga of the scrum at Jerry's, remember. Anyway, it's time we saw each other without having to pretend it's work.'

My stomach jolted, which didn't go well with the status of my late sandwich. 'I'd love to,' I managed.

We fixed a rendezvous and I relaxed into conversation, arriving ten minutes late for my next meeting. Sales greeted me with disapproval, but I didn't care. I was on a high.

Whatever Georgie said, I decided I *didn't* need another dress. The problem with Georgie was, now she was happy again, her bad habits were reasserting themselves. She was struggling valiantly against temptation for herself, but tried to compensate by tempting other people. She had already decided Lin would require a whole new wardrobe for her trip to Scotland, and was only defeated in her attempt to purchase a large section of Harvey Nicks by Lin's obstinate lack of fashion sense. She'd destroyed her credit cards in a solemn ritual in the office one lunchtime, supervised by Cal and attended by Lin, me, and Laurence Buckle, who happened to be in the vicinity at the time. Georgie cut them up into small pieces and dumped them in the wastepaper bin, while swearing never to acquire another. In view of the ease of obtaining a credit card, I crossed my fingers and prayed she meant it.

'Did we ever find out how much she actually owed?' Lin whispered.

'I daren't imagine.'

'Keep an eye on her, will you?' Cal said to me afterwards. 'She really *mustn't* spend any more. We'll only be able to manage this lot because I've got this restaurant job. I don't do that much moonlighting.'

'What's the damage?' I asked.

Cal made a face – in fact, it would more accurately be described as a Face, complete with capital letter. 'Nearly forty thousand.'

'*Shit . . .*'

I'd always rather assumed, whenever she spoke of it, that Georgie was exaggerating. Exaggeration was part of her style. The truth appalled me: I determined that from now on, if she so much as hinted at further expenditure, I would be a walking deterrent. Perhaps that was what Cal intended.

It also meant that if I was going to go shopping for anything, I would have to do it on my own. Since Georgie was doing cold turkey, it would be both unfair and unwise to take her anywhere near the scene of her addiction. All of which resulted in my losing much of my enthusiasm for retail therapy, at least for the moment. It's no fun on your own, and the thought of Georgie's debt hovered over any expedition like a supernatural warning, a phantom in a T-shirt with the legend '40K', moaning: 'Beware! Beware!'

So when I went to meet Todd on Friday evening I was dressed in a skirt and sweater I'd bought some months earlier, both too everyday to merit description. I told myself it didn't matter. He seemed to like me, yes, but he had a girlfriend, and our one night of lust had been a solo effort on my part. Todd hadn't even been there.

We had drinks at 2, Brydges Place, a funny dark little club with a smattering of less well-known literary types scattered through a maze of tiny rooms. Todd had apparently joined a decade or more earlier, and, indifferent to the rise of more fashionable venues, had continued to use the place because he liked it. Afterwards, we went somewhere for dinner, but I don't remember the name or even the genre of food. By then, I wasn't noticing.

'I'm sorry I took so long to call you,' Todd said. 'Life's been a bit complicated. I expect you've gathered Helen and I are splitting up.'

I hadn't gathered anything of the sort, and my heart missed several beats, causing me to replace my drink on a patch of air next to the table, though happily I didn't let go so only a little got spilt.

'Not much light in here,' I said. 'I couldn't see what I was doing . . . You were saying, about Helen . . . ?'

'I won't go into details. It's been going stale on us for a long time. When you get together with someone, your first interest is sex – you don't really discuss what you want to do with your lives. The way Helen wants to live and the way I want to live – they just aren't compatible. I know it's taken us too long to find out . . . I don't like giving up on things, I suppose. We've been papering over the cracks, but they got wider and sex didn't bridge the gap. She had an affair recently, one of her clients – Charlie Nguru. It finished with the case, but it was a symptom of her need to . . . break out. We've been talking it over for the past several weeks. She's moved in with a girlfriend until she can sort out her own flat. The house is mine – I had it before the relationship started and she never contributed to the mortgage, so she's got a lot of money in the bank. She doesn't need to demand palimony, or whatever it's called.'

'She's a lawyer,' I said hesitantly. 'Won't she – do what lawyers do? I mean . . .'

'Sue? I doubt it. Believe it or not, Helen isn't that type. She'd consider it beneath her. It would be different if we'd been married, or children had been involved, but things never went that far. And the break-up's mutual, more or less. I initiated it, but she's been as unhappy with the state of play as I have.'

'I'm glad she's not hurt,' I said, and found I meant it.

'Oh, we're both hurting – a bit. When something's over, you do. But the relationship died a natural death, not a violent one, so you're sorry, you have a sense of failure, of regret, but it's not suicidal agony. Still, I daresay you must have been there yourself, once or twice. Or are you too young?'

'Once,' I said. 'Sort of. I was living with this guy, and then I found out he was seeing someone else, so I threw him out. But I missed him so much I tried to get him back, only he'd moved in with the other woman, and I – I made a fool of myself. It *was* suicidal agony, for a while. Then – it wasn't.' I wanted very badly to be honest with him, but I didn't feel he was ready for the story of the fat estate agent yet. Besides, it was out of keeping with the tempo of the evening.

'Still suffering any pangs?' he asked, and I couldn't help trying to detect a trace element of anxiety in the question. Even if it wasn't there.

'No,' I said. 'None at all. I suppose . . . it wasn't the real thing, because if it had been, I don't think I would have recovered so quickly.'

Did he look more cheerful? I couldn't tell. That's the trouble with these saturnine faces: they don't function as mirrors of the soul. You just get little glimpses, here and there, and it's easy to be mistaken. And the dim lighting didn't help.

'Do you believe in the Real Thing?' he said, with a kind of gentle mockery. 'Love at first sight – the lightning bolt that strikes when you meet the one person in all the world who's right for you.'

'Of course not. That's just romantic nonsense. Love isn't a lightning bolt – it sort of creeps up on you, when you're not paying attention. And it takes a lot of sightings. And getting to know the person. You can't possibly love someone you don't know.'

'Many men would say you're wrong. Not knowing the person is often a prerequisite.'

'That's because men are more romantic than women,' I said boldly. 'It's like *La Belle Dame Sans Merci*, or The Song of Wandering Aengus. Some guys think love is an idealised emotion; they fall for a fantasy woman, an eternal stranger. They can't deal with a flesh-and-blood woman, flesh-and-blood love. So they're always searching for something more than whatever they've got, and they miss out.'

'D'you think I'm like that?' He was looking sardonic.

I'd been drinking vodka martinis on an empty stomach, and as always with Todd I was getting reckless. 'You tell me,' I said.

'Well, they say all writers live in fantasy land, but I think I'm the flesh-and-blood type. Seriously, I'm surprised you think men are romantic; it's a novel attitude. I thought it was women who're supposed to be into flowers and chocolates and stuff.'

400

'Women are into *gifts*,' I said. 'That's got nothing to do with romance: it's sheer hard-headed practicality. We only take flowers and chocolates if we can't get diamonds.'

'I'll strive to bear that in mind,' he said, and I hoped he meant in relation to me, then realised the phrase could've had a general application. 'Now, are you going to explain what was going on at Jerry's party, or d'you want to wait till we get to dinner?'

I told the story like a professional, of course – starting at the end, leap-frogging over the middle, going back to the beginning. By the time we got to the restaurant I was relating how much work I'd done on Jerry's book, and my gratification when the reviewer called it a page-turner.

'If you can do that,' he said, 'you can do anything. How do we celebrate? I expect you're a champagne girl.'

'I don't mind,' I said, 'as long as it's alcohol. What do you like?'

'I prefer burgundy, but—'

'Burgundy is fine.' My only reservation was that it stained my lips, leaving me looking like a maenad after a particularly heavy bacchanalia. But I was *feeling* maenad-like already.

Glancing through the menu, I wondered about ordering asparagus tips so I could suck them erotically, but decided against it as they would be bound to drip butter on my skirt. Seductive food is all very well in theory, but I suspect the practice lets you down. And then there were the stomach-butterflies that fluttered away every time he quirked an eyebrow or looked at me in a certain way. I remember thinking: It wasn't like this with Nigel. (Nigel didn't take me out to dinner, for one thing.) But then, I'd never been out to dinner with a man I fancied madly in my whole life. I hadn't realised how much it would affect my appetite. We ordered wonderful food, and I hardly ate a thing. No wonder I used to be overweight – I'd never been really in lust. Lust is a very slimming emotion. Someone should write a book about it: the L-Plan Diet . . .

The burgundy was rich and heavy and much sexier than champagne, which always makes me burp. I started off sipping cautiously, hoping to let the wine slide past my lips so they would remain unstained, but after the first glass I didn't bother any more. I went to the Ladies and sure enough, I looked like a maenad, all tumbled hair and purple mouth. I didn't care.

I forgot that red wine and vodka don't really mix. There came a point in the evening when the air turned sparkly and the restaurant seemed to be floating around me. I knew I was having a very good time – an amazing time – but the small cold voice of sobriety at the back of my mind told me I should call it a night.

'I'm a bit pissed,' I said. 'No – I'm awfully pissed. I'm sorry.'

We'd been talking about D.I. Hatchett, and where he should go from here. I'd been suggesting a trip abroad, by way of variety. Affiliation to a foreign police force. Todd had said his character was too firmly rooted in his own mean streets; he'd be at a loss in New York or LA. I said that would be interesting, wouldn't it, and Todd added ruefully: 'What I mean is, *I'd* be at a loss.'

'Maybe you need a break,' I said, and that was when the alcohol kicked in.

'I'd better take you home,' he said. 'It's my fault – I shouldn't have suggested martinis.'

In the taxi, I flopped against him. Booze was definitely making a maenad of me, but he didn't respond. Still, perhaps the driver put him off.

When we reached the flat he took me inside, deposited me on the sofa. (The same sofa where we . . . well, you know.) I let my arms slide around his neck, thinking that now, *now*, at last, he would . . . He gave me a peck on the cheek. 'You okay to get to bed?' he said with no sexual undertones.

'I – yes . . .'

'I'll call you.'

He was gone, leaving me racked with disappointment and hurt, and so drunk I fell asleep almost at once.

I woke in the wee small hours and tottered from the sofa to the bedroom, where I was plunged into dreams of rejection and personal inadequacy. I was back at the dinner party in Hampstead and Todd, minus Helen, was getting off with Laura. 'It's all right,' he said. 'You and Roger will make a lovely couple.' The nightmare deepened, and I saw him with a string of other women – Jocasta Tate, the It girl, even Georgie – all of them more glamorous and successful than me. And then somehow I was in bed with him, in Jerry Beauman's fourposter, and all around us the party was raging, and people were scrabbling on the floor for money. He sat up, and it wasn't Todd, it was Jerry himself, fixing me with his beady black stare, and I shrank in horror – waking with a jerk to find myself sweating and feeling extremely sick.

I made it to the bathroom just in time.

Todd phoned around midday, by which time I had plumbed the depths of hangover and depression. I'd always found a hangover was a useful distraction from other miseries, but not this one. This hangover was just *part* of the misery – not a purgative hangover after a night of drowned sorrows but the result of the cause of everything going wrong. I'd had a whole evening with him – a whole magic evening – and I'd got idiotically pissed and he hadn't even kissed me. Our moment of lust would remain forever in the realms of fancy. Quite possibly my chances of experiencing real lust with a real man – the complete flesh-and-blood deal – had gone for good.

The first time the phone rang, it was Georgie. 'How'd it go?' she said.

'Don't ask . . .'

I was feeling too awful to go into details, and said I would get back to her later.

The second caller was my mother. I don't know why it is, but she invariably phones at the worst moment, when my luck is out and my nerve is gone and I feel like a barnacle on the bottom of the great cruise-liner of life, while everyone else is on the main deck having a ball. She can be sympathetic (my mother often is), or bracing, or scatter pearls of wisdom which are too late to be of any use – even if I was prepared to listen to her advice, which of course I'm not – but the effect of this timing is that she always makes me feel a failure. It's a bit like Sophie, accusing me of bulimia when I've gone on a diet. For my mother, too, whatever I do turns out wrong. She's never worried about my sister (even when she was shacked up with a photographer in a state of Parisian decadence), but she worries about me constantly. I could feel her worry trickling down the telephone. I listened to a mixed grill of the sympathy/bracing/pearls stuff, dredged up a few filial clichés, and escaped, claiming I was running a bath. (It seemed like a good idea.) When the phone rang again, almost immediately, I nearly didn't answer it. I'd given up expecting it to be Todd.

But it was.

'Hello? Are you all right? I didn't like to call too early – I thought you'd need some time to sleep it off.'

'I – yes, thanks. I'm so sorry—'

'I had a great evening. I wanted you to know that.'

'– so sorry I . . .'

'Stop saying you're sorry. What is there to be sorry for? Didn't you enjoy yourself?'

'Yes, I . . . of course I did. But . . .'

'But what?'

You didn't make passionate love to me.

'I was horribly drunk. I only hope I didn't embarrass you.'

'Don't be silly; of course you didn't. I was counting on getting points for chivalry, actually.'

Chivalry?

'Chi–chivalry?' I said.

'I didn't lay a finger on you, in the taxi or at your place. I even resisted giving you a goodnight kiss.'

'I thought that was because you didn't want to,' I said, shock depriving me of all normal restraint.

'A gentleman,' he said with a note of irony, 'does not take advantage of a lady in distress.'

'So you're a writer and a gentleman.' I was struggling to recover my *sang-froid*. If I had any. 'I'd never have guessed. The two don't usually go together.'

'I see you're feeling better.' Now, the irony wasn't just a note: it was a whole chord. For some reason, it made me feel wonderful.

He went on: 'I'd like to have seen you tonight, but I've got my son for the weekend – a sort of pre-Christmas session – and I think it's a bit soon to inflict him on you. I don't want a moody teenager putting you off me. How busy are you next week?'

I'd like to have seen you – a *bit* soon to meet his son – how busy are you . . . ? As the import of all this sank in, my hangover evaporated into the ether. Now, all I had was a headache and a vague lingering nausea, but it didn't matter. I wasn't going to die of unrequited lust after all. He hadn't kissed me because of *chivalry* . . .

'Oh, not too bad,' I said, floating up into the air on a pink cloud of happiness. A couple more Paracetamol and I'd be in heaven. 'You know how it is at this season. The usual social round.'

'How about Tuesday? It's the annual dinner for previous winners of the Golden Bludgeon—' a prestigious award for thriller writers '– but I can give it a miss.'

'I expect I could manage that . . .'

This time, I didn't drink too much. I didn't flop in the taxi or expire on the sofa. I lit a candle and removed the cat, lest his icy stare prove discouraging. I put Ravel's *Bolero* on the sound system, but never got around to switching it on.

This time, Todd kissed me.

But I'm not going to tell you any more about that, because this is reality, which is so much better than fiction – so much deeper and wilder and *sexier* – I'm just going to trail off into a row of dots, the way they did in the old days, before erotic scenes became obligatory. If you don't yet know what I'm getting at, then go and find out . . .

. . .

. . .

!!!

And now we're nearly at the end. When I started telling this story, I never thought I'd get as far as a middle, let alone an ending, and I certainly didn't expect it to be happy – not for me, anyhow – though I hoped, because hope is the nature of man. (Or woman.) Of course, it isn't really the end – in fact, it feels more like a beginning – because things go on happening, and stories unravel indefinitely. But we're reaching the point where I'm going to leave off. I've got writer's cramp, and repetitive brain syndrome, and on my screen the words are running into each other like athletes at a sporting event when someone has spiked their feed. I need a small drink, or a large drink, and about a year at the gym (I'll have to join one), and now all I have to do is decide whether I'm going to show it to Todd . . .

(Sorry, but I can't write his name now without putting dots after it. Association of ideas.)

Just a few more details.

Lin came back in the New Year, looking radiant. She'd had a wonderful time, Andy was wonderful, the children thought he was wonderful (or at any rate, they thought the castle was wonderful, which was the same thing), everything was wonderful. Actually, yes – um – they were engaged. She wasn't rushing into anything, honestly she wasn't – after all, they'd known each other more than ten years – so we couldn't say she was going too fast, could we? We didn't. And she was going to leave work, and live in Scotland with the children, and we must all come up for the wedding, and lots of visits (castles have plenty of room), because the one thing she would *really* miss was her friends. We hugged her, and congratulated her (and ourselves, just a little), and went out to crack a bottle of champers, without any of the men, and drink to Charlie's Angels, or whatever.

'All for one!' said Georgie. 'One for all!'

'Farrah Fawcett!' said Lin, who'd never really caught up on that one.

'Toil and trouble!' from me.

We drank enthusiastically. The champagne – courtesy of Andy Pearmain – was vintage.

'It's been an amazing year,' I remarked. Time for a quick retrospective. 'It was last January when we went to the Wyshing Well – d'you remember? After that lunch at the Bel Manoir with Jerry Beauman.'

'At least one wish came true,' Lin said. 'You don't have to work with Jerry any more.'

'Did we wish for that?' I asked.

'We must've done,' said Georgie. 'Anyone would.'

'Actually, all our wishes came true, in the end,' Lin said pensively. 'I've met my true love – even if I already had and

407

didn't know it – and Cal's helping Georgie clear her debts, and Cookie's become Todd's own personal sex goddess.'

'Did I say so?' I was rather startled. After all, they hadn't seen the dots.

'No, but it's obvious.' Lin gave me a sweet, knowing smile, which wasn't what I expected from her. 'We should've trusted the fairy from the start.'

'It wasn't the fairy,' Georgie said. 'It was us. We did it ourselves.'

I was silent. I thought of Georgie's millionaires, and her break with Cal, and Lin and Ivor and Meredith, and my one night as a vamp when I nearly lost my friend. Beware the day your wishes come true. And we did it ourselves . . .

Now, Lin was marrying Andy, whom she *hadn't* loved at first sight, and Georgie was paying at least part of her debts herself, and I was a bit slimmer and much more confident and seriously involved with a gorgeous man, who'd said to me the other night would I mind *not* wearing that red dress any more, except in private, because it was awfully revealing and he wanted to keep me all to himself.

If wishes *do* come true, it's never the way you expect.

'It's a funny thing,' Lin said, reverting to the subject of Andy, 'but I often wonder why it took me so long to fancy him. If I was blinded by being nuts about Sean, and then Garry, or . . . D'you know, he's shaved off his beard? I think all men should shave off their beards. He looks so much younger . . . and he's got a lovely chin.'

Chins, I remembered, had always been an important issue for Lin. I met Georgie's eye, and she smiled a smile of unholy glee.

'I wonder what made him do that?' she said.

THE END

408